Erik Fosnes Hansen is one of Norway's most renowned contemporary authors. His works have won multiple awards and been translated into more than 30 languages, and have been reviewed in journals such as *The New York Times Book Review* and *Frankfurter Allgemeine*. His debut novel, *Falketårnet* (*The Falcon Tower*) was published in 1985, when he was only 20 years old. The second, *Salme ved reisens slutt* (*Psalm at Journey's End*, 1990), was a major bestseller which established him as one of the leading European writers of his generation. A later novel, *Løvekvinnen* (*The Lion Woman*, 2006), about the life of an outsider, has recently been made into a film. Fosnes Hansen is also a literary critic, journalist and biographer.

Janet Garton is Emeritus Professor of European Literature at the University of East Anglia, Norwich. She has published books and articles about Nordic literature, including *Norwegian Women's Writing 1850-1990* (1993), *Contemporary Norwegian Women's Writing* (1995), *Elskede Amalie* (2002) and a biography of Amalie Skram, *Amalie* (2011). She has also translated Bjørg Vik, Cecilie Løveid, Paal-Helge Haugen, Kirsten Thorup and Henrik Ibsen.

GW00645480

Some other books from Norvik Press

Johan Borgen: *Little Lord* (Translated by Janet Garton)

Jens Bjørneboe: *Moment of Freedom* (Translated by Esther Greenleaf Mürer)
Jens Bjørneboe: *Powderhouse* (Translated by Esther Greenleaf Mürer)
Jens Bjørneboe: *The Silence* (Translated by Esther Greenleaf Mürer)

Vigdis Hjorth: *A House in Norway* (Translated by Charlotte Barslund)

Amalie Skram: *Betrayed* (Translated by Katherine Hanson and Judith Messick)
Amalie Skram: *Fru Inés* (Translated by Katherine Hanson and Judith Messick)
Amalie Skram: *Lucie* (Translated by Katherine Hanson and Judith Messick)

Anton Tammsaare: *The Misadventures of the New Satan* (Translated by Olga Shartze and Christopher Moseley)

Ilmar Taska: *Pobeda 1946: A Car Called Victory* (Translated by Christopher Moseley)

Kirsten Thorup: *The God of Chance* (Translated by Janet Garton)

Selma Lagerlöf: *Mårbacka* (Translated by Sarah Death)

Viivi Luik: *The Beauty of History* (Translated by Hildi Hawkins)

Dorrit Willumsen: *Bang: A Novel about the Danish Writer* (Translated by Marina Allemano)

For our complete back catalogue, please visit
www.norvikpress.com

Lobster Life

by

Erik Fosnes Hansen

Translated from the Norwegian
by Janet Garton

Norvik Press
2019

Original title: *Et hummerliv* © Erik Fosnes Hansen, 2016. Published by agreement with Copenhagen Literary Agency ApS, Copenhagen.

This translation © Janet Garton 2019.
The translator's moral right to be identified as the translator of the work has been asserted.

Norvik Press Series B: English Translations of Scandinavian Literature, no. 79.

A catalogue record for this book is available from the British Library.

ISBN: 978-1-909408-52-4

Norvik Press
Department of Scandinavian Studies
University College London
Gower Street
London WC1E 6BT
United Kingdom
Website: www.norvikpress.com
E-mail address: norvik.press@ucl.ac.uk

Managing editors: Elettra Carbone, Sarah Death, Janet Garton, C. Claire Thomson.

Layout and cover design: Essi Viitanen.

This translation has been published with the financial support of NORLA.

1

They had got as far as the cakes when Herr Berge, the bank manager, suddenly slumped down at the table and started to die. It didn't seem real. He didn't clutch his chest or anything like that, he just looked altogether unnatural and artificial, with protruding, staring eyes, as if he was taking part in a little play. In any case, he had just sat down after making an after-dinner speech. To start with, my grandfather was smiling, and my grandmother too, for Berge had not only praised the meal – he had also, and not least, praised my grandmother's imposing *Gugelhupf* in light and amusing terms, and now it seemed for a moment as if he was just carrying on with the joke. His wife was the first to understand that something was really wrong.

'Bjørn!' she exclaimed, springing up to run round the table and come to his aid as he sat there, but there was no-one who could aid Berge the bank manager any longer; the next moment he began to change colour, and then it dawned on everyone else too. He sank slowly forward in his chair, but was too fat to end up with his head on the tablecloth; instead his chin merely dropped onto his chest as he produced a small gurgling croak, and, basically, that was that.

For a few more long, unreal seconds the other grown-ups stayed sitting motionless at the table, whilst Fru Berge seemed for a moment to hang completely still in the air, invisibly suspended, as if she too didn't want to believe what none of us could believe, but then she tore herself free and the next moment she was at her husband's side, shouting 'Bjørn' again.

The first of the grown-ups to get up was Grandfather, as the attentive host, but even before he had finished pushing his chair back, Jim and I, who had been standing against the wall by the kitchen door ready to receive our thanks and clear the table, came storming over.

'Come on, Sedd!' Jim had shouted, 'he's ill!'

So that by the time Grandfather had reached the bank manager, and whilst his wife was still calling desperately for someone to come and help her, or rather her husband, Jim and I had already pulled him upright in his chair. Jim looked into his eyes and muttered something about he's a goner, we need to lay him flat, which provoked whimpers of despair from Fru Berge and comforting or incredulous exclamations from the others, but we managed to lay him down and loosen his collar and tie. As a member of the Red Cross I'd learnt first aid and resuscitation, and I realised that my moment seemed to have arrived. I was already sitting by the chest of that large, wildly staring man, who was still making some strangled gutteral noises, and I knew I had no time to lose, but nevertheless I cast a desperate glance around, looking up at the shocked, formally dressed grown-ups who were crowding around us, dinner jackets and long dresses, to make certain one final time of what I'm afraid I already knew, which was that the local doctor, Dr Helgesen, and his wife, who otherwise would normally attend these private dinners here at the hotel, were by an exceptional chance not present on this occasion, but were unfortunately on a post-Easter holiday in the South, the infernal South, as Grandfather called those parts of the world, in other words that they were not here, that no-one else was present who was better qualified, and that nothing and no-one could take this cup from me, and I bent down and put my lips to those of the bank manager.

He tasted slightly of raisins and coffee, of cake dough and cigarettes, and what was left of his breath met my open mouth like the draught from a dying fire, but I overcame my distaste, realising that the mucous reality of a body was different from the training dummy for Red Cross first-aiders, pinched his nostrils together and started to blow air into him. From far away I could hear Grandmother saying worriedly: 'Sedgewick, dear', but she could not reach me and the bank manager, we were in our own little world, he and I, on our own island of air, where the dying man's breath mingled with my own and became one single entwined breath, where I breathed in his spirit and he mine, and we were fighting for life together, in fact I was fighting for my own survival and that of us all.

It was hard, like blowing life into a church organ with just the power of your lungs, and as soon as I sat up to begin the first chest compressions I could feel I was dizzy, but I just closed my eyes and counted silently and calmly as I carried out the heart massage. Someone said something about phoning; hurried footsteps disappeared in the direction of reception, but it wasn't Jim, thank goodness, even though he was otherwise always the one who did what someone said needed doing. Jim remained beside me, somewhere close by, and his very presence had a calming effect on me; he undid the cufflinks and belt around this huge, slack lump of a body which was lying under me, but said nothing, and I dived down for the second time and blew as hard as I could.

We continued in this way for what felt like an eternity on that late winter's evening, to the accompaniment of Fru Berge's quiet sobbing because she was not the last person to kiss her husband – at least that's what I thought in my foggy state – whilst Jim, who was a practical person and had observed closely what I was doing, gradually took over the heart massage whilst I sat and got my breath back and belched sour burps before throwing myself over the dead man with death-defying courage, because I could tell he was a goner, it was only an empty raisin-scented shell I was blowing into, and he was still staring at me, incredulous and with wide-open, beady-blue eyes, almost accusingly, every time I raised my head, but without having anything further to say, either about Grandmother's imposing *Gugelhupf*, about stocks and shares or credit balances or splendid future prospects for the village, the district and all of us, or about the Falklands crisis, or for that matter something disapproving about my attempts to rescue him, or about my lung capacity – but he did not look happy. 'That's enough now, Sedd,' said Grandfather in a strange voice from somewhere far distant, but I carried on regardless, because I had learnt at the course that you mustn't give up too soon, you must carry on until help arrives, so I carried on, whilst something wet ran down my face and mingled with the cold sweat on Berge's face, with spit and mucus; carried on whilst the tramping of boots in reception and then into the dining room announced that there was at last someone present who could relieve me and release the grown-ups from their humiliation at not having taken a Red Cross first-aid course themselves, and thus not being a part of the new times; carried on until someone firmly but carefully pulled me away and took over, helped me to my feet, and there was only one thing I could do before things went black, and that was to call out with what little air there was left inside me, 'I HOPE I'VE DONE IT ALL RIGHT AND NOT DONE ANYTHING WRONG', after which my legs gave way and darkness took over.

When I came round on the sofa in reception they were in the process of wheeling Berge out on a stretcher, the *real* Red Cross brigade, closely followed by a still sobbing Fru Berge, whilst Jim held the door open; the flashing lights from the ambulance threw long blue gleams into reception from the winter darkness outside, and then it disappeared, without sirens.

Grandfather was standing helplessly at the reception desk. But Grandmother was sitting, gently stroking my hair, soothingly, affectionately. I think I must have cried, because she was whispering little endearments to me; *Schatzerl, mein braver Bub, mein Held* and so on. And she had her arms round me. My kind grandmother, with her strangely attractive, slightly distant presence, was suddenly close to me with her Viennese phrases and her lilting accent; grandmother with earrings and pearl necklace, her neat, curly brown hair and her elegant make-up. Grandmother with her large, brown, almost golden eyes and her scent, the faint scent of eau de cologne and oil of bergamot. Until she said, finally, 'You did so well.'

Grandfather, who had to go in and wind up the remains of the ruined dinner party, all those friends who must have been waiting in there in shock, also came over to the sofa where I was lying. Put his hand on my head, large and reassuring. Then he said the same thing: 'You did so well.'

Then I was helped up to bed.

That night I dreamt about the lobster. About the lobster Erling the Crooked.

It's not true that lobsters make no sound. Firstly, lobsters make a noise when they scrabble on the gravel at the bottom of the aquarium. If you put your ear against the glass you can hear it like soft bumps. Or when they beat helplessly with their tails on the bottom and begin an equally helpless flight through the water, until they crash into the glass at the other short end of the tank and sink just as helplessly to the bottom. And when they bump their bound, disproportionately large nutcracker claws against the glass: then they look at you, whilst they take a bearing on you with their antennae. Something or other close to their bodies, where their claws meet, whirrs and buzzes at breathtaking speed. Whirr, whirr. I'm afraid it's their mouths. They don't exactly wink at you, but they look at you with their black orbs, and you can tell that lobsters are intelligent creatures.

Otherwise they walk around on the bottom in there, staking out small territories, each occupying its own corner. They glare at one another. They lunge at one another, then retreat rapidly with bound, disabled claws. Most of the time they want to murder one another, but they can't manage it. So they just lie there, hoping that the bindings round their claws will slip, so that one day they will have the chance to attack first. Waiting patiently, anticipating an opportunity.

That's why you always have to make sure that their claws are firmly fastened with a broad, blue, tight, high-quality elastic band. Otherwise there would be a reckoning, Jim explained; he was always careful to check that the bands were in place and could not slip.

One day Jim happened to release a lobster from its polystyrene box into the aquarium, and the bands were not properly secured. It was a monster, and Jim was in a hurry and didn't check. I was helping him carry in the other provisions. When we came back in, it had maimed four of the other lobsters in the tank, at God knows how many kroner a kilo; it was a dreadful sight. Chopped-off claws and legs, antennae and strips of meat were bobbing on the bottom. Three opponents lay dying on the field of battle, and the gangster had set about enjoying the fourth, which was trapped in a corner and had already lost its right claw. However, in its cold-blooded submarine fury the murderer had inadvertently cut through the band on its left claw, so that the injured beast had got that one free, and with that left claw it was now defending itself valiantly.

With a shriek of horror Jim thrust a practised hand into the tank, grabbed the sinner by its back and hoisted it out. Shouted that I should stand back, since its claw was free. He took it to the counter and flipped it onto its back, so that it was helpless. Swearing, he fished out the floating elastic band and with exaggerated arm movements manoeuvred it into place around the free claw. Once it was safely in place Jim began to breathe more easily and handled the creature like his normal laid-back self. You could see that he felt like throttling it, but the cost per kilo entered his mind, and he tipped it head-first back into the salt water aquarium without sentimentality. After that Jim put his hand in for the other one, which had recovered from the amputation, and was now also looking round for someone to murder. It had already begun to nibble at a helpless wretch at the other end when Jim, still swearing, got hold of it, lifted it out of the OK

Corral and over into a more prosaic reality, and inspected the damage to its right claw.

'Lousy fucking critter,' said Jim. 'Bugger. Bugger bugger bugger.'

He coaxed a band over this lobster's claw as well and tipped it back into the water.

'What d'you think, Sedd,' said Jim.

'Bugger,' I said. 'Lousy fucking critter.'

'Now Zacchariassen will be mad,' said Jim.

(Zacchariassen is my grandfather.)

'I'm sure he won't,' I said.

'Yes he will,' said Jim. 'That fucking shitty little sea creep has ruined two thousand kroner's worth of lobster.'

'Well, we can eat that last one, even if it's lost one claw,' I said to comfort him.

'You thick or what, Sedd? Course we can't. Only one half, anyway. Can't serve Lobster Thermidor with just one claw, can you?'

'Can't you cook the other claw?'

'Oh no,' said Jim. 'That's not on.'

'Why not, Jim? I mean, can't you fish it out and freeze it and then cook it together with the rest of the lobster when the time comes?'

'No,' said Jim, and he had to laugh. 'The whole lobster has to be alive when you cook it,' he said. 'Lobster has to be alive. Otherwise it goes bad, and you'll be ill if you eat it. Why do you think we boil them alive?'

I had no answer to that. I almost said, because it's horrible but a bit thrilling too, but I said nothing. I hadn't thought about it before.

'Oh no,' said Jim, 'we've lost lots of money here. Sodding fuckup.'

And he was right. Grandfather was angry, but I pleaded Jim's case, so he wasn't half so angry as he would have been, Jim said when he thanked me afterwards, and he didn't dock Jim's wages, but Jim had to help Grandfather repair the gutter on the roof outside the private quarters one Sunday morning when he should really have had time off, and it was lovely sunny autumn weather, even though it was late September, so the two of them actually had quite a good time taking it in turns to stand on the ladder and repair the gutter. Grandfather had a dram afterwards as well, while Jim had coffee as usual, and peace was restored.

The large lobster aquarium was mounted in the partition wall between the restaurant kitchen and the dining room, so that the guests could see and choose their dinner. From then on it was called the OK Corral. The murderer – which was a monster – we called Wyatt Earp. It carried on walking round the tank for several weeks, thinking it was the master of the aquarium, until the director of a children's home from Larvik fancied a really large lobster, and Wyatt Earp was brutally yanked out of its fantasies of domination and hung from its carapace in Jim's hand, struggling for all it was worth. When it saw the boiling water in the large aluminium pot, it was as if it sighed in anticipation, because no doubt it thought it was going to be put in a new aquarium where it could be in charge. Just before it met the surface it realised that that was not how matters stood, realised that something quite different was about to happen, stopped waving its antennae, and stoically, without a sound, with its boots on, it met its death and was eaten by the director of the children's home.

The other lobster, the one that had survived, we called Erling the Crooked, after the Viking warrior who was lopsided after a blow from an Arabian sword, because it looked so strange with just one claw. It had a considerably longer life there in the OK Corral than did Wyatt. For there was no-one who wanted to eat it. Especially after Wyatt had been raised to a higher plane with mustard sauce and everything, Erling the Crooked felt that it could relax properly. It positively strutted around the bottom of the tank, and despite its handicap it conquered a record-breaking territory. It lived to see generations of kinsmen come and go, some on just a short visit, a day or two, whilst others could be there for weeks and months. But all disappeared. Rose up. While it remained. It became a clever and stoical old lobster, and its shell was covered in algae. It's true that Grandfather wanted to eat it on New Year's Eve, and on Easter Sunday as well, but I pleaded for it, just as I sometimes pleaded for Jim, and Grandfather let himself be talked round, and spared it from being eaten in-house. Erling the Crooked carried on walking round the OK Corral for months, to the great enjoyment of the children who saw it and thought it funny without a claw, and it gave me a certain pleasure too. When it looked at me, it didn't look as if it felt like murdering me; on the contrary, it seemed that it regarded me with a kind of understanding. Perhaps not gratitude, that would have been too much to ask of such a cynic – a lobster is a hardened soul – but with detached recognition. Until one day in May, when a lady teacher from Oslo proclaimed in a loud voice that it was cruelty to animals to let *that poor, poor dumb animal* walk around like that with only one claw. '*It* can't complain,' she said to Grandfather, whilst she made it clear that she was taking on the role of that poor dumb animal's extremely vocal spokesperson. She was asking to die, so to speak, on the animal's behalf.

But it's not an animal, I thought, it's Erling the Crooked. Grandfather smoothed things over, whilst Jim and I in the kitchen, on the other side of the partition wall, listened to her cries for help on behalf of the suffering animal world. She had already embarked on the seals on Jan Mayen Island and the elephants in West Africa, poor dumb creatures with their skulls bashed in and their tusks sawn off, and Jim muttered that soon she'll start on about wolves, and about the bacteria on surgeons' hands, but she calmed down when Grandfather assured her that something would be done about the matter as soon as possible, in fact at once. The next moment he was standing in the kitchen and saw that we had been listening, so he just jerked his head, and with a nod Jim flipped Erling the Crooked out of the tank, so that the pedagogue from Oslo on the other side could have peace in her soul. Erling wandered about the large steel sink for a few hours, somewhat nonplussed, suddenly aware of its own mortality and disability, but was returned to the aquarium after the teacher had left, and was immediately perfectly happy and seemed to have forgotten the whole affair.

However, it was clear that it was living on borrowed time.

'We can't keep it there like that,' said Grandfather, even though I begged for it. 'One day another lady will complain, and then another. One of them may refuse to pay. Or write a letter to *Aftenposten*.'

'No-one would write a letter to *Aftenposten* about a lobster,' I objected. But Grandfather looked at me with a dark expression:

'Young man,' he sighed, 'you have no idea what people write letters to *Aftenposten* about. And with the full name of the hotel. Cruelty to animals at Fåvnesheim Mountain Hotel.'

'Then let them write,' said Jim.

'Jim,' said Grandfather, 'you don't know, but *I* do, what small margins we run on. It's not like it was in the fifties and sixties, when I took over from my father. At that time this was the ultimate luxury. People streamed here in flocks, Jim. In crowds. To let themselves be spoilt. Now it's the eighties, and people are travelling to the South, the infernal South, not to mountain hotels. The staff costs, Jim, have also increased markedly.'

Jim looked down. Not just because he had heard it before.

'So the contribution to running costs is hardly – is hardly – in short, we need every single customer. Every single guest. If just one person stays away because they've read in *Aftenposten* ... .'

Every single customer, that was Grandfather's mantra. He said it every single day.

Jim nodded heavily.

'I can keep it in my room,' I said.

'Under the bed, Sedd,' said Jim with forced gaiety. 'In a bath.'

'I can have my own aquarium,' I said, but the suggestion fell on deaf ears.

From then on Erling the Crooked's days were numbered. Grandfather ate him in-house at Whitsun. I didn't even want a taste, but Grandmother ate quite a lot of him.

He was prepared *au naturel*, with just lemon, dill and melted butter. And it must be admitted that he did not meet his death as bravely as Wyatt Earp. When he saw the furiously boiling salted water coming closer, he flailed about in terror, he hissed and whined, and for a brief second he screamed, before he sank down into the boiling, scalding water. So it is obvious that lobsters can make sounds. When he came up again he was dead, and quite pink inside, unnatural, red and wounded. It is obvious that lobsters can make sounds, I heard him scream, and I never forgot it.

The sound of scrabbling lobster claws followed me through the night.

2

The first day after that unfortunate dinner, which had ended so badly for all of us, but of course worst for Fru Berge, not to speak of Berge himself, I stayed in bed. I had a temperature. Whilst I lay there dozing, I had the impression that I was wandering around the empty restaurant. It was actually empty in reality, for it was the week after Easter and the dinner the evening before had been the traditional annual gathering of local dignitaries, in order to celebrate the successful Easter influx into the district. We could never put on a dinner for them in Easter week itself, because we were too busy then, even though the hotel had not even been half full this year. But now there was not a single Easter guest remaining; the hotel was empty, and it had been the time for the year's festive gathering at Fåvnesheim, when everyone came along, every single one – well, except for Dr Helgesen, who had gone to the infernal South after a long Easter week with broken legs and sunburn, and who had thus played truant, the villain.

In my dream the restaurant was just as empty as it no doubt was in reality, and the rest of the hotel too; in my feverish half-sleep I walked from one wing to another, two steps up and three steps down, along wide new corridors and narrow old ones, through all the small and large buildings which had been joined to one another as the years passed. There was not a person anywhere in the whole of Fåvnesheim. Nevertheless I was not afraid, but I think that was a result of my having a temperature.

Grandmother came along at regular intervals to sit with me. Like she always did when I was ill. If I was asleep, she would sit there with a book or a magazine, and if I was awake, she would chat to me. As well as that she brought me fruit, tea and buns. I thought it was a bit strange that I had a temperature now, because I wasn't ill, but Grandmother obviously thought there was nothing remarkable about it at all. So when I was awake, and not sleepwalking through the empty mountain hotel, she talked about things which preoccupied her. Grandmother was very preoccupied by the various European royal houses, for example. She always maintained that she had great respect for our own royal family, but she thought it was too new to be taken entirely seriously. Queen Elizabeth of the United Kingdom of England, Scotland, Wales and Northern Ireland was a clear favourite, and not only because her name was the same as Grandmother's. In the House of Windsor you could really talk about tradition. And now that Princess Diana was expecting an heir, the future of the House of Windsor was assured for yet another generation. It was important to hold the flag high, especially now when war was threatening in the South Atlantic, on the windswept Falkland Islands where sea and sky meet.

It is not unusual for people to have some knowledge of dynastic history. There are many, especially women of a certain age, which Grandmother absolutely could be said to be, who know quite a lot about dynastic history, but in Grandmother's case the knowledge was even more extensive. She knew a lot about dynasties which no longer even existed, and she could hold forth at length about them too, over several generations. For example the Habsburgs, the Austrian dynasty.

Actually it's a shame that there aren't more people than Grandmother and I who are so knowledgeable about Austrian dynastic history. Austrian dynastic history is incredibly rich and exciting. Most events and phenomena in this life, or at least a large number of them, can be illuminated with the aid of examples from Austrian dynastic history. Especially the last part, which concerns Franz Joseph, who was Emperor for almost a hundred years and was married to the noble and lovely Sisi, the Empress Elisabeth, after whom Grandmother was named, the loveliest of all, whom all Austrians love to this day, and who wrote poetry and translated Shakespeare into Greek and had an anchor tattooed on her shoulder. In a way it's wrong to call this period dynastic history, because Franz Joseph was practically immortal and simply went on and on. Whilst the rest of the royal family around him died.

That poor, noble Crown Prince Rudolf, for example. The one who killed himself at Mayerling.

Every time Grandmother got to the Mayerling drama she shook her head sadly, and I understood her, because the Mayerling drama was known as a fearful drama which shook the whole world.

'Together with that disturbed little girl,' said Grandmother, *'die Vetsera.'* She shook her head sadly yet again over the young, disturbed baroness who had met her death together with that poor Crown Prince Rudolf, only seventeen years old, that is to say, first he shot her and then he shot himself, but she wanted him to.

'And why?' asked Grandmother rhetorically, because I knew the answer already.

'Because his father hated him,' I said.

'Because his father hated him,' said Grandmother darkly. 'He mistrusted him and thought he was a dangerous rebel. It was a *Tragödie*. Simply a *Tragödie*. But Seth, darling! What am I doing? I'm sitting here talking to you about death and such gloomy things, today of all days, without thinking of what you've – '

'It doesn't matter, Grandmother. It's really nice. You always talk about this when I'm ill.'

'I think we ought to talk about something else. Or perhaps we should listen to some music.'

'That's a good idea,' I said.

'Wait,' said Grandmother eagerly. 'I'll fetch some of my own records. And I can check at the same time that everything is all right downstairs.'

'Yes, do that, Grandmother.'

'I'll only be a few minutes.'

She disappeared. I dozed. Now I should have dreamt that poor, noble Crown Prince Rudolf, incarnated for the occasion in the figure of Berge the bank manager, considerably rejuvenated, was lying shot dead in, for example, room 217, together with Baroness Vetsera, but I didn't. In my dream the hotel was just as deserted as before. I was the only one there, and I glided from hall to hall, from wing to wing, room to room. From the windows a pure white light was streaming into Fåvnesheim.

Grandmother was back.

'Are you asleep, darling?'

'No,' I said.

'Look what I've brought you. I've baked *Zwetschgendatschi*.'

My grandmother had attended a training course for hotelliers in Linz. That's where she met my grandfather, and he swept her off her feet and then swept her over here, as she used to say. But before that Grandmother had worked at Demel's in Vienna, famed for its cakes. But I didn't feel much like sugar-glazed prunes, they reminded me too much of raisins.

'Just leave it there, Grandmother. I'll eat it later.'

She laid her hand on my forehead.

'Poor *Buberl*,' she said. 'I'll put some music on, then I can read and you can doze.'

'That's a good idea, Grandmother.'

I expected it to be something with Wenche Myhre, Grandmother's and my absolute favourite, but instead it was a record of the German singer Rudi Schuricke. *Wenn bei Capri die rote Sonne im Meer versinkt*, and with that I sank down into sleep again. This time I didn't dream, and when I woke up my temperature had gone.

Grandmother was not sitting there any more.

I lay there thinking. I was very careful not to think about yesterday's events, but focused on the long view. Being able to see the long view in history is actually really important. Without the Mayerling drama, history would have looked completely different. It was *more* than what Grandmother called a *Tragödie*. It was a *great Tragödie*. Because if Rudolf had lived there wouldn't have been any Sarajevo, and without Sarajevo no First World War, and without the First World War no Lenin, and no collapse of Austria, and with that no Hitler and no Second World War and no Cold War, and that's where we are today.

From history's long perspective you can see how important it is to have a good relationship with your father. Now I don't have a father, because my father, Dr Kumar, is dead and I never knew him, but if Dr Kumar had been alive I would have made sure I had a good relationship with him, so that he didn't suspect me or believe me to be a dangerous rebel.

Fortunately, I thought, I have my noble grandmother and grandfather. That's more than a lot of people have.

In the meantime Grandmother had been in with some more baking. A whole row of hotel plates stood on my table. There was *Kaiserschmarrn* and *Marillenknödel* and *Millirahmstrudel* and *Mohr im Hemd à la Sacher*. I could see that she was having a baking orgy. She had them frequently. Regardless of whether Fåvnesheim had many or few guests, there were always at least six different masterpieces from the Viennese tearoom on the dessert trolley.

Grandfather grumbled and said we couldn't afford it, at least not in the periods when we had few or no guests, wasting so many expensive masterpieces. We and the staff couldn't eat all that ourselves. But Grandmother said he could grumble all he liked. It was a matter of keeping up her skills, and besides a good place was judged more than anything else on the quality of its cakes. 'It's important to maintain a certain standard,' she said, and reminded Grandfather that he himself always said that you need to maintain a certain standard.

And masterpieces they definitely were. But today I left them alone. When I thought about it, I couldn't really understand why I was lying in bed. I didn't feel as if I had a temperature any more either. So I got up and ventured forth into the hotel.

The strange thing was that the hotel was just like it was in my dream. Just as quiet, just as empty and with the same clear white light streaming in through the windows. There was no-one in reception, neither the reception manager Synnøve Haugen nor Grandfather nor anyone else. It was completely quiet and empty in the dining room and the lounges. In the kitchen there was a pan of stock bubbling slowly, but Jim was not to be seen. There was no-one in the private quarters either. For a moment I started to think they were all making a fool of me, playing hide-and-seek in Fåvnesheim's rooms and lounges. A couple of times I called out quietly for Grandmother, Grandfather and Jim, or uttered a hollow 'Is anyone there?' But no-one came forward. The hotel seemed deserted. The light was white. I registered that I felt worse and went into the private quarters again, up to my room, got undressed. When I was lying under the duvet I could feel that I was shaking and feverish. I fell asleep at once.

When I woke up it had begun to get dark outside. Someone had lit the lamp in the corner. I looked round the room. The cakes had gone, but Grandfather was sitting in the chair.

'Well now,' he said cautiously, 'how are you feeling, my lad?'

'A bit weak.'

'That's not surprising,' he said. 'That's not surprising. That's not surprising.'

'Maybe not,' I said.

'I must say that you behaved very well last night, Sedd.'

'I'd rather not talk about it,' I said.

'No. No no. But you did behave very well. When you've recovered a bit and we've got time, we must give you some kind of reward for your efforts.'

'There's no need for any reward.'

'Oh, but there is. A visit to Oslo or something like that. One of *our* trips. Where we can expand our horizons. And have a bit of fun.'

'Do you think we can talk about it some other time?'

'Yes, yes, of course. Of course. We can do that. We'll talk about it some other time. I just wanted to check that everything's OK. Is everything OK?'

'Oh yes, Grandfather. Everything's OK.'

'Is there anything you need?'

'No, Grandfather, I think I've got everything I need.'

'Sisi was a bit concerned when she saw that you hadn't eaten any cake.'

'I don't feel much like cake today, Grandfather.'

'She has spent much of the day baking, Sedd.'

'I know that, Grandfather.'

'Well. Well well. Just rest, then. If you need anything, we're downstairs.'

We both disappeared, Grandfather out through the door, and I into a new dreamless sleep.

The next time I woke up it was quite dark outside. I felt fine, my temperature was normal. This time it was Jim sitting in the chair.

'Hi,' he said. 'How's it going?'

'Good, Jim. I'm fine, actually.'

'Fucking hell, Sedd. Fucking hell. I thought I'd seen everything. But yesterday: fucking hell. Honestly, fucking hell.'

'Yes,' I said. 'Fucking hell.'

Jim was a man of few words. That can often be fine. For a while we sat there shaking our heads whilst we swore fervently about yesterday's events. Then Jim said: 'I've brought soup.'

'Have you, Jim?'

'Yes. Proper broth. Consommé.'

'I didn't think there was any left in the cooler?'

'I made some fresh. Today. Since you weren't too clever.'

'Oh thanks, Jim,' I said. 'That's a big job.'

'It's turned out all right. Quite all right really. I started at the crack of dawn. There you are. Sit up and I'll pour some in a mug.'

It was a perfect consommé. Hot, strong and the colour of a dark, shining jewel. Jim had chosen the topping I liked best, ribbons of crêpe and chopped chives.

'Really good, Jim.'

'Mm. I know. It's proper sick food.'

'But I'm not sick, Jim.'

'Haven't I always made you consommé when you've been sick?'

'Not always, Jim.'

'Nearly always, then. At least when you were little.'

'Yes, always then.'

'You did good yesterday, Sedd. Fucking hell.'

'I think I'll get up now, Jim,' I said. 'I feel fine.' I passed him the mug.

'I should stay in bed a bit, Sedd. It's not often you get the chance to take it easy in this place.'

'That's true,' I said. 'Thanks for the soup.'

'If you get up now, you'll only be mobilized to help me wash down the kitchen. Things have been at a bit of a standstill today.'

'In that case I think I'll stay here in bed.'

'You do that,' said Jim. Then he was gone.

Before I fell asleep again I thought about Jim's Great Seafood Feast. I had only seen him make it two or three times.

He was an expert at seafood, even though we were so high up in the mountains. He made the last Great Seafood Feast the summer I was twelve. Two extended families were to be joined together in a mountain wedding, which Fåvnesheim had come to specialize in, and they had ordered a seafood feast. Unfortunately people didn't splash out on things like that any more. It was more normal to have soup and steak. But this time Jim was given free rein.

He made full use of it. Jim was a dreamer. You could see it in his spreads. They were always extravagant. There is no better word for it. It wasn't exactly *nouvelle cuisine*. The aforementioned seafood feast took him four days to plan and assemble. We went to the stores and brought out polystyrene boxes and bubblewrap. After that he sent me off with a wheelbarrow to a stream where there were lots of stones, and told me to collect all the round stones I could find, large and small, and fill the wheelbarrow. I collected. Large and small. Rhomb-porphyry and quartz, gneiss and granite. When I wheeled them into the dining room, Jim was standing there dreaming with wide blue eyes, and on a sturdy long table by the wall he had constructed the basis of an underwater panorama with bits of polystyrene and bubblewrap. Even a little hosepipe wound its way through the service hatch, up onto the table and under the bubblewrap.

Next we brought the sand. More precisely, sand for spreading on the ice in winter, kept in the container by the garage. The whole supply for December was used up. With the sand and with dark green acrylic paint we covered the polystyrene and the bubblewrap, and when we had scrubbed and rinsed the round stones we had an impressive sea bottom, with a large standing rock in the middle made of green-painted polystyrene, taller than a fully-grown man. From his store-cupboards Jim extracted large numbers of props he had squirrelled away over the years, empty clam shells, mussel shells, as well as plastic crabs, lobsters and seaweed.

'Do you know what these are, Sedd?'

'No,' I said.

'Deep-sea creatures, that's what. I keep them for occasions like this. Plastic, but lifelike,' said Jim, wiping the dust off them and beginning to arrange them in the underwater panorama we had constructed on the table. A bit of sand and gravel trickled down. I swept it up. He had made small caves and crevices for some of them. Took a step back, a step to the left, a step to the right, peered, inspected.

'There, don't you think the guests'll be surprised? Just here under the big plastic lobster we'll put the platter of smoked salmon. Don't you think they'll be a bit alarmed if they look up bang in the face of that lobster?'

'You bet they will, Jim,' I said.

'Not a bad idea to frighten guests a bit,' said Jim. 'How about putting Octopussy here, so they get a shock when they want a bit of crab?'

I looked at him enquiringly.

'Look in that other box,' said Jim.

There lay Octopussy. Octopussy was a rubber octopus the size of a yearling lamb, and if you stretched out its tentacles it must have measured a metre in each direction. It was a slightly sickly, purplish-blue colour with splashes of fluorescent green, and had two large, mean eyes painted on it.

'Great, innit?' said Jim.

I was thrilled. Together we laid out its tentacles along the whole of the shorter end of the table where the crab platter was to go.

Jim had more in his stores: five genuine conch shells he had appropriated when he worked at a hotel in Sandefjord.

'Do they have conch shells in Sandefjord?' I asked in disbelief.

'No,' said Jim, 'I think the manager brought them from the Mediterranean. He'd been on boats there. But they're great, aren't they?'

'Super.'

'If you hold 'em to your ear,' said Jim, 'you can hear the rushing of the Mediterranean.'

I looked at him sceptically.

''S'not something I dreamt up,' said Jim. 'It's true. Try.'

I held a conch shell to my ear, half expecting one of Jim's animals in lifelike plastic to come popping out of it.

'It won't hurt you,' said Jim.

27

He was right. There was the sound of the Mediterranean in there.

Jim picked up a conch shell as well and held it to his ear. We stood there for a while, listening to the waves.

'I wonder which beach we can hear,' I said. Jim hadn't thought about that.

'Waikiki beach,' he said.

'Bora-Bora,' I said.

'Bora-Bora's good,' said Jim. 'Oh listen, here comes a big wave. Can you hear it breaking?'

'Yes,' I said.

I could hear the wave running towards the shore, roaring like faint thunder, and could almost see it crashing onto the beach, white and foaming.

'Fucking hell,' said Jim. 'That was a whopper. D'you hear it breaking?'

'Yes,' I said, 'it was enormous.'

For a while we stood there surrounded by breakers.

'OK, come on,' said Jim. 'We haven't got time for this.'

We put the conch shells in their places.

''S'not easy,' said Jim, as we stood and looked at our work, 'being a seafood specialist up here in the mountains. But I've ordered extra things,' he said slyly. 'It'll all be here with the van on Saturday when they deliver.'

No-one who was present at that wedding can have forgotten that feast. There were oysters and scallops, crab and lobster, mussels, crayfish and shrimps, halibut and salmon, smoked mackerel and herring, little cockles and large horse mussels. Over the whole presided a regal Octopussy and a proud, beaming Jim in immaculate chef's whites. The guests' awe at their meeting with the depths of the sea was tangible.

But since then we have never again experienced Jim's Great Seafood Feast at Fåvnesheim.

3

When, like me, you've decided to write your Memoirs, you immediately confront a range of difficulties, not least when it comes to what ought to be remembered. However, it is certain that the future of Literature lies in autobiography. Making things up becomes more and more difficult from one year to the next, because more and more has already been made up. If you just cast an eye over the books that are given as Christmas presents, that soon becomes obvious. Grandfather, for example, definitely preferred a good autobiography to anything else.

But when, like me, you want to write your Memoirs, you soon discover that it's not just a matter of remembering away.

Because what happened first, and what happened last? What was important and what was unimportant? The Seafood Feast, for example, is that important? If you're a famous politician or a significant figure in public life and set about remembering, you have an archive to draw on, perhaps some diaries too.

I only have a few photos from the year I want to write about, and no diaries to draw on at all.

In my Norwegian textbook it says that in a good Norwegian essay you have to aim at a coherent argument. But how early do you have to start in order to create coherence? Right at the beginning?

My mother disappeared early on and is therefore impossible to remember. It seems she was a witch. Not a real witch, of course, but she wanted to be one. That's what Jim told me, because he knew her. A bit, anyway. He thought it all came from listening too much to that Donovan song 'Season of the Witch', and then reading too many weird books about witches, before she made her mind up and set off to find Bloksberg or inner peace and was taken by Time. That's why I have such a strange first name, Sedgewick, because there was a famous witch whose surname it was, until she was burnt. But what's in a name, as the saying goes, and anyway names are invisible. At least they are if you don't wear a name badge. So when I helped out as a piccolo and wheeled luggage on the continental baggage trolley made of brass which needed polishing the whole time, I had no name badge on the equally continental red uniform which Grandmother insisted I wore.

Grandmother originally wanted me to wear a sort of fez as well, but there she met a natural resistance from both Grandfather and me, so I rendered my assistance bare-headed.

So there we stand. I remember that. Ready to welcome guests. Behind the counter is Synnøve Haugen, reception manager. Grandmother, relaxed yet alert in the lobby, and I myself in my uniform, ready to open doors and lend a hand with all kinds of luggage. At the sound of expected buses or cars we straighten ourselves up; Grandfather checks his tie knot one final unnecessary time, Grandmother reaches two hands up to her perfectly manicured hair and lifts it another millimetre, lets a hand glide over the pearls in her necklace which are already lying in perfect order around her neck. Then she takes her place by the column, actually a camouflaged outlet for the central heating system, at a perfectly-judged distance from the entrance. Thus she is not standing obtrusively near to the guests the moment they come in, but is at the same time welcoming. Synnøve behind reception tests out her whitest gleaming smile, so that the silver brooch on her national costume seems to shine a little more, and I am in position just inside the outer of the two main doors, in the porch, ready to hurry out purposefully the moment the bus swings round in front of Fåvnesheim, but not a moment before. It mustn't look as if I've been standing waiting, but as if, despite all my important and urgent tasks in a bustling continental hotel, I am nevertheless on the spot at precisely the right moment. So at the very second that the bus begins to swing into the front drive, I hurry energetically – but without running – out of the door, so that firstly the whole starboard, then the whole port side of the bus can register the essential thing: that here, in this hotel, high in the mountains, there is still class and discipline, here everything is still as it was in the good days, the fashionable days, that time in the fifties, that time before the war, that time before the war before the other war; in brief, here they even have their own, uniformed, elegant and exotic-looking piccolo. The front steps and the flagstones by the door are swept, the flags are streaming from the flagpoles in the breeze. If it is a group from abroad arriving, their flag is hoisted as number two from the entrance, whilst The Norwegian Flag always hangs closest. That was the rule, that was in the rules of etiquette, that was what Grandfather had once given me to understand in the clearest possible way when I had flown the French *tricolore* nearest to the house. On the other side of the foreign flag which matches the contents of the bus I have hoisted an exotic one, for example a Portuguese flag, that always looks pretty. Then the row of four flagpoles is rounded off by Austria's ancient red and white flag, in permanent honour of my grandmother, who just now is adjusting her pearl necklace once more and bringing her high-heeled shoes together in first position over there by the column, whilst I am in the process of assisting elderly ladies on their way down the bus's steep steps, gallantly lifting my brown hand in its red sleeve up to them, like a living bannister, whilst I say, 'Careful down the last step.'

Discreetly in the background, having changed quickly into something other than his chef's whites, stands Jim, a little sulky at having taken over the tasks he thought really belonged to Lars, the caretaker, whom we couldn't afford to keep on any longer, ready to heave suitcases – many of them still too heavy for me – so that I can push the big trolley in a visibly efficient way into the lobby, where the guests have now been given a glass of sekt. Synnøve and Zacchariassen (because he's Zacchariassen now, not Grandfather, and must be addressed as such) allocate the rooms and deal with the formalities, whilst Grandmother converses elegantly with the guests about the magnificent mountains, or *die grausamen Berge*, as she called them in private; she hated them wholeheartedly.

Often the passengers on the tour buses were in a hurry and just wanted to have lunch. Grandfather was only moderately in favour of modern road-building policies – at least if they extended further up the mountain than just as far as our entrance.

'It gets easier and easier to cover the whole distance in one day,' he said gloomily, 'and people are more and more rushed. That's the thing. You would think they would relax a bit, now that there's time to spare, and stay around to admire the mountains, but no. The quicker everything happens, the less time people have. That's Human Beings for you, Sedd,' he added, 'that's Human Beings. It was easier in my father's time. Progress was something which happened more slowly, it gave pleasure. But now? Only ten years ago things were different. People came to stay. People weren't going anywhere.'

'*We're* not going anywhere,' could be heard caustically from Grandmother, but by then Grandfather was long gone, often out into the drive to cast an eye over the building, an activity which on good days inspired a mood of intense joy, but on bad days one of gloom; for example, he knew exactly how many windows there were to be cleaned in each wing, but nevertheless he counted them all once more. He didn't really need to look, he could see every single pane in his mind's eye, down to the smallest peephole, just as the 170,000 litres of water which had to be warmed up in the swimming pool were almost visible, resting on his shoulders with their 170 chlorinated tons. But a mountain hotel had to have a swimming pool if it was to survive in our days, that much was certain.

But on other days, when the hotel had a reasonable number of guests, he could light his elegant little Dunhill pipe, which he had inherited from his father, puff away contentedly and begin to tell the story of each wing and each annexe, right back to the time when his grandfather and so forth, and the British queued up in their carriages to get here and so forth. Then you just had to let him carry on through the afternoon, think about something else whilst he talked, whilst the guests relaxed in their rooms or drank coffee in one of the lounges or bathed their travel-weary bodies in biblical amounts of heated pool water, or sweated in one of the two large comfortable saunas, or had a free game of golf on the minigolf course because it would not have been used if people had to pay to borrow clubs, as the investment calculations had assumed. But at least there were guests in every nook and cranny, happy guests with their clubs, and soon Grandfather would begin to talk about the autumn hunting and fishing trips we would undertake, he and I, and that meant that it would soon occur to him to straighten his tie and stroll through the rooms, being his usual friendly and hospitable self, and I would be able to shoot off to the kitchen and begin to help Jim with dinner.

Jim had always been my best friend.

He had been appointed before I was born, thus in Historical Time. It was impossible to think of Fåvnesheim without Jim. At regular intervals Jim would threaten that he could certainly imagine an existence without Fåvnesheim, but those were just empty words. Fåvnesheim was Jim's spiritual home, as he liked to say. After one year in the Navy, two years at sea, one year in France, one year in Bristol and six months in prison because of a bagatelle, he had finally got himself sorted out when he came up here, and after that he never left. Jim had a weakness for drink, but he never drank, or rather did so at the most once a year. Where Jim ruled, order and cleanliness also ruled. Above all cleanliness.

If Jim had nothing to do for a few hours, he would clean the kitchen, even if it had been cleaned the day before. 'Oh, not *again*, Jim,' I would complain or pretend to complain, but Jim just laughed. 'You never know when there'll be an Inspection,' he would say, throwing me a brush, and we would set to. Everything out of cupboards and drawers, and then back in again, after every cranny had been disinfected. There was a calmness about Jim when he was cleaning, just as when he was cooking, for Jim was the sort who had to be doing something all the time. He never got tired, just washed and scrubbed steadily as he whistled tunefully, 'Three Coins in the Fountain' or the song from the 1966 Oslo Winter Olympics. Usually one of those two. If Inspection had awarded an annual trophy for the cleanest kitchen, Jim would have won it for keeps.

Sadly, inspections happened very rarely. There could be years between each visit. But as the inspector said on one such occasion: 'It's so clean here that it's clean boring.' Jim smiled happily. He would live on that for a long time. Which did not prevent him commanding another kitchen clean the next day.

It was only when Grandmother was going to bake that Jim reluctantly had to surrender control of his gleaming kitchen. Then everyone else had to make way.

I liked being in the cleanliness and order of Jim's kitchen. I grew up there. When I was little I liked being there as a cat would have done, because it smelt good, because it was warm and safe, a place where you could find treats and comfort. And later because there was order. Jim could chop greens and root vegetables into perfect, minuscule cubes, all exactly alike, quickly and efficiently, and at the same time calmly, so that even the ingredients for a basic clear stock were like a work of art, despite it being completely unimportant for the taste. Those vegetables were only going to be boiled down in order to add flavour, and in all the cookery books to this day it says: roughly chop the vegetables. But if I asked why he bothered, Jim would just take his eyes away from his knife and board for a moment whilst he looked gravely at me. 'There's a right way,' he said, 'and a wrong way to do things.' Then he chopped the rest of the kilo of carrots and scattered them like orange crystals into the large pot.

There's a right and a wrong way, that's for sure. Presumably it's like that with Memoirs as well.

4

The funeral was dreadful. Fru Berge cried so bitterly, and I'm afraid I cried too, more than I had planned, even though I didn't know the bank manager at all, had hardly given him a thought, just seen him as one of the grown-up friends of my grandparents who came to visit a couple of times a year and perhaps in the hunting season, like the sheriff and mayor, leader of the district council and doctor, wholesale merchant and head of the travel bureau and perhaps a few more, all with their wives; and now he was dead, and his wife was crying, and since it was through his death that we had come so close to each other, as close as two raisins in a packet, his wife was sobbing for both of us. I was not crying for Berge myself, at least not much, but more for my mother, I think, who is also gone. Taken by Time, as Grandmother said. Afterwards Fru Berge held my hand for a long time there by the grave, after they had lowered the coffin and thrown earth on it; we were all standing there by the hole, not quite knowing what to do, as you do next to holes like that, and then she came over to me, before anyone else, and I thought it was embarrassing. Couldn't she have gone over to one of her own people, or at least one of the grown-ups? She held on to my hand for a long time, there by the hole in her black suit, her face was white, and when she smiled at me it was as if it came from inside her face. She thanked me for everything I had tried to do for Dear Bjørn – for a moment her face threatened to break up from inner pressure, but then she pulled herself together and said I must come and see her one day when I had time, oh no, it was nothing urgent, but she had something for me, wanted to give me something, oh no, there was no rush, but she would be very glad, she said, and looked if possible even sadder. And she carried on holding my light brown right hand in her white one for a good while longer, while she looked down, and her left hand fingered the right glove she had taken off. You don't need to take your gloves off at funerals, not if you're a woman, I thought, and I wondered for a moment whether I should say so, but I reassured myself that it is not a break with good etiquette *not* to know such a thing. That last point is also in *The Guide to Etiquette and Modern Manners*, just like the one about the gloves. There are a huge number of rules about gloves that people don't know. What you should say and not say if you are wearing gloves at the wrong moment and so on.

Someone wanted to talk to her and she let go of my hand.

'Sorry for your glove,' I heard myself say; I'd been thinking too much about the *Guide to Etiquette*. She looked at me distantly and a little wonderingly, and I hurriedly corrected it to 'Sorry for your loss', even though that is not really Norwegian, it's more Swedish. In Norwegian you say 'Condolences'. Actually not everyone knows that either. But then she turned away from me and it was over for my part.

Dr Helgesen, who had been in the infernal South, and in that way avoided his duty as a doctor, was standing beside me. I think he had been standing there for a while.

'You did very well there, Sedd,' he said.

'Oh no,' I said, 'it was just a slip of the tongue.'

'Slip of the tongue,' he said, 'I mean what you did that evening.'

'Oh, right,' I said. 'Right.'

'You must understand,' said Dr Helgesen in a grown-up way, as he walked alongside me down the gravel path, where the snow was rapidly melting and the crocuses were beginning to emerge, back up towards the church and freedom, 'things like that just happen sometimes.'

'I understand,' I said.

'Sometimes,' said Dr Helgesen, 'it's so sudden and massive that not even the heart unit at the National Hospital can do anything. Bjørn' – he hesitated – 'our friend Bjørn was probably not in good health. I think you should know that.'

'Yes,' I said. 'I mean no.'

'But you did everything you could,' said Dr Helgesen.

'No,' I said. 'I mean yes.'

'No-one could have done more,' said Dr Helgesen.

And no-one did more either, I thought; they just stood around watching, but I just said:

'I really did try.'

'Yes,' said Dr Helgesen, 'you were quick on your feet. I must say that. I've heard that the Red Cross are going to give you a silver medal.'

'I'd rather not,' I said.

'Are you sleeping all right?'

'Yes,' I said, a little surprised, because it was a strange question; everything was exactly as usual. I had had a few days off school and gone on a few hikes to get rid of the taste of the bank manager, and Grandfather kept talking about taking me on a trip to Oslo, when the days got a little longer and milder and there was less to do, before there was hopefully more to do again, but otherwise everything was almost like before.

'That's good,' said the doctor, 'just pop in and see me after school, though, if there's anything you'd like to talk about. Well, at any time, actually, at any time. My door will always be open for you, Sedd. Always open.'

'Yes,' I said, and then Grandmother came along to rescue me and we finally escaped from the cemetery.

I definitely did not want to go along to the reception afterwards, even though Grandmother insisted, but the more she insisted, and the more she emphasized what was the correct thing to do and what was not appropriate, and that we, of all people, despite everything, it was at our place that this had happened and so on, the more adamant I was that I had had enough, and I just got into the back seat of the car. 'Elisabeth,' said my grandfather, and it was rare for him to use her Christian name, normally he called her Sisi: 'Elisabeth, I think the lad has had enough now.' For a moment it looked as if she was going to argue, but then on this one rare occasion she gave way.

'You're right,' she said. 'You'd better drive him home, and I'll go to the wake.'

'Are you sure you're not coming with us then, *Liebling*,' said Grandfather, but she just shook her head.

'One of us *has* to go,' she said firmly. 'It would look odd otherwise.'

I knew that she would sing my praises again, and Grandfather looked worried, but then we left it to her. That was the best move.

'In that case I'll come back down in a couple of hours,' he said gently, 'and pick you up.'

So Grandfather drove me into the mountains, whilst Grandmother remained with the bereaved and their coffee and their pitifully amateurish cakes.

'It's just as well we left, Sedd,' said Grandfather in the car. 'I've never liked feasting off the corpse afterwards.' He bit his lip when he realised what he'd said, but I didn't react. He looked relieved.

'The end should be the end, that's what I think,' he said. 'You know what, Sedd, it'll be great for the two of us to have a trip to Oslo during the spring. Or the summer. When there's less to do. Before there is hopefully more ...'

'Do you think ...' I began.

'Think what, Sedd?' He kept his eyes fixed on the road, even though he knew it well.

'Do you think there'll be a fuss at school when I go back? Like the teacher wanting to say something and that sort of thing?'

'Well,' he said. 'It's difficult to know. They must be wondering why you've been away. Whether you've been ill or something.'

'I don't think they're wondering any longer,' I said.

'No,' said Grandfather. 'You're probably right.'

'Do you think you can have a word with Mr Dahl,' I said, 'so I don't have to listen to him saying something in front of the whole class when I go back?'

'Well,' said Grandfather in an attack of honesty, 'I'm fairly certain your grandmother has already had a long conversation with Mr Dahl, but I can always have a word with him too.'

'Yes please,' I said. 'That would be good. I don't want any fuss.'

'OK.'

'I just want everything to be as it was. Dr Helgesen said the Red Cross are giving me a medal or something.'

'But isn't that great, Sedd?'

'No,' I said. 'I just want everything to be as it was. If I'm given that medal, I won't raise a single finger for the Red Cross any more. I just want everything to be as it was. It's nothing to talk about.'

'I understand,' said Grandfather. 'I'll see what I can do.'

5

But he couldn't help himself anyway, Mr Dahl, of course he couldn't. I thought it was a bit feeble of him, since he'd been asked not to do it. I really didn't want my utterly useless rescue attempt to receive any more attention; I would much rather have forgotten the whole thing as quickly as possible, and I was quite convinced everyone else should do so too. Well, not the ones who were personally involved, like the widowed Fru Berge and others; it would have been asking too much for them to forget it. But in general I didn't think this was anything which deserved further attention. It wasn't exactly a historic moment.

Despite that, Mr Dahl made a proper little speech about me and to me the first morning I was back in school. He excused himself later, saying that I had after all been away for some time, that people already knew most of what had happened, and that there had been talk. Personally I thought that if there had been talk and people already knew most of what had happened, then it was even more meaningless to bring it all up in class, yet again, as if to rub it in, for the sole reason that I was back in school, but Mr Dahl must have seen it differently. Perhaps he was even a bit proud. It almost seemed as if he was, as he stood there at the lectern and welcomed me back, at the same time as he explained to my classmates what had happened, what I had experienced, what I had tried to do, and how, despite the fact that the outcome had not been – um – optimal, I had nevertheless done exactly the right thing and that I could serve as an Example. And that I, everyone ought to understand, all of them, despite everything, had been a little upset by what had happened, that much is certain, because it's not every day you experience something like that, and we should thank the powers that be for that.

All this Mr Dahl explained, and it was very handy, because quite by chance the first lesson that day was Social Education, which until secondary school had been a part of General Studies, which I think is a much better description. This is the class in which the Norwegian School System enlightens pupils about greater and lesser events and inventions, from the Black Death to Einar Gerhardsen, from the Structure of the Atom to Electricity in the Home.

I found it best to stare down at my desk whilst he was holding forth, and I just answered briefly, in the affirmative, when he asked if I had not benefited from everything I had learnt in the Red Cross first-aid course, even though it had been of no help at all when it came to it, and in the same way I answered briefly, 'Thank you very much', when, after a lengthy appeal for more people to sign up for a first-aid course, he welcomed me back to the land of the living, or so it seemed, and exhorted all the others to be a bit considerate, boys and girls, to Sedd in the first few days. Remember he has been through something dramatic. Something you don't experience every day, and we should thank the powers that be for that. And so on.

It went on and on, but at last it was done with, and we proceeded to investigations of less personal topics. But no less relevant ones for that. The rights of indigenous peoples, for example. Who owns the water, the sun and the earth, as the textbook enquires? Is it the Norwegian state, which simply marched into the kingdom of the reindeer, or is it the Sami and their reindeer, who are much older than the Norwegian and Danish states combined? What does ownership actually mean? It's important to have thought these things through in order to understand the world of today. And Mr Dahl exerted all his powers to get a discussion going, although I must say my classmates did not exhibit much enthusiasm. It was mostly a matter of the usual 'I-dunno-really' and 'Well-yeah-I-suppose-so', so not particularly rewarding. In the end, in order to make it a bit more rewarding, I put my hand up.

'Yes, Sedd?' said Mr Dahl sympathetically.

'How about the Falkland Islands? Is it the British or the Argentinians who are the indigenous people there?'

Mr Dahl looked desperately at me.

'That is a very good question, Sedd, but it's perhaps a little peripheral to the text we're talking about.'

'Yes,' I said, 'but even on the Falkland Islands, even if there aren't reindeer there, someone must have the rights to the sun, the water and the earth.'

'You're right about that, Sedd, absolutely, absolutely. But it wasn't really the Falkland Islands we ...'

'The question is quite straightforward, actually,' I said. 'Who was there first? The Argentinians or the British?'

Someone behind me groaned, but I carried on regardless:

'I mean: one of the two must have been there first?'

'Yes, Sedd, that's quite right. One of them must have come first.'

There was a short pause, whilst the question, as it were, hung in the air between us, trembling. Definitely an important question, if you ask me.

'Yes?' I said when the trembling had lasted long enough.

'Yes?' said Mr Dahl encouragingly. 'Yes, Sedd?'

Another groan from somewhere at the back of the class.

'Well, who was it then? The Englishmen or the Argentinians?'

Mr Dahl fixed me with a look which endeavoured to convey that this was a complicated question.

'This is an extremely complicated question, Sedd,' he declared.

'But it's the same as it is with the Sami,' I declared, 'and the Norwegians. Either the former came first and the latter last, or the latter came first and the former last. There are no other possibilities.'

Another groan astern.

'That,' I continued, 'is how it must be with the Argentinians and the British. Either the latter came first and the former last, or the former came first and the latter last, unless there is a third party involved, which – '

The groans were louder now, but neither Mr Dahl nor I took any notice. You should always rise above such things. So we rose above it.

'Yes,' said Mr Dahl, 'you're quite right, Sedd. That's how it is. Either one group came first, or the other group came first. But which?'

'Yes, which?'

'It's really not easy to say ...'

Unfortunately the bell for the end of the lesson rang just as he had said that, so that the question remained unanswered. I would like to have continued the discussion with Dahl during break, but unfortunately Dahl didn't have time. I thought that was a pity, because ever since the Argentinians landed their troops on those small windswept islands in the South Atlantic, where earth and sky meet, the question had divided our house. Grandfather thought that Margaret Thatcher and Great Britain were quite right to reject all attempts at compromise, and that they ought to go to war to get the islands back, because just think if the Americans had just allowed the Japs to help themselves to Hawaii in 1942, and slunk off? '*Quatsch*,' declared Grandmother on her side, pointing out that war is in all cases an evil to be avoided, especially when it's about something as meaningless as the ownership of some small windswept islands in the South Atlantic, where earth and sky meet, and anyway what were the British doing there in the first place? Weren't the Falkland Islands rather a long way from home? Imperialists, that's what they were, the British, and that's what they'd always been. That's what she said, even though she had the deepest respect for Queen Elizabeth and the House of Windsor. 'You don't grasp the complexities,' said Grandfather, but Grandmother just expelled air from her nose triumphantly.

Neither of them could say with certainty who had come first, the British or the Argentinians. 'It's really not easy to say,' that was Grandfather's answer as well when I asked.

On the way out into the schoolyard, as I was thinking through all these important geopolitical questions, Hans caught up with me.

'You're potty,' he said, thumping me lightly on the shoulder in what was meant to be a friendly way. I think this was his way of saying welcome back.

'Potty? But it's an important question, Hans. When there's a threat of war. War in the South Atlantic.'

'Like I said,' said Hans. 'You're potty. How's things?'

'OK,' I said.

Hans was the son of the quarry manager, and therefore belonged to the small group of pupils who came from what Grandmother called an acceptable background. He collected stamps as well, just like me. So we spent time together. It had been like that since primary school. We went to each other's houses and such-like, though we didn't really talk to each other very much.

Neither Grandmother nor Grandfather was at all keen on quite a few of the pupils, and Grandmother expressed her opinion forthrightly. She thought they were uncultured, boorish, badly brought up and degenerate, budding criminals, with no trace of knowledge or breeding.

I thought Grandmother was going a bit far here. Many of them could be quite pleasant if they felt like it. And several of them had healthy interests. But that they were boorish and ignorant, that I had to agree with Grandmother about. Yet the fact that they had such limited tastes, for example when it came to music, was not necessarily their fault. Here I agree with Grandmother, who thought it was the fault of the Times. Grandmother had had her own painful experiences earlier in life because of the Times, so she knew what she was talking about, even if she didn't actually talk about her experiences because they were too painful. On the other hand it is not easy to take a stand against the Times. Many artists of the

Times are gifted and attractive. ABBA, for example. So in this case I think Grandmother was too conservative. And even though I agreed that Wenche Myhre was really great, I thought it was saying a bit much to claim that she was the greatest in Europe. In Norway, yes, but Europe? On the other hand, one should not underestimate how large the German-speaking area of Europe is. That has been shown to be dangerous. And there Wenche Myhre is really great, that's a fact.

Nevertheless – I think one ought to take a broader view than that, but when it comes to songs like Pink Floyd's 'We don't need no education', I was in complete agreement with Grandmother that this was a destructive text. There could be no doubt about that. Everyone needs an education, that's what I think. It's obvious. Anyway, it should be *any* education.

'You coming round to my house after school?' asked Hans.

'OK,' I said, 'if I can get someone to drive down and pick me up.'

This was always the problem. It was so far up to Fåvnesheim. Or rather, if you prefer, down from Fåvnesheim. So that if it wasn't actually an obligatory birthday party, and certain birthday parties are in fact obligatory, it was always a complicated operation to get up and down. Normally Grandmother drove me down to school in the mornings, occasionally Jim, and then Grandfather usually picked me up after school, when he had to drive down anyway and do various errands, go to the bank and so on. All trips up and down which fell outside this schedule had to be planned and agreed beforehand, either with my grandparents or Jim or with Synnøve or one of the other employees. I could walk it myself in good weather, or go on skis in the winter or by bike in the summer, and I did that now and then, but it was a long way and steep. I had to allow an hour on the way down and at least two on the way up, depending. So if I did it under my own steam, those hours ate enormously into the rest of the day, into homework time and the time I was supposed to help with running the business. In our line of work the business always has to come first. In the winter, when the days were short, it was no fun trudging up the long road on heavy skis, and then across the plateau and over the mountain range to Fåvnesdal where the hotel lay. Once when there was a fog I got lost, even though I was following the road. But in one place the ski track cuts across open country before joining the road again a bit further up, and that's where I lost it. I was in the wilderness. The fog was like porridge, no, like sauce, white and impenetrable. But I didn't panic, I just followed my tracks back the way I had come, and hey presto, there was the road; I clambered over the bank left by the snow-plough and followed it until I'd got past the difficult bit. It was no worse than that. Unfortunately I mentioned what had happened to Grandmother. Complete ban on setting out on my own either up or down, or in fact on going anywhere on my own. That was more or less the reason I started attending the Red Cross training course, mainly to convince Grandmother that I was a sturdy mountaineer who could rescue myself.

But the fact remained that the distance was great. Not just to Hans's, but also to my other classmates. Like the two who wandered across to Hans and me in the school yard, and who most likely had some sarcastic comments up their sleeves. They did too. I was not wrong there. Not that it was so difficult to predict either, because they belonged to the kind of youths who always have a sarcastic comment for their fellow humans, without themselves having anything particularly constructive to contribute. This time they contented themselves with calling me Mrs Thatcher as they went past, but actually I thought that was almost flattering. Margaret Thatcher is after all an admirable woman. It's quite a feat for a housewife from Grantham to become prime minister of the United Kingdom, with all the responsibility that involves. Even though we are not in sympathy politically, I respect Thatcher. She was a female prime minister even earlier than Gro Harlem Brundtland, and everyone agrees that Gro is a shining example. Besides, I had been called worse things. You just have to rise above such matters. Jim said you should give people like that a smack in the face, but I am not an advocate of unnecessary violence, and in this case violence would not only have been unnecessary but mortally dangerous. So they went their way and I went mine.

It turned out that I could go home with Hans after all. After some quick-fire negotiations with Grandfather via the phone booth in the entrance hall, I managed to arrange that Jim would drive down and pick me up at Hans's around half-past six.

The rest of that school day passed as usual, without any dramatic events. I had been worried that I had missed important parts of the curriculum whilst I had been away, but all the teachers assured me that I had not missed anything at all, and it didn't seem as if I had. All the teachers said they were glad to see me, and that they thought I had been quick-thinking and brave, and even a few of the pupils said something similar, which I found embarrassing, even though it was meant positively.

At Hans's house things were as they always were. His mother had started working again now the children were older, and his older sister was out 'gadding about', as Hans put it, whilst his father was at work as manager of the quarry, so we had the house to ourselves. We went into the kitchen and made ourselves cheese sandwiches and hot chocolate, as we always did, and as always I refrained from remarking that Hans's family used powdered chocolate which they stirred into hot milk, instead of melting a dark chocolate bar in a water-bath and then slowly adding hot milk while whisking with a hand-whisk, which was the correct way. But it's the thought that counts, I always reminded myself. We manoeuvred the tray with cocoa-jug, cups, four cheese sandwiches and plates up to Hans's room, a thing which always had to be done with care, for most of the floors in the family home were of stone, so that if you dropped anything it shattered without a by-your-leave.

Up in his room we ate, drank hot chocolate and admired Hans's last two model aeroplanes, which I had not seen before. It was actually quite a while since I had been there. Hans played a couple of records which I made no comment on, out of politeness, because it's the thought that counts. We ate cheese sandwiches and drank hot chocolate.

After a while Hans wanted to know if it had been ghastly.

'Ghastly,' I said, 'what do you mean?'

'You know, with old Berge...'

I had to think about it.

'No,' I said, 'it wasn't really ghastly. More dramatic. 'Cos you don't think anything like that's going to happen. You don't expect things like that.'

'No,' Hans nodded. 'Of course not.'

After a while he said: 'Is it true they shit themselves when they die?'

'No, Hans. It's not true. At least bank managers don't do that.'

'Are you sure?'

'Yes, Hans. I'm quite sure.'

''Cos I've thought about that a lot. It's disgusting to think about. Fucking hell. It's one thing to die, but something else if you're going to shit yourself at the same time. I don't think I could stand that.'

'I wouldn't worry. I didn't notice anything like that.'

'You sure?'

'Quite sure. You remember Herr Berge. He was far too polite to do anything like that.'

'D'you think so?'

'Yes. I think if you're properly polite, it means you have iron self-control.'

'Like fighter pilots.'

'Yes, just like that. And that's a self-control which lasts until death and even longer.'

'Banzai,' said Hans.

'Banzai,' I agreed. Banzai was what the Japanese kamikaze pilots shouted as they steered their flying bombs to their deaths in the war in the Pacific. As everyone knows, Japanese kamikaze pilots were abnormally polite, and had iron self-control.

'So I think,' I added, 'that if you just work on your self-control enough while you're alive, that sort of thing won't happen when you die.'

Hans looked reassured. He said no more. Instead we read comics in silence for a good while, apart from the fact that Hans changed records at regular intervals, so it wasn't completely silent. But we said nothing. We read *Agent X-9, The Phantom, Commando* and *The Silver Arrow* whilst we lounged on Hans's sofa and listened to Boney M and Supertramp. I knew that Hans had a secret passion for Kiss, but there I put my foot down.

When we couldn't be bothered to read comics any longer, Hans asked if we should look at his stamp collection. He'd got some amazing new stamps from San Marino. That would be OK, I said. Hans got out his albums and showed me his latest additions. His father had contacts with marble in Northern Italy, where San Marino lies, and they made sure Hans got the stamps from there. San Marino stamps are spectacular but not worth much. It doesn't mean it's not worth collecting them, it just means they're not worth much. Here too you can say it's the thought that counts.

After we'd admired the San Marino stamps for a while, and they were amazing, a series with illustrations of fruit, we looked at some Soviet stamps with combine harvesters that Hans had discovered, and after that at some really pretty Swedish fairy-tale stamps.

Then Hans said suddenly:

'Did he go green?'

'Green? What d'you mean?'

'I mean, did he go green?'

'Who go green?'

'The bank manager? Berge? I mean, when he – '

'No. He didn't go green. Of course he didn't.'

'Oh – .'

'Have you got any new Italian stamps, Hans?'

'I thought they did. Go green. Corpses.'

'I don't think that happens until later.'

'Oh – .'

He looked almost disappointed.

'I see,' he said. 'Did he go white then?'

'White?'

'I mean, white as in deathly white?'

I thought about it. 'Yes,' I said, 'I think he went a bit white. I'm sure he did.'

'Oh,' said Hans again. 'How white? Like chalk, or more grey?'

For a moment I felt I was back on the floor in the dining room. My grandmother's *Gugelhupf* suddenly filled my nostrils. Moist, that's what it had been. Everything had been moist.

'You know,' I said to Hans, 'everything happened so quickly. I didn't have time to think. And I really didn't have time to notice very much. Not colours or things like that.'

'Oh. Perhaps he went a bit blue?'

'Yes. I think he went a bit blue.'

'What was it *like*? I mean, really?'

I pretended I was thinking for a while. Then I said:

'It's not easy to say. It's really not easy to say.'

'Oh,' said Hans again.

He was disappointed. He didn't ask any more. Jim picked me up at exactly half-past six.

6

In the car on the way up Jim was quiet, something he was good at when he noticed I had a lot to think about.

I was thinking about the stamps I'd seen at Hans's. Perhaps they weren't worth much, that may well be, but at least Hans kept his collection updated and honed his collector's instincts in his dealings with stamps from foreign parts.

Philately is a fine and useful and educational hobby from which you can learn a great deal. For example about animals and astronomy, space exploration and technological advances, since stamps often illustrate things like that. If you also collect slightly older stamps, you can learn a lot about countries' geography and history.

There are many countries in the world. I think that's a plus. Some people think that having borders isn't such a plus, and when it comes to certain borders, for example the Iron Curtain, we can agree that it does cause a number of problems. On the other hand, if it hadn't been for the Iron Curtain, the Russians could just have marched in here, and that would have been no laughing matter, as Grandfather would say. It would have been 9th April 1940 all over again, except that this time we wouldn't have understood what they said as they marched in.

Take Grandmother, for example. She was what you might call a living example of the fact that, when it came to borders, there were plusses and minuses. When she was young, Vienna was a divided city. There were Americans and British, Frenchmen and Russians. The same story as in Berlin, actually, although the Viennese were let off after a few years. Grandmother really didn't like Russians. She didn't like Americans either, even though they had been perfectly OK; the British had been the most OK of all, the French were OK too, but the Russians were just cruel.

Hungarians she quite liked, but not Hungary, which she thought had stabbed Austria in the back after the first World War. MAGYAR POSTA it says on Hungarian stamps, and that's because Hungary is the land of the Magyar. The Magyars are heroic but treacherous. For the same reason she didn't like Czechs or Slovaks either, and definitely not Serbs, Croats, Montenegrins, Ruthenians, Albanians, Slovenes, Bosniaks, Romanians, South Tyroleans and Triestines. They really belonged under the Empire, together with the Kingdom of Hungary, which had been a recognised Kingdom within the Empire. That's why it says KuK Post (*Kaiserlich und Königlich*) on old stamps from that time. Since 'kuk' is the Norwegian word for dick, certain immature philatelists think that is an amusing pun. If only Austria had been able to hold together, it would have been a major power in Central Europe, and as a result there would have been no Iron Curtain and no atomic bomb. Of course, you might think that the world would have been filled with KuK atomic bombs instead, I often thought to myself, but I refrained from saying so. It was not all that simple to discuss Central European questions with Grandmother, since she was a Central European.

The people she really hated were the Germans, but they weren't Central Europeans, she said, not in *that* way. They were a bunch of upstarts who wanted to take the credit for Beethoven but not the blame for anything at all. The mere fact that they had allowed a wretched corporal to rise to the highest office of state showed what sort of country it was. Austria would never have allowed a *German* corporal to become head of state in Austria, *much less* an Austrian corporal. The Swiss she disliked in a more generalized fashion. She believed that the only thing which kept Switzerland together was all the mountains, which meant they didn't have to see one another. In order not to begin arguing in their four different languages they had to write HELVETIA in Latin on their stamps. The Swiss were stingy as well, but people from Liechtenstein were even more stingy. The Italians were just ridiculous. So perhaps borders aren't such a bad idea, when you come to think about it, so that people can keep themselves to themselves.

In order to be a country you have to have other things as well. Not just borders. For example, you have to have a language, or several, as in the case of Switzerland. Then you have to have a different currency, but there are countries which have the same currency as other countries, like Monaco and France for example. Not everyone knows that. Some countries have Kings or Queens, two countries have Emperors, other countries have Princes, some have Presidents whilst others have Chairmen, and one has a Pope. But one thing you *have* to have in order to be a country, and that is stamps. Otherwise nothing would work and people wouldn't be able to write to one another. It's a really practical system, when you come to think about it.

It was the British who invented stamps, and it was a very smart way of sorting out postal problems. That's why the British never write the name of their country on stamps. They were first. Everyone else has just copied them. Since then the whole world has been grateful to the British, and will always be so. Not least we millions of philatelists in countless countries.

Philately is not a particularly expensive hobby. All you need is an album to put the stamps in, transparent envelopes for swaps, a good pair of tweezers and a magnifying glass. As well as a basin to soak the stamps off envelopes. And someone to supply the stamps, of course.

In my case I had Grandfather. We got masses of post at the hotel, from all the countries you can think of, and Grandfather kept the envelopes for me. Grandmother got letters from family and friends in Vienna as well, even though she complained that there weren't many left, but there were some at least. So I had gradually amassed a fine stamp collection. It was a good thing to have in the winter, when not so much was happening and the weather in the mountains was bad. From abroad I collected anything and everything, not very systematically, but from Norway I had begun to be more choosy, concentrating on Post Horns and On Official Business.

But, it occurred to me as Jim was driving me home, it was a long time since I'd had any.

So when I got back from Hans's, I sat down with my collection in the sitting room in our private quarters. There was a good strong lamp on the writing table, and you need a good light when you're looking at stamps. Besides, I could borrow Grandfather's large magnifying glass, which was considerably clearer than my own amateurish one.

I liked these evenings, when all the countries of the world spread open like a picture book in front of me, via the miracle of philately, whilst the old clock ticked away in the corner, Grandfather rustled the newspaper and Grandmother gave the occasional little chuckle when she came upon something she thought was particularly fine in the book she was reading. Cities, countryside and lakes. Animals and insects. Monarchs and dictators. ESPAÑA. SUOMI FINLAND. POSTA ITALIANA.

For a while we sat there peacefully, the three of us, each doing our own thing.

Just as I had reached the album page for Norwegian Post Horns, which still had a regrettable number of empty spaces, there was a knock at the door.

'Come in,' said Grandfather.

It was Jim.

'Good evening, Jim,' said Grandfather warmly.

'Forgive me for disturbing you, Zacchariassen,' said Jim. Grandmother looked up from her book.

'That's all right. What's the matter?'

'Well,' Jim cleared his throat, 'it's just that it's only four days to our next wedding. Families Carstensen and Jensen.'

'Yes,' said Grandfather. 'We know.'

'Well, it's just that things are starting to get a bit busy. On Wednesday we're expecting a busload of Germans, and I have to do the prepping on Thursday, so we need to arrange the food order now. Preferably for tomorrow, or the day after. And it's starting to look a bit empty in the cellar as well.'

'*Ach was*,' exclaimed Grandmother, '*Schatz*, haven't you ordered a delivery from the off-licence yet? You should have got round to that long ago.'

'There's not much left down there apart from the vintage wines,' Jim announced; he knew the stock intimately. 'We're getting short on spirits as well.'

'It's a good thing you told us, Jim,' said Grandmother.

'And I need the food delivery from the butcher, the fishmonger and the dairy by the day after tomorrow at the latest,' Jim repeated. 'It doesn't look as if that's been ordered yet either.'

'But you should have got that done ages ago, dear!' said Grandmother to Grandfather, exasperated.

'Yes,' said Grandfather. 'Of course. It's just that I still haven't had the deposit for the wedding.'

'So?'

Grandfather looked down at his newspaper again:

'Until we've had the deposit, we don't know for sure that there'll be a wedding. They're leaving it very late to pay, I must say.'

Jim said: 'That's as may be, but we must order the stuff in now.'

'The thing is,' said Grandfather again, 'that it's not very sensible to pay out so much from our reserves without being sure that it's necessary.'

'*Aber wirklich*. It's even less sensible to put on a wedding without having any drinks for the guests. Are they to drink Pommac with their steaks? Not to mention the fact that we need the steaks as well. It's not the sort of thing you can do at the last moment, *Schatz*.'

'No, no, we need to order the food in time, that's obvious,' said Grandfather. 'It's just the drinks I'm uncertain about. If the wedding doesn't go ahead after all, and as I said they haven't paid anything yet, then we'll be left with a large consignment of wine and other drinks that we don't need.'

Grandmother looked at him as if he had said something remarkably stupid.

'Fortunately, wine doesn't go off,' said Grandmother. 'We can just sell it at our next *vedding*. Or you can return it to the off-licence. Anyway, have you ever had anyone cancel?'

'You must remember the Birgersen and Brekke families a couple of years ago. When young Brekke broke it off with Frøken Birgersen, or was it the other way round.'

'But they paid anyway, *Schatz*.'

'In the end, yes.'

'I remember it *extremely* well,' said Grandmother. 'First of all the Brekkes thought it was the Birgersens who ought to pay, since it was Frøken Birgersen who broke off the engagement, but then the Birgersens pointed out that it was young Brekke who had had an affair with Frøken Birgersen's bridesmaid, who was her best friend, and that was why Frøken Birgersen had broken off the engagement, understandably. Oh yes, *Schatz*, I was the one who had to talk to all of them over the phone. First the mothers, then the fathers and after that the lawyers, but the point is that they did pay in the end, though I can't quite remember who paid what.'

'In the end, yes,' Grandfather repeated.

'Honestly,' said Grandmother, 'I think you're being very difficult. You're not getting old, are you?'

'Perhaps. But you, Sisi, you never get a day older.' Grandfather looked down at the newspaper with a strange expression on his face. Jim was hovering impatiently.

'Very well,' said Grandfather. 'I'll sort out the drinks order tomorrow morning. First thing. I'll ring Skarpjordet at the off-licence and see to it. There's no problem. And you just order what you need, Jim.'

'Sure thing, Zacchariassen.'

'Grandfather,' I said, trying to introduce a lighter note, 'weren't you going to find some used stamps for me?'

Grandfather smiled, put down the paper and said it would be a pleasure. He got up and went down to the office to fetch the shoe box he kept used envelopes in. Jim said goodnight.

Grandmother disappeared into her book again, but I could see that she was too irritated to read properly.

After a while Grandfather came back. He put the shoe box on the writing table.

'There you are, lad. Sisi, you're quite right of course. Wine doesn't go off. I'll ring Skarpjordet tomorrow morning, it'll be fine.'

'I should hope so,' grumbled Grandmother.

Grandfather sat down with his paper again.

It was a couple of months since I had had a new supply of stamps, so I had expected the box to be full. But it wasn't. It was barely half-full. And when I had emptied it and started to sort the stamps, I noticed something strange. They were almost entirely foreign stamps, and from Norway there were just picture stamps, puffins and stave churches and things like that. Hardly any On Official Business and no Post Horns at all.

'Grandfather,' I asked cautiously.

He grunted behind his paper.

'Aren't there fewer stamps than usual?'

'No,' said the voice behind the paper, 'why do you think so?'

'I just think it feels like that,' I said. 'For example, there are hardly any On Official Business stamps.'

Grandfather lowered his paper: 'That must be just a coincidence, Sedd,' he said.

'And no Post Horns either,' I said.

'Mm,' he said. 'I thought you had enough of those.'

'But Grandfather,' I said, 'those are exactly the ones I'm collecting. You know that.'

Grandfather chuckled and stood up.

'It must be true, what your Grandmother says, that I'm beginning to get old. I'll remember to keep them from now on. So that everyone is happy. It's important that everyone is happy. Well, it seems to have got rather late. I think I'll go to bed, then I'll sort out the orders tomorrow first thing. Good night.'

'Good night,' we said.

He went. Grandmother sat reading. I sat with my stamps. Neither of us said anything. Neither of us moved. Outside the wind blew over the hills. After a while Grandmother went as well, after reminding me not to stay up too late.

I turned on the old radio and listened to medium wave. I moved the dial from one gleaming name to the next: *Hilversum. Motala. Kalundborg.* In each place in the dark night there was a person sitting in a little brightly-lit room, like a quiet pocket in those great towns, being the voice of those towns. *Köln. Stuttgart. Es ist zehn Uhr. Hier ist der Süddeutsche Rundfunk mit den Nachrichten.* Somewhere in Stuttgart there was someone, perhaps a boy like me, listening to the news. Perhaps he was worried because he had a grandfather who was out driving a car in the bad weather, and there had been an accident on Autobahn 81 in the direction of Ludwigsburg. Or perhaps someone understood what it meant when they heard that in Bonn the Bundeskanzler had agreed to reopen negotiations with the opposition. Perhaps someone was reassured by that.

Soweit die Meldungen.

7

Grandmother couldn't stand weddings, and that was a bit of a problem when it came to it, because she had to arrange quite a few. It must have been ten a year, although this year it looked as if it would be fewer.

Grandfather had explained to me how it came about that the Wedding Package had become such an important part of the hotel's economy. The thing is that many young women spend so long dreaming about their own wedding that it becomes a kind of illness. They live the whole thing in advance in their imagination. It begins at the age of six with a wedding game amongst the lilac bushes, where a poor boy of the same age is enticed into joining the game and thrust into the bushes, sobbing, to say yes, where Siv is the vicar and Karianne the congregation, whilst Tonje is the bride he has to kiss. Later, as they get older, the wedding dream grows larger and more realistic, they draw churches and brides with pink felt-tip, and wedding dresses and bridal cars. In those pictures the bride is large and beautiful and takes up a lot of space in the picture, sometimes accompanied by a roughly-sketched bridegroom, a little smaller than the father, who is of course giving the bride away, but who is not important either. The important thing is the dress. Later still – if I had understood Grandfather correctly – these dreams turn into obsessive neuroses, which imperceptibly occupy more and more of their inner life, and by the time they have taken their final school exams they have already made dozens of guest lists which include every single girlfriend and relative, drawn up seating plans which take into account all the social niceties, thought up menus, designed the cake, designed the dress and drafted the invitations: Managing Director Weikman and his wife have the honour to invite Auntie Tulla to the wedding between their daughter Tonje and A N Other. RSVP. The only thing missing is A N Other. But before long they'll get their claws into him, as soon as they start moving in new circles where there are young men to be had. As soon as he has been snared and prepared, and brainwashed into proposing, the wedding will take place, the wedding they have been dreaming of since they were six years old in the lilac bushes, and it is an inescapable fact that the wedding has become more expensive since then. It involves not only a magnificent shiny car and costly bouquets, but also a three-course meal for 150 people, a free bar and live music, and this can become a bit much even for a managing director. So then they go to their mothers crying, sobbing, shaking, because this is what they have been dreaming of their whole lives, a girl's wedding is a once-in-a-lifetime happening, and what kind of a father are you, says the managing director's wife in a scene over the fish pie at home in Grefsen, what kind of a father do you think you are, denying your only daughter her one big day, which she has been dreaming of all her life, this one single day of her life, unforgettable and unrepeatable, so really, and if father then says that in that case little Tonje should have found herself a father who is a shipowner, then there is an explosion. As he lies there on the sofa for three nights, unable to sleep, he can work out what is to be done.

It was for the sake of these nights on sofas in Grefsen, Grandfather explained, that he had devised the Wedding Package, an exceedingly cunning plan which would fill Fåvnesheim's many empty rooms. There are economies of scale to be had; if everyone eats the same thing there is minimum waste, much less than with à la carte, and if the florist is to decorate both the church and the hotel, and supply the bride's bouquet, it can be ordered and delivered in good time, and such a florist has easy access to wild flowers and cotton grass. The local vicar was fond of roast veal, and if invited to the meal he would be happy to assist in scheduling the wedding on a day convenient for high-class guests from elsewhere. In addition, the church was old and beautiful and atmospheric. A fiddler and a group of folk dancers who could prance around on the turf looking picturesque could also be rustled up. A most satisfactory arrangement in every way, which even including overnight stays for all the guests worked out at a price competitive with the costly banqueting rooms down in town, especially if the managing director lying on the sofa calculated that he could request a small sum from each guest towards their accommodation.

And even if the limousine was not the latest model, but the oversized American gas-guzzler belonging to Vestby, who owned the local garage and petrol station, it was nevertheless exotic and unusual enough for Tonje to get her dream wedding without ruining Father. You could also get a horse and buggy up from the village if you wanted to spin things out. Within this specialism – society weddings at economy prices – Grandfather was quite successful, and it went some way towards making up for the guests who now went to Benidorm. There were more and more of them, he said. 'They go to Benidorm. Is there perhaps something wrong with the Norwegian mountains?' That's what he would say as he flicked irritatedly at the paper with one of those irritating adverts: *Tired of winter cold? It's summer in Benidorm.*

'*Es ist nur ein Übergang*,' my grandmother would say. 'They'll get tired of it. Who wants to lie on a beach and fry themselves for weeks on end? When they get tired of it they'll want to go skiing again. And enjoy the glorious Norwegian mountains. And the glorious Norwegian mountain air.'

Grandfather knew very well when she was being ironic. *Die widerlichen Berge*, she would otherwise call them. But he just said:

'I'm sure you're right. It's just a passing phase.'

'It's the fashion,' she said. 'They want to try something new. You shouldn't be so worried. It will all work out, *Schatzerl.*'

'I worry too much,' said Grandfather. 'But for the time being we have to rely on the weddings.'

'Bah,' said my grandmother. '*Veddings.*'

Grandmother really didn't like weddings; she consistently called them *veddings*, so that the guests thought she had a speech impediment. There was nothing Grandfather could do about it.

'Sisi,' he said, 'my sweet, don't call them that.'

'*Quatsch*,' said Grandmother, 'they don't notice.'

'Sisi, my dear,' said Grandfather as cautiously as he could, 'they might be offended.'

Then the skies darkened around Grandmother, there were signs of an approaching storm around her upswept brown hair, her eyes were first black, then fiery, and everything around us withered. She didn't *say* anything. She just looked at him for a long time.

'Oh well,' Grandfather might say hurriedly on such occasions, 'it's time I got on.' On which he would make haste to disappear. And if I had an attack of self-preservation, I would make haste to disappear too. Get myself off to school, for example, if it was a weekday, or do something else urgent. If I felt generous, I would stay there and listen to the fairytale Grandmother would now tell me.

The fairytale told of how she and Grandfather met in Historic Time and so forth, how they had their *vedding*, but above all everything that happened afterwards.

But not this time. She didn't have time. The Carstensen and Jensen families were to be united.

Willy Carstensen was the poor father who was to pay for the privilege, a fat and resigned man who looked as if he had been middle-aged since immediately after confirmation, which was the time when he met his teenage sweetheart Evy, who for most of the roughly three hundred years which had passed since then had been Fru Carstensen and the mother of Carstensen's daughter, the little treasure Svanhild. Svanhild was blonde. I'm trying to think of something else to say about Svanhild which can provide a fuller description, but basically I can't think of anything other than just this: she was as blonde as spun gold. Wearing her voluminous wedding dress, she advanced through the rooms like a horizontal avalanche. At her side walked her intended, Egil, already exhausted, looking down at his patent leather shoes as often as he could. Everyone agreed that they radiated love's young dream. The wedding lasted for three whole days, with arrival and the usual girlfriend hysteria on the Friday, panic and primping on Saturday morning, followed by the wedding ceremony down in the picturesque wooden church in the village, then afterwards a three-hour reception for the bussed-up guests whilst Svanhild was photographed down in the village with and without Egil, with and without church, until they finally sat down at around six o'clock for a three-course meal which lasted for five hours, because there were many speeches and they were all equally good. In other words: Carstensen and Jensen's wedding was indistinguishable from all the other weddings up here. Had it not been for the unfortunate fact that something happened.

Perhaps it happened in the course of the crème caramel, whilst the meal was in its death agonies as Fru Evy's third cousin on her father's side finally had his turn to speak. Perhaps it was then. Or perhaps it was earlier. It must have happened at some point during the meal, whilst Herr and Fru Carstensen, Svanhild, Herr and Fru Carstensen's family and friends, Egil's parents, their family and friends, and of course also Svanhild's bridesmaids, and Egil's best man, as well as Egil, were sitting at table enjoying the speeches together with Jim's mushroom velouté, roast veal with jus of rosemary and crème caramel with fruits of the forest. In the course of this fairly lengthy period an unknown criminal gained access to Fru Evy's room and removed from her dressing table a gold brooch with three pearls, which she had been given by

Carstensen on their plutonium wedding anniversary, and which at the last minute she had put aside in favour of a brooch with less symbolic significance, but which showed up better on her new gold lamé dress. Then at some time during the course of the evening the first brooch had disappeared, the one which had been left on the dressing table.

Such things are often not discovered until the next morning, but Evy Carstensen was a member of a temperance society and discovered what had occurred the moment she and Carstensen had retired for the night, after cake, dancing and drinks. Whereupon she was standing, with Carstensen in tow, shocked and indignant, not least for Carstensen's sake, in reception at one forty in the morning demanding that the hotel manager should take action.

She could be heard right through in the kitchen, where I had been helping to clear up and was now drinking a Coke. I walked quietly through to reception, positioned myself behind the postcard stand and picked up most of it, since Evy Carstensen described the sequence of events several times.

Not again, I thought behind the postcard stand.

My grandfather was an experienced hotelier. He knew that there was one thing and one thing only he had to do now, and that was to agree with Fru Carstensen about absolutely everything, to applaud all her good ideas and suggestions, and to assure her that he would move heaven and earth so that the Carstensens could relax and sleep the sleep of the innocent. Not a stone would remain unturned, every single member of staff, both hired and permanent, would be subjected to long and thorough third-degree interrogations in the course of the night; he would personally supervise the matter. The sheriff would be alerted that very night. The criminal police as well, if the sheriff advised it. No, hotel detectives were something only large hotels in foreign metropolises went in for, but he could assure them that nothing of that nature had ever happened on any previous occasion here at this hotel, not in his time, not in his father's time, and not in his grandfather's time, if you make a small exception for the German officer who, according to his own statement, had been robbed of his iron cross with oakleaf and sword in 1942, but that one might describe as more an act of resistance than the action of a criminal – and here Herr Carstensen agreed. Carstensen was in fact just as much in agreement with his wife as Grandfather was, and recommended that they should now go up and sleep the sleep of the innocent and leave it to the efficient hotel manager to deal with the matter. 'But the brooch, Willy, that precious brooch which you gave me on our anniversary, it's gone!' 'Yes, my dear, it seems so.' 'We must do something, Willy!' 'Yes, my dear, Herr Zacchariassen has said that he will move heaven and earth.' 'Yes,' Grandfather nodded seriously, 'heaven and earth.'

In the end they went up to their room, Grandfather shut up reception and sent the staff to bed.

'Not again,' muttered Jim as we washed the kitchen surfaces and mopped the tiled floor. Grandfather was standing by the kitchen door smoking, somewhat tired; he nodded seriously. 'Yes,' he sighed, 'again.'

Jim and I cleaned up, finished off and put out the light.

I followed Grandfather up the stairs to our private apartments and could see that his left hand, in which he always carried his key ring, was trembling as it always trembled on such occasions. At the same time he was whistling softly, 'Volare'. So everything was just as it usually was. Outside my door he muttered goodnight and went up to his own room. Grandmother had gone to bed early.

The next morning Grandfather was standing behind the reception desk, impeccably dressed as always (somehow he managed to be extra impeccable in his impeccability on such occasions), rested and fresh as the morning, but with a serious expression, anticipating the next meeting with the Carstensens. In my red uniform I blended in so well with my surroundings that it didn't seem at all conspicuous for me to stand just within hearing distance in reception, waiting for cases and messages to carry; I have in fact always had very good hearing, it's something all men in our family have according to Grandfather, although Grandmother maintains that broccoli is the most important thing to develop your sense of hearing.

The Carstensens arrived. On the way down to breakfast. And like the experienced hotelier he was, my grandfather beckoned the plundered couple over, took Fru Carstensen by the horns, so to speak, with an expression which simultaneously conveyed responsibility, regret and frankness. Looked seriously at them. Placed both hands flat on the reception desk and assured them that he had done everything in his power, but that still more would be done; that he had called in every single employee, both permanent and hired, for a serious interview, one by one. That the sheriff had been informed of the event by telephone and took the matter extremely seriously, as was indeed the duty of the highest police authority in the district, of course, it was the very least he could do, and that the sheriff would personally interrogate every single person who could conceivably be suspected of having filched the Carstensens' room key from the board in reception at an unguarded moment. Herr and Fru Carstensen expressed understanding and indeed a certain degree of satisfaction. However, said my grandfather and leaned his weight more heavily on the desk whilst he humbly lowered his head, however, it was in the nature of the circumstances that a matter such as this unfortunately, and this was deeply regrettable, was difficult, not to say almost impossible to clear up. My grandfather could not remember having experienced anything like it, and the staff were highly trustworthy and had the best references, in short: anyone at all could, and so forth. In a hotel as large as this there were furthermore thousands, not to say tens of thousands of hiding places for such a brooch, not to mention pockets and bags. Of course, he was not referring to the toilet bags of Carstensens' guests, that went without saying, and the couple nodded in unison; that went without saying, but I could see that they had got something to think about. In his calm and reassuring way my grandfather, as an experienced hotelier, now delivered the coup de grace, as he resorted to the most reassuring of all reassuring devices: he activated them. Could Fru Carstensen possibly be so good as to produce a rough sketch of the missing object from memory, as accurately as possible, with an indication of distinctive markings, colour and approximate dimensions? Deftly he took out pencil and paper, as they say in competitions on Children's Hour; the drawing materials had been lying ready under the desk. Faced with the empty sheets of paper together with the coloured felt-tips, the Carstensens also nodded, bewildered, to my grandfather's very down-to-earth request for a provisional valuation of the lost item of value; not, of course, as a binding estimate, of course not, but for the hotel which had never experienced anything like it, this was no less than a matter of honour. No less. Sentimental value, said my grandfather as he lifted his hands from the desk towards his chest, sentimental value can in any case never be measured in kroner and øre. It is a value which resides *here*. He pressed his right hand carefully against his left lapel, just beneath the Rotary badge, and there came as it were an answering golden glimmer from Herr Carstensen's identical Rotary badge on his own lapel. For a moment they were two lone men, two fur trappers, Nansen and Johansen, Scott and Oates, Crosby and Hope, together in the wilderness, and I could see from where I stood that Grandfather had solved the case. Not perhaps in the way that Derrick or Columbo would have solved it, but still, it was solved. There remained now merely a certain amount of tidying up and a few unpleasant aftershocks, and those would be expensive in the form of compensation for the brooch – but he had solved it. By showing himself to be the reliable, solid and honest person he actually was, by *inspiring* confidence, without demanding the impossible either of himself or of others.

And sure enough: after breakfast the Carstensens returned with the paper with a sketch and description of the brooch, without having provoked any excitement amongst their guests, but possibly having regarded each and every member of their friends and family with fresh eyes – how do I know? One never knows about such things. It is altogether difficult to know anything at all with certainty. Innocent until you are proven guilty should not only apply to the suspect, it should apply to the whole world; that is my opinion. It is difficult to say whether this brooch was actually to be found in the striped toilet bag of a light-fingered guest, or in the anorak pocket of a hired waiter, or whether Fru Carstensen herself was perhaps not a member of the temperance society after all, but had a secret vice which she could not afford, opium for example, and was stealing from Herr Carstensen by stealing from herself; in short, you can't be sure about such matters.

But as Herr Carstensen discreetly but solemnly passed the sheet of paper to my grandfather, like a guarantee of safe passage between men, and my grandfather received it, just as solemnly and with a steady hand, I saw that he swallowed and glanced down at the desk for a brief moment. I myself looked down at the toes of my shoes. So much is certain.

Then I looked up again.

The morning light in reception was cold and clear, and everything was as usual.

8

Grandmother went on about it, as she habitually did. I pretended not to notice. 'Aren't you going to,' she said. 'Oh yes,' I said, 'I'll do it tomorrow.' It wasn't that I *hadn't* thought about doing it, but why now exactly? Or why tomorrow exactly. Actually it's pretty meaningless in my opinion. I mean, if you've *thought* about doing something, that means precisely that you've *thought* it, and not that you've actually forgotten it; that seems to me to be a decisive difference. Sometimes it can be an advantage to wait with what you've been thinking about, not because you're dreading it, possibly, it may be because you're looking forward to it, no-one else can know that. No-one can see into someone else's heart, that's for sure. It has to be up to you, and anyway spring had arrived, at least here and there, and I had expeditions to make, and I found valuable things that spring. For example I found a dead cock ptarmigan lying on top of the snow, it was completely white, still in its winter plumage, so it must have been lying frozen in the ice a bit higher up, and no animals or insects had attacked it. It was perfect, and I took it home and put it in the freezer so that Grandfather could make a start on it as soon as he had a free weekend.

But Grandmother went on, as she habitually did about such matters. 'Aren't you going to,' she said, and I said yes I was. 'Tomorrow,' I said. *'Morgen, morgen, nur nicht heute, sagen alle faule Leute,'* Grandmother just murmured, and pinched my ear. That was something she normally did when she was displeased with me, but it was quite a while since she had done it, in fact, so it was a bit unexpected, but I liked it, because it meant that things were beginning to return to normal, and that was exactly what I wanted. So Grandmother's pedagogic pinch, which was a pedagogic winch with which she had been raised with great success in her endlessly wonderful and eventful childhood in the cosmopolitan city of Vienna, had an entirely positive effect on me. Such things do no harm to children, that's for sure, on the contrary it's actually a great method, and quite pleasant too, if the truth be told, in its own way, at least.

So basically I thought things were fine as they were and let Grandmother pinch. In the end she stopped doing it, she didn't even change strategy, just gave up, stopped going on. That was a situation I could live with, because I *was* going to do it, it *was* in my thoughts, but not in the thoughts I thought every day, and that was a positive thing. Besides, it would soon be exam time, and there was a lot of homework. Especially in German. Of course, my German was exceptionally good, but it's one thing to be good at German and something quite different to know by heart all the verbs you have to know in order to prove that you are good at German.

Beweise, bewies, hat bewiesen.

But one day at the end of May, when the summer holidays were already beginning to be visible, like a huge mountain peak on the horizon, white and glistening with sunshine and empty days, it came again: 'Aren't you going to?' I prevaricated. But then Grandfather said it too: 'Aren't you going to? Shan't you do it soon?'

'You see, Sedd,' he said, 'Yvonne is moving.'

'Yvonne?' I said, because I didn't know who he meant.

'Fru Berge,' said Grandfather, irritated, and his face went a bit Zacchariassen. 'You know that.'

I did know it actually, when I thought about it. 'Grandfather,' I began, but he just looked sternly at me and became completely Zacchariassen, and then he went on, and my heart sank, because I understood that there was no escape:

'You have no idea,' he said, 'how much we owe to her and poor Bjørn. When we were going to build the swimming pool in '74, for example. Who do you think it was who supported us with finance when everyone else refused?'

I nearly said Santa Claus, but then he said it himself: 'Do you think it was Santa Claus? And who do you think it was who gave us credit when we were going to build that dreadful waste of money that the minigolf course turned out to be? That was Bjørn Berge, that was, Bjørn Berge and the savings bank, and more Bjørn Berge than the bank. Sedd,' he said, and was still Zacchariassen, 'you must understand this. One day you're going to take over here. You must understand that *connections* are everything. If Bjørn came here so often to eat dinner, him and the others, a hundred times, then it's because *connections are important*, Sedd. And then he goes and dies up here of all places ... .'

Suddenly he became Grandfather again. 'I know, Sedd,' he said. 'I can understand that you don't think this is much fun. I can understand that you'd rather get out of it. But Yvonne is moving, she's moving to Oslo.'

'What's she going to do there?' I asked, mostly for something to say, because I understood that there was no way out and had already begun my mental preparations. 'She's going to live there,' said Grandfather. 'Their daughter lives there with husband and grandchildren, so she wants to be closer to them. Besides, it's the bank that owns the big house.'

'How strange,' I said, 'they've always lived there.'

'Not always,' said Grandfather.

'But for a long time,' I said.

'Yes,' said Grandfather. 'For a long time, Sedd. It's strange to think of, really.'

For a few seconds he was far away. 'You know,' he said, 'Yvonne didn't want to press you. But she would like to give you something of Bjørn's.'

'Can't I get out of it?' I asked.

'No,' said Grandfather. 'She just wants to show you that she's grateful. You must understand that.'

'But it was nothing,' I say.

'Perhaps that's how it seems to you now,' said Grandfather. 'And perhaps you're right. But because Bjørn was always so helpful to us, and because Yvonne is so kind, and because Bjørn went and – well, you understand. So that's why you must do it, Sedd, and not mess about and put it off any more.'

'I'm not messing about,' I said.

'No, I'm sure,' he said. 'But now you have to take the responsibility and just do it.'

As I said, I had already begun my mental preparations, because that's how it is sometimes with things like that, you just have to swallow the bitter spoonful, realise that the race to the Pole is lost and begin your mental preparations. I could already see it in my mind's eye, how the next day, which was a Saturday, I would have to face up to it and make my way down to the village; perhaps I could use my bike if I got the tyres pumped up and oiled it. I could glide down the valley side and swerve a little daringly round the bends, down to the built-up area, find the right turning, cycle up the avenue in the fine weather, past all the ugly prefabs and further on to the grander houses, then up to the grandest of all, the imposing yellow bank-manager's house, where the bank manager had lived since time immemorial, right up till he passed away, put my bike down inside the gate, stroll slightly reluctantly and nervously up to the majestic oak front door, and ring the brass bell beneath the brass plaque on which it said BERGE in brass letters, so that when the next day actually arrived and I did all that, it was as if I had already done it. It must be strange to have just one front door, I thought, it must make people different, they have one door with a bell and a plaque which explains that they live there, and only they do, and they can close that door behind them and be just themselves, and no-one – apart from themselves of course – can see or hear them, and that must be what makes them different, whilst we have loads of doors and there are people living with us the whole time, or a large part of the time, or at least some of the time, and Jim is there and Synnøve and the others, and the front door leads in to where everyone is, whilst a much smaller one on the lower side leads into the entrance which leads to the corridor which leads to the office and our private apartments, which don't really have a door, just a normal staircase which you can go up and down.

Fru Berge opened the door in a light-coloured dress. I was almost dazzled. It was yellow too, just like the house.

'Sedd,' she said, 'how nice of you to come.'

Schwimmen, schwamm, hat geschwommen, I thought.

'Come in,' she said. 'Would you like some tea perhaps? Coffee? No, do keep your shoes on, people are coming in the whole time now to pick things up.'

I looked around. Apart from a couple of cardboard boxes in the corner of the entrance there was nothing to suggest that there were any removals going on, but I thought that she was no doubt the sort of lady who did everything very efficiently and neatly and in the right order. Some people are like that; they can't make a mess, however hard they try. On the chest of drawers in the entryway, or presumably it's called an entrance hall when it's as big as that, there was an impressive display of tulips, which were yellow as well.

'Or perhaps you'd rather have a Solo,' she said. 'You must be thirsty after your bike ride.'

'Yes, please,' I said, and we went into the sitting room. The crystal glittered, the polished mahogany shone, and the parquet floor creaked expansively.

'Well, you've been here before, Sedd,' she said. I nodded. I had been there. But never alone, and not in the middle of the day, and seldom without a *Donald Duck* or a *Silver Arrow* magazine, or more highbrow reading material I could immerse myself in whilst the adults were doing their own thing, so I hadn't really noticed very much on earlier visits. Not as much as now, at least. And now it was over, I thought, strange that now that I had finally discovered this room and how attractive it was, and how distinguished, now it was to be packed up and taken away.

'Will there be a new bank manager coming now?' flew out of my mouth. A quick grimace of pain crossed her face, and I regretted what had flown out of my mouth, and she saw that, and hurried out to the kitchen and brought the Solo which she served in a narrow crystal glass with elegant curves. Farris, it said on it, and the glass was on a tray with a coaster together with the Solo bottle, which was yellow as well. Flies, flew, has flown.

'Yes, it will be strange,' she said. 'I could no doubt carry on living here as far as the bank is concerned, but I don't think that would be right. It was Bjørn who had his professional life here, after all. His long professional life.'

'I understand,' I said.

'And now it is over,' she said.

'Yes,' I said.

'It's eighteen years, you know, from when we arrived until now. Janne has been living in Oslo for a long time now, of course. You remember Janne?' She nodded at a picture of the family, and I nodded affirmatively, because I probably remembered Janne if I thought about it.

'That's a long time,' I said.

'Yes,' she said. 'It's almost forever.'

This was not as bad as I had feared, to be honest. In my opinion this demonstrates the importance of thorough mental preparations. I drank Solo and conversed fairly acceptably as I sat there on the sofa. One has learnt something after many years in a hotel. It wasn't so bad to talk about Bjørn Berge either. Fru Berge fetched another Solo and sat down beside me on the sofa; I steeled myself, because I could tell that it was coming now, and it came:

'Sedd,' she said seriously.

'Yes,' I said seriously.

'I would like to thank you,' she said, 'for everything you tried to do for Bjørn that evening.'

I had prepared myself mentally, and I knew what I wanted to say:

'Everything is in God's hands,' I said.

She was startled. No doubt she had expected that I would say something like I just wish I could have done more, or that I only did what any lifesaver from the Norwegian Red Cross support group would have done, or that I would like to have done much more, but my mental preparation had already worked out that in that case the conversation would be interminable, because she would immediately say no, you could not have done more, or that everyone should take a course in resuscitation with the Norwegian Red Cross support group, or there was really nothing more you could have done, upon which I would have had to repeat that oh no, I really wish I could have done more, and as a result we would have sat there haggling about my efforts, how much they were worth, as it were, bargaining about their value, and I thought that would have been undignified.

She looked at me, a little confused.

'There is something in that,' she said thoughtfully. 'In God's hands, yes.'

'Yes,' I said, thoughtfully.

'Well,' she said after a while, 'I would like to thank you in any case. It was courageous of you.'

Again we could have finished up in negotiations, where I would have to emphasize how uncourageous it was actually, upon which she would have to insist on how courageous it actually was, but I answered:

'Courage is a relative thing.'

Once again I thanked my thorough mental preparations, because this was an absolute and incontestable statement, which fortunately meant nothing at all, and I thought suddenly, Grandma, what big teeth you've got – teeth are a relative thing! But I didn't start smiling, because I could see that she thought I was being very grownup, and I liked that. Grows, grew, has grown. But then she said:

'You acted very decisively, Sedd, I must say that. Bjørn would have been grateful.'

That I had not anticipated, but my thoughts moved at lightening speed. Something which is only possible when you have steeled yourself and are ice-cold because of your mental preparations. But despite the lightening speed of my thoughts, no breakthrough occurred.

'If only he had survived,' I said finally.

Flies, flew, has flown.

She looked at me for a long time. Laid her hand on my knee. Then she patted my cheek. I could feel my face getting hot.

'We'll not talk about this any more,' she said. 'I've got something for you.'

'That's not necessary,' I said.

'Yes,' she said, and put her hand on my leg again, a bit further up this time. 'There's something I'd like to give you.'

'Right,' I said.

'You're very handsome,' she said, 'you know that? A handsome boy.' Then she got up. 'Come, I'll show you.'

I went up to the first floor with her. The rooms here were smaller, the ceilings not so high, and there was a smell of cleaning products and lavender. Through a half-open door I caught a glimpse of a large, yellow double bed and an open wardrobe door which she was in the process of clearing out.

'Come and see,' she said, and opened the door at the end of the corridor. The room behind it looked like Bjørn Berge's snug. There was a writing desk, there were shotguns and trophies everywhere, there was a carafe with something brown in it on the mahogany chest of drawers. Against the wall stood a narrow bed.

'It'll be good to get away from all this,' she said. 'This was where Bjørn lived the last few years, you see.'

I nodded.

'Here you are,' she said. She opened a cardboard box. 'It's for you,' she said. 'All this equipment was Bjørn's, I think they are quite professional things. I would like you to have them.'

The contents of the box gleamed metallically and expensively.

'I can't take all that,' I said.

'Oh yes, do,' she said. 'Otherwise it will only be sold or thrown away. I don't take photographs. And Janne and her husband don't either. So just take it. Bjørn would have wanted it.'

'I can't carry it on my bike,' I objected. Then I hurriedly added, so that it only seemed to be a practical objection: 'I'll have to get Grandfather to drive down and collect it one of these days.'

'Yes, do that, Sedd,' she said in a strange voice. 'Do that. I'm moving next week, so do it soon.'

'Thank you,' I said. 'Thank you very much.'

'It's a pleasure,' she said. 'I know you like going out walking and finding things. Perhaps you can start taking photos as well. Bjørn used to say that as long as you have a camera, you can always find something attractive to photograph. Perhaps you'll find something attractive, Sedd?'

'Thank you very much,' I said. 'It's really too much.'

'Oh,' she said. 'It's nothing.'

She came down with me and said goodbye, shook my hand first of all and then gave me a hug. When I turned to go out to my bike, she touched my backside. Almost like a little smack. It could have been by accident, but I thought I heard a slight noise from her, like a breath, a hiccup, a giggle. I turned round wonderingly.

'Goodbye and good luck, Sedd,' she said.

'Goodbye,' I said. Then I was outside and could see my bike.

Gehen, ging, ist gegangen.

The following Wednesday I drove down with Grandfather and collected the equipment, but then we weren't alone, Yvonne and I, so I saw no more of the merry banker's widow.

9

I think it would be a good idea to write a few words about myself. Or rather, not about myself exactly, but about what Grandmother would call my provenance. That is a precise and useful word, although apart from Grandmother and myself, and perhaps Kåre Willoch, I doubt there are many who understand it. Most people probably know less about their provenance than they realise, and that's a good thing for them. But I definitely know more than many people do. More than is good for me, Grandfather would say. Jim would say that too. That it's not good for me. But that's just the way things are in this life; once you know something you know it, and you can't stop knowing it just because the knowledge isn't good for you. It's like a door on an Advent calendar you've accidentally opened too early, and seen that there's a picture of an angel inside; however hard you try to close the door again convincingly so that no-one notices anything, you've seen it now. This is one of life's really great mysteries. When you know something, you can't force yourself to unknow it. You can of course pretend you've forgotten it; that's often the best course. But if you don't actually forget it, so that you can't remember it any longer, then you remember it because you can't help remembering it, and things like that you can't decide for yourself, and that as I said is one of life's mysteries. And what I know about my provenance, that is my origin and parentage, that is what my brain has pieced together entirely of its own accord from what it has picked up here and there, mostly here, from what I have heard from Grandmother and Grandfather. That's the strange thing about the brain. It adds two and two together without anyone asking it to, and fills out the picture, like if there has already been an angel behind one of the doors on the Advent calendar, you can work out that the next picture won't be another angel, but perhaps for example a sheep, or a lamb as they say in the Nativity story.

Although certain things one does not know. I was aware of the fact that my mother wasn't *here* any longer. That was something everyone knew. That was nothing new. She had been taken by Time. But I didn't know, for example, *why* she wasn't here any longer (apart from the fact that she wanted to be a witch), and also where she was now. The last thing was something that no-one else knew either, I am convinced of that. But their eyes flickered when I asked.

So there is a lot we don't know. But I can begin with what I did know: that my mother had once lived here, in the same room as I do, and had grown up here, in the same way I did. With a sense of responsibility and helpfulness as her immutable guide. I can just about remember her, as a foxy-red sheen in the air, a soft warmth brushing past. Occasionally I dream about it. Then I usually dream that I'm standing in my cot, and that she's there. I know she's there, because I can see her, but only from the side or with her back half-turned. I can't see her face. It irritates me, because it always makes me wake up when I dream that dream. I think I must be sad in the dream, because I can hear someone crying. I think I would have remembered her face if I got to see it, but I can never manage it. How typical. The confirmation picture which stands on the sideboard in a glass frame doesn't look like her at all. I'm sure of that. Even Grandmother has admitted it's not a very good likeness. I think she looked completely different. There are no pictures of her to be seen anywhere else. Not in the albums either. I think perhaps Grandfather has removed them. Well, actually, Grandmother has one, in her bedside drawer, but I've only sneaked a look at it two or three times. Or perhaps four or five. It's a picture of her as a little girl, but it's so unfocused and faded that it looks as if it's painted with watercolours. The only thing you can see is the red hair, and two thin lines as she screws up her eyes against the sun; she's facing the sun in the picture, of course. A portrait in which you can't see the pupils tells you nothing. That's what I think.

My mother was called Elisabeth as well, after Grand-mother and after a whole dynasty of Elisabeths, mother and daughter, mother and daughter, and so on backwards for all eternity, until about as far back as Charles V. That's the custom in Austria. The mothers are called Elisabeth and so are the daughters. She grew up and all went well – I'm speaking here about my mother, the last Elisabeth in the line so far – but then something dreadful happened. I'm not really clear about what this dreadful thing was, but according to Grandmother it was Time. That, and perhaps Norway. If my mother had grown up in Austria, for example, where everything is a little more organized, and the effects of Time are not so terrible, everything would no doubt have been different. But Norway is a land where people have too much licence to behave as they want to, and things are too lax. There's no precision about anything. Just take the people who demand that Norway should go in for nuclear disarmament – they say we should become 'an atom-free zone'. Of course I understand what they mean, but there's no denying it would be rather a problem if all our atoms disappeared. It's atomic weapons they want to get rid of, and that you can understand, but then that's what they should say. On the other hand, without atoms there wouldn't be any Norway here either, and sometimes I think Grandmother would be more than pleased about that.

So it is not entirely clear what happened. But she was taken by Time, the witch, and disappeared never to return. Down in the village they said she had gone to Amsterdam. Jim for his part had had a postcard from India, which he had unfortunately mislaid. Grandmother and Grandfather said only that they didn't know where she was. They didn't want to speculate about it either. Whatever: she was gone. Without me. I wasn't gone. I was still here. But before that things must have happened which neither Grandfather nor Grandmother would talk about. Their faces just looked strange. 'Your mother had a difficult temperament, Sedd,' Grandfather would say. 'A difficult temperament.' Then he clammed up and wouldn't say any more. Grandmother said: 'She was just too nice, that was the problem. Too nice and too gullible for her own good. Too nice for the Time.'

But before she was taken by Time she had managed to have me. For a long time I thought that this must have been a kind of high point. That's what you believe in the springtime of youth, isn't it, that your own birth must have been a triumph in your parents' lives, for what else could it have been? But I'm past the springtime of youth, as a matter of fact, and I understand the whole thing better now. But, no hard feelings, as Hemingway says. Now, for example, I can understand that my birth, however positive a thing it might have been for me, was one of those things my mother got up to which must be called problematic, before she was taken by Time.

And this is where I must talk about my provenance. After all, I do look a little special. Exotic, that's what Grandmother calls it. Perhaps it was my exotic appearance that Fru Berge was referring to. I read somewhere that children don't notice skin colour, but that's rubbish. Blind children no doubt don't notice skin colour, but there's nothing they can do about that. It's not so easy to be blind. But all other children notice it, I'm sure about that. I certainly noticed my skin colour, which had a completely different brownish hue than everyone else I knew, both children and grown-ups. So I began early on to ask how it could be that I looked so exotic. The answers I got varied from year to year. First Grandmother said that I was *ein Schmuckstück in Gottes Augen*, which being interpreted means that I could thank God for a favourable appearance, which was all the more favourable because it was unusual, and not similar to the appearance of most Norwegians, and especially not Grandfather's. Later on she had different variants of this, which generally speaking related to the fact that I should be glad that I deviated in a positive way from the mountain norm. Eventually this became that I should be glad, and of course thank God, that my mother had had such good taste. This made me think that mothers have a special internal mechanism which makes it possible for them to form the children in their stomachs according to their own wishes, with reference to a kind of vision as it were, and this created serious problems in my dawning understanding of how children are born. That wasn't how it was described in Lennart Nilsson's excellent book of that name, i.e. *A Child Is Born*, for example, or in the extremely informative *Show Me!*, two most helpful books, especially the latter, which were available from the library when they weren't out on loan, which they frequently were, especially the latter. So her answer confused me. There wouldn't have been any point asking Grandfather, because he thought that human reproduction didn't belong under natural processes. Natural processes were everything which had to do with hunting and fishing, together with plants and the weather, and he knew everything about all of those, but if you asked him about anything to do with people, he just said that he didn't know anything about things like that. But Jim knew. With a deep sigh which clearly announced that he thought something was hopeless, he explained to me how it all hung together. At the time I imagined that perhaps he thought it was hopeless of me to ask, but now that I am much more mature than I was I have understood that he actually thought it was rather hopeless that he was the one who had to explain it to me. It is even possible that he didn't think that this formed part of his contract of employment, which in any case was exceeded long ago. So, after his deep sigh Jim quickly sorted out my ideas by explaining that my father had not been Norwegian but Indian. Pure and simple. That explained as well why my surname was Kumar as well as Zacchariassen, something I hadn't thought about before, in fact.

'So that's how things stand,' said Jim.

'But Indian,' I said, confused. 'Did he come from India, then?'

'No,' said Jim shortly, 'he came from Bergen.'

I must have been about twelve when we had this conversation, so I don't remember everything. But I do remember that I asked Jim: 'Who was he?' And Jim looked at me with an expression which clearly indicated that he thought that the limits of his contract of employment had now been stretched excessively, and answered:

'That's something I think you'd better ask your grandparents about.'

'I don't think they know,' I said.

'Don't you think so?'

'No,' I said. 'There's a lot they don't know.'

'Well,' said Jim. 'You'll have to ask them first.'

No sooner said than done. Although it was easier said than done. I thought about it for days. What was the best way to approach this? It was important to be clever and not ask in a way which gave them to understand how much I understood, or to understand that this preoccupied me particularly, or God forbid to understand that I had talked to Jim about this, or that I had read *A Child Is Born* by Lennart Nilsson, and definitely not *Show Me!* We didn't have books like that in our house, but I was sure that Grandmother knew there were books like that. I thought and I thought, until finally I just blurted it out one day over dinner:

'Is it true that my father was from Bergen?'

As nonchalantly as I could, I reached out for the cranberry jam, seemingly concentrating all my attention on the wild berries, whilst I pretended not to notice my grandparents' frozen faces.

'From Bergen?' said Grandfather, alarmed. 'What on earth makes you think he was from Bergen?'

'It's just something I heard,' I said lightly, or at least as lightly as I could, for I could see where this was going.

'And where on earth did you hear that, young man?'

'Now now,' came warningly from Grandmother.

'I thought at first that he came from India,' I said, and helped myself again to Grandmother's lovely homemade jam. 'But India is a very long way away.'

'I see,' said Grandfather.

'Yes,' I said desperately. 'It's 6700 kilometres to Bombay. That's a very long way. Bergen is much nearer than that. It's only – '

'Yes,' said Grandfather, relieved to have been rescued by geographical facts. 'He did come from Bergen.'

Grandmother cleared her throat, but Grandfather didn't say any more. Then there was a pause, after which it seemed natural that it would be Grandmother's turn to say something, but she didn't say anything either; she just asked me to pass the jam.

In this way, with equal amounts of ingenuity and luck, I had it confirmed that my father came from Bergen. But in actual fact I was not much the wiser.

I had certain facts, and facts are good. What would we do without facts? Solid knowledge is the key to all progress. When people in olden days believed that the stars were fastened to a crystal sphere which surrounded the earth, it was because they lacked facts. But when you don't have *all* the facts, but just two or three, it can be more frustrating than if you don't have *any*. Then you might just as well have carried on believing in the crystal spheres. Isolated facts can actually be very confusing, if you can't see the whole picture. Often it leads to social unrest. People get agitated if there are one or two facts which indicate that the fixed stars are not glued in place after all, and then they get worried and that leads to social unrest. I think that's what's called a paradigm shift.

My paradigm shift lasted over many years, as such paradigm shifts usually do, and was accompanied by much unrest. I knew two things:

1. My father was Indian, and
2. He came from Bergen.

More than that I didn't discover for a long time. It was most frustrating. My grandparents said nothing more about the matter, and Jim too was watertight, however much I dug around.

'I don't want to get involved in that, Sedd,' he said, 'so I know nothing about it. I'm sure you'll find out when you're a bit older.'

'But Jim,' I begged, 'I really do want to know! I mean, when did they get married, for example?'

Jim looked at me for a long time:

'They weren't married,' he said.

So now I could add a third fact to my list of facts, which were growing in number, namely:

3. They weren't married.

So it was quite a while before I got things clear. For a long time I thought about it almost every single day, I dreamt about it at night and worked out theories about it in the daytime. After a while I was so exhausted from thinking about it the whole time that I actually stopped thinking about it. I wasn't getting anywhere anyway. The social unrest was replaced by a period of passivity and unrelieved darkness. That's how it often goes when paradigm shifts don't get a proper opportunity to break out. Paradigms are like viruses: they have an incubation time while they're lying there dozing before they break out with snot and pestilence. But if the strength of resistance is too great, the sickness doesn't break out, and you can go around feeling under the weather for months, like some of our top skiers. Many of them are actually too strong for their own good, and they can be under the weather for years, sometimes even for the whole of their careers, without getting the pestilence out of their systems.

But truth will out, as the saying goes, and in the long run it carves itself a path, first as a slow dribble, then more and more, stronger and stronger, until in the end it pours forth as a triumphant hymn-like song, like for example 'We Are Alive', written and sung by Wenche Myhre. In the long run you can't suppress the truth. So now I know. I know my provenance. The first drip happened when I was thirteen, and consisted in it leaking out of Grandmother that my father had been a doctor. She called him Dr Kumar. It came as rather a surprise to me, not least the fact that Indians could be doctors, but when I thought about it, it was a perfectly natural thing.

I asked Grandmother whether he had been a good doctor, and what kind of doctor he had been in that case, if he'd been a brain surgeon for example, but she said that he'd been a perfectly normal GP further up the valley – but had he been good? She didn't know that.

'Didn't you know that, Grandmother?'

'No,' said Grandmother and looked guiltily at me. Yes, she actually looked guilty.

'We didn't know him, you see, Sedd.'

'You didn't know him?'

'No,' said Grandmother, 'or rather, we did. But not properly. Just very – what's the word? – *oberflächlich*.'

'Superficially,' I said.

'Superficially, yes. Like you know your guests. Or don't know them,' she added.

I could see from her face that she understood she'd said too much, and that the avalanche had started rolling. Her attractive brown curls seemed to curl up even more as she shook her head gently. She glanced around, and I realised that she was looking for something to do, so that she could escape from the corner she'd painted herself into. But I didn't let her off so easily; I was much older now and had waited a long time for this paradigm shift. So I struck at once:

'So perhaps he was a regular guest here, then?' I asked in as innocent a voice as possible, despite the fact that my voice was breaking, although perhaps that fact helped me in some way.

Grandmother looked at me for a moment with the same alpha-female wolf gaze she always mobilized if someone said something highly inappropriate, but then she gave the accused the benefit of the doubt, and the wolf retreated.

'Yes,' she admitted shortly. 'He was. He used to stay the night here when he was driving over the mountain.'

Once again she glanced around desperately for a diversion; I could see that she'd already fixed on the glass-fronted cupboard with cut-glass vases, which no doubt needed cleaning. But I wasn't giving up so easily:

'Was it here he met my mother, then?'

'Yes,' said Grandmother shortly. 'It was here Dr Kumar met your mother. Good gracious, how dusty these vases have got.'

'But,' I began.

'It must be the spring light, things like that always show up so much clearer in the spring light.'

'But,' I tried again.

'Salt and vinegar,' said Grandmother, 'and a good chamois leather, that's the only thing that helps. Sedd, *mein Büblein*, can you be a good boy and pop up to the broom closet on the first floor and get the chamois leather that's hanging on the third hook on the left inside the door, under the shelf of spare blankets?'

'Yes, Grandmother,' I said, satisfied that I had after all progressed much further in my investigations, and that now the whole truth would soon break forth with supernatural force; I was convinced of that, so I went and fetched the leather.

It was Grandfather who was responsible for the next drip, almost without me having to lead up to it. I suppose I did lead up to it a bit, but only by talking generally about medicine. The thing is, Grandfather had sore heels, which at times bothered him a great deal, and which he'd got because he was on his feet all day in hard shoes. It is a very common complaint amongst us hotel people, and it's not dangerous, but extremely painful. The only thing that helps is to sit on a sofa with your legs stretched out, wrap a long scarf around your toes and pull the scarf with all your strength in order to stretch out all the tendons and muscles in the sole of your foot, whilst you grunt and groan. You have to do that for at least five minutes with each foot. Morning and evening. And even so it's not certain that it will help. But it does hurt. Grandfather had got through the torture of foot number one and was about to stretch out foot number two when I said it would be interesting to become a specialist in orthopaedics. That is, if by any chance I became a doctor. Clearly Grandmother had not warned him about our conversation, because he looked at me in genuine surprise.

'Or I could become a brain surgeon, for example,' I said. 'There are so many possibilities.'

Grandfather, who had hitherto never heard me talk about an alternative career choice to hotelier, let go of the scarf. He looked seriously at me:

'It's not the worst thing you can be, a doctor,' he said, 'they earn well too.' He looked at me thoughtfully. 'Your father was a doctor,' he said, after thinking about it.

'Yes, I know,' I said.

'Oh – '

'Grandmother told me that a long time ago.'

'Did she, right. Yes, of course she did.'

'Yes,' I said, 'he was a perfectly normal GP.'

'Yes,' said Grandfather. 'That's right. He was a GP. Or at least a locum, if I remember correctly.'

'But where is he a GP now?'

'Now?' Grandfather looked at me, taken aback. Hesitated for a moment. Then he said: 'He's not alive now, Sedgewick. Didn't you know that? He died before you were born.'

'I didn't know that,' I said, and felt that I was going quite numb.

'Well, that's how it is,' said Grandfather in a low voice, and wrapped the scarf round his foot again. 'That's how it is.'

'Yes,' I said. 'That's how it is.'

Thus I could add two new items of knowledge to my list, namely

4. He was a GP, possibly a locum, and
5. He was dead.

In that way I both found and lost a father in a short space of time, but in reality of course I had never had one.

I hadn't had a mother either, as I said, but she was in a way more tangible, and presumably not dead either, although she had gone away. I lived in the room which had been hers, where she had been small and had grown up, and the room bore traces of that, if you looked closely and thought about it. For example, I would never have hung up that poster of the Stones. Nor was the glass snow globe from Vienna, *Originalmanufaktur Erwin Perzy*, with a white Lipizzaner horse in the snowstorm, one of the things I would have chosen to exhibit, but I couldn't bring myself to put it away. After all, Erwin Perzy's invention, *Glaskugel mit Schneeffekt*, was an important one. And there were a few books left behind by my mother too; I once found a green hair ribbon used as a bookmark in one of them. The end which protruded from the pages was faded, but the part that had been inside the book was still dark green shiny silk, as if it had come straight from my mother's head. The choice of literature was of good quality, but it was undeniably coloured by the fact that my mother had been a girl. That is not something you can reproach her for, even if you can reproach her for other things. Books about Heidi, Toya, Nancy Drew, Worrals and other heroines were in the majority. In the bookcase in the corner there was also her old Garrard record player, and I could actually remember that from the time when I was very small, before she was taken by Time and when she was still living at home. I remember that she used to play her singles on it. That's not so remarkable, but what I remember is that in the middle of the turntable, around the spindle, she used to put a small, shiny merry-go-round. She put it on when the single records had large holes in the middle, like American ones did. So this shining merry-go-round was a collar. I could watch it for hours, I think, as it went round and round, shining, as the music played, whether it was the Stones, Herman's Hermits, Creedence Clearwater Revival, Donovan's 'Season of the Witch' or simply Petula Clark. The merry-go-round was especially fine when Petula Clark was singing 'Downtown'. It and the song seemed to go together. Perhaps I wasn't staring at that merry-go-round for hours, perhaps it was only for a few minutes, but I remember that I was looking at *it* and not at my mother, so that that is what I remember. Her records were still there after she'd gone, in the small paper-covered record case in which she had glued magazine pictures of The Fab Four inside the lid, and written the names of the Apostles under the pictures: St. Paul, St. John, St. George and St. Ringo. She'd written some boys' names too, Gunnar, for example, and Per, followed by a heart. But not the name of an Indian GP who was working as a locum. So the records were still there, but not the merry-go-round. Perhaps she had taken it with her off into Time.

So there were traces of her in my room. And I'm not thinking of large traces like the Stones poster or the records with music I didn't like, or the fact that my bedside table lamp had a pink shade, no, there were many small traces as well. From a crevice or from behind a shelf a scrap of paper could suddenly fall out with a message:

'Meet me tonight. Gunnar.'

That Gunnar again. Under the bed, wedged in behind the bed leg, I found a crumpled-up fortune teller made of pink paper. It was so crumpled that it could unfortunately no longer be used as a practical instrument for foretelling the future, but I could open it and see which predictions my mother had had. Number of children: 4. Not exactly accurate there, then, as far as I knew anyway. Name of the boy you'll meet: Gunnar. Not so surprising perhaps, but once again my mother had been a poor fortune teller. There were of course other boys' names in the fortune teller, and varying clutches of children, but there was no number 1, and neither did any Indian doctor from Bergen make an appearance. Another time I found a different note, this time under the paper lining of one of the drawers. This was written in a hand which had become a little more grown-up; it had no address or signature, but I recognised the handwriting as my mother's. It said: 'Meet me in Olympus this evening.' And then, in a different handwriting, which presumably was Gunnar's, someone, presumably Gunnar, had answered: 'OK.'

This note really stopped me in my tracks. What could she have meant by Olympus? Of course, Olympus is a high and significant mountain in Greece, or Hellas as Grandmother says it should be called, since it is the Hellenes who live there, and this race believed that Olympus was the home of the gods, but there was no mountain in the vicinity of Fåvnesheim which had ever been called that. So it was impossible to deduce what she might have meant. Who was she going to meet in Olympus, what was Olympus, and where was Olympus?

Little did I suspect that a new discovery would quite by chance lead me directly there.

That's the way it is in general with all significant discoveries: they arrive unexpectedly, like a thief in the night. For tens of thousands of years human beings went around believing that the stars were fixed in place. But all of a sudden, while everyone was minding their own business, along comes this Galileo and takes a closer look. Everyone was naturally frightfully surprised, and some became angry, but nothing could be done about that. It wasn't Galileo's fault that it was all a bit sudden. It's just a matter of keeping your eyes open, and then the discovery can come along and ambush you before you know it.

10

In my case the discovery arrived like a thief in the night one fine day in February of the year I became thirteen. Although fine is pushing it a bit. It was cold and windy. The winter holidays were over, but it was not yet Easter. This was what Grandfather called an interregnum, and as always we used this interim period to undertake major spring-cleaning with the associated annual clearout. People who aren't in the business can't possibly understand how much has to be cleaned in a hotel with 132 rooms, and how much has to be cleared out. Unbelievable masses of things can accumulate in 132 rooms, plus public areas consisting of restaurant, ballroom, eight lounges, reception, swimming pool and sauna, cloakrooms and toilets, billiard room, bar and corridors, not to mention outdoor areas in the form of terraces, barbecues, ski waxing stations and ski stores, cycle shed and toolshed and storage shed, and even then we haven't mentioned kitchen areas, offices, cold storage and freezer room. In all these places you find a large number of misplaced objects, not to mention dust. You have to clear up and wash and dust the whole time, and we hotel folk do that twenty-four hours a day. My grandmother was continually, every single day of the year, busy with a greater or lesser cleaning or clearing-up project, together with the four room-maids, two permanent and two who came as needed. If it wasn't the dessert forks, it was the flower jugs. If it wasn't the carpets and the wall hangings, it was the dusty books in the library which needed going over with one of our trusty Nilfisks. The shelves could be impregnated at the same time with a teak oil called Pallisto-

Lux, which was applied via a sponge in the cap and spread with a soft cloth. Grandmother smelt of Pallisto-Lux, green soap and eau de cologne. That's how it was for the rest of us as well: Jim, whatever waiters we were employing at that moment, Synnøve and the reception staff, and Grandfather and me; we cleaned and cleared up. For example, one of my tasks from when I was very small was to sort out the postcards in the racks in reception. At any moment a guest could come along and mix them all up. The Americans were the worst. When a group of Americans had plundered the postcard racks, all of a sudden Geiranger Fjord had been put together with Urnes stave church, the Crown Prince and his bride had ended up behind Polar Bears and Other Norwegian Animals, whilst King Olav himself had been disrespectfully moved from the topmost holder of the highest rack, where His Majesty had his rightful place, and across to the rack which contained the new postcards which Grandfather had had made of Fåvnesheim, a series which to be honest was not entirely successful, but which at least demonstrated that the hotel had a large indoor swimming pool, and a great number of windows. But you can't see anything of the landscape, Grandmother had sighed when she first saw the cards, just the windows. You could tell that her immediate thought was that they needed cleaning.

So there was enough to get to grips with. Cutlery had to be sorted, towels changed, cloths folded. And even though the sound of the vacuum cleaners rang out from all floors every blessed morning, like a song of praise as the sun reached its zenith, there were plenty of areas where the daily folding and hoovering was not enough, and which had to wait until the great cleaning sessions.

It was during this February spring-clean that Grandfather asked me to take down a row of old, framed, attractive but unfortunately faded tourist posters from one of the side walls in the lobby and take them up to the second floor of the old wing, which was the attic floor. There had been rooms up there in the old days, before the west wing was built, but they were too small and not fit for purpose, said Grandfather, who set great store by meeting Modern Standards. So these attic rooms were therefore now used for storage, for example the box files of the hotel's invoices and receipts were carried up there, each in turn, to room 6, as the year's accounts were finalised, to be laid to rest.

So I carried the pictures up the steep narrow stairs to the attic floor of the old wing. There were a lot of them, and they were heavy, so I had plenty of opportunity to look at them more closely every time I took a breather. It was true that they were faded, I had to agree with Grandfather there, but nevertheless it seemed rather a pity to remove them. It's a strange thing: pictures you've seen all your life, ever since you were tiny, become as it were a part of the landscape. In a way it was as if it was only now that I *saw* them, saw them for the first time as I saw them for the last time, carrying them to the waiting room for the rubbish tip. They were glorious motifs, all of which underlined the various splendours of our Native Land. A trim coastal ship, slender and elegant, drawn with the sensitive touch of an artist, was crossing a stylized Arctic circle against a horizon where a glowing red sun was just kissing the sea. The ship was called *Midnight Sun,* of course. Another poster, which I was especially fond of, showed the happy little blond Sami boy who didn't really have any face or eyes beneath his big blue fool's cap, but just a single big, white, triangular smile. NORWAY via SAS Land of the Midnight Sun! it said. Then there was the one of the Geiranger Fjord, where a sporty man was standing silhouetted in a dynamic pose on the very edge of a shelf of rock. Deep beneath him, far below, a white cruise ship was floating on the ice-blue waters of the fjord. NORGE NORWAY NORWEGEN NORVÈGE NORVEGIA NORUEGA it said on the poster, so that no-one could be in any doubt as to where in the world you might find such a dramatic landscape. There were quite a few more, and I carried them one by one up to the attic floor and stacked them in number 7. I padded the frames carefully with newspaper, so that they wouldn't get damaged.

When that was done I went out into the corridor and locked the door behind me. For a few moments I stood there, listening. From the living parts of the hotel far below I could hear the sound of the vacuum cleaners. But up here under the roof what you could hear most clearly was the sound of the mountain wind, whistling in the crevices and the eaves. There was quite a gale outside, and at regular intervals the wind seemed to tug at the building so that the roof trusses groaned.

It was cold up here. In the narrow corridor two weak lightbulbs glowed in old-fashioned globes. The rest didn't work. The broad floorboards were painted with shiny grey oil-paint which was peeling here and there. On top of them lay a worn, striped runner. The brass fittings of the runner needed polishing.

Instead of going downstairs to the others and carrying on with my duties, as was right and proper, I walked further along the narrow corridor. I'd been up here several times before, of course. But we professionals who have grown up in a large hotel are actually not greatly interested in deserted corridors and unused rooms. From reading ghost stories or watching horror films I am aware that deserted corridors and unused rooms have a thrilling effect on ordinary people who aren't in the hotel business, and who haven't grown up in a large hotel, and that is after all most people. But it's not like that for us, it's not thrilling at all, and that's why I hadn't been here all that often. But I knew that the corridor turned a corner a little further on, and carried on for a few metres after that with another couple of rooms until it ended in a gable wall with a window, by which there was a fire rope. This was another reason why this wing was no longer in use; fire escapes had to meet Modern Standards, and had to be capable of being used by everyone, even Americans; that was Grandfather's credo. He was no doubt thinking of that dreadful hotel fire at Stalheim long ago. Lots of Americans and others perished in that, even though fire ropes were available. So I thought I would check that the fire rope up here was OK, that it wasn't rotten or anything – but actually I think that I just wanted to look out at my familiar surroundings from the gable window, and see the wind blowing white crystals of ice over the crusty, greying winter snow in what looked like being the last winter storm, or the first spring storm, depending on how you looked at it; Grandmother used to say that it was all the same to her.

So I rounded the corner of the corridor. The floorboards did not creak; this was solid carpentry such as is no longer seen in our day, built for frequent traffic of guests with heavy luggage.

At the end of the corridor the fire rope lay on the floor as it should, fastened according to regulations to a trapeze hook on the wall. I stood there for a while, looking out. I could see half of the large terrace in front of the dining room, and could see that Jim was toiling away, wiping the benches in the suntrap next to the wall, something I was happy to have escaped. In the far distance Fåvne peak had disappeared in the gathering mist, and at its foot lay Geirvann Water, still frozen but with blue-grey puddles where it had begun to melt.

I stood like that for a while. After that I turned and started to walk back. Then I noticed, although I don't really understand how, that there was something about the door of the room on my right. Something that was different from the others. I stopped and turned towards it. Looked at it without really knowing what I was looking for. And right enough: there at the top of the door panel, high up on the left-hand side, in the corner above the room number, something was different. Someone had written in red biro, so that the writing made a small groove in the surface of the grey oil-paint, in neat round handwriting: *Olympus.*

For a moment I stood as if paralysed. I recognised the word before I recognised the handwriting, and then word and writing came together in a wave of amazement and recognition. I could feel my heart hammering in my chest, I had to take an extra breath. Then I grabbed the handle.

Locked. Of course. I pressed the handle down a second time, the way you do when a door is locked, without it becoming any less locked.

With numb fingers I took out the keyring for that floor. My heart was beating. I fumbled from one key to the next; they were numbered from 1 to 11. I looked up at the door, at the old-fashioned numberplate on the door panel. 12. Of course. Nevertheless I tried all the keys in the door, from number 11 and down to number 1, and then up again to number 11, one after the other, whilst I jiggled the lock and turned the handle authoritatively each time, in the hope that the door to the abode of the paradigm shift would open. But to no avail. I tried the key to the corridor too, but that I couldn't even insert into the lock. The keys for the linen cupboards in the corridor were obviously too small, but I tried them anyway, just to have done so.

I took hold of the door handle one last time, glancing up at the top left-hand corner of the door. *Olympus.* There was no master key on the keyring.

But now I knew where Olympus was.

Slowly I went back down the corridor, down the steep stairs, and came out in the hotel's lived-in quarters, where Grandfather told me off for taking so long. I explained that I had had to clear a space for the pictures, and that I didn't want to just throw things around, but to be tidy and organised, as he had taught me to.

Whilst I helped Jim wipe the benches, I wasn't thinking of anything at all. But my heart was beating.

In a hotel there are many keys. I know that, because I tried all of them. I hadn't really given any thought to the matter before, how many there were, but to tell the truth my grandfather and grandmother, as well as Jim and other employees, had always jingled as they walked. They had keys everywhere. Large rings and small rings, long keys and short keys, private keys and public keys, room keys, cupboard keys, swimming pool keys, storeroom keys, chest keys, fuse cupboard keys, and a range of other keys for all the large and small openings and mechanisms people can furnish their surroundings with. There were keys hanging in reception, keys in the office, keys in our private apartments, in the bar, in the kitchen, in the service area and in the toolshed.

It wasn't too difficult to walk off with some of them at an unguarded moment. The difficulty lay in being able to hang on to them for long enough so that I could get upstairs to try them on Olympus, and then down with them again before someone who needed them discovered that they were missing. There was always someone who needed them; not all of them at once, of course, but most of them hung on rings which were in constant use. After having almost been caught in the act a few times, I decided the solution was to slip a few keys at a time off each keyring, so that I could try them on the locked door as soon as I had the chance. However, this created a different problem. The kind of key I was looking for had to be like the other room keys up in the attic, that is a common-or-garden standard Yale key. Unfortunately this kind of key was in the overwhelming majority on all the keyrings. After trying three or four keys at a time in the way I have described, I lost count. Had I already tried *that* precise key from the keyring with room keys? Didn't *that* key from Grandmother's private keyring look very much like one I had already tried from the same bunch? Yes. Perhaps. Perhaps not. At night I dreamt that I was drowning in keys. They were like small metallic insects which crept into my ears and nostrils.

But fortunately I'm not stupid. I am actually of above average intelligence, and I found an intelligent solution to the problem. It happened when I noticed that almost every single key had a number stamped on it. And these numbers differed from key to key. So I could write down the numbers from the keys I had tried in a notebook, and in that way keep a tally of which keys I had tried. The few extra keys which didn't have a number, but where the top of the key was blank, I could furnish with a small v-shaped mark which I scratched on with a pin, to show that the key had been tried.

So far so good. But gradually, as the number of keys I had tried began to exceed a certain amount, and filled several pages in the notebook, it became impossible to keep track of them. Therefore I worked out a different intelligent method of registering which keys I had tried by systematizing the series in a squared notebook according to their initial number, as well as their length. My bad luck was that Grandmother came upon me one day as I was sitting entering three new numbers in the notebook; I just managed to sweep the keys into my pocket, but the book was still open. Unfortunately my grandmother was the kind of woman who sees everything, a thing my grandfather would no doubt have confirmed, and that was because she was born in Austria, where you are trained from very young to see everything if you are a woman. I did hope for a moment that she might believe it was maths homework I was doing, but she saw at once that it was no maths homework, but some kind of table, so she said:

'What kind of table is that?'

The essential thing was not to hesitate. I thought like lightening. For a fraction of a second it occurred to me that I could say that I'd started collecting car numbers, like people used to do in the old days, but the fact that the length of the numbers varied wildly, plus that they had no initial letters, made me realise that that explanation had to be rejected. For the next fraction of the same second I considered saying that I was learning by heart the distances between central geographical locations in our beloved country, like for example between Oslo and the North Cape, Trondheim and the Arctic Circle, the Arctic Circle and Lindesnes, Lindesnes and Oslo, Oslo and Bergen, Bergen and the North Cape and so on all the way round, all of them extremely useful items of knowledge for someone who is going to work in tourism, but I understood simultaneously that I couldn't use that explanation either, because there were no place names by the columns, and because my grandmother belonged to that rare class of people who have actually learnt all such distances by heart, completely off their own bat. If you asked her how long the Hardanger Fjord was, she would be able to say at once that it was 180 kilometres, that is 82 kilometres longer than the river Sjoa, but that both of them of course paled by comparison with the Danube, the river of rivers, which was 2860 kilometres in length, from its source in the Black Forest to its mouth in the Black Sea, and a whole 357 kilometres of it ran through her beloved Austria. So I said:

'I'm trying to learn Trachtenberg's system of calculation.'

Grandmother nodded approvingly.

'That's a good idea, Sedd,' she said.

'Yes.'

'I've always wanted to learn Trachtenberg's system of calculation,' she said.

'It's a really smart system.'

'Yes,' she said. 'Really smart. Anyone who knows Trachtenberg's system of calculation can work out large numbers in their head, or at least very quickly on a small piece of paper.'

'Yes,' I said. 'It's very practical.'

'And with all four basic maths operations,' said Grandmother, impressed. 'When I was a youngster at the hotel school in Linz there were several who were learning Trachtenberg's system of calculation.'

'There you are,' I said.

'They went far. I often regret not having learnt Trachtenberg's system of calculation myself. Then perhaps I would have gone further. At least further than – this.'

She glanced up from the tables and looked meaningfully in the direction of the elk's head. 'So it can be a good idea to learn Trachtenberg's system of calculation,' she concluded.

'That's what I thought,' I said.

'*Mein braver Bubi*. You're so intelligent and forward-thinking. Perhaps you would be so good, when you've learnt Trachtenberg's system of calculation, to teach your old grandmother something about the system too?'

'Yes, Grandmother,' I said. 'Of course.'

Grandmother smacked her lips, satisfied, and glided off towards new surfaces which needed to be kept dust-free, whilst I breathed out in relief. She had accepted my explanation without more ado. The only snag was of course that I now had to learn Trachtenberg's system of calculation as well, which by all accounts took just as long to learn as it otherwise takes to become proficient in maths in the normal way. I knew there was a textbook about Trachtenberg's system of calculation in the science lab at school, and I assumed – in fact I counted on it – that no one would miss it if I borrowed it for private study for a few months. Who knows, perhaps I would even be encouraged to borrow it. Not all pupils exhibited such natural ability for maths as I did, that's what my teacher Mr Dahl had said to my grandmother during a reception, and he said it loudly enough to be sure that I picked it up too. In other words I didn't really need to learn Trachtenberg's system of calculation, but it could be fun to learn it anyway, I consoled myself as I sat there.

By this time I had managed to try perhaps two-thirds of the Yale keys I had access to, and I was beginning to lose heart. My greatest fear was of overlooking one of the keys on a ring, and I checked and double-checked the key numbers until it almost became a mania.

Another possibility which had begun to dawn on me was that it might be that the key to Olympus was not actually on all the keyrings I had been able to locate, but that it might also be, indeed that it was highly probable that this precise key was *not* on any of the rings or bunches. After all, it wasn't on the keyring together with the other keys belonging to the rooms in the attic. It was possible that this very key I was looking for, not to say fanatically searching for, in a never-ending idiot's game of patience with no apparent solution, was actually in a completely different place, for example in a drawer or a cupboard, or in a desk or a chest somewhere else in the house, and that this drawer, cupboard, desk or chest in its turn was locked with a *different* key, which wasn't a Yale key at all, but one of all the many other keys which *also* lived (or even worse: perhaps *didn't* live!) on one of the rings or bunches I had access to, but which I hadn't tried precisely because they were not relevant.

My dreams about keys at night got worse. At the same time I couldn't stop trying all the Yale keys, one by one, until I was certain that I had tried them all. If I didn't do that, all my systematic work would be completely wasted, not to mention the laborious study of Trachtenberg's system of calculation, which I had managed to get quite good at as Advent approached that year. In the meantime a spring, a summer and an autumn had passed by, with constant secretive visits to stand in front of the door to Olympus.

By the third Sunday in Advent it had become irrefutably clear to me that all, absolutely all the Yale keys I could get my hands on had been tried, without success. The whole thing felt fairly hopeless. Now what remained was to begin from the beginning again with all the keyrings, but this time with all the rejected keys, different in form, type, function and appearance, and which for the most part could not be categorized by any numbering system; and what was worse, it was completely impossible to see whether they related to cupboards, drawers, chests, padlocks or any of the other barriers which people erect in front of the openings they surround themselves with.

I was at a loss.

At regular intervals, when I was on an errand outside the building, I would glance furtively up at the window on the top floor which I had worked out must be the right one. It was completely black. I couldn't quite decide whether that was because there was a dark curtain over the window, or whether the room itself was so dark. But it was definitely darker than the neighbouring windows. Like a coal-black hole in the row of windows. Of course I considered whether it would be feasible to get in through the window with the help of a ladder, but that didn't seem very realistic. Not that I wouldn't be able to get hold of a ladder; ladders we had in plenty. But I do believe that Grandfather, not to mention Grandmother, would have been most puzzled as to why I should suddenly put up a ladder by the wall just there. Of course I could say that I suspected there was a wasps' nest under the eaves, and I wanted to investigate it more closely, or that I thought woodpeckers had started to damage the wall beneath the gable ridge, but there was a considerable risk that they would then take matters into their own hands and investigate themselves, or even worse stand down below and follow my exertions admiringly, and then I would not only have to abandon my plan of climbing in through the window, but in the worst case scenario have to produce a wasps' nest or at least a poor woodpecker; it would turn out exactly like Trachtenberg's system of calculation. Besides, it was winter, wasps and woodpeckers had flown south, and anyway I didn't believe I would be able to open the window from outside, not without damaging it. It looked like a solid window with inner and outer glass panes and old-fashioned catches, no doubt of the same high, old-fashioned quality as the rest of the carpentry up there.

So I carried on searching. In cupboards, drawers, chests and bureaus. I found a large number of interesting things whilst I was engaged in this, amongst other things Grandfather's love letters to Grandmother, an old Luger pistol from the war, some black-and-white photos of an attractive young lady I can't remember Grandfather ever mentioning, together with a fine collection of postcards from the 1930s. I found cigarette holders, champagne whisks, ear-wax scrapers, petrol lighters with mother-of-pearl handles, hairpins, tourist association badges, old glasses, pendants and rings – but no key.

Every day, or nearly every day, I sneaked up to the attic and tried that door handle. Every time the door was just as locked, and would not give way. Not so much as a millimetre. It was as if it too was black, as if it was a dam holding back the black darkness inside. Each time I stood there for a few seconds as I tried to look into the door's eyes, as it were, but it wouldn't meet my glance. It was silent and uninterested.

In a casual tone, so that it would seem just a passing remark, I asked Jim, who was experienced in the school of life, including reform school, if he knew how you picked a lock.

'Why the hell would you want to know that?' asked Jim, looking up from the vegetables he was dicing.

'Oh,' I answered innocently, 'I'm reading a detective novel. It's very popular. *The Deceased Requested No Flowers* by Gerd Nyquist, Norway's answer to Agatha Christie.'

It was the only title of a book in the detective fiction genre I could think of at the drop of a hat, though I was well aware that there is no break-in in that novel, only two extremely elegant murders, but also well aware that Jim never read books.

'And in that novel the villain picks the lock of a door, you see, Jim,' I said. 'I just wondered if it's as easy as that in real life. I mean, as Fru Nyquist makes out?'

'And you think I would know about that?'

Jim looked at me a bit sharply. I felt uncertain. I pretended that I was less intelligent than I am in actual fact, and said:

'I thought perhaps you might have learnt it at sea, if the captain for example had locked himself in his cabin …'

'Listen,' said Jim. 'I have no idea how you pick a lock. Neither at sea nor anywhere else. But locksmiths use special picks or universal keys if they need to open a door where the lock is stuck or if someone has lost the key.'

'In *The Deceased Requested No Flowers* it says that the villain uses a hairpin,' I said.

'Hairpin?' Jim looked at me doubtfully. 'Well,' he said, 'I doubt that it's possible to open anything at all with a hairpin, but you can try.'

'I hadn't thought of trying,' I protested forcefully, whilst I could feel that I was going bright red. 'I just wondered how –'

'No,' said Jim, 'I think that's best. It's best not to try things like that.'

He was quiet for a while. Cutting tomatoes. When he had cut eight tomatoes into perfect boats, he said:

'Is it thrilling, that *No Flowers By Request*?'

'*The Deceased Requested No Flowers*,' I said. 'Yes, it's frightfully thrilling.'

'Perhaps I can borrow it when you've finished with it?'

'Yes,' I said desperately, 'of course you can, Jim, as soon as I've finished it.'

The next day I supplied myself with a good selection of hairpins and went up to the attic. Jim was right. Hairpins no doubt have many uses, but picking locks is not one of them. Especially not Yale locks. Most of them couldn't even be inserted into the lock, and none of them would go in far enough to reach the interesting part of the lock's mechanism. I had got no further, and now to top it all I had to find a copy of Gerd Nyquist's *The Deceased Requested No Flowers*; a book I had read the previous summer, which had been left here by a female guest and had been returned to her long ago. Also to hope that Jim wouldn't remember the break-in which didn't happen in Fru Nyquist's elegant novel.

This matter of not finding things is a problem. I'm not just thinking of keys. I'm thinking of all the large and small things you can't find when you need them. Grandfather estimated that he had walked around twenty-five miles during the course of his life, merely to look for his glasses. Grandmother was always wondering where she had left her knitting, whilst Jim was normally looking for the meat thermometer. Apparently it was never in the same drawer as he had put it in last. Guests too can search and search. For disappearing brooches, pendants, rings and bracelets. Sometimes they look for more important articles of property too – or it may happen that they *don't* look for them. We had a whole chest full of personal effects which no guests had asked after and which no one had asked to have sent on. In that chest there were the most incredible things, things you really would believe people would miss, like family pictures, electric razors, false teeth and even an artificial arm with a right hand. You would imagine that people would miss their teeth, at least when they looked in the mirror, but no. We had enough artificial teeth for half a curling team, and you might well think that they would need teeth, given the amount of time they spend on the ice. Curling is actually a sport with a high risk of injury. And you would imagine that an artificial right arm, or rather the lack of one, would be noticed by its owner, for example when he was sitting on the bus on the way down to town and had time to collect himself, or at the very least the next time he went to shake hands, but no. It is of course possible that the owner was left-handed, but even so. After a while you really would think that the lack of an arm would be noticeable. The strange thing was that none of us could remember that we'd had a guest with an artificial arm, and even less that any guest had departed armless.

But the artificial arm lay there in the box, together with transistor radios, watches, hernia supports, glasses and a good assortment of medicines to treat sometimes life-threatening illnesses, waiting for someone, an owner, a relative, to remember their loss at some point in the future and get in touch to reclaim the objects. Only jewellery was sought after. That, on the other hand, had disappeared without trace. But jewellery is so small, it can easily slip down and be lost in the cracks of this world.

Around New Year I gave up trying to find the key to Olympus. I stopped making plans as to how I could get into the room with no one noticing. It could quite simply not be done. I was unable to pick locks, and breaking in by force was out of the question. It would be discovered at once. Neither was it possible to gain access through the neighbouring room; I had checked that. The wall panels were not only solid but also wallpapered. So I just accepted that Olympus, whatever it might be, was forbidden territory for me, or would be so until by some chance at some point in the future I was in a position to gain entry to the room.

It could be a very long time until that happened. In the worst case it wouldn't happen until Grandfather and Grandmother were dead, and I had taken over up here, and could do what I wanted with my doors. Because that's how things stood: at some point I would take over up here, and stand behind reception in an immaculate suit in order to welcome guests, and take on the mantle of inheritance from my grandfather and his father and grandfather. It was a proud and weighty inheritance, but nevertheless I was dreading it a little, because it is a wearisome job to be a hotel manager, that's for sure. Nothing is more sure than that. You have a heap of worries, and you have to be on your feet the whole day long. You can't go off on holiday either, because you have to make a living from other people's holidays in the holiday season, and outside the season you have to clean and clear up, gather up abandoned teeth and so forth. Fortunately that wouldn't happen for a long time. That's how I normally thought. Besides, it wasn't very pleasant to think that one day Grandfather and Grandmother wouldn't be there any more, because there were only the three of us, if I don't count Jim. When I was small I was often very frightened if Grandfather came home late from one of his trips into the mountains. I would actually become quite terrified, so terrified that Grandmother had to calm me down. 'He's just a tiny bit late, darling,' she would say. 'It's nothing to get upset about.' Of course she was right about that, and I didn't understand at the time why I was getting so upset.

The only bright spot about the thought that I would take over one day was really the fact that I could finally open that door. But that was a long way off, a very long way, hopefully. In any case, a number of things might happen before then. Suddenly one day the key might be found in a place where it hadn't occurred to me to look, like a bright shiny gift from fate, or perhaps at some point in the course of the long future between now and when I was to take over I would pluck up the courage to ask Grandfather or Grandmother what Olympus was, and whether it was possible to get into it.

Although I doubted it. If I'm to be completely honest, I didn't believe that I would ask at all.

If, like me, you make long trips into the mountains, either on foot or on skis, and generally in the evenings, you will often have noticed the following: in the time just after sunset the clear sky is still full of colour, as if the twilight is something the sun pours into the huge round glass of the sky, a colourful farewell drink. In all this colour you can make out one star. Clear and still, before all the other stars are lit. It is Venus.

I don't know why. But when I saw Venus hanging there like that, the evening star, I always became very calm and stopped thinking both about the door which could not be opened and about my provenance. Instead I thought about the few things I could remember about my mother, whoever she was before she was taken by Time, and as long as Venus was lit these thoughts didn't upset me, they just gave me peace. When the sky had swallowed its last mouthful of the sun's gleaming Driver's Special, and thousands of other stars appeared in the darkness around me, I turned round and set off for home, lonely now, but not anxious. There weren't that many memories to speak of either, actually, when it came to it. Just a very few simple, detached, meaningless pictures. Often it wasn't even a picture; a scent of henna, a foxy-red sheen in the air. As long as I had been going away from the hotel, and the sky was still gleaming and Venus was hanging there alone, I had felt a kind of trembling desire to follow, to find Time and ask it to take me with it, to take me too, to that place and that state which I felt I could sense the existence of at that moment. On the way back to the hotel, as the darkness closed in, I was simply longing to see the lamps shining out in front of Fåvnesheim, and to see the myriad of windows, most of them black, one single one blacker than all the others, but a few of them lit up.

11

All this had happened the previous year. I still made a trip upstairs every now and then and tried the door to Olympus, just to confirm that it was as locked as ever. But I did it more and more rarely. After Herr Berge's death I hadn't been up there once. I devoted myself to my philately hobby instead.

However, there was still a deficit in the stamp box in the office behind reception when I examined it. Just a few frivolous, colourful, foreign stamps, torn from postcards or booking letters, eked out a miserly existence at the bottom of the shoebox. Not a single On Official Business and only two miserable Post Horns at 50 øre each.

I went out to Synnøve in reception. As reception manager she ought to have a good overview of the hotel's incoming post, I was pretty sure of that.

She was busy filling out some foreign visitors' forms.

'I say, Synnøve,' I said.

'Mm?'

'There don't seem to be many stamps in the box?'

'Mm,' was all she said.

'Don't we get any post any more, or have you forgotten that I'm collecting them?'

'Sorry, Sedd, what was that? I'm a bit busy.'

'I said there are hardly any stamps in the box, and I wondered if you've stopped tearing them off for me?'

She looked up from the forms. 'No,' she said, 'I'm still tearing them off and putting them in the box.'

'But what about the On Official Business and Post Horns?'

She thought about it. 'You'll have to ask Zacchariassen about that; he's the one who takes care of most of those letters.'

'I have asked him. He says he's tearing them off and putting them in the box when they arrive.'

'So that's all right, then.'

'It's just that there aren't any.'

'I don't think I can help you with that, Sedd. Sorry.'

'But do we get fewer letters like that at the hotel now?'

She thought about it again. Considered the question for a while. 'No,' she said pensively. 'No, I don't think we do. Now that you ask, if anything it's the opposite.'

'So where are the stamps then?'

'I have no idea. You'd better ask your grandfather. Perhaps he's beginning to get forgetful. Anyway, I have to get on with this.'

I thought that was strange, but said no more. The following day, a Saturday, when Jim had been down to town to collect supplies and brought the bundle of post back up with him, I made haste to undertake an investigative survey whilst it was still in the basket in the office. Eight letters with Post Horns, two On Official Business. After that I sat down in the lobby and pretended to read an ancient magazine which was lying there. After a few minutes Grandfather came past. 'Don't sit there doing nothing,' he said. 'I'm not doing nothing, Grandfather,' I explained. 'I'm reading an article about investigative journalism.' 'Oh, are you,' said Grandfather. 'It's actually really interesting,' I said.

He made no answer to that, and disappeared behind reception. 'The post's here,' Synnøve trilled. 'Many thanks, Miss Haugen.' I lifted the magazine up above the tip of my nose and tried to follow what was going on. If anyone looked at me they would just see a young man reading an absorbing article in *Women's Weekly*.

Soon after, Grandfather came past again, going the other way. Synnøve didn't look up as he passed, and if he'd looked over at me, which he didn't do, he would just have seen a young man reading an absorbing article in the aforementioned magazine. But I could see that he had a carrier bag in his hand.

When he had left the lobby I nipped into the office again. The brown business envelopes had gone.

I looked in the wastepaper basket. It was empty. I looked in the shoebox again. No new stamps. There was only one possible conclusion: Grandfather had taken the letters with him in order to read them elsewhere, which he sometimes did, but he had forgotten to tear the stamps off first.

Sunk in deep thought, I went out into the fresh air to think about the situation. With the help of a simple investigative ploy I had confirmed that Synnøve was right: letters did come to the hotel with both Post Horn and On Official Business stamps. But Grandfather had become forgetful.

I was not a little shaken by this discovery. Grandfather, who up until now had remembered everything, every detail, every room, every promise and every unpolished window, had now seemingly begun to forget so simple a thing as to tear off stamps for me. And that despite the fact that I had reminded him of it repeatedly. It wasn't like him at all, and precisely the fact that it was so unlike him was cause for concern in my opinion.

A hotel manager cannot be forgetful. There are far too many urgent things to remember. Grandfather himself had said so, and that many times, so that I shouldn't forget how important it was to remember. Was he now in danger of losing his memory?

The thought made me more frightened than I would have expected beforehand. Everything here at the hotel depended on Zacchariassen being one hundred percent on the ball. That was something we all knew, without actually having talked so much about it. The idea was probably – that is to say if I myself had thought correctly – that I should finish school, and make an excursion out into the world, more precisely to the hotel training school in Linz, in order to return home and gradually take over Grandfather's duties.

I was fairly certain that this was the plan. We must have talked about it, in driblets, or tacitly worked our way towards it. Besides, there was no other possibility. Not if the whole thing was to continue. History is just one damned thing after another, as Ibsen says.

I took deep breaths of the clear, cool morning air. Suddenly I felt, in a completely different way than before, an adult responsibility. But above all a concern for Grandfather. Fåvnesheim could not cope if the manager became senile.

My first impulse was to take my suspicions to Grandmother, but a moment later I rejected the idea. I knew Grandmother. She would just be plunged into a whirlpool of worry. So I decided to wait. These stamps were after all pretty scanty evidence to build such a serious case on. I would instead keep a vigilant eye on Grandfather from now on, keep him under observation without him noticing, so that I could ascertain if there really were grounds for actual concern. But I was already concerned.

In the absence of any stamps to collect I began to take some photos with the splendid equipment I had acquired. Inherited.

But even if photography is fantastically interesting, it is also fantastically difficult, I had to admit to myself. At the start I thought it was just a matter of inserting a film, looking through the viewfinder and clicking away, but that was not the case at all. If you insert a film and click away, you can get back for example a film with completely black frames. Or at least really dark ones, I have to say.

So I had asked Grandfather, who had a small box camera himself, if he could show me, but he didn't know enough to get anywhere. Bjørn Berge's camera had a series of rings with numbers on; Grandfather's camera didn't have that. Grandfather stood there for a long time, looking thoughtfully at those rings. Then he rotated them a little, inserted a film, and gave it back to me with a nod. As I said, pictures like that can be extremely dark. I asked Jim, but he just shook his head. 'It would be nice,' said Grandmother, 'if you could get so good at photography that you could take group pictures. Then your grandfather could make it part of the Wedding Package.'

That was a good and useful idea. Nevertheless I understood that I had to draw a dividing line here between usefulness and art. I decided immediately that my photographic art would have nothing to do with the Wedding Package. In the long run I would prefer to take pictures like the ones Sverre M. Fjelstad and Rolf M. Aagaard took for *Aftenposten*'s weekend magazine. Large, impressive photos of flora and fauna. I imagined for example a series about the secret life of reindeer. But I wouldn't manage as much as a dead lemming if I couldn't get to grips with the technical side.

Fortunately help is never far away for a young person with resolve, as Grandmother would have put it so aptly. I could of course have gone directly to Titlestad Photographers in Storgata, where I had had the first film developed, and asked for help from Titlestad himself, but I thought it was embarrassing to be completely ignorant, because you then have no chance of being on anything approaching equal terms. I would rather find out some things *first*, so that I could stroll into the photoshop after that with a film which needed developing, and *then* ask for advice, from one professional to another, so to speak. I could also have the Leica hanging nonchalantly around my neck when I entered, in order to underline the equal relationship.

Visit your Local Library, as their publicity says. In libraries they have taken a vow of silence, as is well known. That's why it's so quiet there. For that reason I reckoned on them treating my enquiries with discretion, so that I could learn something before I sought out Titlestad Photographers again.

So the day we had our German exam and finished early I popped into the library. I went over to the one male librarian. The other two librarians are women, but to be honest I believed that a man would have a better grasp of which books they had on technical subjects. The last time I had been there, in order to borrow *Little Lord Fauntleroy* again, one of the women had tried to palm me off with a Swedish teenage book about a black person.

'I think this might appeal to you,' she said, and held it up in front of my face. '*Omin Hambbe in Slättköping*, it's called,' she said. 'It's by a Swedish author called Max Lundgren.'

I could actually read, but I just nodded. I thought that perhaps librarians become like that with time, that they have to say all the names and titles out loud. It may be that they do it in order to remember better which books they have on their shelves. In any case, I explained that I already had what I came for, but she didn't give up. 'It's about a black person,' she said, 'he's called Omin Hambbe, and he comes to a small town where everyone is white. And this small town is called Slättköping.'

'Perhaps it's a town in Sweden, then?' I said, and she nodded eagerly. 'I'm not so keen on Swedish books,' I said.

'But it's really amusing,' she said. 'I thought it might appeal to you,' she said. 'The black boy Omin Hambbe gets off the train in the small Swedish town of Slättköping, where everyone is white, you see.'

As it happens I'm not particularly fond of amusing books, and besides I was born here and didn't arrive by train, but I didn't say that, I just said that I might borrow it when I'd finished reading *Little Lord Fauntleroy*, and since then I hadn't been there.

So now that I was looking for a book about photography, it seemed most efficient to go straight to the one male librarian, who was over in the adult section. He was standing by a shelf with his back to me, and looked as if he was memorizing names and titles.

'Excuse me,' I said as quietly as I could. Then we stood there for a while, he with his back still turned to me. He let his eyes follow the book titles, clearly sunk deep in mnemotechnic ecstasy. I wondered how long it would be right to give him. But then it occurred to me that he had perhaps taken a vow of silence so many years ago that he had become a little deaf.

'Excuse me,' I said again, a little louder. He jumped.

'Sorry,' I said. 'I didn't mean to disturb you.'

'Can I help you, sir?' he said.

I was taken aback. It wasn't every day I was addressed as sir.

'I'm looking for a book about photography,' I said.

'Right,' he said in a friendly tone, 'OK, yes, we have a number of books about photography as well as books of photographs. Perhaps sir could describe more closely what kind of book it is you're looking for?'

If I'm to be completely honest, I did think at first that it was slightly disappointing that a representative of a progressive and democratic institution such as a lending library should use such a formal means of address – after all their publicity invited us chummily to Visit your Local Library – but on the other hand that was the way grown-ups spoke in business dealings and the more serious aspects of life's negotiations. I had gone into the adult section after all. So I thought it was most appropriate that the librarian addressed me formally.

'That is indeed the case,' I said. Since I've grown up in a hotel I'm not entirely unfamiliar with formal language, so I could reply in the same tone.

'Are you looking for a book *of* photographs, for example a book of art photographs or nature pictures? Or do you need a book *about* photography?'

'Well,' I said, 'the former would of course also be of interest, as I am for example enthused by the photographs of Rolf M. Aagaard and Sverre M. Fjelstad, but for the moment I have more need of a book about photography. Or perhaps several, if you have several good ones.'

He nodded. 'I think we have at least one which is quite good,' he said, and walked over to the drawers of index cards. There was a vast number of drawers, but he knew exactly which drawer to pull out and quickly thumbed through them to find the right card, nodded to himself and wrote down some numbers and letters on a white slip of paper. I felt like asking him what they meant, but decided that that could wait for another time, as it could well be that this was something most people ought to know.

'Would you perhaps know whether the photographers Rolf M. Aagaard or Sverre M. Fjelstad have ever published any books with pictures of the secret life of reindeer?' I asked instead.

'I don't know,' he said, 'but I can find out for you.'

He pulled out another drawer. Then a third. He shook his head.

'No,' he said, 'not that I can see. Nothing specific about the secret life of reindeer.'

Then we went over to some slightly larger shelves, where he located two books.

'Here,' he said, 'these two should be good.'

'Perhaps you take photographs yourself?' I asked.

'No, only amateur snapshots,' he said. 'But my wife takes photographs. She takes very good pictures.'

'I see,' I said. 'That must be practical.'

'Practical?'

'Yes,' I said, 'for christenings and similar family occasions.'

'Oh, yes,' he said. 'It's very practical. Is there anything else I can help you with?'

'No,' I said, 'not today. Many thanks.'

Life had taught me that it could be heavy work riding a bike all the way up into the mountains if you'd borrowed too many books, and today I was on my bike, since I had to get home early.

We went over to the counter.

'May I have your borrower's card?' he said.

I passed him my card. A child's card. He looked at it.

'I think we'll make you a new one,' he just said, and sat down at the typewriter. He entered the information from the old card, asked for my phone number, and we were all set. 'You can throw your old card away,' he said, 'the new one will work in all sections.' I threw it away immediately. He fed the new card and the punch cards into the machine which registered the loans with its gulping sound, slotted them with practised ease into the pockets at the back of the photography textbooks, gave me the books and I thanked him and left.

A library is an extremely democratic institution, that's true enough, but as I toiled up the hills on the way home I thought that it is actually a fantastically distinguished institution in many ways. Knowledge is marshalled there together with high-quality fiction, like the book about Omin Hambbe and other works, and even though the laws of nature mean that not everyone can gain access to all of it, it is accessible for most people, if they just make a little effort.

The first pictures I took, as I mentioned earlier, were not particularly good. At least, not from a technical point of view. But practice makes perfect, as the master says. The very first roll of film consists mainly of shadows. Only I know what these shadows are meant to represent. They represent Grandmother, Grandfather, Jim and Synnøve and other familiar subjects from the hotel. But I hadn't really understood about the shutter at that point. However, the books about photography gave me solid technical guidance, so that the pictures on the second roll already show some improvement. Here you can clearly recognise amongst other things Grandmother's profile and the back of Jim's head, as well as the flagpoles at the entrance and some of Grandfather's stuffed animals. The last-mentioned had the advantage that they stood completely still whilst I took their photographs. That's because I was still having problems with the exposure times. The little pine marten came out especially well in the light from the window.

But then, from the third roll onwards, the pictures become noticeably better. That I can assert without fear of contradiction. I can see photos of everything I did that spring, until the end of the school year. A trip into the mountains. The confirmation dinner for the mayor's daughter, 120 guests. As for me, I couldn't be confirmed because my mother, who was a witch, hadn't had me christened, and I didn't want to be christened as an adult. In June another wedding. The last meeting at the Red Cross before the holidays. Completely ordinary things. And ordinary people. Grandmother smiling with the sun in her eyes, not all that good, and quite a good one of Grandfather in a sports shirt.

It seems strange, looking at these pictures now. Not simply because they show me what enormous strides I had made technically, but also because they show the last time when everything was as it had always been.

I examine them carefully, hoping that something in them, anything at all, a little detail, a shadow across a face, an unfocused object in the background, might betray something, give a hint about what was happening, but of which I had not the slightest suspicion. But I see nothing. Nothing special. Just ordinary things. Unless it is the case that the ordinary things in themselves are an indication, just difficult to read. So that the sunny Sunday afternoon, the rainy grey sky over the mountains, the hotel far below, tiny when seen from Fåvne peak, are in themselves indications.

Or perhaps the very existence of the pictures is the most concrete indication, seeing that they were taken with the deceased bank manager's camera. Through Bjørn Berge's eyes, so to speak, which I would not have had the occasion to exploit if the bank manager had not been so dead, so buried, so unreasonably early. When I passed the bank manager's house it was empty and closed up. No bank manager, no widow. Perhaps I should have taken a picture of it, but it didn't occur to me. When I look at these pictures, it is obvious to me that there are a number of things it didn't occur to me to take a picture of. Important things. Significant things. But it is remarkable how difficult, indeed how extremely complicated it can be to see which things are significant and important then and there. And then to take a photo of them. I assume that is what is meant when it says in the photography book that the gifted photographer is always on the watch, always prepared. In other words you have to seize objects in flight, seize the subject, see it the moment it arrives. That is the art of photography, capturing the moment as it flies, as the inspired saying goes.

On the last school day before the holidays I noticed that there were workmen in the bank manager's house. I didn't take a picture of that either.

On the other hand I did take a picture of my class. Both as a group and as individuals. 8A, on the way into the future, or at least on the way into the summer holidays. I'm afraid that it would be incorrect to say that any of the members of 8A showed much talent as models. Basically it's odd how unrecognizable even people with attractive and regular features can become if they screw their faces up hard enough. Not even Mr Dahl could resist pulling a face when I got the camera out. So that roll was not especially successful. Or rather I would say it was completely wasted.

Mr Dahl said some well-chosen words about the school year we had behind us, about our development and so forth, and added some further well-chosen words about the world situation in general. In particular he expressed his pleasure in the fact that the Falklands War was now over. That was a pleasure it was not difficult to share, just as it had not been difficult to share the pleasure Queen Elizabeth must have felt in her heart when she was informed that The White Ensign – the flag of the Royal Navy – was once more fluttering proudly in the breeze over Port Stanley, where sky and sea meet. After that we emerged into the school yard, where the headmaster basically said the same well-chosen words, and then it was officially summer.

I went home with Hans.

Hans admired Berge's Leica.

'Super cameras, Leicas,' said Hans. 'Cost the earth.'

'Yes, I've started learning to take photos now.'

'Christ,' said Hans. 'Doesn't that cost a lot of money?'

'Yes,' I said, 'films are expensive. Cost the earth. Films and getting them developed, not to mention the prints. But Grandfather has an arrangement with Titlestad's Photographers, so that I can take a certain number of films a month on Grandfather's account.'

'Christ, you're lucky. Dad would think it was far too expensive. Is it difficult?'

I thought about it:

'Well, obviously taking photos with a Leica isn't the same as clicking away with one of those box cameras for housewives. There's lots to watch out for. Lenses and shutters. Film speed. Light levels. It's quite difficult actually. Really advanced stuff.'

Hans gave a low whistle, impressed. 'I can imagine,' he said.

'So the thing is, I'm not going to have so much time to spend on my stamp collection from now on.'

Hans looked at me, surprised.

'Not that I'm going to stop doing it,' I hastened to add. 'But there are only 24 hours in a day, and if I'm going to learn photography properly I'll really have to prioritise it in the coming months, if I'm going to get anywhere.'

Hans looked a little bit disappointed.

'Besides,' I said, in order to have an explanation, 'there are far fewer letters with stamps coming to the hotel than there were. So the supply is not what it was.'

'That's strange,' said Hans.

'Well, you know, people use telex much more nowadays.'

'Do they?'

'Yes. In the travel business anyway. Nearly everything comes by telex now.'

'I see,' said Hans. 'Got it.'

'If you got a camera, a half-decent one, we could take photos together. I'm sure Grandfather wouldn't mind you taking two or three films a month from Titlestad's as well.'

'Do you mean that, Sedd?'

'I'm quite sure,' I said.

Jim picked me up in the afternoon. In the car on the way up he asked if end-of-term had gone well. Oh yes, I nodded.

Was it good to be on holiday? Oh yes, I nodded. 'That's good,' said Jim. 'Let's hope we have a few guests this summer, so that you have something to do.'

12

My grandfather was a man of his word. At least, that's how he used to express it. 'If you're not a man of your word,' he said, 'you won't succeed at anything. No-one will trust you. Do you understand? If you break your promise just once, then your suppliers will never rely on your promises again. If you've promised a guest a particular room, and the guest doesn't get that room, then you're finished. Just as a clock mechanism promises that the clock will strike three when the big hand is on twelve and the little hand is on three, that's how a man must be too.'

Yes, I nodded, agreeing with him. That was the simplest thing to do. He liked to recite this speech about promises and clock mechanisms to me if I'd forgotten to do my homework, or even worse: *said* I'd forgotten my homework, when in actual fact I had ignored it deliberately. Then out came the whole lecture about the value of a man's word. Then it was best to agree. Especially because I knew, as I said, that Grandfather was indeed to the ultimate degree a man of his word. No guests at Fåvnesheim Mountain Hotel were ever offered anything they didn't get. If he had promised Jim a day off on a particular day, then Jim had that day off, even if it was inconvenient. It is true that Grandfather had his own tragic way of granting Jim his day off at times like that, so that Jim often relinquished the privilege, but I understood from Grandfather that it was the *intention* that counted. He had *wanted* to keep his word. If he promised Grandmother a holiday, an excursion, a new coat, jacket, piece of jewellery, handbag or similar – and it happened not so seldom that he had to do that – she always received the promised gift, which was presented along with the exchange of the following ceremonial phrases:

Grandmother: '*Aber Schatzerl!* How lovely!'

Grandfather: 'The pleasure is mine. Glad you like it.'

Grandmother: 'Exactly the one I wanted! To think that you remembered.'

Grandfather: 'The most important thing for me, my darling, is to see you pleased and happy.'

At moments like that, when he had said precisely that, Grandmother could look at him with strangely glistening eyes, and with a sweet, almost child-like smile which meant that for a few seconds you could understand, without any words being spoken, why she had chosen to follow him all the long way from the hotel training course in Linz in civilized Austria as far as the rugged Norwegian mountains, in a country inhabited by cross-country skiers and hydroelectric engineers. It was at moments like that I was most fond of them. A warm, peaceful atmosphere settled over them and over the whole hotel in the hours after such redeemed promises. Grandmother would wander around humming, slightly dreamily, whilst she glanced at regular intervals at the tribute Grandfather had brought, letting her hand gently caress a grey squirrel stole or admiring the play of light in a green stone. If the redeemed promises had been particularly propitious this atmosphere could gild our existence, drop by drop, for days at a time.

So I knew that Grandfather was a man of his word, and in my case too he never shirked a fishing trip he had promised me, a model plane which needed building or the delivery of a shiny new bike when my legs had definitely outgrown the frame of the old one.

But recently there had begun to be a longer interval between the timing of Grandfather's word and the timing of its fulfilment. Almost unnoticeably there had started to be a kind of quarantine between the moment when the promise dropped anchor, so to speak, and the moment when it finally disembarked. Had he actually become forgetful? I didn't want to remind him about it either, because after all he was always a man of his word, and would get upset if he had actually *not* forgotten the visit to town he had promised me just after the bank manager's demise. So I said nothing, even though time was passing. Besides, Grandfather was extremely busy during this period, it seemed, even if bookings could have been better. Besides, summers were always a bit complicated; most people who were up in the mountains walked from cabin to cabin, whilst those who wanted to stay put preferred to holiday on the coast or in the infernal South. But as Grandfather said – and he had a habit of saying things like that – sloth is the root of all evil. So he busied himself, made himself a bit unapproachable, started clearing out and catching up with postponed projects. He commanded Jim and me to varnish an enormous lounge floor and joined in washing down and staining two of the wooden partitions on the terrace which were worn by sun and wind. The minigolf pitch too, which no-one used, was industriously attacked: the concrete channels were cleared of greenery where necessary, cracks were repaired, the red numbers got a new coat of paint and even the clubs were polished with stainless steel cleaner so that they shone like new. But when all this was done Grandfather announced one day that he and I were going to town, that the hotel room was booked and that he had drawn up a little Programme.

Grandfather loved drawing up Programmes. As opposed to my grandmother, who preferred Serendipity. Grandfather believed that a good Programme, precise and well thought out, was not only the best way for a man to stick to his word, but also the best way to get the most out of the day. This applied to days off as well. Sloth, as mentioned earlier, being the root of all evil and so forth. Grandmother on the other hand thought that a day off was a day off. That's why they rarely went to town together nowadays; it would simply end in what Grandmother called *Krach. Krach* is a German word which is self-explanatory. So that when

Grandfather announced his Programme, it was just for himself and me that he had drawn it up. The Programme was indistinguishable from those we always followed when we went to Oslo: one part cultural enrichment and broadening of horizons, one part outfitting and one part gastronomy. So this was not an especially sensational Programme, but I hadn't expected that either. The sensational thing about my grandfather was how unsensational he actually was. I think it is difficult to imagine anyone who would be less likely to do anything sensational than precisely my grandfather. It caused a sensation the one time he wore a pink tie on a Sunday with his manager's suit, so that just goes to show. Normally it was blue with gold stripes.

The date of departure was fixed in good time as 12th July. I began to count down to it immediately after Midsummer. I don't know whether Grandfather was counting down, but I wouldn't be surprised. For however happy he was to be in the hotel business, and however happy he was to be standing immaculately dressed in his place in the lobby, there would nevertheless be something unusually lively about him when he could get away for a while from the daily grind, as he put it with an expression borrowed from the science of dentistry. Presumably in the same kind of way as when a horse emerges from its stable and rediscovers all the greenery and is suddenly reminded that there are other things than oats. From all his greater and smaller preparations, together with a certain vivacity in his movements and a little whistling now and then, I could deduce that for Grandfather too, the countdown had begun.

Grandmother was counting down too. But in her case the expectations were of a slightly more mixed nature. She said the whole time that it would be lovely to get rid of us for a few days, and it would be good for us to get away for a few days, and that it would be lovely to have Fåvnesheim to herself, but at the same time it was quite clear that she was not altogether happy about it. In part I think it was because she would have liked a trip to town herself, because when I thought about it, it was nearly two years since the last time. And in part I think she was actually worried about Grandfather and me. Normally you couldn't tell.

You could never really tell with Grandmother. She said one thing, but did she mean another? I had never properly understood that before. And if I came to understand it now it was because terror came to Oslo on 2nd July.

It was on the news bulletin straight away. The newsreader's voice trembled with seriousness as he slowly read the announcement. An unknown perpetrator, no-one knew who, because he was unknown, had placed a bomb in a luggage locker in the hall of Østbane railway station, and in the middle of the afternoon it had exploded and killed a person, a young girl who was sitting in the photo booth beside the lockers, taking a passport photo. Right in Østbane railway hall, that thousands of passengers pass through daily. I had passed through there myself many times.

Perhaps, I thought, she was going travelling, and needed a passport photo. Or perhaps she just wanted a passport photo to give to her boyfriend. Whatever; Norway had for the first time been hit by blind terror, and Norwegian radio revised its programmes. Perhaps, some thought, it was people from the Middle East who were behind it. Perhaps, others thought, it was far right forces who were on the attack. 'Far right,' said Grandmother, 'I know them. That's the kind of thing they do.' 'Middle East,' said Grandfather. 'Bah,' said Grandmother. But there was no point arguing about it so long as the perpetrator was unknown. The grown-ups were serious, shaking their heads over the newspapers and news bulletins. For the next few days Grandmother followed all the bulletins and read all the papers. After just the first few hours of news coverage she began to hint that Norway was no longer the friendly, peaceful corner of the world it had been until now, and that nothing would be as before, even that Oslo had now become a risky place to spend time in. It didn't get any better when it soon emerged that the unknown terrorist had placed *two* bombs in the lockers, but that only one of them had exploded.

Then Grandmother marched in to where Grandfather and I were sitting at breakfast, and said:

'Just think, you're sitting here as if nothing has happened. But things *have* happened. They really have.'

Grandfather took a sip of his coffee.

'I wouldn't say this,' Grandmother went on, 'unless I meant it, but I mean it. I know you've promised Sedd a trip to town, but I honestly think you should consider whether Oslo has not become too dangerous a place. Accompanied by a minor and all that.' She glanced in my direction.

'Sisi,' said Grandfather calmly. 'We're not going by train.'

She looked at him with an injured expression: 'That was not at all funny,' she said. 'You know perfectly well what I mean. Just think if anything happened to Sedd. Or to *you*,' she added.

'Nothing's going to happen, Sisi. Stop worrying. Well, I can't just sit here, I've got to get ready for the trip.'

'Well!' For a moment Grandmother seemed choked with tears, but only for a moment: 'Well, now I've said it! I just wanted to say it.'

On that she marched out, with *Aftenposten* under her arm. She said no more on the subject that day, and Grandfather got down to his preparations.

For someone who was in the hotel business, Grandfather made very extensive preparations for travel. First of all he got out his suitcase, dusted it, opened it and surveyed the number of cubic centimetres he had at his disposal. Then he got out the clothes he was taking, which he placed in neat rectangular bundles on the bed beside the suitcase. This took the greater part of a day. For he spent the whole time exchanging one item of clothing for another, as he thought about the possible changes in weather he might encounter in the course of the trip. 'You're only going to Oslo,' Grandmother objected. 'And it's baking hot, and if there's a change in the weather you can just buy a sweater.'

But Grandfather was of the opinion that it was best to be equipped for all eventualities. Should he take his galoshes or not? Should he take that thin cardigan or not? Or would it be enough with a knitted woollen waistcoat? Which he could wear under his jacket? And in the latter case: which jacket would it be most sensible to take? Should he also take the short poplin coat, to be on the safe side? And an umbrella? It was also important to have the necessary medical equipment in his sponge bag. 'Oslo is full of chemists,' said Grandmother, 'on every street corner', but this didn't stop Grandfather being on the safe side: mosquito oil, antihistamine, suntan lotion, aspirins, Alka-Seltzer, charcoal tablets and Vademecum mouthwash had to be there, after weighing up the possible risks on the journey. In addition a small first-aid kit, just in case. When all this was sorted, and the miniature shoe-cleaning set together with the elegant travelling manicure case had been put out, and the spare shoes were cleaned, had shoe trees inserted and been encased in bags, the whole lot could be placed carefully and gently into the suitcase in symmetrical patterns. Personally I travelled light and packed quickly, but Grandfather always advised me on the importance of painstaking and meticulous packing. On the morning of 12th July, when he had checked the oil gauge on the Vauxhall and measured the tyre pressure, always a sign that departure was imminent, Grandmother made fresh objections to the trip. It really was too risky, all things considered. The bomber had not been caught yet. And he could attack again at any moment.

'Calm down,' said Grandfather. 'We're not going anywhere dangerous.'

'No-one knows,' said Grandmother, 'which places are dangerous. Don't you see, I'm worried about Sedd.'

'It'll be fine,' Grandfather said. 'The police are keeping an eye out.'

'You can't rely too much on the police. It's especially in public places you have to be on your guard, it says in the paper. People should be vigilant, it says in the paper.'

'It's all right, Sisi,' said Grandfather. 'We'll just do what we normally do when we're in town. Expand our horizons.'

'Promise me that under no circumstances will you let Sedd go anywhere near Østbane station!'

'Yes, Sisi, I promise.'

'Under no circumstances! And you, Sedd. You must promise me that you'll go nowhere near the place.'

'Of course, Grandmother. Under no circumstances. Grandfather and I are just going to expand our horizons.'

Then we drove off.

In the car on the way down to Oslo the mood was, as always, good, even if not chatty. This was another thing about Grandfather: he didn't talk for the sake of it, and when he talked, he most often said something he had said before. About the hotel, about how to behave in this world if you wanted things to go well, and you did want that. Such things as that the world is wisely divided, my boy, not everyone can do the same thing, you know. That's how it is. Some people have to be served, and others must serve. Some have to sleep in a bed and others have to make it. All of us are at some point masters and at another one servants. That's how it is, that's how it has always been, throughout the ages, and it cannot be otherwise.

If it so happened that you had recently read in English class a flaming torch of a book with the title *Uncle Tom's Cabin*, it would be easy to raise some objections here. But you wouldn't get anywhere with them. Firstly because it would put Grandfather in a bad mood, and secondly you would risk it leading to nothing more than him repeating his point, just with a great number of extra words, or finally you might risk him going quiet and saying not a single word for the rest of the day. So I answered with monosyllabic assent, and Grandfather was content. After that it was agreeably silent in the car right until we had descended to the plains of Eastern Norway, the traffic was building up, and we'd soon be able to see Oslo. Then Grandfather said: 'The traffic's building up, that means we'll soon be able to see Oslo.'

Oslo. It was a long time since we had last been in Oslo. In the past we used to visit at least once a year. Oslo for me meant three things. The first was the hotel. As a respected member of the profession, Grandfather always stayed at the best hotel, Hotel Continental. The stylish piccolos, the impeccable service, the heavy coffee pots and the smell of shoe polish and floor wax inspired him and put him in a good mood. The second was the restaurants. Grandfather insisted on eating exclusively at the best places, so that he could see what was going on amongst the foremost representatives of fine dining. The third was outfitting. Every visit to Oslo normally included a lengthy visit to Ferner Jacobsen's in Stortingsgaten, a place where even the royals do their shopping. But this time, Grandfather had explained, there was to be no outfitting expedition there. Hard times, Sedd, he said, hard times.

But as always, the Continental.

We tramp in from the sun-warmed Stortingsgaten, through the double doors where an adult piccolo in a dove-grey uniform raises a finger to his cap in friendly fashion, and into the cool, hushed shade of the lobby. Everything in here is as it always is, even if the guests are never the same. This, as Grandfather has said, is the secret of a really first-class hotel. Hotel Continental in Oslo is a really first-class hotel. We make straight for the reception desk, where Grandfather, in his impeccable grey suit, introduces himself and explains that he has booked a room. Zacchariassen. Yes, that's right. With a Z.

The receptionist smiles obligingly at Grandfather, and then looks in his book. Holds today's page between the tips of two soft, slightly nicotine-stained fingers; looks firstly at one side of the page, then at the other side, then at the first side again. Columns, lines, hand-written names and numbers. He does it again, checks up and down today's two pages. 'Hm, yes, Zacchariassen,' he says again. 'Yes?' says

Grandfather, slightly surprised. 'I think it would be best, sir,' says the receptionist, 'if you have a word with Pedersen.' 'I don't understand, young man,' says Grandfather in a puzzled but firm voice. 'I made the booking over two weeks ago.' 'I understand, Herr Zacchariassen, two weeks ago, of course, but as I said, I think it would be best if you had a word with Pedersen.' 'Young man,' says Grandfather a little more distinctly, 'have you or have you not received my booking? And have you or have you not our usual room ready for us?' 'Herr Zacchariassen,' begins the receptionist, and Grandfather says: 'I am the owner of Fåvnesheim Mountain Hotel, you know,' and the receptionist continues: 'I do apologise, sir, it may be there has been some mistake, but I think nevertheless it would be best if you have a word with Pedersen.' 'Very well,' says Grandfather politely, 'my old friend Pedersen, why not, why not?'

The receptionist disappears behind a door which he makes sure to close behind him. Another receptionist, busily engaged in dispatching two Scottish-plaid-wearing Americans, sends Grandfather a quick glance from the middle of Wisconsin, but looks down hurriedly as soon as Grandfather notices it. Grandfather doesn't notice my glance at all.

Pedersen arrives.

'Good morning, Pedersen, old chap,' Grandfather announces warmly, and the other man flashes a wide smile and greets Grandfather just as warmly. They shake hands. They ask how things are going, Pedersen asks after Grandmother, after the hotel, and then pretends he has only just spotted me and exclaims at how much I've grown since last time. 'Good heavens, it's just amazing, how time flies, and how is business these days,' he asks Grandfather. 'Oh, you know, not too bad,' answers Grandfather, 'things are a bit up and down now that people have started travelling south on holiday, but we are very flexible and are reaching new markets. New markets, yes.' I understand that he is referring to the Wedding Package. 'I imagine you notice the same kind of ups and downs even here in town,' says Grandfather. 'To some extent,' says Pedersen. 'And how are things with Borghild and the children?' Pedersen gives a detailed account of Borghild and the children, and then he asks whether the skiing was good in the mountains last winter, and the receptionist sends another quick glance in the direction of Pedersen and my grandfather, before he returns to explaining to the Americans the practical difficulties of arranging a day trip to The Fjords.

'It seems there has been some misunderstanding about my booking,' says Grandfather, breaking the stalemate. 'Your *younger* colleague seemed unable to find it? A very obliging young man, to be sure, very promising.'

'Well,' said Pedersen, 'to tell the truth …'

Abruptly Pedersen stops and looks worriedly at me, then meaningfully at Grandfather.

'Sedd,' says Grandfather, 'that's an idea. Why don't you go over to the lobby bar and order a Solo?'

'Or a coke,' Pedersen interposes. 'Just say that Pedersen in reception says you're to have one.'

I stand still for a few seconds, bewildered, looking at the two of them. I've been here many times before, not a hundred times, but many, many times.

'Yes, off you go, lad,' says Grandfather. 'You know where it is.'

I know where it is. I've been here a hundred times. Know the place in and out. At Hotel Continental, a first-class hotel, everything is unchanged and as it always was, and yet everything is different.

I sink down into one of the easy chairs in the lobby bar, with a little table just next to me. A waitress comes tripping over straight away with a friendly smile. Would I like anything?

I'd like things to be the same as before, I think, but I don't say that. Instead I say: 'What do you have, then?'

'Oh … We've got most things, but perhaps you'd like a soft drink?' She looks at me with blue eyes.

'Actually I would really like a gin and tonic,' I say, 'but I don't suppose you'll give me one of those?'

As I say this, I make sure to smile my friendliest and most polite smile, and the joke doesn't fail to have the intended effect: partly she is a little impressed by my impudence, partly I have made it clear to her that I'm well aware of what a gin and tonic is, that I'm not unacquainted with gin and tonic, and possibly not with other forbidden drinks or grown-up delights either, but that I am at the same time mature and responsible, I know the rules of the world and obey them, accept them and understand them, but not without humour. As I said, it doesn't fail to have an effect, and the blue eyes take on a deeper shade of blue, she giggles, and I say: 'So I think I'll have a Solo. With ice. Crushed. Perhaps a slice of orange.'

Impressed, she takes my order, disappears, and returns at once with my Solo, exactly as specified, and in addition a bowl of peanuts which I didn't order, but which are provided for welcome guests at a place like the Continental. That's what I like about places like the Continental. As a guest you get exactly what you have ordered, plus a little extra. This place is unchanged, it's always been like that, I can't remember anything else, ever since the first time I was allowed to eat my fill of the house's homemade strawberry ice cream, which just kept on coming, one portion after another, for as long as I wanted, and with as many chocolate sprinkles as I could desire, as if from a deep-frozen cornucopia. Grandfather and Grandmother sitting contentedly at the table, slightly tipsy, watching me drowning in ice cream, whilst they themselves are bathing discreetly in Cointreau. That's how it was then, and that's how it is now. The Solo tastes more Solo than other places, the ice is crystal clear and the slice of orange rests on the glass's horizon like a setting sun. Now I raise my eyes.

I haven't wanted to do so before. I've always been a bit frightened of those pictures. Those prints. Edvard Munch's pictures. I don't like Edvard Munch's pictures. I think there's something unpleasant and repulsive about them. All those contours which melt away. The faces which are so unformed. Especially I think the picture called 'The Vampire' is unpleasant. The one where she's sucking blood from the neck of the man who's lying with his head in her lap. It's the sort of picture which is impossible to forget, it's so unpleasant. The walls in this lounge are full of these pictures, and it has always amazed me, and it amazes me now, as I'm sitting here with my Solo, that none of the other guests seem to see or notice how nasty and unpleasant these pictures are. They are so unpleasant that it almost hurts. One of the first times we were staying here, I think it was that time with the strawberry ice cream, I had a nightmare that night in which the figures looked like the people in these pictures and all the contours melted into one another. But now that I'm older and haven't been here for a long time, I think that I don't need to be frightened of these pictures any longer. So I look up. But it's no good. They are still positively nasty and unpleasant.

I look hurriedly down at my Solo again, away from the Vampire.

Then I become aware of Grandfather's grey, lightly herringbone-patterned suit trousers on the right of my field of vision, beside my table. I look up. Grandfather looks down. 'Come,' he says. 'I'll just finish my Solo first,' I say. 'We're going,' he says, without meeting my eyes. I don't answer. 'There's been a misunderstanding,' he says. 'Come on.' 'But Grandfather …' I begin. 'Just come,' says Grandfather, irritated.

So we go. Leave the Solo and Munch's dreadful pictures, the peanuts, the lift, the marble floor, Annen Etage restaurant, Pedersen, the Theatre Café and the whole Continental. The piccolo opens the door for us, but he doesn't salute us, just looks at us.

Out in the street Grandfather starts to look for his car keys in all his pockets, including the pocket where he keeps them, that is the left jacket pocket, but nevertheless it seems to take a while before he discovers them, and then he does something he otherwise never does: he swears.

'Fuck,' he says. Then he finds the car keys and we get into his Vauxhall Viva. He turns the key in the ignition, and swings the car competently out into Stortingsgaten, calm and controlled.

'Very annoying, Sedd,' he says. 'It was a stupid misunderstanding. Things like that should not happen.'

'No, Grandfather,' I say. 'Things like that are unprofessional.'

'That's certainly true. Such discourtesy.'

He says no more, just expels his breath between his front teeth. Makes that little s-sound he often makes when he is exasperated about something, and then there's no more to be said, because it's a short car journey, and now we are pulling up in front of the Grand Hotel.

There he asks me to wait in the car, so I do that, whilst he goes inside to make arrangements. I look out at the busy summer-clad life in Oslo's main street, this street in which writers and artists have walked with sombre steps, depressed unto death, and all with the feeling that they were on the wrong planet, but just today there are none to be seen. Just strolling people in summer clothes. Some are eating soft ice, some of those with sprinkles on. The only sign of artistic activity is a man with a cowboy hat and a drum on his back, who has taken up a position outside Freia. There he is playing and singing, in a piercing voice, a ballad in American with such an endless number of verses that I assume it must be Bob Dylan, the whole time drumming on his drum with the help of a clever mechanism which is fastened to the heel of one of his cowboy boots. From the other heel there is a wire leading up to the cymbal on top of his drum, and at every fourth beat he activates that too. In between the verses he blows his mouth organ, which is fastened to a kind of scaffolding he has suspended from his shoulders; there are other wind instruments on it as well, amongst other things a kazoo, and thus the man in the cowboy hat is a whole orchestra on his own. He doesn't look Norwegian.

Perhaps he's American, or English, or I don't know what, but there he stands, and passers-by let coins rain down into the guitar case he has lying open on the pavement in front of his ceaselessly-tramping cowboy boots.

From out of the watchmaker's shop an angry man comes running, suit and tie, red in the face, arms in the air. He goes straight over to the artist and places himself between him and his guitar case, says something, the music stops. They stand there discussing matters for a short while, fairly agitated, but not so loudly that I can hear what they are saying through the open car window. I reach back into the back seat and find my camera bag, open it, take out the camera and hold it up to my eyes. Through the viewfinder I can see how the people around are following with interest. A couple of them want to join in the discussion, but it's already over, for the musician disconnects his mechanisms, nods resignedly, gathers up the coins in his case, puts the guitar in it, closes it, makes a sweeping bow to his public and to the angry man from the watchmaker's, who is now obviously in a friendlier mood, because he gives him a coin as well, and then the musician sets off with his whole orchestra in the direction of Egertorget. I follow him with my camera, craning my neck. Grandfather has still not returned. If I crane my neck still further I can see the Storting building on Løvebakken, a splendid and distinguished building which houses the parliament of the Kingdom of Norway. All power shall reside in this chamber, it proudly declares. I had hoped there would be some Sami on the lawn in front of the building, amongst the lilac bushes, as we saw them continually on the news last year, but they're not there. The Sami were arrested long ago, they've given up, or perhaps they have a summer holiday as well, I think, or do they have to look after the reindeer on the summer pastures? It's difficult to know. Or perhaps they have starved to death because of all their hunger strikes? It's quite a macabre thought, so macabre that I almost have to laugh. It's much more probable that they're under arrest somewhere. And I begin to think about what you give to

Sami who have been starving for a while – probably not reindeer spam, but perhaps you give them nourishing soup, the kind of consommé Jim cooks from bones and vegetables, four hours it has to cook, then it's sieved and cooled, after which you remove the fat and heat it up again, but this time you clarify it by adding a mixture of mincemeat and egg white. The clarifier rises to the surface in the large stockpot and collects there as a dirty grey foam before it is removed with a couple of slotted spoons, leaving behind the clearest consommé. Just the thing for someone who has been hungry for a long time, Sami or not, and good with the addition of a little leek, or croutons, or strips of crisply fried crêpe, and where's Grandfather got to? I am actually quite hungry. I could have done with a soft ice, with or without sprinkles.

Grandfather came marching out through the hotel entrance, noticeably less stressed. He opened the door on my side and leaned in:

'All in order,' he said with satisfaction. A piccolo came out to collect the suitcases and Grandfather leaned across my seat and removed the key from the ignition. He smelt, as he always did, of Old Spice aftershave mixed with a faint scent of lavender. When I was little I thought that it was his skin, that it was Grandfather himself who smelt like that.

We floated in through the enormous lobby – in many ways finer, Grandfather said, than at the Continental, and it's here at the Grand that Nobel prizewinners normally stay. 'Yes,' he said as the lift slowly vibrated up to the third floor, 'Sir Charles Chaplin himself stayed here at the Grand.'

'And Sophia Loren,' said the piccolo.

'Yes, Sophia Loren as well,' said Grandfather.

'And Danny Kaye,' the piccolo went on informatively.

'Yes,' said Grandfather, slightly irritated, 'Danny Kaye as well.'

'He's stayed here twice,' said the piccolo as we passed the second floor.

'Twice? And there was I thinking it was only once,' said Grandfather.

'Third floor,' said the piccolo.

Room 425 was perhaps not as large as the corner room Grandfather and Grandmother used to have at the Continental, but it was a really nice room, I could see that with my practised eye.

'Actually Erik Bye has stayed in this room a couple of times,' said the piccolo after putting down the suitcases, as he drew back the curtains.

'Many thanks for the interesting information and for your help,' said Grandfather, and gave him a whole shiny ten-kroner note as a tip.

The piccolo thanked him almost too effusively, as a bonus showed us for the second time how to regulate the air conditioning, and disappeared.

'It's always good to get into your room after a long journey,' said Grandfather with satisfaction. 'Especially in a good and reputable hotel.'

'Yes, Grandfather,' I said.

'I'm sure I can wait a few minutes to park the car,' Grandfather said. 'Don't you think it can wait five minutes? I'm sure it can wait five minutes, Grand will keep an eye on it, you know.'

He walked a few paces round the room and looked out of the window which looked over Karl Johans gate.

'Yes,' he said, 'well yes, perhaps a little smaller than we are used to, but that's how it is. That's how it is. The view is actually better than at the Continental.'

I looked out of the window. I had to agree. The view was actually better than from the Continental. I took a new photo.

'A little smaller,' he said, looking over the bathroom with a professional eye. 'Still. All in all an excellent room. An excellent room.'

Again I had to agree. It was, all in all, an excellent room.

Then he went out to park the car.

13

It is often said that knowledge is important and that knowledge is power, but knowledge is definitely much, much more than that. Knowledge broadens your horizons. Grandfather and I always used to broaden our horizons by visiting a museum whilst we were in Oslo.

There are many such horizon-broadening institutes of knowledge in Oslo, as there generally are in a large and vibrant capital. During the period when I was an active stamp collector we often went to the Postal Museum, a really interesting museum, where they have not only complete collections of Post Horn stamps but also actual post horns which postal riders have blown, as well as message sticks made to fasten to walls and fences and all sorts of other things. Another very interesting museum is the University Coin Collection, not to mention the Norwegian Museum of Technology at Ensjø, where you can admire the largest model railway in Northern Europe, as well as a model of a Wankel engine, King Olav's first car when he was a little prince, Tryggve Gran's plane in which he made the first flight over the North Sea, together with a number of other interesting exhibition objects. But the museum which, in my opinion, broadens your horizons more than any other is the Kon-Tiki Museum.

Thor Heyerdahl was a man who was not afraid of broadening his horizons. In fact he broadened them continually. No sooner had he broadened one horizon than he set about broadening the next one. He began like that as a child, and after that he just carried on with horizons. All this is documented in the extremely interesting Kon-Tiki Museum on Bygdøy in Oslo. There you can also see Thor Heyerdahl's academic distinctions; the most eminent of these must be Norway's only Oscar, which is placed in a glass case above the ticket office. Above all, at the Kon-Tiki Museum you can follow Thor Heyerdahl's many daring expeditions. Here there is irrefutable proof of how civilisations have migrated over the world's oceans by means of primitive but intelligent vessels, and it is strange to think that no-one understood this before Thor Heyerdahl.

It is warm and full of Americans when we enter the museum. As always, we begin chronologically with the Kon-Tiki raft, and as always Grandfather has to say a few words about how incredible it is to think that seven grown men could cope in such a restricted space for so long.

'They must have been extremely polite to one another,' I say, 'since they didn't fall out.'

'Yes,' Grandfather agrees, 'that is well observed, Sedd, very well observed. It just shows how important politeness is in all of life's situations. Tremendously important.'

'I don't suppose many people think much about that, Grandfather,' I say, to get him started.

'No, indeed they don't. Indeed they don't! There are really not many people who think about it. Most people today wouldn't last three days on a raft like that. Some can't even manage in a hotel. These chaps on the Kon-Tiki could serve as role models.'

'Perhaps they could be used as role models in school books,' I suggest.

'A brilliant idea, Sedd, a brilliant idea. Unfortunately they have abolished order and good behaviour in schools. It is a catastrophe. A catastrophe for the country. It's the Labour Party's fault. How will it all end? I'm not worried about you, though, my boy. You have mastered the art of politeness, generally speaking. That's how it is with people from good families. They always manage. Just look at Thor Heyerdahl. A good family. A very good family.'

'Do you think I would have coped on a balsa raft across the Pacific, Grandfather?'

'Yes, Sedd, I'm quite sure you would. At least when you're bigger. Even bigger.'

Grandfather looks away for a moment from the coils of rope and boxes of food on the Kon-Tiki's coconut-matting-covered deck, places his hands on the railings which separate us from the raft and the artificial water it rests on, looks at me, and registers me visually, as it were.

'A big boy, yes, Sedd,' he says, almost a bit embarrassed. 'Good Lord, how time flies.'

He lets his eyes wander along the walls and up towards the roof, where Kon-Tiki's mast is pointing towards an artificial zenith.

'It's really fine,' he says, 'how they've put this together. Clever. Really clever. With those beautiful clouds and everything. Really clever. You could almost believe you're far out at sea, blown by the trade winds.'

'They must have had a fine trip,' I say.

'Oh yes, they must. Undoubtedly. Surrounded by flying fish and with mutual politeness on all sides.'

Down in the basement, under the raft, in the half-light which filters through the artificial water surface, it's just as interesting as I remember. Now we're down in the vast depths of the Pacific Ocean, where they show all the interesting and fearful sea creatures which followed the Kon-Tiki on its epoch-making voyage. It's like being down in an aquarium, apart from the fact that there's no water behind the glass walls, and no lobsters either. All the sea creatures, from the enormous whale shark via the glittering silver swordfish down to the smallest pilot fish, have been mounted on thin wires and threads which can hardly be seen. It's really cleverly done. Everyone who has read the Kon-Tiki book will recognise it. Unfortunately it's too dark to take pictures. Grandfather and I observe the mysteries of the deep in what I would call devout silence. I say devout, because that word is connected to devotion, and I don't mean devout as in the

Morning Service on the radio, but a real feeling of reverence in the face of Greatness. And the Pacific Ocean is great. It is the greatest and deepest ocean on earth, and contains sea creatures and beings of all kinds, in enormous numbers, with several species which haven't even been discovered yet. It gives you pause for thought when you – as we were doing – look into a part of this enormous world ocean, regardless of how small the part is. In front of the narrow jaws of the whale shark swim the small pilot fish, as always. From the Kon-Tiki's enormous balsa logs, which are lashed together, the sea grass is hanging down and swaying in the current, as always, and on the centre boards which are slotted into place and which the polite crew of the Kon-Tiki used to steer with, barnacles and shellfish are growing, as always. And it strikes me that this raft is always on its way westwards, eternally, like the Pacific, like the Humboldt current, like the South Equatorial current, as it follows the sun's course over the heavens towards a sunset it can never catch up with and distant atolls and islands of green palm trees far, far ahead, their position unknown. I look at Grandfather's profile in the half-light, and think suddenly how awfully he resembles the larger of the two Easter Island statues up on the ground floor, with his long sharp nose and his deep eye sockets. He is peering into the mysteries of the Pacific and looking devout and unfathomable. Perhaps, I think, I resemble the smaller of the two statues, the one with a ship with three masts carved on its stomach, and I try to look just as unfathomable and devout, looking into the deep, where the reflections of the equator's powerful sun are playing in the waves above us and endless shoals of small fish are gliding past, like glittering veils which toss and turn unpredictably.

Afterwards we eat soft ice in the shade of the Fram house, and then we inspect the maritime memorials which have been placed on the lawn outside the Maritime Museum, down towards the sea. For example the huge round mine with spikes like a sea urchin. 'One spike snapped off,' says Grandfather, 'and farewell ship! Just think, Sedd,' he says, 'what it was like when the whole North Sea was like a soup filled with meatballs like that.'

'Yes,' I say.

'One single explosive soup,' says Grandfather sombrely. 'From Stad and all the way over to Rockall.'

'Dreadful,' I say. 'Gunpowder soup.'

We go over to the monument to the dead seamen. I take a photo of Grandfather in front of the memorial. Then we stand there looking up at the silent bronze screams.

'They gave everything for their country,' says Grandfather in a thick voice. 'Everything. Do you understand, Sedd?'

'Yes,' I say solemnly.

'No, you don't. No-one understands completely.'

'But we can try,' I suggest.

'*Dulce et decorum est pro patria mori,*' says Grandfather. 'It is sweet and noble to die for one's country. That, Sedd, is the highest way to serve. The ultimate act of service.'

'It is,' I say.

'You know, Sedd,' – and I know what's coming now – 'you know, Sedd, the human race is divided into two categories.'

'Yes, I know, Grandfather.'

'Two categories. Those who serve and those who are served. For some reason the Labour Party doesn't understand that, though it's not just the Labour Party either, a lot of people, a really large number of people nowadays will not understand or accept this. That the human race consists of two categories. And that there's nothing wrong with that! It's entirely natural.'

'It's entirely natural, Grandfather.'

'That's what's best for people. Sometimes we serve, and other times we are served. It makes us happy and content to know what we should do, to know our place. That makes the servant a good servant and the master a good and responsible master.'

'It's important to be responsible,' I say.

'And we all serve something greater! A greater goal. A greater purpose. Something more than ourselves. That is humanity's duty. That's the only way they achieve anything.'

'The only way, Grandfather.'

'The only way. The only way. For example by serving their native land in wartime, like the seamen on warships. Or in another fashion. For example in the hotel and restaurant business.'

I nod.

'The country wouldn't have coped during the war without our seamen and crews on warships. But the battle continues today. The country would collapse overnight, or at least in the course of a week, if it wasn't for the hotel and restaurant business.'

'I've never actually thought of that.'

'No, not many people have. But just imagine: no-one would be able to stay the night anywhere. No-one would be able to rely on finding a clean warm bed. No travellers would be able to get a hot meal. Or get their shoes cleaned. Or their trousers pressed. Commercial travellers. Conference participants. The crime department's mobile units. Emissaries! Ambassadors of foreign powers! No-one would have any- where to live any more! Do you understand? We would be back in the Middle Ages, in the darkest Middle Ages, when people had to make do with the hospitality which was on offer when they turned up; sleep in barns and outhouses, in haystacks and animal shelters, and eat what the residents could spare, gruel and porridge, flatbread and rancid cured mutton. Do you see?'

'Yes,' I nod, because it's always interesting to hear Grand- father draw up broad historical perspectives, even if he often repeats the same broad historical perspectives.

'Civilisation would come to an end, at least civilisation as we know it. Because what is our civilisation without the people who travel and those who serve them? It wouldn't be much of a civilisation, Sedd. There are lots of people who don't understand this, not just the Labour Party.'

'It wouldn't be much of a show,' I agree.

'No, Sedd, but people aren't good at acknowledging who they are indebted to. That's just how it is, unfortunately. Neither when it comes to the sailors in wartime nor the hotel and restaurant trade. Well, I can see the boat coming. What do you think, Sedd? Shall we take a trip to Ferner Jacobsen's and get kitted out?'

I nod eagerly and stuff the last of the ice-cream cone into my mouth, because I understand that it was just a joke, all that about times being too hard to go to Ferner Jacobsen. Going to Ferner Jacobsen to get kitted out together with Grandfather is an amazingly positive experience. I don't know anyone else of my age who has a Grandfather who is dressed by Ferner Jacobsen. Being dressed by Ferner Jacobsen, as Grandfather expresses it, is the apex of civilisation. So I am in high spirits as we board the elegant vanilla and royal blue Bygdøy ferry to be transported to City Hall quay; I watch the cloudy but glittering waves washing past the hull as we shoot in towards the ancient towers and time-defying walls of Akershus Fortress, and towards the imposing form of the monumental City Hall. Almost as if it was prearranged, we pass by the royal yacht, 'Norge', and it suddenly becomes clear to me that I am in the middle of The Reward. The reward for my efforts. My service, you might say, in the attempt to save the life of the bank manager, and all of a sudden it is as if the sight of the royal yacht is like the conferral of a knighthood, a warm, golden stream of recognition and praise which runs through me from the top of my head all the way down to my trainers. Those who serve will be rewarded. That's how it is. And that's how it is too to order clothes at Ferner Jacobsen, a renowned and noble establishment where the kingdom's foremost men have ordered their finest clothes throughout history. We steer a course straight up to the first floor, where well-dressed assistants are standing at each counter, as if eagerly waiting to take orders, with their tape measures round their necks. Grandfather steers directly towards the oldest and most dignified of the gentlemen, and is greeted as a long-lost friend, or as the esteemed customer he is. Almost all of Grandfather's suits, apart from the two bespoke ones from London, hail from Ferner Jacobsen. We have been here before, so I know what's going to happen; first of all the elderly assistant utters some phrases of a general friendly nature, such as you are most welcome, Herr Zacchariassen sir, we haven't seen you for a while, and here is young Zacchariassen as well, goodness me how he has shot up, well, I suppose at that age, to which Grandfather replies yes, at that age, me, I'm only growing sideways, ha ha, but you are as slim as ever, Malmberg, I must say, I must say, and Malmberg answers that he gets out into Nordmarka as often as he can, and Grandfather sighs and says that there's too little time to enjoy Norway's glorious nature, even for us right up in the mountains, times are so busy, many visitors, a full house and you can imagine. To which Malmberg will reply that you have to be pleased to have plenty to do; there is no shortage of examples of respectable businesses where things have gone very quiet these days, times are not what they were, that much is certain, to which Grandfather replies that that's the way it's going, that much is certain. But perhaps we should see that this rascal here gets something smart to wear, so that he doesn't disgrace us in front of all our visitors? And Malmberg answers ha ha, such a well-brought-up young man cannot possibly embarrass anyone, and let's see, let's see, I've just had a delivery of some fine blazers for young men from the spring collection at Corneliani, quite by chance; it's a difficult age to dress, but these might do the trick. Let's see, young man.

And I follow him, stand over by the mirror with my arms held out diagonally from my sides, as Malmberg and one of the younger assistants, who is nameless, measure my arms, shoulders, waist and legs efficiently and with a light, stroking touch; here we are gentlemen amongst gentlemen, surrounded by a scent of superior aftershave and expensive woollen material, the measuring is finished almost too quickly, and then the fitting begins. Two blazers find favour for Grandfather's critical gaze, the one grey and classical, the other red and rather more youthful, says Malmberg; yes indeed, Herr Zacchariassen, it's important for young people to feel youthful, and I can see that he'd like that one, and it's precisely the sort of jacket young people today go for, most popular, I have a nephew of exactly the same age out in Bestum who has been a hit with all the Bestum girls in that very jacket.

And I think to myself that it's not exactly the kind of jacket worn by youngsters in our locality, but then they're not from Bestum, so in fact that's their problem. I think the jacket is great, elegant and stylish, it makes me look older and more mature, slightly racy, and I look appealingly at Grandfather, so this jacket too gets the seal of approval.

Next: slacks! Malmberg clicks his fingers whilst his name-less assistant inserts safety-pins into the left jacket sleeve to indicate how much it needs turning up. In between Malmberg makes notes on his alteration pad, and then we are offered slightly different trousers which go with the one jacket or the other, or perhaps just with a simple sports shirt, so I have to have that as well, and gradually, as I walk to and fro from the fitting room, the pile of purchases grows on Ferner Jacobsen's polished wooden counter.

'And you, Herr Zacchariassen, would you be looking for anything new?'

'Well, yes, I could perhaps use a lightweight autumn suit, if the truth be told. If the truth be told, the one I have is beginning to feel a little tight round the waist, ha ha, it must have shrunk, ha ha; you know how it is, Malmberg.'

'It's the advancing years.'

'Indeed, the advancing years.'

'Now, let's see,' begins Malmberg; his eyes take on a slightly hectic gleam, and Grandfather clearly feels in his element, because it's an occasion when Zacchariassen the hotel owner is in town to make purchases, oh yes. That doesn't happen every day. Oh no. And soon his pile of clothes has also begun to grow on the counter, because once you buy a suit you need shirts to go with it, and in our business you can get through two or three shirts in the course of a busy representative working day. In our profession you can never be too representative, that much is certain. The slightest little deviation from a high standard on the sartorial front will be noticed immediately – not merely by the guests, who will form a bad impression of the place, but also by the staff, who will lose respect, and in that way the falling standards will be transmitted down through the ranks and then everything's on the slippery slope, as Grandfather would put it. Malmberg converses with Grandfather as he plucks pins with a practised hand from the little pincushion he is wearing on his left arm like a watch, measurements are confirmed, Malmberg asks whether Grandfather might not consider a sports jacket too, and I can see that he'd like one, but then common sense asserts itself and he says: 'No, Malmberg, it's very tempting, but we must be sensible. Besides, I don't have the leisure time to wear one.'

At which Malmberg smiles obligingly, glances at his real watch just below the pincushion, and informs us that he can have the clothes ready by 2 pm the following day, unless Herr Zacchariassen would like them sent?

'No, there's no need for that,' says Grandfather; 'we're in town until the day after tomorrow. And in any case we have a social engagement tomorrow afternoon.'

'Do we, Grandfather?'

He winks slyly at me: 'It was supposed to be a surprise, Sedd. But never mind. Never mind. Tomorrow is 14th July. I'll say no more.'

He looks at me with an air of mystery. Malmberg's face lights up with a conspiratorial smile of recognition. It is clear that Grandfather rises even further in his esteem.

'Ah yes, ah yes, I understand, Herr Zacchariassen, I understand. We have had several customers in here the last few days who will be attending.'

'Attending what, Grandfather?'

'You'll have to wait and see.'

'Ah yes, ah yes,' says Malmberg.

'But tomorrow is 14th July. As I said. If you paid enough attention in history lessons you will perhaps be able to guess. Although it's called "General Studies" now, I suppose.'

'No, Grandfather, that was in primary school. At secondary school General Studies is called sociology, history and science.'

Malmberg and Grandfather look at each other with an air of resignation, and both shake their heads gently.

'What do you think of that,' says Grandfather. 'No history any more. Soon they probably won't have maths any more either.'

'No,' says Malmberg diplomatically, 'it's all very peculiar.'

'We *do* have history, Grandfather. General Studies is a group of subjects. The terminology is just more up-to-date,' I tell him.

'Oh, is that so,' says Grandfather.

'It's because everything is connected to everything else,' I try to explain, but I can see at once that there's no point. In a place like Ferner Jacobsen the very walls are steeped in history. Literally. Here, as I mentioned earlier, many of Norway's leading figures have acquired their garments throughout the ages. Both on the occasion of the dissolution of the union and on the occasion of national independence day, Roald Amundsen's triumphal homecomings and other great days in our nation's saga, but however hard I concentrate I cannot call to mind that any of those things happened on 14th July.

14

After that we went back to the hotel. On the way through Studenterlunden Grandfather said little. The satisfied smile he had displayed the whole time we were in Ferner Jacobsen's slipped away; the hotel manager disappeared and only Grandfather remained. When we got back to our room he declared that he was tired and wanted to rest. But I didn't want to. So after a little parleying, as Grandmother always calls it, he handed me a whole hundred-kroner note and said I was to go out and have some fun, have an ice cream and go to the cinema or some such thing. But no violent films. Do you hear?

'Yes, Grandfather. No violent films.'

'Violent films are not good for children and young people. They make them aggressive. And callous.'

'Yes, Grandfather. Callous. I know.'

'And they don't sleep well. Just remember what happened when we let you see *Psycho* in the Monday film series. We should never have done that.'

'I remember.'

'What we see during the day remains with us in our dreams, you know. You didn't sleep properly for several weeks after that terrible film. You need your night's sleep, now you're growing so fast.'

'I know.'

'Yes, because it's at night that you grow. Just like potatoes and tomatoes. They grow at night.'

'Do they?'

'That's something everyone knows. But I suppose it's not a part of General Studies yet.'

I just wish he could stop going on about General Studies, I thought, but out loud I said: 'Perhaps they'll get round to it next year.'

'Just remember to be back here at the hotel by eight at the latest. We're going out for dinner.'

'Right, by eight.'

'And be careful. Watch out when you're crossing the road. All right, make yourself scarce.'

I took my camera with me and made myself scarce.

The town air outside the hotel hit me like a wall of heat. I thought I might drift along the street a bit and observe life in the town, perhaps find some photogenic subjects, before I went to the cinema, so I did that. Firstly I drifted up towards Egertorget, where there was a different street musician than the first one, also standing outside a goldsmith's, this time David-Andersen, dressed in exactly the same fashion, and singing the same songs. This one was wearing a stetson. 'The times they are a-changing,' he sang, over and over again, in a piercing voice. People in the crowd seemed to appreciate the message. I'm not so sure myself. That times are changing the whole time is of course a fact. But I'm not so sure that people are changing so much. According to Grandfather's view of history, if they are changing it's for the worse. But I think that people are basically changing very little. If there's anything we can learn from history, it's that people basically change very little, and that much of the change we notice is simply superficial or imagined. That's my view of history. It's important to develop your own view of history. So if the selection of violent films is so broad and upsets the internal life of young people, this is in principle no different from the selection of gladiatorial battles during the time of Caesar, which no doubt also resulted in some bad dreams and disturbed sleep, in the same way as *Psycho* by the outstanding British-American film director Alfred Hitchcock.

I took three pictures of the singer from slightly different angles.

After that, without really thinking about it, I walked along the whole of Karl Johans gate and down to Østbane railway station. But there was nothing to see. The three large green wooden doors under the neon sign of Oslo Ø, which normally stood open, were closed and locked. There was a police car outside. A few curious people were standing around, and a couple of them were trying to look in through the glass panes in the doors. I walked up the five steps to the doors and peered in too. But the inner doors, between the entrance and the large reception hall where the bomb had exploded, were also shut. Through the windows you could just make out a little of the long, narrow, illuminated advert for the Norwegian Credit Bank, which runs right across the hall just before you get to the platforms. That was all.

'Nothin' to see here,' said a policeman, getting out of his car and sauntering over with deliberate steps. I had to agree with him about that. I don't know if I was disappointed, but I don't think I was. It was actually eerie enough to see the closed doors in a place where so many people are normally coming and going, on the way to and from their daily tasks, as they always are at a railway station in a busy metropolis like Oslo. The closed doors looked solemn, almost stern.

I couldn't bring myself to take a picture of the doors. Even though they were just doors. It was the fact that they were closed.

I thought once more about the girl who'd been sitting in the photo booth. Perhaps, I thought again, she was taking a passport photo. Perhaps a picture for her boyfriend. Or perhaps just for herself. It was troubling and sad to think about. Perhaps, I thought suddenly, the flash went off at the same moment as the bomb? But that was a horrible thought. Most troubling of all was the thought that the terrorist had still not been caught, but was still walking around in our midst.

Suddenly I turned and descended the station steps. As I crossed the street towards the station square, I began to run. I don't know why. I just had to. The camera bounced up and down against my chest.

'Hey! You there!'

That voice. The policeman's voice.

'Yes, you! Where are you off to? Wait a minute!'

But I pretended I hadn't heard him. On my left there was a goldfish-bowl tram with its back door open, ready to depart. I steered straight for it. At any moment I expected to feel the long arm of the law reaching out for my shoulder, because I had the impression that the policeman was right behind me. Perhaps he believed I was the terrorist, who had been back to admire his gruesome handiwork.

But I made it onto the tram after an appreciable sprint, just as the doors slammed shut. I stumbled over the rough rubber matting on the floor and grabbed hold of the central pole, but I didn't turn round. Not until the tram swung left over to Fred. Olsens gate did I dare to throw a swift glance over my shoulder. Right enough. The policeman was standing at the tram stop, looking after the tram. I hope he thought that I just needed to catch that tram, so that I was on an entirely law-abiding mission. And not, as my appearance might lead him to believe, that I was from the Middle East, for example. There aren't so many who come from the Middle East, so in that sense it was good that he was on the alert, but I could just imagine what would happen if, for example, he had taken me in for interrogation, and I had had to explain everything, and he had had to ring Grandfather at the hotel, who would most certainly have rung Grandmother, and then all hell would have been let loose. No question.

Law-abiding, yes. It was important to be law-abiding right now. So I walked quickly forwards in the completely empty compartment, as far as the tram driver.

'Thank you,' I said, 'I only just managed – '

He merely pointed at the sign which said Do not disturb the driver, as he stared stolidly in front of him, concentrating on the traffic.

I stood there waiting politely, because I didn't want to disturb the driver, on the contrary I wished to be law-abiding; then I discovered that the stripes on the rubber matting here by the entrance door were painted in alternate shades of yellow and black, and that there was another notice which declared that you should not stand in the yellow and black-striped area when the tram was moving, so I hurriedly sat down on the front seat until the tram stopped at a red light. Then I stood up and walked forwards to the driver again.

'I didn't manage to buy a ticket,' I said, and held out the hundred-kroner note.

He glanced at it. Shook his head. Pointed to another notice, a smaller one, which informed the traveller that Oslo Trams could not change any amount larger than 50 kroner.

'I'm afraid I don't have any less,' I said, as politely and law-abidingly as I could.

'Then you'll have to get off at the next stop, lad,' he said simply.

'Oh,' I said.

'Jup,' he said. 'Where you off to?'

'Grand Hotel,' I said.

'This tram don't go to the Grand,' he said.

'Oh,' I said. 'I'm staying there.'

'Stayin' there?'

'Yes. Just visiting. With my grandfather. Herr Zacchariassen, the hotel owner.'

'Is that so. Zacchariassen the hotel owner.'

'Yes.'

'Right. You can stay on till Wessels plass,' he said. 'That's not far from the Grand.'

'Thanks,' I said, 'that's good of you.' I thought: well begun is half done. That's how the old saying goes, and if the police car which was standing in front of the railway station had followed the tram and me, and stopped us, and demanded an explanation, I now had a representative of Oslo Trams as an upstanding and sober witness, who, even if he couldn't give change for notes over 50 kroner, could now state on oath that I definitely:

a) had tried to pay my fare, even if the note was too large, and

b) had a perfectly plausible and lawful reason to catch the tram, since I was on my way to the Grand, even if this tram didn't actually go there.

I thought perhaps I ought to give the driver some more information about Grandfather waiting for me and that was why I was in a hurry, just to be on the safe side, in case the policeman actually came, but I decided it would seem too conspicuous. I would be making too much of it. When you watch realistic detective series, for example *Derrick*, you can see that one of the mistakes criminals most often make is to make too much of things. So I decided to say no more, other than a final short thank you, and sat down again.

'Wessels plass,' announced the tram driver, as the tram swung to the right and braked with a screeching sound outside the Storting.

'Thank you,' I said again, and was about to walk back through the tram, because I had noticed that there was a sign on the front door saying Exit at the rear, but the tram driver nodded at the front door.

'You can just get off here,' he said.

'Thanks,' I said. 'Sorry. Thanks.'

'Bye,' said the tram driver. Then the doors shut with a bang and the tram disappeared.

For a few seconds I stood still, listening. But no. No sirens. Nothing. Nevertheless, I thought, it was probably best to start walking. I looked at my watch. It was a long time until the cinemas opened. So after taking a picture of the back of the Storting, I sauntered up Akersgaten, where the day's newspapers hang in the windows of the editorial offices. As always, there were lots of people here, reading the newspapers for free. It must be because they had no money, even though many of them were perfectly respectably dressed. But appearances can be deceptive. You can't always tell by looking at people whether they have money problems. Quite the opposite. Grandmother explained that to me. When the money runs out, the façade is the only thing you have left. It's called keeping up appearances, and is apparently a widespread phenomenon in parts of central Europe, according to Grandmother. But it seemed it occurred here in Oslo as well, to judge from the crowds who wanted to read the evening papers for free, even though there was hardly anything in them now in the middle of summer. Or perhaps they had just forgotten to renew their subscriptions. They read and read, as if the Third World War was about to break out at any moment, but I suppose it was the bomb attack they were reading about. Personally I'd had enough of that and was only interested in the cinema listings, so I went straight over to the last section of *Aftenposten* on the farthest right of the windows. I couldn't help noticing that *Aftenposten*'s evening edition was carrying the kind of story which shows how on-the-ball this newspaper is, a most serious incident from London, as a matter of fact. There a man had made his way uninvited into the bedroom of none other than Queen Elizabeth II of the United Kingdom, in Buckingham Palace itself, completely unobserved. The Queen had to observe him herself. And so she did, when he sat down on the edge of her bed. This shocking story shows not only how poorly protected Queen Elizabeth II is, but also how brazen people have become. They have no respect for anything any more, that is certain, if they don't even have any respect for Queen Elizabeth II. This report would no doubt be on the evening news on television as well, and I knew that Grandmother would find it hard to bear. It could be too much for her on top of the bomb attack. But for a few more hours she would be in a state of ignorance about the terrible thing that had happened, since we don't get the evening papers at home any longer. They are only distributed in the Oslo area. Unless she picked it up on the news on the radio at six o'clock, but she hardly ever listened to that, because then she was having an after-dinner nap, or resting her eyes, as she used to say. I decided then and there to remember to ring Grandmother as soon as the TV news was over at five past eight, so that we could discuss it.

I found the cinema listings and discovered immediately that a number of cinemas unfortunately were closed for the summer, so the choice was not great. I didn't know where many of these cinemas were either, so I had to limit myself to those which were on Karl Johan or nearby. There weren't all that many violent films on offer either, so I plumped for *Arthur*, age rating 12, which was showing at the Victoria. That left me exactly half an hour to eat a soft ice, and I did that outside an ice kiosk in Rosenkrantzgate. I consumed it without chocolate or sugar sprinkles, just the pure, white, soft taste of ice cream.

Arthur turned out to be a very entertaining film after all. I hadn't expected it to be so entertaining. In brief, the film is about a young man from a good family. At bottom he is good enough, but he drinks too much. He can afford to. His family is so important and so old that he has access to 750 million dollars, and that is quite a lot of money. Converted into Norwegian kroner it becomes a great deal more. Arthur thinks it is great fun to be so rich, especially since everyone thinks it makes him extremely attractive, even though he's just a little squirt and an alcoholic into the bargain. But Arthur is lonely. His family – and it is not big, just an ice-cold father and a dreadfully brutal grandmother – treats him with ice-cold and brutal disdain. Fortunately he has his loyal butler, Sir John Gielgud, who in reality is his friend and spiritual father. If Arthur refuses to marry Susan, he risks losing the 750 million. That would be a harsh blow, but Arthur is in love with an unemployed actress, who steals from shops, something Arthur finds charming. But fortunately, as I said, he has this butler, Sir John Gielgud, or Hobson as he's called in the film, not forgetting the chauffeur Bitterman, a kind black man, who do their utmost to help him and serve him.

In the butler's case it really is the utmost, all the way to the grave. There was a really sad moment in the film when Arthur turned the key in the door to his deceased butler's little room. I'm sure Grandfather would have liked this film. It illustrated his view that the world is divided into those who serve and those who are served in a way that was ten thousand times better than words. It also showed the importance of coming from a good family, not just outwardly, but also and above all inwardly. But the most important thing this film has to teach us is that love conquers all. Including the loss of 750 million dollars. You have to follow your heart at all times, and then all will be well. If you don't follow your heart you simply become a liar, to yourself as well. Another thing you can learn from this film is that a butler's love also conquers all. As I said, I think Grandfather would have been very enthusiastic about this film. But I don't think he'd have liked Liza Minnelli stealing gentlemen's ties. Grandfather has experienced far too many such vanished ties and other valuable articles in his professional life, as I recounted earlier. So that was a weak point in the film. It seems to me that Liza Minnelli is charming enough in herself, and doesn't need to steal ties to get attention, and that the director here had too little confidence in the actress's ability. After all, Liza Minnelli is quite a star, and also the daughter of the legendary Judy Garland, though actually not everyone is aware of that, since Liza Minnelli for one reason or another doesn't use her mother's surname but her father's, whoever he was. But that's how it goes with surnames. I myself, for example, use my father's surname, Kumar, even though he and my mother only met very briefly and weren't married, and he died before it could develop into anything else, and even though I have grown up and been brought up in all ways as a Zacchariassen. Finally I would like to say that the music in the film was very good. So that as I left the Victoria together with the handful of other cinema-goers who had defied the summer heat this evening in order to devote themselves to their film hobby, we were all audibly

159

humming the film's theme tune, which describes the distance between the moon and New York City.

When I was standing outside on Karl Johan again it was a quarter to eight, so I wandered around for exactly ten minutes, so that I could be back at the room at precisely eight o'clock. Not too late and not too early. Grandfather doesn't like people being late, but he doesn't like them being too early either, especially not for dinner. It places unnecessary stress on the staff.

And right enough. As Grandfather opened the door, he was wearing an impeccable suit and had just shaved, I could tell that from the scent of Old Spice.

'Good,' said Grandfather, 'excellent, Sedd. You're on time. That's good.'

As usual, he didn't need to look at his watch to see what time it was. Grandfather had an internal clock. It was equally impressive every time. He used to say that he had developed it over many years as a manager. And as if to underline how accurate Grandfather's internal manager's clock was, the city hall bells began at that moment to chime eight o'clock. Grandfather glanced swiftly at the mirror, straightened his lapels, glanced swiftly at me and asked if I was ready.

'Yes, Grandfather.'

'Did you go to the cinema?'

'Yes, Grandfather.'

'Was it a good film?'

'Yes, very good. You'd have liked it.'

'Good, good. You can tell me more over dinner. I think you'd better comb your hair.'

'It was called *Arthur*,' I said from inside the bathroom as I combed my hair in front of the mirror.

'What did you say? You know I can't bear anyone having a conversation with me from another room.'

'Sorry. I just had to comb my hair.'

'Come on then. We have a table at Blom's at a quarter past eight.'

15

Blom's is the Artists' Restaurant. That means quite a lot. Amongst other things it means that if you are an artist, you can have your coat of arms hung in the restaurant, which has a fountain in the middle, even though it is indoors. And there are hundreds of coats of arms. Even Charlie Chaplin has his coat of arms hanging here, at Blom's, the Artists' Restaurant. Grandfather showed me the coat of arms when we arrived. Grandfather thinks that Chaplin is one of the greatest film stars the world has seen. And the world has seen many film stars, that much is certain. But even if Chaplin no doubt was a great film star, the problem in my eyes is that he didn't speak. He was as silent as a library. Myself, I would back Dudley Moore. However, he has no coat of arms hanging in Blom's Artists' Restaurant, as far as I could see. But Sir Charles Chaplin did, with his motto 'Stand on your own two feet', and he must have felt it was an enormous honour when he had it hung up in 1964, during a visit to Oslo. Because it's not everyone who gets his coat of arms hung up here.

However, we didn't see very many artists in the restaurant that evening, just a few American tourists. The artists were presumably on their summer holidays.

On the other hand, we did have the pleasure of meeting the manager of Blom's. This is how it happened: the head waiter, an elegant little Hungarian with grey hair, decided it was preferable to chat to us rather than the American tourists. Then he realised that we were in the hospitality business. That's the kind of thing professionals understand. So he enquired as to whether we were in the hospitality business, and Grandfather confirmed it and introduced himself, and with that Stefan, as the head waiter was called, immediately went out to fetch the manager of Blom's, who introduced himself in his turn and was large, breathed heavily and smelt of sherry, and Grandfather introduced himself, and all was mutual honour and rejoicing. Furthermore, Blom's manager could inform us, since I asked, that it was not easy to get your coat of arms hung up here, it's not something just anyone can do. That much is certain. For that, young man, you really have to belong to the Upper Crust. Grandfather laughed.

I asked the manager whether he thought that Dudley Moore would be accepted as Upper Crust if he too came to visit Oslo, and the manager laughed and said that it was not inconceivable, not at all, provided he did actually visit Oslo, and you have a clever grandson there, Herr Zacchariassen.

The manager of Blom's thought it was excellent that Grandfather and I had visited them, he said. But he hadn't met Grandfather before, and that he thought was a pity, and when he found out that Grandfather had been there before, he expressed deep regret that Grandfather had not sent word of his presence, but Grandfather said that he didn't want to make a fuss and so forth. But the manager of Blom's breathed heavily and heartily and asked the head waiter Stefan to bring him a glass of sherry, just a wee drop, and Stefan nodded and disappeared and returned, and the manager said we professionals must stick together, and it was an honour, he added, an honour to have a visit from the manager of such an ancient and respected place as Fåvnesheim – just as ancient and respected as Blom's, if not older, but up in the mountains, and he had been there himself as a boy, a place which had always attracted the cream of society, just like Blom's, and what are times coming to?

'They're changing,' sighed Grandfather. 'Regrettable, but a fact.'

'That's how it is,' said the manager of Blom's. 'Regrettable, but a fact. But I have confidence,' he added. 'Confidence that the cream of society will always find the places of real quality and pre-eminence.'

'I agree entirely,' said Grandfather, 'pre-eminence. Pre-eminence is the word.'

I took note of the word, because it's useful to know words like that. But you have to look them up after you've taken note of them, so that you use them properly, otherwise it can be embarrassing. Pre-eminence comes from the Latin *eminere*, and means outstanding superiority. So it's quite straightforward.

The manager of Blom's remained at our table throughout our dinner, which consisted of crab cocktail, lamb cutlets in port sauce and crème caramel with Norwegian berries. Grandfather and he discussed all the tribulations of the profession, including how difficult it is for high-class places to keep the flag flying as it is meant to fly.

'Herr Zacchariassen, I am so pleased,' said the manager of Blom's, 'that you let us know you were here this evening.'

'It was your excellent head waiter Stefan here who unmasked us,' Grandfather said with a smile of acknowledgement as Stefan brought the manager of Blom's another glass of sherry.

'And your well-behaved grandson.'

'My daughter's son,' said Grandfather, smiling.

'Is that so,' said the manager of Blom's.

'Yes, I'm afraid his mother is dead,' said Grandfather, looking hard at me. 'And his father too. He was an Indian professor of medicine. Professor Kumar. So his grandmother and I are *in loco parentis*.'

'Oh my goodness!' said the manager of Blom's in astonishment. 'Oh my goodness. I am sorry to hear that. That explains his exotic appearance.' He looked at me.

'Yes,' said Grandfather, 'that explains it.'

'I must say,' said the manager of Blom's, 'it really is marvellous that you and your wife have done that. Taken it upon yourselves to bring him up like that. And at your time of life.'

'Needs must,' said Grandfather seriously. 'That's life.'

'Yes, that's life,' the manager of Blom's nodded. 'That's life. Sometimes you just have to.'

We had got to dessert, which I was picking at. I could understand that it is sometimes necessary to simplify history a little, I really could. But nevertheless I didn't like Grandfather saying that my mother was dead. We didn't know that. No-one could know that. So I asked politely whether Grandfather had a couple of kroner, because I said I'd promised to ring Grandmother.

'What a good boy,' said the director of Blom's. 'He wants to ring his grandmother.'

'I'm sure that's not necessary, Sedgewick,' said Grandfather.

'I promised her.'

'Listen, my boy,' said the manager of Blom's, 'why don't you ask Stefan if he can show you – Stefan! There you are. Can you show this young man the way to the office. He's promised to ring his grandmother.'

'But it's long distance,' Grandfather objected.

'No matter. No matter.'

'Come this way,' said Stefan.

'Grandmother?'

'Is that you, Sedd?'

'Yes. Did you hear about Queen Elizabeth?'

'Yes. *Du meine Güte*. I heard it. On the evening news.'

'I thought I should ring.'

'It's just terrible. *Schlimm*. And in the middle of the night. A stranger.'

'Yes, but everything was all right, Grandmother.'

'Yes, it was. Fortunately. What a scandal.'

'Are you all right, Grandmother?'

'Oh yes. It's sweet of you to ring, Sedd. Is Grandfather all right?'

'Grandfather is fine. We're at Blom's. The Artists' Restaurant.'

'Oh, it's lovely there. *Sehr anmutig*. Your grandfather and I used to go there often, years ago.'

'The manager of Blom's is sitting at our table. I'm using his phone.'

'That's nice. Is the food good?'

'Very good. I went to the cinema and saw *Arthur*.'

'Who did you see?'

'*Arthur*. It's a film.'

'You'll have to tell me about it when you get back. I'm a bit tired. I'm going to bed.'

'Sleep well, then. I just wanted to make sure you were all right.'

'That was sweet of you, Sedd. *Mein braver Bub*.'

'Good night then, Grandmother. Oh, by the way, Grandmother, is there anyone in the royal family who has a birthday tomorrow?'

'Tomorrow? No, I don't think so.'

'July the fourteenth. Are you sure?'

'The fourteenth?'

'Yes, the fourteenth.'

'Now that you ask, I think Crown Princess Victoria of Sweden will be five years old tomorrow. Five. How time flies.'

'But none of the Norwegians?'

'No. Sedd, you haven't been to the railway station, have you?'

'Oh no, Grandmother.'

'Are you sure?'

'Yes. Quite sure.'

'Well, that's good. That's good. You're a good boy, Sedd, keeping your promise.'

'Goodnight then, Grandmother.'

'Goodnight. Give my love to Grandfather.'

'Yes, I will.'

I hung up.

'You must be really fond of your grandmother,' said Stefan, who had been standing waiting in the doorway.

'Yes,' I said. 'She's so kind. From Austria.'

Stefan brightened.

'*Sehr schön,*' he said.

When I returned to the table I passed on Grandmother's love. I added a greeting to the manager of Blom's while I was at it.

'His grandmother is Austrian,' Stefan announced as he held my chair.

'No, is she really? Austrian? Fancy that. Skål, by the way.'

'Yes, that's right,' said Grandfather. 'Yes, skål. We met at the hotel school in Linz. My beautiful Sisi and I. And would you believe it, I managed to carry off this beautiful lass to the Norwegian mountains! There she is an ornament to our house. A first-class hostess. They only make them like that in Austria.'

'Remarkable,' said the manager of Blom's. 'You are extremely lucky. Well, what do you say, Zacchariassen? How about a little one for the road?'

'It's most kind of you,' said Grandfather, 'but I'd better get back to the Grand with this young man.'

'Rubbish,' said the manager of Blom's. 'He's a grown lad. If he gets tired, he can just walk to the Grand on his own. It's only *due passi*, as the Italians say. Stefan. Two Upper Tens.'

'Then I accept with pleasure. Sedd, are you tired?'

'Not at all,' I said.

'I hope you enjoyed the meal, Zacchariassen.'

'It was exceptional,' said Grandfather. 'Don't you agree, Sedd?'

'It was delicious,' I said. 'Both the crab cocktail and the lamb. A suitable balance between richness and tartness in the cocktail, and the cutlets were perfectly grilled, just the right shade of pink.'

'Ah, the young man is a connoisseur! Imagine that!'

'Say thank you, Sedd.'

'Thank you very much.'

'And I would like to inform you that Blom's will be delighted if you and your fine grandson here will accept this evening's meal as our guests.'

'Oh no, no, that's too much. We can't accept that.'

'I insist,' said the manager of Blom's. 'It's the least we can do.'

'You're too kind,' said Grandfather.

16

14th July arrived, the day of the surprise, associated with some red-letter day or other about which I had no idea. Unfortunately, on the trip to Oslo I did not have access as I usually did to the *Almanac for Norway*. To be precise, the *Almanac for Norway for the year Anno Domini 1982*, as calculated by the Department of Theoretical Astrophysics of the University of Oslo. This almanac is extremely useful. It is definitely a publication which most people ought to invest in every year. The thing is, the Department of Theoretical Astrophysics works out all the calculations for the almanac long before the year in question, so that people have plenty of time to buy it for one another for Christmas. It is a really super Christmas present to get. One year Grandfather gave all the hotel staff the *Almanac for Norway* for Christmas as a reward for the year's efforts. Many of them were pleased, and expressed their pleasure, but there were unfortunately a few who clearly did not understand what a useful present they had received. It's not always that people appreciate the difference between superficial tat, as Grandmother calls it, and what really is valuable in this world, especially in Norway, which the Almanac is designed for. Anyway: in addition to the times of sunrise and sunset, new moon, first quarter, full moon and last quarter, charts for high and low tide, significant movements of the planets and astronomical events, as well as indications of the precise dates of the spring and autumn equinox and the winter and summer solstice, the *Almanac for Norway* also contains a miniature government yearbook, practical information about hunting regulations, and an overview of both religious and secular festivals and commemorations. So if you are wondering when Septuagesima falls, the Almanac can give you the right information. And there is no doubt, I thought, that it would also have been able to inform me of what this 14th July was all about, but unfortunately I had left it in my room in Fåvnesheim, although it was quite a small almanac. Actually it's small enough to carry with you all the time.

Besides, the *Almanac for Norway* is an official publication, and is completely without any form of advertising. This is a definite advantage in our day, when there is more and more advertising and branding everywhere. In the *Almanac for Norway* we meet Time, Norway and the phases of the moon just as they are, uncontaminated by adverts for Bergen Bank. I don't believe that the banking system should own Time, or put its brand on it.

When we had eaten breakfast we proceeded to Ferner Jacobsen's, where all our clothes lay ready in attractive carrier bags. Malmberg greeted us ecstatically. We tried on the clothes, even though it was surely not necessary, as Grandfather said, but Malmberg insisted. 'Better to be on the safe side,' he said. 'That is always best. If anything should be wrong, we can see it here and now, instead of you possibly having to send the clothes all the way to Oslo and us having to send them back again. And it's not certain they would be right then either.'

'I understand,' said Grandfather.

'And if we need to adjust anything now,' Malmberg said, 'and you leave before the adjustment is finished, then we would of course send the clothes on without any extra charge to you.'

'Splendid, splendid,' said Grandfather, studying himself in the mirror.

Of course no adjustments were required, but at least we had tried on all the clothes one final time. All that remained was to pay.

'Perhaps you would be so good as to send me an invoice, as usual?' Grandfather enquired.

At that moment a kind of veil was drawn over Malmberg's ecstasy. He threw out his hands with a friendly but apologetic gesture, and his face assumed a courteous expression:

'I very much regret, Herr Zacchariassen, I very much regret.'

'You can't send an invoice?'

'Changing times, sir, I regret to say; the firm has discontinued that practice, to all intents and purposes. I very much regret.'

'That is a pity.'

'I do understand, sir. But it's on orders from – the highest authority.' Malmberg inclined his head in the direction of the Royal Palace.

'I wasn't aware of that, unfortunately,' said Grandfather. 'I see. I suppose you will take a cheque?'

'Of course, Herr Zacchariassen. Of course.'

'Then I'll write you a cheque on the spot, but to be honest I was not entirely prepared for this, so it may well be that this will give rise to – how shall I put it – a slight embarrassment.'

'I understand, sir.'

'Might you be so good as to wait to present the cheque until after midday on Monday, so that I can transfer sufficient funds to my private current account?'

'Of course, Herr Zacchariassen, no problem. That's perfectly fine.'

'Many thanks. And if you could in addition be so good as to allow me to add seven hundred, no, just a moment, let me see, seven, eight, nine hundred kroner to the total, and cash that for me, then my grandson and I will have enough money for the rest of the day; because I don't think I will have time to visit the bank, as we're on our way to …'

'No problem, Herr Zacchariassen sir, I understand. I understand. And you're on your way to … Yes. Should we not say a thousand kroner while we're at it, just to round it up?

Better to be on the safe side. And once again I regret that our firm has a new policy.'

'Very good of you, Malmberg. Very good of you. Indeed, it's all about policy now. It seems to be a sign of the times.'

Grandfather wrote out the cheque and gave it to Malmberg with a polite nod, which Malmberg reciprocated:

'True, times are not what they were. Many thanks, here is your receipt. I'm pleased that you and the young gentleman here found what you wanted; thank you so much for your visit. Just a moment, I'll get someone to help you out with your bags.'

'Many thanks, Malmberg. Until next time.'

'Until next time!'

So off we go. The elegant white carrier bags with gold lettering from Ferner Jacobsen are shining exclusively in the sunshine. We are kitted out, and ready for most things. A man who is properly kitted out has one thing less to worry about, Grandfather always says. It's best to have the fewest worries possible. This July the fourteenth has already achieved an intense warmth, and I could really fancy something cold to drink or an ice cream in the shade, or perhaps a return to the hotel room in order to cool down a little, but instead of that Grandfather is forging ahead, across the grass in front of the Storting in the direction of Egertorget.

'Come on,' he says shortly.

'Where are we going, Grandfather?'

But he doesn't answer. Walks with rapid, energetic hotel-manager strides up the gentle slope towards Egertorget, in the shadow of the parliament buildings, with bags in both hands and me in tow. He doesn't stop until we are standing outside the jeweller's where I heard the second street singer yesterday, singing in a piercing voice that the times they were a-changing. Today there is a thin young man with a shock of blond hair standing here instead, selling poems from a wheelbarrow full of stencils, which must be an extremely impractical way of distributing literature. You see many strange things on a visit to Oslo.

'Grandmother,' Grandfather grunts shortly, leading the way. 'We're going in here. Come on.'

Inside David-Andersen the goldsmith's it was dark and cool. The bags from Ferner Jacobsen gleamed in the gloom like shining white crusaders' shields. A lady in glasses hurried over to us, asking how she could help us. 'Brooch,' said Grandfather. 'I'm looking for a pretty little brooch for my wife.'

'Of course, a broash, of course, and what kind were you looking for? Colour? Size?'

'Brooch,' repeated Grandfather. 'Just a brooch. It's not for any special occasion. Just a little present.'

'A love token,' I said.

'How lovely,' said the lady in glasses. Her glasses were slightly wing-shaped, rising to two points on either side of her forehead which as it were pointed upwards to her stiffly permed hair.

'It's just a present,' Grandfather grunted. 'But anyway. I suppose so.'

'We have some really pretty broashes over here,' said the lady, leading us across to a display. We looked down at the items.

'What about that one?' I said, pointing. 'I think that would suit Grandmother.'

'Yes, why not?' said Grandfather. 'Perhaps. Perhaps. Could we take a closer look?'

'Of course,' said the lady, unlocking the display cabinet and taking out the tray of brooches, which was lined with blue velvet. With manicured fingers she extracted the piece I had pointed to, three twisted sprigs of gold held together by a band on which was mounted a blue stone.

'A really pretty piece,' said the assistant. 'Really pretty. The young man has good taste. This is from our own workshop. The goldsmith is called – '

'And how much is it?' asked Grandfather.

'It is a genuine tourmaline, and the piece itself is unique, so the price is one thousand two hundred and twenty kroner.'

'It is pretty, that's true. But I'm afraid my wife might find it too ostentatious.'

'What about that one then, Grandfather?'

Grandfather leaned over and looked at the brooch I had indicated, a smaller piece with two gold rose leaves held together by an enamelled band.

'Very pretty,' said Grandfather hesitantly.

'I really must say, the young man has good taste in broashes,' said the assistant appreciatively.

When you have grown up, as I have, with the civil engineer Erik Tandberg, the Norwegian Broadcasting Corporation's eminent specialist on space travel, as one of your linguistic models, always speaking distinctly and with exemplary clarity, even when using the most difficult specialist terminology, it can sometimes be an ordeal to talk to people. But I did not react, only smiled as the lady continued:

'Perhaps you would like to have a look at some of our more modern broashes?'

'No, thank you,' said Grandfather. 'My wife's tastes are definitely classical. Don't you agree, Sedd?'

'Yes, Grandfather, definitely classical.'

'Six hundred and eighty kroner,' said the lady, who had taken out the brooch. 'A really pretty classical broash. Really classical.'

'Really classical,' nodded Grandfather. 'Thank you, I think I'll take that one.'

'Would you like it gift-wrapped?'

'Yes, thank you very much. That would be most kind.'

The assistant unfastened the black thread with the little price tag with tiny numbers on it, hung it skilfully around her left ring finger, and asked us to accompany her to the counter. She was really skilled at gift-wrapping. It became a beautiful little parcel, finished off with an elegant little butterfly bow of gold ribbon.

'An excellent choice,' she affirmed. 'I hope your wife is pleased.'

'I hope so too,' said Grandfather.

'How would you like to pay? Cash or cheque?'

'Cash,' said Grandfather decisively. He took out his wallet and counted out eight red hundred-kroner notes and laid them on the counter.

'That's one too many,' said the lady, smiling.

'Oh, is it? So it is,' said Grandfather. 'Many thanks. It's easily done.'

'Don't mention it,' said the lady, giving him the change, together with the little bag with David-Andersen's elegant crest on it.

17

We went back to the hotel, where we first of all ate in the café, just like Ibsen. Ibsen ate a shrimp sandwich and Napoleon cake here every day, and that was what gave him the energy to complete his late plays. It just shows how important delicate open sandwiches are, made in the traditional way. They can awaken even the powers of peevish old men. Not to mention a well-executed Napoleon cake. As Grandmother has often explained, this confection of airy millefeuille combined with a rich buttery cream was a central European classic long before Ibsen's or for that matter Napoleon's day.

Grandfather ate with a good appetite, and drank a cup of coffee, but said little. He seemed distracted. But then he roused himself, checked the clock and said it was time we got moving.

We went up to our room and changed. Grandfather insisted that I should wear the more formal jacket, even though I was keen on trying the red one. Grandfather thought that the more formal jacket would be most appropriate, together with grey trousers, so that's what I wore. I asked whether I should take my camera, and he said definitely, of course, absolutely.

He looked secretive.

'Where are we going?'

'Wait and see,' he said, and smiled just as secretively as before. 'I think it's a bit strange that you've not guessed yet. You're normally so knowledgeable about history.'

'But Grandfather,' I began. 'I've been racking my brains yesterday and today, and I can't think of one single episode in Norwegian history.'

'Norwegian history, hm,' he said slyly. 'Come on, Sedd, let's go.'

We set off through the baking hot town. It was so hot that the asphalt felt soft beneath our heels. At the top of the slope where Drammensveien begins it was gleaming and shimmering like a mirage. The formal jacket felt dreadfully hot, and I asked Grandfather whether we had far to go. No, he said, not terribly far, just a little way. This reminded me of the rather Delphic answers he used to give on ski trips when I was little, so I suspected that it was quite a long way. As we embarked on Drammensveien, I took off my jacket and laid it neatly over one arm as I walked.

'Why did you take your jacket off? Put it on again.'

'But Grandfather, it's frightfully hot. I'm sweating half to death, in my tie and everything.'

'No-one has ever sweated to death,' Grandfather declared. 'It's not medically possible. So. Put it on again. And straighten your tie.'

'But Grandfather …'

'Come on. No nonsense. A gentleman has to be able to control his perspiration.'

'Really?'

'Of course. I learnt that when I was a student and waited on tables in an establishment in Linz with formal dining outside. It could get dreadfully hot there in the baking sun. Much hotter than this. So obviously we perspired, every one of us. We perspired like horses. But the head waiter, Herr Kantorowicz, wouldn't hear of it. He thought it looked indelicate. And it did too, when we were dashing to and fro with faces running with sweat and great damp rings under our arms.'

As if to underline his point, Grandfather increased his speed as we walked.

'But Herr Kantorowicz was merciless. We had to stop sweating immediately.'

'But that's impossible?'

'Not at all. Not at all. It's a question of inner willpower and mastering the art of auto-suggestion. You just have to say to yourself over and over again that in actual fact it's rather cool. And that if you stop and think about it, the temperature is no worse than on a fresh day in the mountains. And that the hot air you're breathing in and out is actually a cool refreshing breeze. Then you have to instruct your organism, every single cell, to cease perspiring immediately. On the spot. You have to get your organism to understand that it cannot allow itself to do something so impolite. Finally there are certain practical things you can do, such as only breathing through your nose, which cools the air a fraction. And the head waiter explained to us that it was a good idea to wear a decent vest. It might sound paradoxical, but a decent close-fitting vest absorbs perspiration and keeps you dry, so that you don't begin to perspire even more. A gentleman, especially when he is engaged in a profession such as ours, must always demonstrate perfect self-control.'

'So you stopped perspiring then, did you, Grandfather?' I asked as I slowly put on my jacket again and straightened my tie.

'I find an outlet for my perspiration when the opportunity arises. On a ski trip or in the sauna. There it doesn't matter if you perspire.'

'Rather the opposite,' I said.

'Exactly. Rather the opposite. That's quite right.'

We had reached Solli plass, and were following the tramlines out along Drammensveien. Here there was more shade, so it felt slightly more bearable with my jacket on, but I sensed nevertheless that I had a long way to go before my self-control was as well developed as Grandfather's.

A goldfish-bowl tram surged past us with its clamour; inside it people sat behind the open windows, avoiding having to move in the heat, and I glanced at it longingly;

perhaps it was being driven by my acquaintance from yesterday, the friendly and sympathetic tram driver who had let me travel for free when I was being pursued by the police in all innocence, but Grandfather and his willpower marched confidently and perspiration-free past all the tram stops and onwards towards Skillebekk. He began to whistle in marching time. A rousing march, as if created for fast walking. In all kinds of weather. In rain and sunshine. I recognised it at once. It was the Marsellaise. The glorious and revered national anthem of the Republic of France. A march in which the rapid rhythm and the bold melody imaginatively reflect the French Republic's revolutionary past. The French are not a people who let themselves be messed about. It's easy to believe that they are only concerned with cheese and wine, not to mention fashion, but if anyone messes them about, they throw down their sewing needles, strengthen themselves with a sip of wine, gobble down a piece of Roquefort and begin straight away to build barricades in the streets. Preferably with a rousing song.

And at that moment a light went on in my head; it was as if the *tricolore* itself in red, white and blue was waving inside me, for now I understood. Or I thought I did. Grandfather marched onwards, like a division of *La Grande Armée*.

'Now I think I know where we're going, Grandfather!'

He carried on whistling steadily, striking the ground extra hard with his heels on every fourth beat.

'It's the fourteenth of July today,' I said. He stopped whistling and half turned his head:

'It is indeed. It took you long enough, I must say.' He began to sing: *'Allons enfants de la patrie! Le jour de gloire est arrivé!'*

I joined in the song. And sure enough: after walking past a number of embassies, which lay one after the other here on Drammensveien like national anthems on a string, we arrived at the French ambassador's elegant and imposing residence. A crowd of people were on their way in through the wrought iron gates and strolling down the curving drive towards the house. The *tricolore* was hanging from the flagpost, and from inside the garden you could hear a buzz of voices. The French in Norway had no intention of letting the fourteenth of July pass like any other day, that much was clear.

'This is where we're heading,' Grandfather announced.

He patted his breast pocket happily and looked at me. Stood still for a moment. Then he put his hand in his pocket and drew out the invitation:

> *On the occasion of Bastille Day*
> *His Excellency the French Ambassador*
> *M. Frédéric Sylvain and Mme. Sylvain*
> *have the honour to request the presence of*
> Herr F. Zacchariassen and guest
> *at a reception in the Ambassador's Residence*
> *Wednesday 14th July 1982 from 2 to 5pm*

I looked admiringly at the card, which was of shiny white cardboard embossed with the French coat of arms. The same text was on the other side, but in French.

'The French ambassador is an important contact,' Grandfather declared. 'And a good guest. Very gracious. You remember him, Sedd, don't you?'

Yes, I remembered him.

'Twice, Sedd, twice he and his gracious wife have visited Fåvnesheim. His Excellency takes his duties as ambassador seriously. As French ambassador to Norway he wanted to learn to ski. Nordic style.'

'Was that why he and his wife came, Grandfather?'

'Yes,' said Grandfather as we showed our card to a stiffly uniformed officer at the gate and proceeded inside onto French territory, 'that's why he was there. He has, so to speak, learnt cross-country skiing from me personally.'

I stared at him in disbelief: 'Did you teach him, Grandfather?'

'Indeed I did, as good as. As good as. A gentleman who picked it up very quickly. Ah, he's over there greeting people. Come on.'

We followed the stream of guests, who were mostly Norwegian, which in a way was a little disappointing, in the direction of Monsieur and Madame Sylvain. When it was our turn, Grandfather extended his hand and said:

'Uuh…'

The ambassador looked at him in some confusion for a moment, but then Grandfather summoned up his French and got going: '*Bonjour, monsieur l'ambassadeur, et la madame aussi.*'

'Ah, Mister Zacchariasson!' the ambassador replied in English. 'How very good to see you. Welcome. Glad you could make it.'

'*Et voilà mon grandfils.*'

'*Comment?*'

'Grandson,' I said.

'Ah, yes. I remember him. My Lord, he has grown, hasn't he?'

'*Il a, il a,*' Grandfather agreed.

'Yes … Well, I hope you'll enjoy yourselves. Both of you. There's refreshments in the garden.'

'*Très merci, merci.*'

We made our way into the garden, and now we were deep inside French jurisdiction. Here no Norwegian authorities could reach us. Not that they had any reason to reach us, but if they had, they would in fact not have been able to reach us here, but would have had to wait outside the gate. Here you were only admitted with an invitation.

A waiter in a white jacket with a black cravat came towards us with glasses of champagne on a tray. Grandfather helped himself to one.

'*Merci beaucoup, monsieur,*' he said.

'You're welcome,' came the answer in Norwegian.

'Do you have anything non-alcoholic for the lad?'

The waiter nodded discreetly in the direction of the large buffet. We set off towards it. On the way we were accosted by yet another waiter in a white jacket, who offered us a tray of canapés. We took two each. A tiny pastry case filled with what couldn't be anything other than pâté de foie gras, and a triangular canapé with smoked salmon and cream of horseradish.

'Superb,' said Grandfather, licking his lips. 'Incomparable. French cuisine is and always will be the best.'

'I agree,' I said, chewing. 'A pity Jim's not here.'

'Yes, a pity. You'll have to try it all and see what you think of it, so that you can pass on some ideas to him. Perhaps you could take some pictures.'

'Will do.'

'It would really be a good idea to serve canapés when we have tourist buses and other small groups who just call in briefly. I'm thinking about the cost.'

'Cost is important.'

'There's always such a dreadful amount goes to waste with the big buffets Jim puts on. A dreadful amount. I mean, I know they are his pride and joy, but …'

'But you do need lots of waiters if you're going to serve canapés.'

A new white-clad figure was standing in front of us with new varieties; this time it was small biscuits with brie, round canapés with cream cheese and radishes, and tiny stuffed tomatoes. I had never seen such small tomatoes.

'That's true,' said Grandfather. 'Oh, these are delicious. *Mange takk. Merci beaucoup.* I'll have to think about it and do the sums. Oh, look!'

'What?'

'Over there! Can't you see?'

'See what?'

Grandfather pointed cautiously:

'There. Yes, there. Can't you see who it is?'

He was pointing at a group of men in suits who were drinking and smoking.

'Who, Grandfather?'

'The bearded one with the glasses. Can't you see it's the journalist Jahn Otto Johansen?'

'Yes, you're right. It must be Jahn Otto Johansen.'

'That's incredible,' said Grandfather. 'Jahn Otto Johansen, no less.'

'Isn't he in Moscow?'

'I suppose he comes home now and then, once in a while.'

'Oh yes,' I said. 'Of course. Perhaps he comes home to see his wife and that.'

'Fancy that,' said Grandfather. 'Jahn Otto Johansen. He looks just like on TV. Perhaps a bit smaller.'

'Yes,' I said, 'I think so too. I had imagined Jahn Otto Johansen would be bigger.'

I took a photo of him, discreetly and not too close, so that he didn't notice.

A new waiter came past with a tray of glasses, and Grandfather picked up one of them with his left hand, whilst at the same time putting his empty glass down on the tray with his right hand, all in one practised, gliding movement.

'I think I'll go and find a soft drink,' I said, 'I'm really thirsty.'

'Oh yes, do that. Poor you. I forgot you were so over-heated.'

I went over to the buffet and got a glass of Fanta. On the buffet there were even more platters with different kinds of canapés. I began tasting them. Systematically. But there were many different kinds, so I decided to concentrate on four or five sorts and really try to understand how they were constructed, what they looked like, how they tasted and what they were made of. I took pictures of the ones I thought tasted best, but I had to ration the film, because I didn't have all that many exposures left. Actually it was strange that Jahn Otto Johansen was here, I thought, and not in the Russian embassy, where he properly belonged. It was of course possible that Jahn Otto Johansen also had a concealed passion for France, which most people didn't know about.

When I had tested enough of the canapés I set off on a journey of discovery through the groups of smartly-dressed people. Further down the garden you could see over the train line and the motorway down towards Frognerkilen Bay, and on the other side of the water you could make out the pink castle of Oscarshall, towering up in the distance like a royal monument. But here we were on republican territory.

On the terrace there stood a lady in a flowery dress, admiring the view over Frognerkilen. It is important to say hello politely, so I did so.

'Good day,' I said.

'Good day,' she replied.

'You are admiring the view?'

'Yes,' said the lady. 'And this, if I may remark, is a classical view.'

I could hear immediately from her accent that she was not Norwegian. But she didn't sound French either, because she didn't have a throaty 'r'.

I took a picture of Oscarshall, but I knew as I was taking it that it was too far away to come out well.

'A literary view, I must say,' said the lady. 'Very literary. It always hholds the same fascination for me.'

'Yes,' I agreed, 'very literary. Impressive.'

'When I think that perhaps it was hhere, precisely hhere that hhe stood…'

Her h's were extremely throaty.

'Yes,' I said, 'it is incredible.'

'… looking out over Frognerkilen Bay whilst the train passed by below, on the way to Skarpsno in the dark … Whilst sparks danced from the funnel of the locomotive. What a way to begin! Fantastic! Genius!'

'The train is electrified now,' I informed her. 'No sparks any more.'

She looked at me uncomprehendingly.

'Do you know that I learnt Norwegian just because I was so entranced by this book?'

'No, really? That is impressive.'

'I think I hhave read this book forty times in its Russian translation. In the end the pages fell out. A book of genius. So that when I learnt Norwegian I could just start at page one in the Norwegian edition, because I knew the text almost by hheart in Russian.'

'How fascinating,' I said. 'Are you Russian?'

She held out her hand:

'Olga Nazarenko,' she introduced herself. 'From the Soviet embassy. Cultural section. Pleased to meet you.'

'Pleased to meet you,' I said. 'Sedgewick Kumar.'

'Ah,' she said. 'From the Indian embassy? They hhave a commercial attaché there called Kumar, I believe.'

'Yes,' I said. 'He's my father.'

'And hhere he stands,' said Olga Nazarenko from the cultural section of the Soviet embassy, 'just hhere, Wilfred Sagen, as the story begins.'

'Who did you say?' I asked.

'Little Lord. In the book. An amazing exposition, don't you think?'

'Yes,' I said, 'absolutely unique.'

It was best to go along with it, since it was possible that she was a Russian propaganda agent. There had been quite a lot about that in the papers, and I thought it was best to be on the safe side.

'Everything is a lie,' Olga exclaimed passionately. 'Everything! And Little Lord, the child, hhe does not only know that, hhe hhimself lives the lie. Yes, you can say, together with the great Russian literary scholar Kaminski, that Little Lord, Wilfred, *is* hhimself the lie. Make-believe through and through.'

'Exactly,' I said. Presumably any Soviet propaganda agent would know a great deal about lies and make-believe, so it was best to be forearmed.

'It is absolutely one of the best novels in the whole world,' Olga insisted. '*Little Lord*. It is actually strange it is not better known.'

'Well, it is quite well-known,' I protested. 'Apart from anything else it has been made into a radio play.'

'Hhas it?' Olga Nazarenko looked at me in amazement.

'Yes,' I said. 'I've heard it. And it's been filmed, though it's not a Norwegian film. I think it's a British or American version. Also, now I come to think about it, it's been made into a Norwegian TV play, I believe.'

Now Olga Nazarenko's amazement knew no bounds: 'Is it possible? Is it really possible? I must absolutely try to see and hhear these dramatizations. Tell me, are you old?'

'Sorry? Am I old?'

'No, no, excuse me. I mean: are they old? The drama-tisations? That's what I mean!' She uttered a dry laugh.

I considered: 'Oh, I'm not too sure. The Norwegian versions are not very old. But I think the English-language version is from the thirties.'

'The thirties? That cannot be right. *Little Lord* was not published until 1955. So that is not possible.'

'Oh no,' I said, 'of course that can't be right. Anyway, it's an amusing book. Exciting.'

'Exciting? Oh yes, absolutely. But amusing? I am not sure that is the right expression. It has a couple of suggestions of comic episodes, but the laughter, hhow do you say, hhangs fast in your throat.'

'Sticks in your throat,' I said politely.

'Yes, that's right! You speak fantastically good Norwegian, Hherr Kumar.'

'So do you,' I said diplomatically.

'But what I mean is, I would sooner call it *hharrowing*. Never has an author better described the life-lie and self-deception of late bourgeois society than in *Little Lord*. Not even Ibsen, not the great Hhhamsun.'

'Yes, there is a lot of self-deception in that book,' I said, 'and a lot of bitterness.'

'Yes,' said Olga. 'Yes, yes, yes! Bitterness! It is not everyone who sees the bitterness behind the gleaming and hharrowing surface. It is really good that you saw that! Really good! Even though you are so young.' She looked over at the sailing boats on Frognerkilen Bay: 'Bitterness,' she said. 'So much bitterness.'

'But then fortunately everything ends well after all,' I comforted her.

'Well? After all?' She stared at me enquiringly: 'Well, yes, on the metaphorical plane ... perhaps you can say that. That is an interpretation I hhave not thought of before.'

'But that is obvious,' I said. 'Love conquers all. Little Lord's love.'

Now Olga Nazarenko was looking at me with an expression as if she had been struck by lightning: 'Love!' she whispered. 'And beauty! Beauty shall save the world! Yes, yes, yes! Yes! That is so well observed! I hhave not thought about it like that before. It is Little Lord's desire for love which drives hhim! It is true that it drives *hhim* into the abyss, but on a deeper plane the perverted desire for love of all this world's little lords leads to the breakdown of bourgeois society. To a new world!'

'There, you see!' I said, beginning to look round for an escape route. Olga Nazarenko's eyes had taken on an intense gleam, and I was afraid that she was seriously engaged on gaining influence over me. It could be risky.

'Excuse me,' I said, 'but I have to find my gr ... someone.'

'Must you? What a pity! Well, many thanks for our conversation.' She held out her hand again. This time she had a hard handshake.

'Thank you too,' I said courteously.

'And thank you for your interesting insights into this material. Into this great novel.' She would not let go of my hand. 'Into *Little Lord*. You have absolutely hhelped to give me a new perspective on this work of genius.'

'Not at all,' I said.

I could feel her eyes on the back of my neck as I walked quickly back up the garden to look for Grandfather. I understood that it was quite complicated to take part in these diplomatic gatherings. Here people really did not just make polite conversation.

I couldn't see Grandfather anywhere. So I wandered around for a while, helping myself to canapés and more fizzy drinks. All around the garden there were people in small groups talking to one another. I noticed that they had a distinctively nonchalant way of discussing any subject, whether it was politics or small talk. With their heads inclined slightly backwards, a glass in one hand and a cigarette in the other, they each listened with a smile to the other's contribution, which clearly should not last too long, and then answered with an amusing comment or agreement, before changing the subject. In one group they were talking about the bomb attack at the railway station, shaking their heads in dismay, agreeing that it looked as if terrorism had now arrived in Norway, that you could no longer reckon on Norway being a safe harbour, before they abruptly changed to discussing the price of strawberries, which had broken all records, and shaking their heads in equal dismay.

Grandfather was still not to be seen, and for a moment I felt a little stab of fear. Grandfather was not a young man any more. And I was worried in addition that he had started to become forgetful. What if he had just wandered off? What if he had had a heart attack from the heat? This was something which crossed my mind now and then, and always had done for almost as long as I can remember, since I had grown up with grandparents instead of parents. Once I explained this to Grandmother, or tried to explain it, that I was sometimes uneasy that something might happen to them, since I only had them and they were so old. I should not have done that. Grandmother denied strenuously firstly that they were old and secondly that anything might go wrong with them. So I must be so good as not to entertain any such thoughts. Besides, I thought between two canapés, if anything had happened to Grandfather, if for example he'd had a stroke, I would have heard the ambulance arriving. And just at that moment I heard his voice as well. It came from inside the villa, where the front door stood open. I walked up the few steps and into the large hall. There were groups of people in here as well, having nonchalant conversations on the elegant creaking parquet floor, and in one group I saw Grandfather. But he wasn't being especially nonchalant. Quite the opposite, in fact. I would say he was rather loud. He was red in the face, and talking to those around him about his work teaching the French ambassador and his wife the art of skiing, Nordic style. The group around him diminished rapidly, and those who remained looked extremely reserved, I must say. None of them made a nonchalant or witty remark, and it was clear to me at once that Grandfather was in the act of transgressing the rules of good diplomatic behaviour.

'Yes,' he burbled, 'it's not just anyone who could have undertaken such a task. No, it is not. Absolutely not. The ambassador himself told me that I deserved some recognition, recognition for this contribution towards the mutual understanding of our two cultures. The French and the Norwegian cultures. Perhaps even the Foreign Legion. But I told him that was too much for such a small service.'

He turned and picked up a glass of champagne from a passing waiter, still with the same perfect gliding movement, quick as a flash, but when he turned back the group around him had vanished, and he was left alone, adrift on a sea of parquet floor.

I went over to him. His face was red, and he was not quite himself. He was sweating profusely. He looked at me with a dejected expression.

'Come on, Grandfather,' I said.

He made no move. Just looked at me as if I was a diplomat from an unknown country.

I took hold of his arm.

'Come,' I said firmly. 'We have to go back to the hotel.' He smiled weakly at me, his eyes narrowed. Emptied the glass of champagne in one mouthful.

'Yes,' he said. 'You must be tired.'

'I am a bit tired. Let's go.'

Grandfather said nothing on the way back to the Grand. He had a long afternoon nap, and in the evening we both had braised steak in the café. The next day we got up early. Grandfather gave his morning gymnastics a miss, and packed. In reception we paid our bill with a cheque, and then we drove home.

18

When we got back to Fåvnesheim everything was in chaos, and after a brief survey of the situation Grandfather decided to retire to bed with influenza. The first symptoms announced themselves while we were still out on the driveway, before we had even got out of the car. When we saw Grandmother bearing down on us with rather too hasty, ominously energetic strides, Grandfather had a nasty coughing fit. He parked the car, switched off the engine and put the handbrake on. Grandmother was already round the driver's side of the car, and well launched into her speech. Grandfather coughed again, then he sighed and opened the door.

'… and I won't put up with it, I don't think I should be asked to put up with it, and you must deal with this at once!'

Grandfather sighed again, undid his seat belt and clambered out of the car, straightened up, and looked seriously at her.

'… and I mean *im Ernst, wirklich im Ernst*, that enough is enough. Enough! I do think, *im Ernst*, as the hostess here and wife of the manager, that I am owed *eine gewisse Achtung*. Yes. A certain respect. Now I have held out up here, without complaint, without a single complaint, for nearly forty years. Forty years! *Ich finde, mir gebührt eine gewisse Achtung!*'

'Now now, Sisi, we haven't even got out of the car yet. What is wrong?'

'But you're standing there! Out of the car! Oh yes, you can just go away in the middle of the season! Whilst I have to stay here, and' – her voice broke for a moment – '*endure* these dreadful people! Yes. Dreadful.'

'Oh dear, Sisi, that's too bad. Which dreadful people do you mean? Are there problems with some of the guests?'

'The guests? The guests are altogether dreadful, just as usual, rude and Norwegian and without any manners, but they're not the ones I mean. You know very well. I do think that after more than forty years, *aber wirklich*, it really is time they stopped treating me like a stranger, like a guest, like a foreigner! A foreigner!'

'Now now, Sisi, is it the staff again?'

'Again? Again? It is *always* the staff! *Immer*! No respect, no deference!' Her voice broke again: 'I can't stand it any longer. It is driving me mad! Forty years. *Ich bleibe hier keinen Tag mehr!*'

Grandfather took a deep breath and sighed.

'What is it this time, Sisi?'

'This time?! You're not even taking me seriously!'

'I am taking you really seriously, my love. It's just that – '

'You're not taking me seriously at all! This time, you say! You say it as if you're not taking it seriously!'

'Oh yes, Sisi, my sweet. I'm taking it very seriously. Oh no, don't cry. Don't cry. Or at least do it quietly, the guests might hear you.'

'The guests! If they do, it's your fault. Here you go, off to town on a pleasure trip for days on end, leaving me with all the responsibility. All the responsibility. And it would all have been all right, perfectly all right, and I would not have complained for a moment, not for a single second, if it had not been –'

'Well, that would have been unlike you,' said Grandfather quietly, but fortunately she didn't hear him.

'- if it had not been for this dim-witted staff who never the smallest thing can do right and never show me any respect! *Nicht im Geringsten*!'

'But Sisi,' Grandfather tried to stem the flow, 'what is it that's happened?'

'Everything has happened! That's what!'

'But Sisi,' Grandfather tried again, 'it's difficult for me to help when I don't know what's happened.'

I had now got out of the car, and was standing on the other side watching my grandparents over the car roof. Grandmother was having what Grandfather normally referred to as a paroxysm. She had a number of these in the course of a year. She had so many that the word had become part of our everyday vocabulary. When I was small and Grandmother had one of her paroxysms, and threatened to stay not a day longer, up here in the uncivilised wilderness, surrounded by layabouts and boors, of whom the worst by a long way was my Grandfather, and that she was going back to the cultivated and civilised Vienna, on the spot, this moment, immediately, without a second's delay, I used to get upset or frightened. Especially because on some occasions when she had her paroxysms it looked as if she was carrying out her threat; she would pack a suitcase, bang the doors, pack some more, bang some more, close the locks on her suitcase with two furious clicks, look contemptuously at Grandfather and me, and announce that she was off now, goodbye, *auf Wiedersehen, schönen Abend noch*, turn on her heel, march out of the hotel, get into the car and drive off. It didn't help if I cried and called Grandmother, Grandmother, and it didn't help in the slightest if Grandfather attempted cautiously to follow her as she swept around in her paroxysm, whilst uttering a calming 'now now, Sisi, don't get so upset'. She marched out. Usually after sending him a final furious look. Then she was gone. Drove off. Stayed away an hour or two, possibly a whole day, but seldom longer. But whether her trip to Vienna lasted for thirty minutes or three hours was in reality all one to me, because each time I believed that she had gone for good. I got terribly upset, and Grandfather was unable to comfort me, no matter how hard he tried. So I would go in to Jim in the kitchen, and sit down on the floor beside the large warming cabinet. That was a good safe place. Jim would comfort me: 'Now now, Sedd, chin up. She'll come back, you know. She always comes back. Doesn't she always?' 'Well, yes, Jim,' I would say, 'but what if she doesn't come back this time?' 'She will, Sedd. She will.' 'It's a long way to Vienna,' I would say, and apart from the one time when Jim answered that it's not bloody far enough, he would otherwise answer, 'Take it easy, Sedd, she's not thinking of going to Vienna, you know that. This is where she lives. She's just having, what does your grandfather call it, a paroxysm.' 'Yes,' I would say, as I swallowed the titbit which Jim had always dug out for me by this point in the conversation, 'I hope you're right, Jim. It's just one of her paroxysms.' 'That's true enough,' said Jim. 'Just one of them.'

But this time, as I stood watching my grandparents with a Vauxhall Viva between them and me, I suddenly realised that I was not at all frightened. I just felt a bit sorry for them, and particularly for Grandfather, who had driven all that long way, just for my sake, and was so tired. So when Grandmother marched inside to pack her suitcase, and Grandfather took sick leave on the spot and shuffled crestfallen and muttering into the private apartments, I decided to sort things out.

In the kitchen I found Jim. He was carrying on as normal, just in the process of emptying a sack of potatoes into a crate. 'Ah,' he said, 'there you are. Good thing you're here. Help me with the spuds.'

'What's going on, Jim,' I said.

'Going on? Nowt. Nowt's going on.'

'Yes it is, Jim,' I said. 'It's not nowt. It's obvious something's going on.'

'Well,' said Jim, 'it's the usual. Just the usual. The woman's potty.'

'What is it this time then, Jim?'

'God knows, God knows.'

'But there must be something, Jim?'

'Must there really?' Jim sighed.

'Besides,' I added, 'I don't like you calling Grandmother potty, Jim.'

'Well, what should I call her,' muttered Jim, looking away; but then he pulled himself together and said: 'All right. All right. But you know what she's like. I'm standing here with my hands full, and I mean really full, without enough help and I'm having to use all the worktops because I've got to have several things on the go at the same time, and she suddenly comes in because she's decided she wants to bake.'

He sighed. I sighed.

'So I said that's fine, Fru Zacchariassen, but could you please be so good as not to take up two of the worktops here, because I'm in a rush, and otherwise there won't be any wedding dinner here tomorrow, Fru Zacchariassen, that's what I said.'

'It sounds like the usual thing, Jim,' I admitted. 'So what happened then?'

'Then? Well, what d'you think? It was a fucking Vesuvian eruption. First of all I was fired. I didn't worry too much about that, because it happens so often. Then I said – well, what I said was – just listen to me, Fru Zacchariassen, I said, if you're going to start firing me all over again we're just going to waste heaps of time, so I don't intend to use as much as half a calorie listening to this, Fru Zacchariassen, I just can't be bothered. Yes, that's what I said. That's what I said.'

'Oh dear, Jim. That was bad.'

'Yes,' Jim admitted, 'I suppose it wasn't too smart. I should have known better. But you know what it's like when it gets really busy here – '

'So what happened then, Jim?'

'Well, it all boiled over properly then. First I was fired again, and then she started firing everyone she met. She even managed to fire a couple of guests she bumped into in reception. Fortunately the firing was done in German, and I don't think they understood. "*Ihr seid entlassen,*" she said, completely furious, but they just looked at her oddly. Then the rest of us. The whole staff. In the end it was a kind of general assembly in the office. Two of the girls, Anita and Big-Anita, who haven't worked here before, began to cry. Sobbed and begged and said "dear Fru Zacchariassen," they said, "we need the money for the autumn," they said, "so that we can start studying," they said, but they shouldn't have said that. Because Fru Zacchariassen explained that no studying, no course, no form of education whatsoever would have the slightest chance of improving their characters and behaviour, which had been ruined long ago, perhaps even from birth, that was what she said, and so they cried even more, don't you know. And then we were fired, every last one. All at once.'

'Blimey, Jim,' I said.

'It was probably because Zacchariassen himself wasn't here. You should have heard the howl of protest which rose into the heavens, like the weeping in Ramah, with wailing and gnashing of teeth, and that's when I told her. That's when I said it.'

'What did you say?'

'I had to put an end to the racket. It was such an uproar. The guests must have been starting to wonder.'

'But what did you say, Jim?'

'I said now you're going to be quiet, Fru Zacchariassen, I said, and go to your room and calm down, so that the rest of us can get on with our jobs, that's what I said, otherwise we'll go, the lot of us, I said, on the spot, I said. Yes, that's what I said.'

'I don't think that was so clever.'

'No, I'm sure it wasn't, but we were facing total breakdown. "Just go!" The woman yelled. "Just go!" And I said that Zacchariassen can sort this out when he gets home, because I'm not listening to any more of this, and we have a hotel to run. So I ordered everyone back to their posts, and we went. Yes, we just went. So she could stand there shrieking as much as she wanted.'

'Grandfather has taken sick leave,' I told Jim. 'He's gone to bed with flu. Grandmother's moving to Vienna.'

'Right,' said Jim. 'Everything's back to normal, then. Are you going to help me with the spuds?'

'Yes, I will,' I said, 'but I think I'd better have a word with Grandmother first.'

'OK. Good luck.'

He turned his back on me and began searching for something in a drawer. His broad white back swayed from side to side, irritated.

'I'll come back soon,' I said to the back.

'Do that,' he grunted. 'Do that.'

I turned to go. When I had got as far as the door, he said:

'By the way, you can tell her I'm sorry for what I said.'

'I'll do that, Jim.'

'Good,' he grunted. 'But not too sorry, Sedd, just so you know. Got it?'

'Yes,' I said, relieved. 'Message understood.'

In reception there was a red-eyed Synnøve, fiddling with the brooch on her national costume.

'Hi,' I said. 'How are you?'

'Don't talk to me right now, please, Sedd.'

I felt that actually I didn't have any choice, so I ignored her:

'Have you seen Grandmother?' I said it in as forceful and grown-up a way as I could. It worked. She answered automatically:

'Not for a while, fortunately.'

'When did you see her last?'

'Last? She was on her way to fetch a suitcase.'

'Many thanks,' I said in as mature a way as possible. Then I added: 'This will all blow over, Synnøve, you'll see.'

She fixed her blue gaze directly on me.

'I know,' she said, 'I know. But I'll tell you something, Sedd, if it wasn't for Zacchariassen and for you, I wouldn't stay here a day longer. That's the truth. And for Jim, of course.'

I didn't know what to say to this, so I assumed a smile which I hoped appeared mature, grateful and understanding all at the same time, and departed to look for Grandmother.

Presumably, I thought, she had gone up to the attic in the private apartments to fetch her suitcase, the elegant little blue case with the Pan Am label on it, which was up there. But when I got there I found neither Grandmother nor the case. I unlocked the door to the old staircase in order to walk down to reception again that way, but before I got there I met Grandmother on the stairs. She was on her way down from the attic floor in the old wing, and was clearly a little startled to see me. She was carrying the blue suitcase with the Pan Am label, the one she always carried when she was making it clear that she intended to leave for Vienna, and which Grandfather called her representative case, because it was mostly used to represent journeys which never happened. Besides, what would she do in Vienna?

'Hi, Grandmother,' I said. 'Are you going to Vienna?'

'Yes! And no-one's going to stop me!'

She assumed a deeply insulted expression and made as if to march straight past me, holding her suitcase tightly to her with both hands, but I simply said: 'Have a good trip then, Grandmother.'

She stopped, taken aback. Then she pulled herself together and tossed her head, ready to continue her representative march towards Vienna.

'What are you going to do in Vienna?' I asked.

She stopped with her back to me. I continued:

'I mean, you hardly know anyone in Vienna any longer? That's what you always say.'

'They're dead,' she said, still with her back to me. Her shoulders seemed to sink a little.

'Not all of them, Grandmother.'

'No, not all.'

'Oh well,' I said. 'I'm sure we'll manage while you're away. We've got a wedding here tomorrow, haven't we?'

'Yes,' she said. She was still standing a couple of steps below me on the stairs with her back to me. I looked down at the back of her head, and saw the grey patches at the roots of her otherwise chestnut brown, immaculately coiffured hair.

'Oh, Sedd,' she sighed. '*Das ist nicht so einfach. Das ist alles gar nicht so einfach.*'

'I know, Grandmother.' She turned on her heels and walked up to the attic again. I heard her open a door up there. She put the suitcase down. Then the door was closed and her footsteps came clicking in my direction again. At the top of the stairs she said:

'How were things in Oslo? Did you have a good trip?'

'Yes, Grandmother, very good.'

'Did you expand your horizons?'

'Yes, Grandmother. We were at the Kon-Tiki Museum. It was super-interesting.'

Together we walked downstairs again, with her in front.

'That's good,' she said.

'And then we got kitted out at Ferner Jacobsen's.'

'That's good.'

'We bought you a present. But I think that's a secret.'

'You weren't down at the railway station, I hope? To see the place where the bomb exploded?'

'No, Grandmother,' I lied. She turned round, and I could see that she had been crying.

'Because you did promise me!'

'I wasn't there,' I said. 'You can relax.'

She carried on walking.

'Do you know,' she said, 'I think I'm a bit tired. I'll have to have a little nap.'

For a moment I felt like saying in that case perhaps you'll go to Vienna tomorrow then, Grandmother, but I didn't. Instead I just said sleep well.

She disappeared into the private apartments and I could hear her going into her own room and closing the door after her so that the lock clicked.

I went down again to Jim in the kitchen.

'Where are those spuds?' I said.

He nodded sideways at the crate, busy tying up a roast. I started on the potatoes.

'Well,' he said, 'has it quietened down?'

'Yes. They're both asleep.'

'Great. Then we can work in peace.'

Jim started to whistle, and that was a good sign. Especially when he whistled the song from the skiing World Championships in Oslo in 1966, the one Wenche Myhre sang.

Then we got through the work like child's play, almost like skiing on crisp new snow. I stood there peeling, and after a while I joined in the whistling. But then, as we were whistling it for the third time, and had got to the place where Wenche Myhre sings 'He knows not that for a thousand years our land has been crossed by the tracks of skis', Jim suddenly broke off and asked:

'Did you say I was sorry?'

'No. It wasn't necessary.'

Jim grunted appreciatively. Then we began whistling again.

Winter and snow. Even if it was the middle of summer.

19

If, like me, you have decided to write your Memoirs, it is important that you have something to remember. Many people who write their Memoirs have not understood this. When you write your Memoirs you have to think of the reader. The reader, after all, doesn't know what is important and what is unimportant, which are the vital things and which are simply supplementary information. The small things which occurred, and which occurred unnoticed in a sea of everyday events, may have been just as important as the large and visible events. The small things may not even have made ripples on the surface of this sea. Nevertheless they might have been of central importance, but it is difficult to unpack them if you are a reader, and all too easy to pack them away if you are the one writing the Memoirs.

It has been said that writing resembles large-game hunting. It was Hemingway who discovered that, and it is mentioned in the school anthology of British and American Literature. It's in a small box at the top of a page, page 77 to be precise, which is where Hemingway begins. There's a picture of Hemingway in a safari outfit, and quite a bit of information about him, like when he was born, which wars he fought in and when he committed suicide, in addition to the fact that he discovered that writing was like large-game hunting.

I have never been large-game hunting. But I have been small-game hunting, and the writing process, at least when it's a matter of Memoirs, is very similar to grouse-hunting. You walk and walk, or you sit and sit, and the dogs don't understand anything or just want to play, and they can't find anything, and time crawls past and the mountain plateaus are unending; you're wet inside your boots and down the back of your neck, the anorak drawstring has lost its toggle and disappeared up into the hole for good so that you can't close the hood, the gun is rubbing and the thermos is empty. Nothing happens. Until suddenly everything happens at once: the flapping sound of wings taking flight, a grey shadow through the air, scurrying like a marten with wings, two or three explosions of shot, and that's that. Often followed by the sound of someone cursing, because the quarry was too quick. Grouse-hunting is an unequal sport. It's the grouse which has the upper hand. But now and then it comes good, and you can return home with aching legs and your quarry dangling from a string, with happy dogs and the satisfaction of having increased the meat supply for the winter by perhaps half a kilo. People in the Stone Age survived on small game. That's why they were so small in those days. Hemingway would never have survived in the Stone Age. Perhaps in the early Iron Age and after, but not in the Stone Age.

It's the same way with Memoirs. Suddenly something flies up right in front of your feet, and even though you have been prepared for this moment for several days, you are not quick enough, not fast enough with arms and hands to take aim at the formless, flapping, brown shadow in the air, so that you can carry it home in triumph for a grouse dinner and Grandfather can stuff the carcass in time-honoured fashion and place it in his collection. And even if you do manage to hit it, you are often unlucky because the bird has been ruined by the shower of shot, its beak is crushed, the head is spoilt or the plumage so damaged that it would only bring shame to the collection. Because it no longer resembles a bird.

The thing is to be ready. The memory of the one vital thing suddenly flies past you, full of life, and you want to catch it. So that you won't have to keep on walking with wet feet. In the endless silence. There are no gnus or zebras on these plateaus; the streams have no water buffalo and there are no lions lying behind the heaps of stones. Just now and then this flickering through the air.

And that's how I saw them for the first time, like a movement in the air, a hint of colour which quickly passed. I can't even remember any faces, just that someone passed by me in reception on their way in, mother and father and child, three guests.

I was busy, or I was lost in thought, I'm not sure. But I know that it was fine weather that day, like it was the whole of that summer. Grandmother had not left for Vienna. Grandfather had recovered, and had given her the brooch from David-Andersen:

(Grandmother: *Aber Schatzerl*! How lovely!

Grandfather: The pleasure is mine. Glad you like it.

Grandmother: Exactly the one I wanted! To think … etc.)

It was Saturday, the time was perhaps just after one o'clock. If I assumed anything about the three guests who had just arrived, it was probably that they belonged to the wedding party. The large daughter of Herr Sørensen the paint-store manager was to be united with the small son of Herr Hjort the butcher. They had ordered the Extra Large Wedding Package, and the hotel was almost full, so there was plenty to do.

I carried their cases up. I remember that well. But it was only the older couple, the parents, who came up to the rooms with me. They were a stylish, friendly couple in their forties. She was small and pleasant, with a silk shawl and shoulder-length hair, discreetly made up, whilst he was tall and blond. Jeans and a poplin coat, blue eyes, calm voice. They chatted behind me as I walked along with the cases; I didn't listen. When we got there I entered the room quickly ahead of them, drew back a curtain which the maid had forgotten to draw, and explained the usual things in quick succession, the bath, the shower, minibar here, corkscrew there, telephone like this, outside line like that, reception zero, kitchen eight, light switch in one end and thermostat out the other, and the cases, should I put –

'You can put the cases there, but not the red one, that belongs to our daughter and she has the room next door; she didn't come up with us, no, she wanted to go for a walk, a walk around the car park, right, ha ha.'

'Right, ha ha,' I echoed. 'Was there anything else?'

'Yes,' he said, 'we wondered whether – oh, what a great view!'

She: 'It'll be good to be here, Christian.'

Me: 'That's Fåvne Peak you can see there.'

'Fåvne Peak, I see. I see. Is it far up there?'

'Well, it's further than it looks. It's almost 1200 metres above sea level, and here we're at 700. You have to walk for five and a half kilometres before you begin the ascent.'

'Right.'

'Coffee, Christian,' she prompted gently.

'Yes, that's right. We wondered if we could have a pot of coffee in our room?'

'Of course,' I said. 'We also started serving lunch a few minutes ago.'

'Thank you, but we'd like coffee first, if that's OK?'

'Naturally,' I said, discreetly accepting the tip. 'I'll put the red suitcase in number 314, then. Should I leave the key in the door?'

'No,' she said, smiling. 'Let me have it. Then she'll have to get in touch with us when she finally comes up from the car park.'

I bowed, thanked them and left. Down on the ground floor I ordered coffee for them. Then I got busy helping Jim and the others.

Later that day I was busy with my own things; I was reading my photography book and experimenting with the camera. I had plans to make myself a darkroom, since the book recommended it. The discerning photographer can control the process much better when he has his own darkroom. The results you get with prints from a shop are practically speaking always inferior, unless you are fortunate enough to find a dedicated, interested and enthusiastic developer. No doubt there are many positive things to be said about Otto Titlestad, the owner of the photo shop down in the village, but specially dedicated he was not. When I went in there before my trip to Oslo in order to drop off a couple of films to be developed and printed, I asked him for example whether he might expose the negatives for a few extra seconds. But all he said was:

'I don't do that.'

'I see,' I said.

'I always do what it says in the book of instructions.'

'Yes, but if you just …'

'Was there anything else,' asked Titlestad, unmoved.

'Two Kodacolour films with 24 exposures, 100 ASA,' I said quickly in order to show which of us was the dedicated and discerning one. 'You can put them on Grandfather's account,' I said. 'He says it's OK.'

'Does he now,' grunted Titlestad, but without showing any signs of looking for the items.

'Herr Zacchariassen, the hotel manager,' I emphasised. 'He has an account here.'

'Yes,' said Otto Titlestad slowly. 'So he does. Not many people have that.'

'No,' I said. 'But he does.'

He got out the films. Put them in a carrier bag.

'Here,' he said, 'you'd better take a packet of lens paper too. It's important to use it often, so that you take good care of the lenses.'

'Thank you,' I said, and realised that he understood that I was a discerning and ambitious photographer who took things seriously, and had good lenses.

'Thank *you*,' said Titlestad, 'and remember me to your grandfather.'

'I will,' I said.

'It's a long time since I've seen him,' said Titlestad.

No, in the long run the best and simplest thing would be to have a darkroom. We weren't short of unused rooms. That wasn't the problem. But the developing equipment cost money, the trays cost money, the tweezers, clips, red light bulbs and chemicals cost money. And not least, the paper for printing photos cost money. However, there is a good deal of money to be saved by the ambitious photographer who develops his own pictures. The kroner you invest in developing equipment can soon be earned back by anyone who takes lots of photos, it said in the book. I was already taking lots of photos and had thought of taking even more. If I contributed most of the money I got as tips, I felt sure that Grandfather would contribute the rest, even if it would still be very expensive. I was reasonably certain that both Grandmother and Grandfather would see the economic arguments in favour. Especially if I became so proficient that my photographic services could be included as part of the Wedding Package. And there was more to it than that: a new idea began to take shape at the same time. An idea so simple and brilliant that it startled me, it was so good. Why should I not simply ask Grandfather, or Grandmother, or both, if I could use that locked room in the attic, Olympus, which clearly was not being used for anything, as a darkroom? Well, why not? Perhaps it would turn out to be as easy as that?

I was so pleased with these thoughts that it was quite a while before I discovered that I had read several paragraphs of the book on photography without taking in anything at all. I sighed, returned to the top of the left-hand page and was about to make a fresh start, clear and focused, when there was a knock on the door.

It was Grandmother. Just as flustered and irritated as she was at every wedding. Sometimes, Jim would say, you would think that she was the one getting married. It's strange really. That she should get so worked up each time.

Grandmother in the doorway was a picture of perfect misery. With a grim expression and eyes like pinpricks she announced that it was twenty to four, and that I should have been down in the kitchen helping long ago. Did I perhaps believe that she and Jim could manage everything on their own? *Was*? Did I perhaps believe that this hotel ran itself? *Wie*?

'Yes, Grandmother, no, Grandmother. I just forgot the time.'

'*Quatsch*,' said Grandmother, 'it's not possible to forget the time if you keep an eye on it all the time.'

'No, Grandmother,' I said. I refrained from mentioning that she had given Jim the sack just the day before.

'Why do you think we have clocks in all the rooms otherwise?'

'I know,' I said.

'*Immer aufmerksam sein!*'

'Yes, Grandmother,' I said, and realised that it had occurred to me for the first time to wonder whether my mother, back then, had not been taken by Time, but had run away from it.

'Come on then, don't hang about here. Jim is waiting in the kitchen. But dinner at eight, and all the guests, the bride and groom, the witnesses, the parents, the brothers, sisters, cousins, grandparents, friends and enemies – they will *not* wait!'

'No, I'll get a move on.'

She turned on her heel and marched off; then, without turning round: 'Eight o'clock precisely!'

I struggled into my white jacket and hurried off. I ran across the yard behind the house, between the private apartments and the kitchen, all the while fumbling with the buttons on my jacket. That's why I didn't see her until I literally ran into her.

'Sorry,' I exclaimed in alarm. But she laughed.

'Is there a fire?'

'A fire?' I said, even though you should never answer a question with another question, not unless you're a criminal investigator like Derrick. He can do it the whole time. But not the rest of us, it gives a bad impression.

'Since you're in such a rush, I mean,' she said.

'A rush?' I said, confirming the bad impression. I looked her up and down. Estimated that she was around ten or eleven. Dark blond straight hair, grey-blue eyes. Pink corduroy trousers and a green T-shirt with Garfield. She looked at me teasingly:

'Yes, perhaps you're going to save the hotel?'

'Yes,' I said, 'I mean no, of course not, I'm just running late.'

'OK.'

I hastened onwards. Her voice reached me:

'Excuse me, I just wanted to ask …'

I stopped and half turned:

'Yes?'

'Is the minigolf open?'

'Minigolf – ?' I asked, and realised that I was being Derrick again.

'Yes, is it open?'

'Yes, it's open. Do you want to play?'

'Yes,' she said, 'I'd love to!'

'You'll have to get your mother or father to ask in reception,' I said; 'you have to pay for it.'

'Fine. Do you want to play with me?'

'I'm not allowed to play with the guests,' I said. She pulled a long face.

'That's stupid.'

'Besides, I don't have time,' I said. 'They're waiting for me in the kitchen.' As I was about to turn away again, she called out:

'I'm Karoline. What's your name?'

'Sedgewick,' I said.

'That's a funny name,' she said.

'I know,' I said. 'They just call me Sedd.'

'Sedd is funny as well,' she said, and giggled. 'Really odd.'

'Perhaps it is,' I admitted.

'Perhaps you're foreign? In my class in town we've got a boy who's foreign. He's called Arkhilokhos. He's pretty stupid. But then he's Greek.' She giggled again.

'No,' I said; 'actually I'm called after a witch.'

It just popped out. This is something I don't normally explain, not to anyone, because it's a bit embarrassing. She giggled even more. Now it was her turn to be Derrick.

'A witch?' she asked, with an expression as if this was the funniest thing anyone had ever said.

'Yes,' I said, because if I had said A, I had to say B: 'My mother was very interested in witches. If I'd been a girl I would have been called Mary. After Mary Sedgewick, who was burnt in 1672 in Scotland. But I couldn't be called Mary since I was a boy.'

'In Finland boys can be called Kari,' she informed me.

A little irritated, I said: 'Hundreds of thousands of innocent women were condemned and burnt as witches. It's a tragic historical fact. It's not so very amusing, actually.'

'OK,' she said. 'OK. I'm called after my grandmother. Who wasn't a witch.' She made an effort not to giggle again.

'Sorry,' I said. 'I have to dash.'

She didn't answer. I tramped across the flagstones and over to the kitchen door. Jim was standing in the doorway, waiting. When I turned round on the steps, the irritating girl had gone.

'Well?' said Jim. 'The grouse season starting early this year?'

'Shut up, Jim. She's just a snotty little kid.'

Jim laughed. Then he said:

'You need to peel and chop a quarter of a ton of potatoes, Sedd.'

'OK,' I said.

As I said. One of the problems with writing your Memoirs is that things don't always happen in the order they should. When you read the Memoirs of famous people you get the impression that all the dramatic and significant things happened simultaneously. As if their lives, and along with that the account of them, were thought out in a definite and exciting way beforehand, with appropriate timing. Many people no doubt believe that authors of exciting stories just sit down and write any old exciting story which occurs to them. But it's not as simple as that. Anyone who has the slightest experience of Norwegian classes at school knows that. All authors start off with:

1) A definite theme for the story they're going to tell.

2) They have decided what the theme is before they start.

3) After that they have decided what is going to happen in the story, carefully constructing the plot so that things happen in the right order and with a calculated increase in tension, so that everything significant happens when it ought to.

4) And finally, they have written out the story exactly as they had planned it, whilst abiding by the normal rules of spelling, grammar and syntax.

That's what it's like being an author. Life, on the other hand, can often behave in a way which is much more random, aimless and quite simply somewhat muddled. Life is like porridge. And anyone who wants to give it a stir in order to try and extract a kind of meaning from it, and then to write it down, must either cheat massively regarding the order of events or accept that he's never going to become famous.

In all stories, including memoirs, timing is all. And by that I don't mean the kind of timing and continuity we professionals in the hospitality business have to observe so closely. That order of events is determined by how the evening unfolds. Each course of food has to be ready at the right moment, everything has to be hot, and each serving has to follow the rhythm of the wedding dinner, so that there is room for speeches and songs. Those of us with some experience of the Wedding Package have evolved a certain routine in this area. A prawn cocktail can be prepared and kept in the fridge a relatively long time in advance. An asparagus soup has the advantage that it can stand in its pan and just get better and better whilst it waits for the bride's father to finish saying nice things to his daughter, and even possibly the first song on the songsheet; it is usual to start with the pink one, which the bride's mother pretends she has written herself, although they are exactly the same each time. After that roast beef with mushrooms, green peas, hasselback potatoes and a glossy dark brown sauce stirred into the meat juices. Finally a refreshing lemon mousse with raspberry coulis, candied citrus fruits and vanilla cream. Apart from the item roast beef, all the timings in this sequence are completely flexible. You can delay the roast as well, either by turning down the oven or simply by letting it rest, and letting the hot sauce and the burning hot plates do the job of warming it up when you serve it. These are the kind of trade secrets which normal people have no idea of and never think about.

You never know quite how a wedding party like this is going to behave once it has sat down to dinner, that's part of the game. It might for example happen, as it did this evening, that there is an uncle who takes the floor. Although *takes* is not the right expression. In cases like this it would be more correct to say that he *seizes* the floor, and has no intention of letting go. This uncle is not on the list of speakers, and has not alerted the toastmaster in advance, so that the toastmaster has not been able to warn the kitchen in his turn, but Uncle feels overcome by an urgent desire to say something to his niece, and invokes all their common ancestors from the preceding four generations, of whom he is personally acquainted with at least three.

This evening's uncle was a proper old and slow one, white-haired and dignified and full to bursting with roots and historical information.

So whilst everything in the kitchen was marking time, whilst the sauce was separating and the mangetout slowly turning yellow and sulphurous, whilst the parsley began to wilt onto the potatoes and the roast turned grey, awaiting the moment when Snorri Sturlason should begin to approach the present day, Jim tapped me on the shoulder as I stood there in the hatchway and whispered so as not to disturb the monotonous droning of historical roots:

'You'd better take the roast in to the others.'

'The others?' I asked.

'Yes,' said Jim. 'We've got other guests. They're sitting waiting in the annexe. Do you think you could sneak past with a dish for them? Then *they* at least will get a reasonably juicy roast this evening. Anita will follow with the potatoes.'

I stole past along the wall of the dining room with the dish, whilst Uncle was declaiming a lengthy poem and his family and friends were staring into the Dark Ages. I shoved open the door to the annexe with my shoulder and manoeuvred the dish inside. That Karoline and her parents were sitting there. Her parents smiled at me. As if I was welcome. Welcome in a special way. Although perhaps they were just hungry, because her father said:

'Ah, food.'

And her mother looked at me with a friendly smile, and said:

'Hello again.'

But Karoline said nothing. Not nice to see you or anything. She just looked sulky.

'Good evening,' I said politely. 'The cook sends his best wishes and apologises that it has taken some time.'

'Oh, that doesn't matter.'

'Really, it doesn't matter.'

They said these two things simultaneously, and I don't know which of them said what, but when you write it down you have to write them one after the other. That is a weakness with a written presentation; when things happen at the same time they have to be recorded one after the other. Not that it is a major weakness, but nevertheless. It is clearly a weakness.

'We're sitting here admiring the hunting trophies,' said the man.

'Yes,' said his wife, 'they really are impressive. Both the big ones and the little ones.'

I began serving.

'That large stag there,' I said, 'that was one my great-grandfather shot. Together with an English lord. Would you care for some carrots? Unfortunately it's a little moth-eaten. But you can't see that at a distance.'

'No, you can't see that. Yes, please.'

'Mangetout? The smaller stag is one my grandfather shot. That's in much better condition.'

'Yes, it looks really good. Almost as if it's alive.'

'It's the eyes that do that,' I explained. 'If you don't get the eyes right, the result isn't very convincing. How many slices of beef?'

'Two,' said the man. 'Yes, its eyes really look natural.'

'I helped to prepare it,' I said. 'Sure you wouldn't like another slice?'

'Oh, why not. Why not.'

'Many taxidermists make the mistake of not ordering glass eyes which are good enough. Mushrooms?'

'Yes, thank you. The smaller animals look good too. Thank you, that's enough.'

'Some roast beef, miss?'

She looked up at me. She had the sulks, just like girls of that age do for a large part of the day.

'One slice, thanks,' she said.

The door opened. 'Here's Anita with the potatoes,' I said. 'Enjoy your meal.'

When the evening was over and I went through reception after hanging my jacket up outside the kitchen, Grandmother was standing behind the counter. She was standing the way she usually did, on one foot, with the other foot raised behind her calf, one hand leaning on the counter and a cigarette in the other. She was reading *Aftenposten*. Sometimes, when I could just see her figure in that position and not her face, she looked young. As if she was ready for action. I went over to her to say goodnight. She looked up and smiled. She looked a little tired, and her face was not so young.

'Na, Buberl,' she said. 'Are you done for the evening?'

'Yes, Grandmother,' I said. 'I just wanted to say goodnight.'

She gave me a hug. The same scent of eau de cologne as always.

The door to the guest lounge opened, and the sound of music got suddenly louder. A confused wedding guest wandered unsteadily into reception.

Grandmother let go of me, and instantaneously became the manageress. The guest said something incomprehensible, and she waited until he had finished, because she already knew what he wanted.

'Back there,' she said. 'Go back, yes. Back where you came from. Then second on the left and down a few steps. That's where it is. Yes, back there. Through the door you came from. That's right. That way.'

She sighed.

'Could you please shut the door after him, dear, so that I don't have to stand here and listen to that dreadful music.'

'Yes, Grandmother,' I said.

I went. Behind me I could hear Grandmother saying what she always said: 'Thank you, Sedd. My feet – '

'Your feet will be the death of you, yes,' I whispered, at the same time as she said it.

'A long day, and extra guests as well,' I said as I went back to reception.

'Yes, a family of three.'

'I saw them,' I said. 'Nice people?'

'Very nice. No trouble with them.'

'I thought they were wedding guests when they arrived,' I said.

'I think they're just having a week's holiday in the mountains.'

She reached for the guestbook and looked them up:

'Let's see ... Christian, Annette and Karoline Ekenes. Oslo 3. Arrived today. No departure date.'

'Right,' I said.

'Perhaps they just love the mountains,' said Grandmother. 'If only there were more like them. Was Jim's lemon mousse a success?'

'A great success,' I said. 'Goodnight then, Grandmother.'

'Goodnight, my dear.' She bent over *Aftenposten* again, and lit a new cigarette. I went through reception and into the private apartments. I was just about to go up the stairs to my room when I saw that the door to the entrance was ajar.

I opened it further and looked out.

Karoline was there. She didn't look as sulky as earlier on.

'Hi,' I said, surprised.

'Hi,' she said. 'Do you have time for minigolf now?'

'Are you mad? It's night-time.'

'It's still light,' she said.

'I'm sure you're supposed to be asleep,' I said. She pulled a face:

'I don't want to,' she said. 'Besides, they won't notice that I've gone out. They've gone to bed.'

'I'm not allowed to play with guests. I've told you that.'

'Oh go on, please? It's so boring here. I've no-one to play with.'

'There were some children in the wedding party. Can't you play with some of them?'

'I'd much rather play with you,' she said, pouting. 'Please, please?'

'I can't do it now anyway,' I said. 'I have to get up early.'

She poked me in the chest with a sharp little fist.

'See you later, alligator.'

'What?'

'You're so slow,' she said.

'Erm – see you!' I replied.

She sighed and gave up.

'I'll teach you it later,' she said.

Then she was gone, just running steps across the gravel. Her voice reached me, disembodied in the twilight:

'See you later, alligator!'

20

I don't know so much about what the morning after, as it is so poetically called, is like for alligators. Perhaps it is a joyful occasion in the rushes on the river bed, with happy cries and broad smiles. Although I doubt it. On the other hand I know a good deal about the morning after with a wedding party which has been celebrating half the night, and which the following morning makes a valiant attempt to appear sober and collected. The moment of departure, with checkout, car driving and bus travel, is approaching at twelve o'clock, and you can see the panic in the faces of those who come down last for breakfast. That's how it was this Sunday morning as well, as the butcher's and the paint-shop manager's families, relations and friends, with faces in varying shades of pale, were gradually reunited in the dining room, which now appeared much less festive than the evening before, without white tablecloths and in the sharp morning light. They greeted each other as brightly as they could, but you could see that not everyone felt too good. We made large amounts of coffee, and kept the scrambled eggs well salted. We had a busy day ahead, many rooms had to be made up. A company of gentlemen from Germany was expected during the afternoon.

Unfortunately the reunion was not entirely complete. An old aunt, the wife of the historically-inclined uncle who had made such a long speech the night before, had lost something. When you are as old as that you can presumably expect nothing other than a fair amount of muddle, where you forget where you have put or what you have done with both this and that. To be honest she did look ancient, and I didn't really think this was anything to write home about, as the saying goes. But as I passed along the tables clearing things away, I gathered that that was precisely what Auntie's younger relations were doing. They were writing home about it: 'Well, I really think you should say something about it, Aunt Gunvor dear, I really think you should.'

Aunt Gunvor: 'Well, yes, perhaps, yes, but I don't want to make a fuss. I hate making a fuss. I might have put it – '

Eager relation: 'But you said you were quite sure where you had it last?'

'Well, yes, perhaps, yes, I did say that. I mean, I am sure. But you know, it does happen that I get things wrong. I've probably just put it somewhere else and made a mistake.'

'But where could that be, Aunt Gunvor?'

'Well, no, I don't know – '

I left the room with a pile of coffee cups. Soon after I could make out through the serving hatch that Aunt Gunvor, accompanied by her historically-inclined husband, who seemed somewhat reluctant, together with two energetic younger female relatives, was proceeding in the direction of reception. I finished what I was doing, and slipped away to see what was going on. In reception I took up my position by the postcard racks and began to sort out the postcards, even though that was not at all necessary, as we had hardly seen a trace of any Americans this summer season. At the reception desk the delegation was already in full swing, and my grandfather was listening understandingly:

'… a diamond pendant, genuine, and an antique as well, a family heirloom, isn't that right, Aunt Gunvor, that it's a family heirloom?'

Aunt Gunvor: 'Well, yes, that's right. A family heirloom.'

Her historically-inclined husband explained further:

'That's right, it is. She inherited it in forty-nine after her great aunt Louise, who had been living in Reval, what we now call Tallinn, and who had received it as a gift on her wedding morning from her Russian husband, who himself – he was born in ninety-four, so long before the revolution – '

'Yes,' said the energetic younger female relatives: 'Before the revolution. So you can understand that it is priceless. Not just valuable, Herr Zacchariassen, but *priceless.*'

'Priceless, yes, I understand,' said Grandfather. 'That is a terrible shame. Terribly upsetting. Are you sure you know where you saw it last? I mean, before we begin a major investigation, we need to make quite sure that the item is actually lost and not – ahem – mislaid?'

Aunt Gunvor: 'Well, yes, perhaps, that's just what …'

Indignant female relatives: 'You're surely not insinuating that Aunt Gunvor is – '

'*Hi.*'

Someone was pulling at my sleeve.

'Hi,' it said again. I half turned. It was that irritating Karoline.

'Have you got time to play minigolf with me now?'

'Erm,' I began.

'You did promise to.'

'Did I? When did I do that?' With half an eye I could see Grandfather behind the counter, spreading his hands out apologetically and nodding seriously and affirmatively.

'You promised last night. You did.'

'I'm a bit busy right now,' I said. The corners of her mouth drooped.

'But you promised. You *promised.*'

That last 'promised' was so loud that I had to take preventative action.

'I can't right now. But perhaps later.' She brightened up.

'When, then?'

'I don't know, later. Aren't you going to have breakfast? Or have you had it already?'

'We're having it *now,*' she smiled.

She ran off, hopping on her left leg, in the direction of the dining room. When I turned towards reception again, the conference about the heirloom was clearly almost over.

Grandfather was spreading out his hands apologetically, and his final reassuring words reached me:

'… and of course we will institute a full investigation. You have my word on that.'

I went out into the yard. Took a few deep breaths. Then I strolled in the direction of the minigolf course. Algae had started growing on the concrete again. The wide channels, like on holes 1, 4 and 6, looked particularly bad. I ought really to go over to the shed and put on some overalls, and get out a bucket and brush and a bottle of Anti-Algon, but I realised that I didn't feel like it. I didn't feel like it in the slightest. After all, when you think about it algae is a perfectly natural thing. It isn't a problem at all if algae grow on things. On the contrary, you can say that algae actually represent Life in its simplest and most basic form. And in any case, it just comes back straight away after you've removed it. Besides, the algae remover eats away the paint on the concrete, so that if you keep on treating it you just make more work in the form of a major paint job. Perhaps, I thought, we could simply paint the whole structure dark green and have done with it, then we wouldn't need to think any more about it. In any case, green is a positive colour, it's the colour of hope, as the saying goes, and what's more: green is the colour of golf, and I'm not talking about minigolf, but real golf, that ancient and noble Scottish game which takes place on endless vistas of green.

Pleased with myself for this idea, I returned to the hotel. It was time to clear away in the dining room, and after that to help with all the baggage as people left. Aunt Gunvor's suitcase would be lighter by a few expensive grams, but after all it was no more than a few grams. It could not be so terribly serious, after all. Not in the grand scheme of things. If it had actually happened at all. Aunt Gunvor was really extremely old, when all's said and done.

In the kitchen Jim and the others had already heard the news.

'Some jewellery has gone missing,' said Jim.

'I know,' I said.

'A pendant this time.'

'I know.'

Jim shook his head gloomily, but said no more. Instead he started to make lunch.

'Only three for lunch,' he informed me. 'That family. The group of Germans isn't arriving until three, and then they want sandwiches for seven.'

'Not much to do, then,' I said.

'Not much, no. So you can have some time off when the wedding party has left.'

The last guests departed at half-past twelve, naturally not before Grandfather had assured them yet again that a full criminal investigation would be undertaken, that the hotel would like to offer its sincerest apologies and would of course pay compensation, and so on.

He looked worried.

I caught sight of that pushy Karoline in reception; it looked as if she was watching out for someone, no doubt with plans for a round of minigolf, and I disappeared hurriedly into the private apartments before she noticed me.

The gentlemen from Germany arrived as announced at three o'clock. Precisely on the stroke of three. They came in a hired minibus all the way from Oslo, and had an appreciable amount of luggage. There were fishing rods, fishing bags, landing nets, waders, gaff hooks, cooler bags, spools of extra fishing line, bags of spinners and even a fishing net. In addition, of course, suitcases with normal luggage. The gentlemen themselves were already clad in sporting gear, with fishing equipment and fishing knives hanging from every available loop on their garments, and with soft-crowned hats from which hung even more spinners and hooks. They had practical rucksacks on their backs and all had a fish-shaped white badge emblazoned on their jackets. *Dortmund Sportanglerverein e.V.* it said.

I transported all their worldly goods on the brass trolley into reception, and they processed after me, already in high holiday spirits, and made a beeline for Grandmother and

Grandfather, who had assumed their normal stations and attitudes in order to wish them welcome.

They addressed themselves first to Grandfather.

'Hello,' began the one who looked like the leader; a cheerful, elderly man with a moon-shaped face and round steel glasses and sparse hair under his soft hat.

'*Herzlich willkommen,*' said Grandfather.

The leader held up a warning hand and stopped him. An expectant hush fell over the others in the group. It was clear that the leader had prepared something to say.

'Good avdernoon,' he said solemnly in Norwegian.

'Good avdernoon,' replied Grandfather.

'We are wery glad to be in Norvay …'

Murmured applause from the rest of the group when it looked as if Grandfather understood their leader.

'I'm pleased to hear it,' said Grandfather. '*Freut mich sehr,*' he said in the direction of the others.

Renewed murmured applause.

'We – ah – wery plised too,' the leader continued. 'Wery plised. We are – eh – we are schportsfischers,' he explained, indicating the emblem from *Dortmund Sportanglerverein e.V.*, in case there should be any doubt.

Grandfather nodded politely.

'*Herzlich willkommen,*' he repeated. 'You're very welcome.'

'We wery plised to be in beautiful Norvay,' said the man in glasses. He half turned towards his travelling companions: '… *dass wir wieder im schönen Norwegen sind, freut uns sehr.*'

'*Ja, ja,*' the others joined in, '*sehr, sehr.*'

Grandfather smiled warmly. 'You are Herr Brehm, I assume?'

'*Doch, doch,*' said Herr Brehm. 'I am it.'

Now Grandmother sprang into action. She sailed into the group wearing her most dazzling hostess smile:

'*Aber die Herren sind doch alle sicherlich von der langen Reise ganz müde und hungrig. Mein Name ist Frau Zacchariassen. In wenigen Minuten werden norwegische Smörrebröd für Sie im Speisesaal serviert.*'

To general exclamations of *wie schön, gnädige Frau* and *wie nett*, I began to carry the gentlemen's extensive luggage up to their rooms.

'Can one in the hotel purchase fisching licence,' I heard Herr Brehm asking Grandfather as the staircase door closed behind me.

They were a pleasant and in all ways very jolly group, but were not very forthcoming with their tips. They had not got round to breaking into their newly-acquired Norwegian banknotes yet. But they were extremely polite. I knew that it would be my job to guide them across to the fishing lakes, so I was as obliging as I knew how. There might well be rich pickings later. When an ambitious amateur photographer is planning to invest in setting up a darkroom, all contributions are welcome. Nowhere near all the rooms were booked for the rest of the summer, so here it was a matter of making the most of every opportunity. After what had happened with Aunt Gunvor's historical pendant, a story which had unfortunately spread around the wedding party all too quickly, there had hardly been any tips at all as they departed.

After depositing the little I had got, I took off my uniform and hung it up in the private apartments and was free. There wouldn't be much to do for dinner either with so few guests.

From the kitchen window I could see Karoline and her parents, now in walking gear, setting off into the countryside in the fine weather. So no minigolf either, thank goodness.

For a few hours I sat absorbed in the book on photography, disturbed by no-one. I had discovered that it was a very good camera, the one I had inherited. Good, but demanding. The thing that was difficult to master was the relationship between exposure time and shutter opening. Besides that, I still didn't completely understand the workings of the light metre I had inherited from Bjørn Berge. Until now I hadn't used it very much, but I could see that I would have to learn to do so. So I attempted to understand and memorise the tables in the book.

At around five o'clock I went out to stretch my legs a bit. I shouldn't have done that. Just outside the door to the private apartments stood Karoline. Brimming with anticipation. I got the impression that she had been standing there for a while.

'Hi,' she said. 'Minigolf?'

'Well,' I began, 'I'm just in the middle of doing something.'

'Uuugh. You're always so busy.'

She kicked irritatedly at a little piece of gravel which had strayed onto one of the flagstones. Hard, so that the innocent little stone flew into the air:

'It's so boring here!'

'Can't you play with your parents?' I suggested.

'They're having a rest,' grumbled Karoline.

'What about playing with some of the other guests?'

'The other guests? Are you stupid?'

'No,' I replied.

'You are stupid. I can't play with those horrible old Germans.'

'What about a swim in the pool?' I suggested.

She looked at me as if I had said something quite unbelievably stupid.

'I can't do that. Haven't you read the notice?'

'The notice?'

'Children under 14 are not allowed in the pool un-accompanied.'

'Oh yes. That notice. I know which one you mean,' I said (I had helped to put it up).

'Perhaps you can come swimming with me? It's so *incredibly* boring here!'

I could see that there was no way out:

'OK,' I said. 'We'll have a game of minigolf then.'

'Oh yes!'

'Normally it costs ten kroner for a round,' I said. 'But the hotel doesn't want guests to get bored, so we can let you have a free round.'

'Oh, good! But I do have money. Look!'

From the pocket of her pink corduroy trousers she pulled a heart-shaped girly purse. She opened it triumphantly. It was full of blue notes.

'I got them from Mummy and Daddy to play minigolf with,' said Karoline brightly. 'We know that it costs money to play.'

'Oh yes,' I sighed, 'you've got enough for lots of rounds there.'

'Oh yes! It's important to pay your way, Daddy says. You must always do that. You have to pay what it costs.'

'OK,' I sighed. 'You can have the first round free anyway.'

'Oh yes!'

'Let's go and get the clubs and balls.'

You can't say that she didn't have a positive attitude to the game. Extremely positive. You could even go so far as to say enthusiastic. Each ball which went down the hole occasioned small screams and outbursts of delight, each miss resulted in corresponding cries of distress and irritated groans. I played as passively as possible, and let her win. That summer when the minigolf course had just been installed, Jim and I had played as often as we could, in every spare hour. It had become an obsession. The course had a full 18 holes, and according to the construction firm it was theoretically possible to get a hole in one on each hole, so that you could get round the course in 18 strokes. Theoretically. By the time autumn arrived that year, Jim and I had got down to 22 and 21 strokes respectively. By the time the winter was past and the concrete structure had again become visible after the snow melted, neither Jim nor I felt any compulsion to rekindle our eagerness for the game. We had been, as it were, inoculated. From then on the minigolf course was mostly a matter of maintenance. But on the rare occasions when I played, like now, I could feel that I knew each hole inside out. Every unevenness, every slope, every single trick. So I played passively, apart from hole 17, quite a difficult one, where the ball had to go round a curve and then down a hole which was in the middle of a round sloping surface. There I felt like

223

showing off a bit, despite everything, so I pulled off a hole in one.

'Gosh! How did you do that?'

'Just luck, I suppose,' I answered lightly.

'Gosh!' said Karoline.

She tried to copy my trick, but of course she couldn't. She had to use six or seven strokes, and got very cross each time the ball rolled past the hole and ended up back in the gutter. Soon she was so far behind that I had to play with almost conspicuous clumsiness on hole 18, so that she would be able to win. I hoped she wouldn't notice that it was a pretence, so I uttered annoyed exclamations every time I seemed to mis-hit. So in the end she did win.

'Another round!'

'No, I don't have any more time.'

'Oh yes! Just one more! Please?'

'I've got lots to do.'

'But you want revenge? Just one more game? Look.'

She held out a ten-kroner note. I looked at it. Glanced over towards the hotel. Then I thought about my darkroom. 'OK,' I said. 'Another round. But this time I'm going to beat you.'

'Oh no you won't!'

That time I did beat her, but I made sure that it was not by much. When we added up the points she had really been bitten by the minigolf virus.

'Best of three?' she suggested, holding out another note. It seemed to me that Fridtjof Nansen was looking reproachfully at me with his heavy, serious, humanist's eyes. Then I took the note and stuffed it in my pocket.

'Best of three,' I said.

21

The next day after breakfast I was to blaze the trail. Already the evening before, whilst they were eating dinner, not to mention as the time drew on towards midnight, Herr Brehm and his travelling companions had been raring to go. Best of all they would have liked to set off on the hunt for fishing lakes immediately, and skipped Jim's delicious stew – constructed from the remains of the wedding roast, and presented as *Der traditionelle, lappische Eintopf* – but Grandfather had assured them that it was a long walk, which was true enough, and that the best thing was to have an early night and meet the next day's exertions with well-rested sport-fisher bodies, advice which they did not take. It was really difficult, as they said, now that they were so far north, to register how late it was, without looking at the clock. They carried on carousing until midnight and beyond before they looked at the clock, sharing their joyous expectations of the number of lively, fresh, leaping and absolutely genuine *norwegische Bergforelle* they were going to catch. The fishing licences were acquired, the cool bags were standing ready. Jim had orders to clear space for the catch in the freezer room. They consumed white wine and beer, together with the odd dram; I didn't follow that closely, but I could still hear them as I went upstairs in the private apartments. Karoline and her parents had been sitting in the lounge for a while playing cards, but they clearly found that the yodelling had got a bit much, and went upstairs early.

So now it was time to blaze the trail. Even if Herr Brehm and his *brave Burschen* were not quite on top form, they were undeniably on time, and were all in reception ready for the off on the stroke of nine, wearing their fishing jackets and with assorted equipment dangling from every belt and every loop. They jangled each time they drew breath. I myself was wearing light walking clothes and boots, and carrying a rucksack of provisions. Grandfather called the gentlemen to order, and presented me as his *Enkelsohn, der sich bestens auskennt*. Which was true enough. If you've grown up in a mountain hotel, there isn't a puddle in the area that you haven't cast a line into at one time or another.

'Even though he may still be young in years,' continued Grandfather lyrically, 'Sedd is someone who knows the secrets of the mysterious waters. He knows where the genuine, pink, leaping Norwegian mountain trout is to be found.'

The gentlemen stared at me sceptically, whilst I made every effort to look as Norwegian as possible, without apparently convincing them. But they trotted along behind me, and Herr Brehm said politely in Norwegian:

'You go first and show us the vay.'

I had done all this before, and had a plan of action. So after we had been walking for an hour, and the company needed a little rest and an energy supplement for the gentlemen in the form of a thimbleful of schnapps from the Flachmann in Herr Brehm's anorak pocket, it was time to create a bit of Norwegian atmosphere.

I asked the gentlemen whether they would perhaps be interested in hearing a genuine Norwegian folk song? They would definitely be interested. So I launched into 'Mannen og kråka', which they thought was just fascinating. Especially since I could explain in my excellent German exactly what each verse was about. 'Mannen og kråka' is, when all's said and done, an extremely moral composition, and that did not escape the company. They particularly liked the verse which describes how the man makes twelve sets of rope out of the crow's guts.

Herr Brehm's happy company of fishermen wanted to hear it again at once. I knew that they would begin to join in the chorus now, so I suggested that I should sing it as we walked, since this was a traditional song composed to be sung as you walked through barren mountains and forests. It's possible that I was stretching the idea of tradition a bit when I said that, but they weren't to know that. Besides, it's true that it's a good song to walk to. So I launched into song, and with regular manly outbursts of 'hei-fara!' and 'falturilturaltura!' we made good progress before it was time for new energy-giving drops from Herr Brehm's Flachmann.

The sun had begun to warm up, and I had tied my jacket around my waist, but an angler's lot is not a happy one, as the poet says: the Germans, poor things, could not remove very many clothes without at the same time removing the sum total of their equipment. But they held out bravely. During this pause I performed for them another traditional Norwegian folk song, and they listened entranced to the fishing song 'Byssan lull'. In a devout and emotional mood, my melancholy rendering of all six verses carried us as far as the first lake, Blåvann.

The impressive thing about Blåvann is that you first have to climb over a small ridge, before you catch sight of it. But when you've done that it appears right in front of you, blue as ever, and if you are for example a German, or for that matter a British, Dutch, Danish or French sport-fisher tourist, you exclaim in wonder. Blåvann is always the same; nothing special about it, about one and a half kilometres long and perhaps six hundred metres across at the widest point, with a fairly sheer mountainside along half of one long side, and otherwise a fairly typical lake. But the Germans, who thanks to my valiant efforts in the field of folk music had accepted me as an Ur-Norwegian, a child of nature and son of the mountains, provided the requisite exclamations of wonder. They called on *mein Gott, meine Güte, Donnerwetter* and other Teutonic gods as witnesses to *wie wunderbar schön* the whole thing was.

And it is true that when you saw Blåvann like that, mysterious and dark and at the same time glistening slightly in the morning sun, it is understandable that it made an impression.

Even greater enthusiasm when I could show them the rowing boat, 'Fåvne II', which belonged to the hotel and was moored at one end of the lake.

It is a well-known fact that there is nothing German sports fishers love more than risking their lives by standing up in a small rowing boat without a life jacket, casting a line. That's why, as Grandfather had many times sternly instructed me to do, I made a short warning speech to them about the dangers of a sailor's life, invoking real and invented regulations issued by the authorities and by the hotel, and showed them where the life jackets lay under the thwarts. Then I pointed out some of the best fishing places on shore, not without a certain air of secrecy, and explained mystically that it would pay to cast towards that headland or that rock, although in reality the fish tended to bite more or less the same anywhere in the lake. But a fishing trip can't be successful without a certain element of magic.

Four of them wanted to fish from land, three wanted to go out in the boat. I put on a life jacket in order to lead by example, but the anglers showed no sign of wanting to put theirs on. It was their own responsibility, and I didn't want to ruin the mood, so I made do with a meaningful glance at the life jackets in the bottom of the boat. I took the oars and we rowed off. Once again I explained to them with many secretive glances where it would pay to cast. They listened to me as intently as if I were telling them where to find the sunken Atlantis.

And then the usual nightmare began. Herr Brehm was the first one who wanted to stand up. I tried to explain, in as calm and friendly a way as possible, that it is not such a good idea to stand up in a low rowing boat which has its centre of gravity about a metre and a half above the gunwale, especially if you are going to make violent throwing movements with your arms at the same time. I explained, as reasonably and Ur-Norwegianly as I could, that you can cast just as well if you remain seated in the boat.

'*Aber*,' Herr Brehm objected, 'you can't cast as far when you're sitting down.'

I had been here before, and I knew that it was impossible to get him to understand that the length of the cast was completely irrelevant when you were already in the middle of the lake; out there it made no difference whether you were casting fifteen metres or two. So I left them to their fate, as they one after the other stood up from their seats and cast their lines in different directions, and the boat rocked alarmingly. I was wearing a life jacket myself, but as always I experienced a slight internal shudder at the thought of what would happen on the day when I suddenly found myself in the middle of an ice-cold mountain lake, surrounded by slightly inebriated continental tourists who were not wearing life jackets, but who were on the other hand hung about with a number of heavy objects which would quickly drag them to the bottom.

'It's extremely deep here,' I ventured, but *Dortmund Sportanglerverein e.V.* just went on casting. 'Legend has it,' I ventured, 'that Blåvann is bottomless,' but the anglers had now become one with nature and had all their senses tied up in their fishing lines which whirred out of the spools time after time, into the far distance over the ripples on the lake. Soon a shout from the shore announced that the first angler had caught a fish, and straight after that one of the men in the boat also made his first catch, an event which almost capsized the whole vessel; but as they were all standing, like a group of passengers on a bus, they fortunately balanced one another out with their movements and their casts.

So the morning passed without any accidents, and everyone caught fish, both from land and from 'Fåvne II'.

It was time to have lunch and swap positions, and we made a small fire. In my rucksack I had sour cream, salt and pepper, as well as Jim's cucumber salad in a large plastic box. We roasted some of the finest trout on twigs over the fire, and the call of the wild became so intense that they asked me to give them a new song. Well, if truth be told I don't know all that many folk songs, but 'En ekte lofottorsk jeg er' is always a winner on such occasions, particularly because it also has a catchy chorus. The seven agreeable Germans caught on at once, and we had a good time sitting round the fire. Especially as it transpired that a couple of them had a bottle of Riesling with them, which they now consumed with even more *fadderullandei*. Herr Brehm's Flachmann did the rounds again as well. They asked me if I would like some, both of this and of that, but I just shook my head gently in child-of-nature fashion, like the son of the mountains I was, and they respected that.

The next group in the boat was clearly more unstable than the first, and just as life-jacketless, but they did catch fish. And without any accidents. Nevertheless, I was very pleased when they started to look at their watches and it was time to suggest that we should set off on the walk home.

No-one made any objections.

Worn out by mountain sun and mountain air, full of lively, fresh Norwegian mountain trout and Riesling plus extras, and very satisfied with the day's catch, the stout-hearted anglers trotted in front of me in a happy group all the way back to the hotel. It had been a successful day in all ways, and Grandfather would be pleased.

In the yard Karoline was standing waiting, already supplied with golf clubs. I saw her from a long way away. She began to fuss even before I had got my rucksack off. Was I ready for the day's tournament?

'Not now,' I said.

'Why not?' Her eyes were shining with desire for a game.

'Because I've been on a long fishing trip with our guests,' I said, peeling off my rucksack. We had arrived in reception, and the Germans were uttering long fanfares of praise about the glorious, wild Norwegian mountains and the fantastic trout, about their fishing successes, about the sun, about me and even about the boat. Grandmother, who was there to receive them, shone like a sun as well and expressed polite enthusiasm that everything had gone so well.

'Just one round, please?' she begged.

Fortunately her father came along to rescue me.

'I think that Sedd – it is Sedd, isn't it? – is a bit too tired right now, Karoline,' he said admonishingly.

She pulled a long face, no doubt partly because he was talking to her like a child.

'Perhaps I'll be able to play in a couple of hours,' I said to cheer her up, at the same time as I wondered why her father or mother couldn't play with her.

She brightened up. Her father said:

'We would like to have played with her' – in an apologetic tone – 'but we both have to go down to the village for a while. We have things to do.'

This was rather strange, because it was unusual for our guests to have any need to go down to the village again once they had got away to the mountains, but I just said that I was sure I could give her a game later on.

After that it was off to the kitchen with the lively anglers, where Jim was standing ready to gut the fish and put it in freezer bags. He kept back some fillets so that the gentlemen could taste their own fish for the evening meal, prepared à la meunière.

I went up to the private apartments, showered away the mountain air and the fish guts, and relaxed for an hour before I had to be in the firing line again.

I could tell that I was tired, because she beat me without any effort on my part in one of the three rounds we played. She paid with a ten-kroner note the first two times, but the last round I let her have free.

'I'm going to be an expert in minigolf,' said Karoline. 'We're staying for three weeks. At least!'

'Are you really,' I said politely. I had a feeling that there would be innumerable rounds of minigolf from now on.

'Another round?' She looked pleadingly at me as she leaned on a putter and rocked eagerly to and fro on her trainers.

'No more today,' I sighed. 'It's dinner time now. I think we're having trout.'

'Trout? Yuck.'

'I helped to catch it.'

'Oh.' She thought a bit: 'I suppose trout is OK. Now and then.'

'Especially when it's cooked à la meunière,' I said. 'And covered in almonds.'

'Oh, that sounds great! Are you having some too?'

'No. We never eat with the guests. We're having stew from yesterday.'

Before the next day's fishing trip Grandfather gave his usual talk about the hotel's Golden Age for the guests.

It was held as always in the Heimdal room. I went along as well, partly out of old habit, partly to demonstrate that I was a loyal and interested heir, but mainly in order to avoid having to play even more rounds of golf before dinner.

On the walls in the Heimdal room there hung pictures and souvenirs from the Golden Age and other times in Fåvnesheim's history. Right back to the first Zaccharias, who with his own two hands had built the first tourist cabin up here, for the entertainment of British lords and other members of the aristocracy, then via his sons, who had improved the place so that it became internationally renowned and had had a road constructed all the way up. There were pictures of the sons, heavily bearded, in their smartest Sunday clothes. A yellowing cutting from *The Times* showed the hotel's first international advertisement. There were also pictures of the hotel as it had been at that time, a large L-shaped house over two floors, but of course without all the wings which had been added later. In the picture an enormous Norwegian pennant was waving from a gigantic flagpole, and there were carriages outside the entrance. The staff were lined up around the flagpole. If you counted them in the picture you got to 27 people, large and small.

'*Ganz Europa*,' Grandfather intoned in a voice which trembled slightly with pride, 'yes, the whole of the fashionable continental clientele was attracted up here into the mountains, just like you are today, gentlemen. Artists as well ...'

Grandfather waved his hand to indicate the two beautiful landscapes on the opposite wall, which both illustrated the area around the hotel, one by Wentzel and the other by Thaulow, both of them significant names in our national history of art, who had each in their turn sought fashionable inspiration up here.

'*Wie schön, wie schön*,' said the gentlemen, who were listening with interest.

Change of scene. Change of period. New wall.

'After the two World Wars and the depression in between,' Grandfather explained, 'Fåvnesheim experienced a fantastic boom during the fifties. As the standard of living in Norway gradually improved, more and more people came to the mountains, and Fåvnesheim was able to capitalise on its solid traditions and its excellent reputation amongst the more cultured classes from earlier times.'

The pictures on the third wall, still in black and white, showed immaculately clad ladies and gentlemen in elegant skiing outfits in bright sunshine, nearly all of them wearing teardrop-shaped sunglasses. From one picture to the next the hotel was growing in the background, wing by wing, extension by extension. A somewhat faded hand-coloured photo in a heavy frame showed a gentleman with no beard but an impressive moustache, smiling at the photographer. In one hand he held a Dunhill pipe, in the other a staff.

'*Mein Vater*,' said Grandfather devoutly.

One of the gentlemen coughed, but Grandfather took no notice. He described developments on into the sixties, when really large numbers of Norwegians, now definitely freed from postwar worries, made excursions into the mountains.

'Easters in those years,' Grandfather was lost in memories. 'Easters in those years ...'

Another cough from the audience.

'Normally we had a staff of up to forty here in high season .... And all the rooms fully booked. Just about always.'

'That's fascinating,' interposed one of the gentlemen quickly. 'Really fascinating. Tell me, Herr Zacchariassen, did the hotel attract significant Norwegian artists during this period as well?'

'No,' Grandfather admitted. 'Not to the same extent.'

Finally Grandfather showed them his great-grandfather's staff, which hung in a display case over the door, the same one which his father had been holding in the photo. The relay baton, you might say, which had passed from father to son for generations, and which had followed the hotel through good times and bad. Mostly good times, thank the Lord. And he expressed a sincere hope that the gentlemen had been satisfied with their stay so far.

'*Ja, ja, sehr schön. Alles bestens.*'

Were the gentlemen interested in hunting? In that case he would be more than happy to show them his collection of hunting trophies, which he had stuffed himself.

No, no, not so interested in hunting. There wasn't much opportunity for hunting in the neighbourhood of Dortmund, which unfortunately was heavily built up. But there were some good fishing ponds here and there, where you could keep your eye in with line casting whilst you were waiting for your year's trip, not to say expedition, to the really free and genuine nature reserves of this world, where it was still possible to feel that that you were a human being; but goodness me it was high time to get spruced up a bit before dinner.

Dortmund Sportanglerverein e.V. streamed as one body out of the Heimdal room in the direction of their rooms. I remained behind together with Grandfather. For a moment he looked small in his suit.

'Just as good as always, Grandfather,' I said. 'It's just like Grandmother says: people appreciate a bit of history.'

'True enough,' said Grandfather. 'True enough. I really appreciate you coming along, Sedd, when I talk about these things. One day it may be your turn to – yes.'

He waved his hand rather vaguely, whether to indicate the staff or Thaulow was not easy to see.

'I caught three trout for us today, Grandfather,' I said as we began walking towards the private apartments.

'That's good, my lad. That's good.'

'Times will always get better, Grandfather.'

'Let's hope so.'

'All history shows us that.'

'Yes,' said Grandfather. 'It does indeed.'

On the last day of the Germans' visit the weather took a turn for the worse. There was a bit of wind, and it was cloudy, but it wasn't raining. And the weather was definitely not too bad for fishing. *Überhaupt nicht*.

For the sake of variety they were going to walk a short way downhill from the hotel this time, where the river Svartå flowed. For quite a long stretch it ran through flat countryside, and it was a good fishing area.

There were fewer fish here than up in the mountain lakes, but the guests appreciated the change of scene. And as lunchtime approached, we could suddenly hear enticing calls from the thicket just above the river, interspersed with notes from a Hardanger fiddle. Out from the bushes emerged a fiddler from the district, in full rig, closely followed by a folk dancer dressed as a wood nymph in national costume and silver brooches, crooning and humming. A little way behind them appeared Jim with one of the temporary staff, carrying two large picnic baskets and a camping table.

The gentlemen from Dortmund were beside themselves with enthusiasm. Whilst the fiddle played and the wood nymph hummed, Jim served up a magnificent cold table, so that the guests' stay in Norway might finish on a memorably high note. The fact that a few raindrops started to appear was immaterial. After an appropriate interval, Grandfather himself appeared to see how things were going, as he said. He was greeted with cries of joy and gratitude. Such an incredible experience. So unique. So unforgettable. The boys back home in Dortmund, those who hadn't been able to come, would be green with jealousy. And the wives. The wives too. Absolutely green. Yes, Herr Zacchariassen, they said as the white wine splashed into their glasses, who knows? Who knows whether they ought not to find their way up here again another year, precisely here, to the pure, unpolluted, fresh and genuine Norwegian mountains, where they had been so well received, and Herr Brehm added in Norwegian: 'I haff alvays loved Norvay. Ever since I vos here the furst time.'

'Yes,' Grandfather smiled.

He was wearing his ancient, elegant climbing jacket with plus-fours, and looked just like a distinguished elderly hotel owner should. He lit his Dunhill pipe, the one he had from his father, and listened with satisfaction to the exclamations of gratitude, even allowing himself half a glass of wine.

The wind made violent billows in the skirts of the re-presentative folk dancers, and a couple of gusts threatened to overturn the camping table. It was not going to be possible to do any more fishing that day, but in any case they were leaving later that afternoon. So we marched as a body back up to the hotel, that is to say Grandfather, the Germans and I, whilst Jim and the others disappeared quietly back to the car which was parked up on the road, a few minutes' walk away.

Outside the entrance stood Karoline, watching out for us. She began at once to wheedle about more minigolf. I did my best to shake her off, but she was pretty insistent. Just for once Herr Brehm addressed me in German; he winked and said: '*Pass mal auf! Sie flirtet mit dir!*'

'*Nein*,' I informed him, '*sie möchte nur Minigolf spielen.*'

'I see, is that what it's called now?' said Herr Brehm, and disappeared upstairs to pack.

I managed to extricate myself by saying that I would be busy until the guests left, but not without promising that I would play a round with her as soon as they were safely on their way, so long as the weather was good enough. I trusted that it would get worse as the afternoon went on. After that I barricaded myself in my room until it was time to help the guests with their enormous quantities of luggage and equipment, as well as the fabulous amounts of frozen fish which were to be transported to family and friends and no doubt the friends of friends back home in Dortmund. Considerably over the legal quota, of course, but there were hardly any others who were going to be fishing up here this summer, so it didn't really matter.

When the last little fish was safely packed away in the minibus, and the time for departure had arrived, it started raining properly. This was most unfortunate, because the gentlemen were suddenly in a rush to climb into the vehicle, so that only two of them, Herr Brehm and another guy whose name escapes me, found time to slip me a note for my efforts. I thanked them politely, but it was only those two. If everyone had contributed then the return would have been in proportion to the effort. But they were already sitting inside the bus. *Falturilturaltura* could be heard from inside. That's just how it is sometimes, I knew that, and that's what I said to myself as I watched them driving away, and if you're a member of the profession you mustn't let yourself be disappointed by things like that. That's no good, if you do that you just become bitter and twisted. But it occurred to me as I stood there that it would have been just as rewarding and not taken up half as much time to play twenty rounds of golf with Karoline. She at least could be relied on to pay.

So it was inevitable that I looked round to try and spot her, but at the same moment a gust of wind threw a shower of rain in my face, and I could see that there would be no minigolf that day. The purring the German minibus's engine died away in the distance, and all that could be heard was the sound of the rain and the low humming of the dynamo from the freezer room. Grandfather and Grandmother had long since gone in, and I was left standing out there all alone. No minigolf today. I could tell that I was a bit disappointed, but I was not bitter and twisted.

Then I went in.

22

Karoline and her parents had a strange way of having a holiday. At times they behaved like most guests, went for walks or used the swimming pool or enjoyed Fåvnesheim's other facilities – whilst at other times the parents or all three of them would drive off down to the village in the burgundy-coloured Saab, and could be gone for hours. It was particularly when her parents were away that Karoline was at her most demanding.

After the Germans' departure we had a couple of days of bad weather when no minigolf was possible, but then it cleared up again. Her parents drove off, and Karoline wanted to play immediately. There were a few other holiday guests who had arrived in the meantime, but I didn't have too much to do, so I was free to play a few rounds with her.

I noticed at once that her playing had improved. Her strokes were more precise and she had picked up some of the finesses on certain holes. It struck me that she must have been practising on her own. But I didn't want to ask. She dutifully passed me ten kroner for each round, whilst every now and then I said that the hotel would pay. When we got to the third round I said to her: 'This is costing you a lot of money.'

She just dismissed it.

'Oh,' she said. 'That doesn't matter. There's more where that comes from.'

'Perhaps we could arrange a sort of en gros rebate,' I said, after feeling a stab of conscience.

'What's that?'

'That's when you get goods or a service at a reduced rate because you buy a lot of it.'

'Oh, yes. An en gros rebate. That's not necessary. You give me just about every fourth round for free.'

'The hotel gives it,' I said.

'I mean the hotel. So that's fine.'

On the seventeenth hole she slipped on the algae, but managed not to fall.

'It's really slippery here,' she announced.

'I know,' I sighed. 'I must pull myself together and do something about it.'

So the next day I went into the toolshed and put on overalls, gloves and goggles, got out a bucket and brush and cloth, and began to look for the bottle of Anti-Algon. Anti-Algon is really disgusting muck, as Jim says. You mustn't get it on your skin and for God's sake not in your eyes, and preferably not up your nose or anywhere else, and when you've scrubbed it into the concrete you have to remove it with a cloth so that it doesn't leak out and destroy the vegetation around the course. Because then it would be a Sahara. I had actually thought I might persuade Karoline to do the job with me, or at least to stand and watch admiringly, because it's always good to have company, but she and her parents had gone off to the village straight after breakfast, whatever they wanted to do that for. Jim was busy in the kitchen.

The Anti-Algon was not where it ought to be. I could see that the whole shed was in need of a good tidying. On the topmost shelf, behind a cardboard box, I could make out some plastic bottles. I climbed up on a stool, lifted down the cardboard box and sure enough: there was the poison-green bottle. Extra Large with liquid death for all micro-organisms which came near it.

It was as I was about to put the cardboard box back in place that I discovered it. The box was carelessly closed, and I happened to glance down into it.

Letters.

I had to look twice. The box was full of letters. I looked for a third time, in order to make sure that it was not just empty envelopes, and that Grandfather had not been preparing a giant surprise for me in the form of a Post Horn bonanza and On Official Business orgy, for example as a Christmas present, but there was no doubt. The envelopes were unopened. And there were many. Most of them were large brown business envelopes. Some were addressed to the hotel, others to the hotel management, others again to Grandfather. Some were from the bank, whilst others were from various public authorities and offices, and a few had no sender's name.

I sat there on the stool for a while, leafing through the shiny sealed envelopes. All had typewritten addresses, all were unopened. There were also a few window envelopes franked by a franking machine. All in all there were certainly more than a hundred letters in the box. That was strange. For a moment I wondered whether I should open some of them, but then I remembered the Privacy of Correspondence.

Not everyone knows what the Privacy of Correspondence means, but I knew. Privacy of Correspondence is the sort of thing experienced philatelists know about. It consists of the following simple but absolute principle: that only the person to whom a letter is addressed, and that person alone, may open the letter. The Privacy of Correspondence is the first commandment of this world's posties, even more important than the ancient motto 'The mail must get through!' The contents of a letter are sacred and inviolable, just like the King's person in the Constitution, and a letter must not be opened by anyone other than the addressee or those to whom he has given permission, unless the address on the letter is so inadequate that it is impossible to find the addressee. In that case the Royal Mail Dead Letter Office is called in. The Dead Letter Office, which consists of twelve men and women sworn to secrecy, is the only one which is authorised to transgress the Privacy of Correspondence. If a letter is irredeemably lost in the sense that it is impossible to discover who it's for and where the person in question lives, the Dead Letter Office can open the letter to see if they can find useful clues in its contents. This happens during a solemn and serious meeting which the Dead Letter Office holds every six months. There letters can be presented which have wandered from town to town, from post office to post office, from postie to postie, often for many years, without the addressee being found, despite all the efforts of the faithful workers. Only then can the Dead Letter Office open the letter. Whether they find the addressee with the help of the contents or not, they are sworn to secrecy for life regarding what they have read in the letters. That's how strong the Privacy of Correspondence is, so you can see that it's not something to be taken lightly.

The letters in the box were for Grandfather, there was no doubt about that, and he must have put them there himself, although it was unclear why he should do so. In any case, there was no doubt about the addressee, and he had to be allowed to do what he wanted with his post, so there was no reason to transgress the Privacy of Correspondence. Nevertheless, it was strange.

I put the box back, and took with me the equipment and the bottle of Anti-Algon. As I stood there scrubbing, or got down on hands and knees to mop up the muck, I thought about how strange it was.

When I was done with the horrible job, I went inside to look for Grandmother. I found her in the kitchen, where she was in the midst of baking. There was a floury cloud of concentration around her, and I could see she didn't want to be disturbed.

'I think,' said Grandmother, 'that I shall put up a poster down in the village and offer one of my classical Austrian coffee mornings. It's a long time since I did so.'

Grandmother had a habit of arranging small gatherings with coffee and a selection of baked goodies for both local inhabitants and guests, when she felt too restless.

'I'm sure that's a good idea, Grandmother,' I said.

She carried on tirelessly throwing together the ingredients for short-crust pastry. She worked quickly and efficiently, with the precision of a professional.

'Grandmother,' I said.

'Yes?' she said, without looking up from her pastry.

'I wonder whether Grandfather perhaps has a bit too much to do?'

'Too much?' She stopped kneading and looked up: 'Too much? My dear, he's never had less to do.'

For a moment she looked at me with something like genuine concern.

'We hardly have any guests,' she said. Then she carried on kneading quickly. 'Haven't you noticed?'

And was it perhaps then, in that moment of truth over the short-crust pastry, that it occurred to me as more than a vague suspicion that not all was as it should be? I don't know, but suddenly I felt a cold stab of worry.

'I just thought,' I went on, 'that Grandfather could perhaps do with a little help with the office work?'

'Office work? What do you mean?'

'Oh you know, correspondence and accounts and such-like.'

She looked up again:

'My sweet *Bubi*. You really are a good boy.'

'Besides, I have to make a start on learning about that side of the business as well.'

'But we have Synnøve to look after the administration.'

'Yes.'

'But I'm sure he'd be glad if you ask. I'm sure he'd be glad.'

'I'll ask him then, when it's the right moment.'

'But Sedd, I don't think you should – how should I put it – express any concern about his capacity for work.'

'No, Grandmother.'

'Just say that you'd like to help.'

'Thanks, Grandmother.' I turned to go.

'By the way,' said Grandmother, 'while I remember: it's very good of you to play minigolf with little Karoline. They're staying here for so long.'

'Yes, Grandmother.'

'Whilst you were busy with the fishermen, she borrowed clubs and balls at all hours of the day so that she could practise.'

'Did she?'

'Yes.' She smiled slyly. 'I think she's trying to make a bit of an impression on you. Her parents seem to have private errands down in the village, so she's left on her own a lot. So I told her she could play for free. They'll be here for another three weeks, so it's the least we can do.'

'Yes,' I said. 'It's the least we can do.'

'Perhaps, if the weather is better tomorrow, you could take her out on a little fishing trip?'

'Oh, I don't know, Grandmother ... I've got so much to do.'

'*Quatsch*,' came the reply. 'You just said you wanted to help. Learn more. Well, things like that are part of the job. *Das weisst du doch*. Besides, whilst you were out on trips with the Germans, she told me she really wanted to learn to fish.'

'Did she say that, Grandmother.'

'Yes. And she also said that she thought mountain trout was so good.'

'Right.'

'The best thing she knew, if truth be told. So perhaps, since they are such good guests, and if the weather is fine tomorrow, you might do us a really big favour – ?'

'Yes,' I said. 'It's the least I can do.'

'Quite, it's the least you can do. Well, I don't have time to talk any more, if I'm going to get this finished before Jim needs his kitchen back.'

When Karoline was ready for afternoon play on a scrubbed, algae-free and shiny white minigolf course, she held out a ten-kroner note as I arrived, without a word. I looked at the note uncertainly, without taking it. But she practically forced it on me. I took it.

'This is costing a lot,' I said again.

'Pooh,' was all she said.

We played. She was getting better and better. And making less and less noise, both when she missed and when she triumphed. On hole seven I said:

'It looks as if you're staying a long time?'

'Mm. Very long.'

She concentrated on her stroke.

On hole twelve I said:

'It seems they've got lots to do, your parents?'

'Mm. Lots.'

She hit the ball. Straight down the hole.

'Ha! It's always like that, anyway.'

'Like that?'

'Yes. Lots to do. Lots to do. Always lots to do.'

She sighed. Before we began on hole eighteen, I said:

'Erm, I wondered if you'd like to come up to Blåvann with me tomorrow and do a bit of fishing, if the weather's good?'

She dropped her club and brightened up.

'Oh yes!'

'I mean, if you're not going to the village with your parents or – '

'Oh no! No, no, I'm sure I'm not! When shall we go?'

She looked ready to set off immediately.

'Oh,' I said, 'straight after breakfast?'

'Oh yes!'

It's actually rare to see anyone look so happy. Suddenly she threw her arms around me and hugged me tight. 'Thank you so much,' she said into my jacket.

'No problem,' I said, and freed myself by bending down to pick up her golf club. I passed it to her: 'My pleasure. Come on, let's see if you can manage number eighteen with less than five strokes this time.'

She collected herself, and pushed her hair back behind her ears. Then she concentrated. She managed number eighteen with four strokes, and was over the moon.

The next day the weather was perfect from early morning, and by the time I had finished breakfast Karoline looked as if she had been standing waiting impatiently for a long time. She had packed a little rucksack and was wearing practical walking clothes. I had two light rods with me, one for her and one for me, together with a spoon lure and a landing net.

On the way out she hummed and sang, clearly bubbling over with joy at going on a fishing trip, so I wasn't called upon to interpret Norwegian folk songs on this trip, at least.

It was hot. All the rocks gleamed silver and grey, and the snow patches were whiter than white. The sky was blue with a faint tinge of yellow.

Once we'd got up to Blåvann, without needing any rests on the way, we pulled off our rucksacks and I put the fishing rods together. I tried to explain to her what I was doing, and showed her the fishing knot I used to fasten the spoon lure, but she was too excited to take much in.

'Haven't you ever been fishing before?'

'Oh yes. With Papa. But that was boring. We didn't catch anything. Besides, it's a long time ago.'

'It's not certain we'll catch anything now either. You can never guarantee that you'll catch a fish.'

'I think we'll catch some fish.'

'Do you?'

'Oh, yes. But it doesn't matter anyway.'

We went down to the edge to try casting. I wanted to make sure that she would be able to cast well enough so that she didn't get it snagged on the bottom straight away, and I didn't risk wasting precious lures. So I took off the hook from her lure, an ordinary light silver spoon with green dots, in order to see how she managed. It went quite well; she soon got the hang of it. Now and then I had to correct her a little, straighten her arm and improve her stance, but she was quick to learn. After she had made eight or ten acceptable casts, I fastened the hook on again, and the fishing could begin.

To start with we caught nothing. It was completely dead. Perhaps, I thought, most of the fish stocks were now in the freezers of Dortmund, so that there was nothing left for us.

But Karoline didn't seem to mind. Her casts became longer and more elegant, and the most important thing after all was that she was having fun. When as part of your official duties you have to round up German fishermen or babysit a pushy little girl, the main thing, as I mentioned earlier, is to keep them busy and provide variety. Guests must not be allowed to be bored. And Karoline was my guest. No doubt about that.

I got out my own rod and made some casts. Straight away she was distracted by admiring my casts, and her hook snagged on the bottom. There of course it stuck fast at once, and for a moment she thought she had a bite, and her face brightened.

'I'm afraid it's a really big fish you've got on your hook there,' I said.

'Oh? What sort?'

'You've caught the earth itself.'

For a moment she looked at me in confusion, then she understood.

'Oh,' she said, looking at me unhappily. 'I'm sorry.'

'It happens,' I said.

Fortunately, with a little jiggling I managed to get the spoon loose. It leapt out of the water like a glittering piece of silver, and Karoline was jubilant.

'Mind you keep your eyes on the lure,' I said, passing the rod back to her.

We carried on casting for a while, but got nothing. After an hour had passed, we moved up to a place nearer the northern edge of the lake. But it was just as dead there.

'No,' I said, 'if we're going to catch anything, we'll have to go out there.'

'Out on the water?'

'Yes. Come on. Wind the lure all the way in. Like this. Then you fasten the hook to the furthest ring there, and tighten the line. That's it. Now it's secure. And you won't get it in your eye.'

'OK. Got it. It would be really stupid to get it in my eye.'

'Yes.'

'Because then I wouldn't be able to see,' Karoline declared.

We went over to 'Fåvne II'. There was no end to Karoline's enthusiasm when she caught sight of the worn old wooden boat. She had never thought it would be possible to go on a boat trip so high up in the mountains.

Unfortunately there was quite a lot of water in the bottom after all the rain, and I had to bale it out. Another problem was that the boat was only equipped with one baler, and Karoline showed no signs of wanting to take on her share of the task. Instead she talked twenty to the dozen about their country place in Denmark, where the beaches were white and endless, but where you couldn't fish, about Legoland and the driving licence she had got there the summer before last, about the church buried in sand and the lighthouse at Skagen and some horses on a nearby farm which were incredibly lovely, by all accounts the loveliest horses in the whole world, and a number of other things, whilst I baled and baled.

When I was finally finished, or at least there were only a few puddles of water left in the bottom, I threw her one of the life jackets.

Of course it was far too big. It drowned her. Karoline giggled hysterically.

'Look! Oh, just look at that! I can't wear *this*!'

I tried to tie it around her, but she was so tiny that she was engulfed by it, and I had to agree with her. She would certainly not be able to cast wearing that.

'Ok,' I said. 'You can drop the life jacket. It's quite calm today anyway. But you must promise me not to stand up in the boat.'

'I promise.'

'The German fishermen gave me the fright of my life. They kept on standing up in the boat.'

'Did they?'

'I think they believed the laws of physics didn't apply to them.'

'I do understand. I've been out in a little boat before.'

She looked at me seriously, and I felt reassured. After that we set off. I rowed, and Karoline sat on the rear thwart and let her left hand trail in the cold dark water. She was humming a little song. I thought about telling her that you had to be silent while fishing in order not to frighten the fish, but I didn't. If she wanted to sing, then she could sing. Arias if she liked, I didn't mind.

When we had reached the middle, I shipped the oars and showed her with my own rod how to cast sitting down. She picked it up fine. In any case it was so deep here that it didn't matter if some of the casts fell short.

When I saw she was getting on all right with the casting, I sat back in the bow with my back to her and started to cast myself. Soon there was a bite, on my rod first and then straight after on hers, so the Germans had not managed to empty Blåvann completely. I had to struggle backwards in the boat with the landing net in order to help her get the first fish on board, and she watched in some alarm as I detached the trout, which was thrashing about strongly, from the hook and killed it. She looked at it for a moment with wide eyes, almost as if she was about to cry, but then she bit her lower lip, smiled bravely and cast her line out again.

I returned to my position at the front. I left the landing net lying on the middle thwart between us, so that we could both reach it if we needed to.

They weren't biting furiously, but at regular intervals we reeled in a fish. Karoline insisted on killing the second one herself, but wasn't quite firm enough, so I had to show her. Numbers three and four she killed sharply and unsentimentally, as if she had never done anything else.

Soon there was an appreciable pile of silvery fish in the bottom of the boat, slightly smeared with blood.

All that could be heard was the lapping of water beneath the keel, the click and swish of our casts, the chatter of the spools being wound in. Karoline hummed. ABBA. 'Dancing Queen.' We were casting back to back.

A while later I got something on the hook which felt like a real monster. It jerked violently and the rod suddenly bent sharply. I turned round towards Karoline to say that she had better watch this, perhaps even help me, because this was a big one; that was what I was about to say, in fact I had already begun to say precisely that as I half turned towards her.

But Karoline was not there. Her rod was lying crosswise across the gunwale, but no Karoline.

For a moment – a moment as long as a day and as short as a petrified skipped heartbeat – I couldn't believe my own eyes. 'Karoline?' I said, staring stupidly at the thwart where she should be sitting. Why wasn't she sitting there any more? She wasn't sitting there any more. She should have been sitting there, just there, on that thwart, casting and humming. Was it long since I had heard her humming? Or casting? How long ago was it? I glanced around over the dark water round the boat, confused, frightened, more frightened than when Bjørn Berge had sunk forwards and died a gourmand's death; I saw nothing. Not a thing. The water was dark, bluish-grey, with small ripples. It was glistening in the sunshine. Everywhere around the boat the water was the same. Everywhere the same, as far as I could see.

Until I suddenly saw, or perhaps more suspected than saw, something pale in the water, a movement, something which shouldn't be there, a small distance away from the boat on my right.

I tore off my life jacket, kicked off my boots and had enough presence of mind to throw out the mooring rope before I let myself fall headfirst over the gunwale and into Blåvann.

It was dark and cold. Terribly dark and unbelievably cold. I've never been especially good at swimming under water, and especially not with my eyes open, and of course not fully dressed, but now I had to do it. And I could tell that I was frightened, more frightened than I had ever been before, and that the depths of Blåvann were opening beneath me as if it really was bottomless. As if there was a crevasse all the way down to the centre of the earth, which would swallow up both Karoline and me and never release us back into light and air again.

I could see nothing. I kicked my way up to the surface again, got my head above water, took a few deep breaths and dived back down. This time I tried to move in the direction of the place where I had seen something. It hurt my eyes, and the water was so cold that it made my bones ache, but I forced myself on. Eyes open. Eyes open. I had to keep my eyes open. They were my only chance, and Karoline's only chance, like two small searchbeams in an endless darkness, two fireflies, two small windows; and there, there I could see a shadow darker than the darkness around me, I could see long girl's hair billowing silently, ghostlike, and I reached out an arm. Couldn't reach her. Too far away. Was she sinking?

She was sinking. Deeper and deeper she sank. And I knew that if I return to the surface now to get the air I need, I will never reach her again. I will get some air, but I won't reach her. Then she'll die. So I tried once more to reach her. Forced myself downwards, stretched out an arm and felt it touch her side, and then I could feel the skin of her neck against my palm, and then she grabbed me.

She grabbed hold of my arm so hard I thought it would break. She grabbed as she sank, not wanting to sink, grabbed because there was something to hold onto.

For a moment I panicked. If she held me so hard, and I couldn't use both arms, I wouldn't be able to pull her up. But somehow or other, in the midst of her own terror, she must have understood: you have to let go, Karoline, you have to let Sedd help you, Sedd has to do his job, Sedd has to rescue you, Sedd is a member of the Red Cross first-aiders, he is a rescuer, and she let me free myself from her grip, let me get hold of her under the arms from behind, and then I kicked upwards. I kicked upwards as hard as I could. Nothing happened. We hung there in the cold, terrible darkness, surrounded by the pressure of the water, close and suffocating like an ice-cold slippery duvet, and didn't move from the spot. I kicked again, and pulled with one arm, but everything was heavy. Our clothes were heavy and she was heavy and neither of us had any air left in us. I looked upwards. The surface glinted like a bluish-grey, milky membrane. A bit further away I could make out the boat. It was like in the depths of the Pacific, under Kon-Tiki, on Bygdøy, except that this was real and there were no living creatures other than us, no whale sharks and no pilot fish, no swordfish and no flying fish, just us, and now we were going to die.

Then I saw the rope. It was trailing diagonally in the water after the boat, and if Karoline could just help me a little bit, just a bit, if we could just make ourselves a bit lighter, lift ourselves, I would perhaps be able to swim the half-metre over to it.

The next moment I had hold of it with my left hand, I had something to hold on to. Somehow I managed to grip it between my legs, and by pulling us along it and at the same time kicking out and making swimming movements, I got us moving, as we hung there, a tangled mass of fear and lack of air.

Suddenly our heads broke surface. I could hardly believe it was true. I coughed, retched and spat out lake water, then finally I could draw breath. Filled my lungs with air, and knew that I had made it.

But Karoline was hanging round my shoulders with her eyes closed. Her eyelashes were like black streaks in a face which was frighteningly pale. We were far out in the lake, and I could see that it would be difficult to get her up into the boat. I couldn't let go of her either. I slapped her cheeks and called her name, but there was no response. Her eyes were still two streaks. Her skin white, cold and wet. I couldn't see any breathing.

Somehow it seemed to me shameful, in fact it almost seemed dishonest, if she were to die now after I had got her up to the surface with such a struggle. So I slapped her again, and said the same thing I had wanted to say to Berge the bank manager that time, you mustn't die. Then I wound the rope tightly under her arms, as firmly as I could so that it wouldn't slip, and tipped her backwards in the water and hoped that her face wouldn't go under. After that I climbed into the boat.

It looks so easy on paper. Climbed into the boat. In reality it was like lifting yourself up by the hair with your pockets full of lead. But somehow or other I managed it. My legs and arms were shaking with the effort when I was finally sitting on the bottom of the boat again, but I knew that the most difficult thing was still to come. Somehow I would have to manoeuvre Karoline up too. I pulled her in to the side by the rope and leant out to get hold of her under the arms; but I realised at once that that would not work. I would just tumble out of the boat myself. And I felt fairly sure that I would not be able to climb up again by my own efforts. I looked round in the boat. Since we had no jetty, and the boat was Blåvann's only vessel, we had of course no boathook either. Nothing with a hook on, apart from the fishhooks, but they wouldn't be any good. Not the oars either, nor the baler.

The landing net. If I sliced the net open with my fish knife, I could bend the two metal prongs slightly apart, and make something which resembled a large hook. I wound the dangling cut pieces of net around my wrist so that I shouldn't lose hold of it, and swept it under the water. I was lucky. It caught at once on a belt loop behind her back. I could hardly believe I had been so lucky. I braced my feet against the opposite gunwale, wrapped my left arm round the thwart, and with the help of the landing net and by pulling on the rope I got her high enough up in the water to be able to get hold of her belt and try to flip her over into the boat, which was listing dangerously. Fortunately she was small and slim, and once I had got a proper hold, it was surprisingly easy.

Suddenly she was lying on the bottom of the boat, white and still, next to all the trout.

And then the terror returned. She looked very dead. And I could not imagine how I would be able to row, much less leave her lying dead on the shore, whilst I ran down to the hotel for help. For a moment I thought that it would actually have been better if we had remained down there in Blåvann.

But then the training from the Red Cross took over, and I did as I had done with Bjørn Berge. I gave her mouth-to-mouth, I tried to force out any water which might have got into her by pressing on her diaphragm, then gave her mouth-to-mouth again, breathed into her. The air which came back was cold and damp and tasted of mountain water and something sweet.

Then suddenly it happened. It was like a bubble bursting, a little hiccup. Then she threw up masses of water, straight into my mouth; it tasted like all the other water I had swallowed that day, and I understood that she was alive.

More water, more coughing, followed by a few long, rattling gasps, and she opened her eyes. They were completely black. She looked at me with an expression which seemed almost reproachful, cross. She was just as pale as before, gasped a few more times, coughed, cleared her throat, and then she said:

'I can't swim.'

'No,' I said. 'Perhaps you should have said that before.'

'Yes,' she said. Then her teeth began to chatter. I got hold of the oars and began to row us to shore, my upper arms trembling with exhaustion.

Even before we were halfway there she began to cry.

By the time we reached the shore she was almost blue with cold, and my teeth were chattering too, even though I had been rowing. Of course I didn't have any towels with me, but I did have an extra sweater in my rucksack. We got out of our wet clothes and she put on the sweater. It covered her almost completely. Then we sat on rocks in the sun to get warm. We said nothing to each other. It occurred to me that I had tea in my flask, and I poured out a cup for each of us. She took hers in both hands in order not to drop the cup.

'Thank you,' she whispered. She took a few sips, and some of the colour came back to her face, but she still looked rather shattered.

I took our clothes and draped them over some bushes. Hopefully the sun and the wind would soon dry them. Then I sat down, a little way away from her, in my underpants, and drank tea.

'So what happened?' I asked.

She shook her head weakly.

'I don't know,' she said. 'I was going to get the landing net because I had a bite. So I stood up. I didn't even stand up properly. Then I just kind of slipped in.'

'Mm,' I said. 'It's easily done. You should have told me you couldn't swim.' She looked at me darkly:

'You didn't ask.'

'No,' I said.

'You should have asked!'

We were silent for a while. I didn't know what to say. She just sat staring in front of her. I thought: shock. So I went over to her and sat down beside her, and rubbed her back through the sweater. To begin with she was as stiff as a log, and I could feel that she was taking quick, shallow breaths, but after a while she relaxed more and her breathing became calmer.

'Bloody hell,' she said. I had never heard her swear before. 'That was horrible. Bloody hell, it was so horrible.'

'It wasn't much fun, no.'

'It was horrible.'

'Oh well,' I said, 'at least we caught some fish.' I said it mostly in order to put her in a better mood, but at first she just looked at me in surprise, almost reproachfully. Then she smiled. A little.

'Lots of fish,' she agreed with a little hiccup.

She leaned against me. I could feel how tired I was. It felt as if I had moved the whole of Blåvann a metre towards the east.

'I say, Sedd,' she said seriously.

'Yes?'

'Do you think we could not tell anyone about this?'

'Anyone?'

'Yes, Mama and Papa and so on.'

'Well, I don't know ...'

'Oh, please don't! They'll just get so worked up. And then they'll be frightened. And then they'll be angry.'

'Perhaps there's nothing so strange about that.'

'But it won't change anything! Not about me not being able to swim, and not about me falling in. It'll just be *more*.'

I glanced over at our clothes, which were fluttering and flapping in the mountain breeze. The water in Blåvann was quite clear, with no sediment in it, and you wouldn't be able to tell from her clothes that she'd fallen in. And if they did notice anything, she could just say that she'd tripped over as we pushed the boat out.

'Please?'

'OK, then. We'll do that. More tea?'

'Yes, please.'

When our clothes were reasonably dry, we got dressed. We stood with our backs to each other. The clothes were still damp, but they'd probably dry on the way down. Her boots were worse, they made loud sucking noises. But we could say we'd trodden in the marsh on the way back.

I made the boat fast, put the fish in a plastic bag in my rucksack and dismantled the fishing rods. I could tell that I wasn't quite myself, because I fumbled with everything I did. Karoline stood a few metres away, motionless, and just watched me without saying anything. When everything was packed, she just turned on her heel and set off.

She didn't sing on the way down. When we got back to Fåvnesheim, her parents were on their way from the car across the front yard. They caught sight of us at once, and waved.

'Did you catch anything?' Karoline's mother asked, smiling.

'Yes, loads of fish,' I said enthusiastically.

'Loads!' echoed Karoline. She forced a smile.

'But sweetheart,' said her mother, 'you look a bit peaky. Have you got a temperature?'

'I think perhaps I'm sickening for something,' said Karoline.

'I think so too,' I said. 'I'm afraid we stumbled into the marsh and got our feet wet.'

'Oh dear.'

'It's important to have dry feet if you start to get ill,' I declared.

'I think perhaps I'll go and lie down for a bit,' said Karoline.

'Yes, that sounds like a good idea,' her father agreed. 'Get yourself warm, so you don't get really poorly.'

'Will you see to the fish, Sedd?'

'Of course. Don't worry about it.'

I suspected that her parents suspected that something was not quite right, because they looked at us and at each other a little uncertainly. Karoline still had large black eyes, and in general didn't look quite as usual. I think Karoline also noticed that her parents were wondering, because she suddenly burst out:

'Sedd, thanks so much for taking me fishing! It was really nice of you!'

'No problem,' I said. 'It was a pleasure.'

'Perhaps you'll take me fishing another day too, if you have time? I mean, only if you have time?'

'Sure,' I said, 'I'm sure I can.'

'Now you must go upstairs and take those wet boots off, young lady,' her father admonished her. Karoline began to walk towards the hall door. Her mother said in a low voice:

'That was a good girl, Karoline, to remember to thank Sedd for taking you with him.' Karoline nodded. Then she turned round:

'See you later, alligator!'

'Yes, cheerio!' I said.

'You're so slow,' she declared. Her mother: 'Karoline, really!'

'See you,' I said, but they had already gone.

Knock knock.

....

Knock knock knock.

'Oh, it's you, Sedd. Nice to see you.'

'I just wondered how Karoline is? Is she asleep?'

'Visiting the sick? That's nice of you. Just knock on her door. I don't think she's asleep. The door's not locked.'

'Because she didn't come down to dinner, so I was wondering ...'

'I think she's much better now.'

'Thanks.'

'And Sedd ...'

'Yes?'

'We're very pleased that you're keeping Karoline company. It's really kind of you.'

'That's OK. I mean, it's a pleasure.'

'We're so busy right now, you see, my husband and I. And Karoline ...'

'Yes?'

'Karoline has never found it easy to make friends.'

'Right.'

'We thought perhaps it would be easier when we came here.'

'Oh?'

But she said no more.

Karoline was in bed, but awake. She still looked the worse for wear.

'Hi,' I said. She brightened. 'Hi. Hi, Sedd.'

'I just wanted to check how things were going.'

'Things are fine, I think.' She looked down at the duvet. Then she said: 'You know, I've been thinking. You must teach me to swim.'

'Well ...' I began.

'Yes, you have to. This won't do.'

'Well,' I said, 'we'll see. Here. I've brought something for you.'

I put my hand in my pocket and brought out the snowy glass globe from Vienna with the white Lipizzaner horse, which I had from my mother.

She took it. Turned it over in her hand. The snow whirled around the white horse in the water.

'Thanks,' she said with shining eyes. She turned it around in her fingers. Bit her bottom lip.

Then she fell asleep as I was watching.

I had done my life-saving mission, my only one, which no-one would ever know about, and for which I would never be awarded a medal.

23

To start with she didn't want to put her face or her head under, and that was really not difficult to understand. But you can be sure she worked on it. Since there were so few guests at the hotel, we practically had the swimming pool to ourselves. That is a definite advantage when you're learning to swim at a relatively advanced age and are ashamed that you haven't learnt long ago. Indeed, Karoline found it so embarrassing that if other guests suddenly came in to use the pool area, we changed straight away to playing water games at the shallow end where she could stand. She admitted to me that she always stayed there in the shallows when she was in the pool, anyway.

I had never taught anyone to swim before, naturally enough, since it does not form part of my usual tasks. But Jim had taught me to swim when I was little. His method had been successful, so I used the same one, since I reasoned that it would probably work with Karoline too. In brief, Jim's method was to hold the pupil under the stomach, whilst said pupil attempted to make various swimming strokes, and hopefully at some point they would begin to float of their own accord. I didn't feel entirely convinced that this was enough, so I varied Jim's method with other exercises which occurred to me, whenever I felt they would help. Floating on your back. Ducking under. Making yourself into a ball in the water and popping up – all the things it is useful and fun to be able to do.

Karoline was stiff with fright the first few times. Her meeting with the depths of Blåvann had not made it any easier, as you would expect. I realised that I had to proceed with caution in order to get her to relax. It is very difficult to become a good swimmer if you don't relax. I explained that to her, and she tried with all her might to relax, which of course only made her even stiffer. But after a while she began to believe that I wouldn't drown her, and she said so too:

'Sedd,' she said, 'I don't believe you'll drown me.'

For a moment she hung there with both hands clasped round my neck, then she stretched out backwards in the water, so that I could hold her from underneath whilst she attempted to float.

The first breakthrough came on the third day, when she suddenly and completely of her own accord managed to swim a few strokes.

She was so happy. I would not have believed it was possible to be so happy for the sake of a few little strokes.

It was a strange feeling of suspension. She had been resting on my outstretched arms, light as a feather in the water, but still as stiff as a branch, whilst she mechanically made swimming movements. As I slowly walked sideways, like a kind of two-legged crab, she 'swam' from one side to the other, but the whole time it was shallow enough for her to be able to stand. Once, without thinking about it, I walked out where it was too deep. As I let her go, I realised at the last moment that her head would go under; she realised it at the same moment as I let go, uttered a sharp hiccough of panic, and I grabbed her under the arms just in time, and manoeuvred her into shallow water. I could feel her toes against mine, searching for ground to stand on, and she held me tightly around the shoulders.

'Promise me you'll never do that again, Sedd,' she said. 'Never, never, never.' Her toe nails jabbed sharply against my ankles.

'I promise,' I said. 'I didn't mean to.'

'Never, never again.'

'I promise,' I said again. 'I didn't mean to.'

'You really must promise.'

'I do, Karoline, but it would actually help you to float if you let me take you out a bit deeper.'

'Never.'

'OK.'

But then, suddenly and without realising it herself, she swam a few strokes, and to start with I don't think she even noticed that that was what she was doing. I followed her, still with my arms beneath her in readiness, but she was swimming. No doubt about it. The time was half-past ten in the morning, it was a completely ordinary Wednesday at the beginning of August, and Karoline could swim.

Then she realised it herself.

'Was I swimming then?' she asked, amazed.

'You were swimming,' I said. She turned towards me as she stood there with water up above her shoulders. All that could be seen above the surface was one big smile.

'Again!'

We tried again. And she was swimming.

That morning she would hardly agree to get out of the pool. I almost had to pull her out. As I said, it's strange that anyone can be so happy just because of a few little strokes.

Once she was out, on the side of the pool, whilst she dried herself, shivering, with a fluffy towel, it was clear that she could say only one thing, and that was:

'I can swim. I can swim, I can swim. Did you see me, Sedd? I can swim, I can swim.'

'Yes.'

'I can swim. I can swim! Good God. Bloody hell. I can swim.'

'Yes, you were actually swimming.'

'Yes, I actually was!'

'Now your parents will be pleased.'

'Oh yes! Oh yes.'

'Not everyone learns to swim up in the mountains,' I said.

'Oh no!' She laughed. 'But Sedd,' she added, 'can we wait a bit?'

'Wait?'

'Yes – to tell them and that.'

'Why?'

'Well, I just thought perhaps I could get properly good first. Properly good at swimming. Underwater and on top and everything. Properly good. Just like you. Or' – she looked at me a little uncertainly – 'even better.'

'OK, we can do that,' I said.

'I mean, if it's all right with you? To keep on practising?'

'It's all right with me,' I said. 'Quite all right.'

She looked at me for a long moment. Smiled slightly, her eyes narrowed.

'You are nice,' she said.

'Nothing is too much for our guests,' I said, because I had to say something. 'Well done for learning to swim!'

'Yes, I did swim, didn't I? Mama and Papa will be so pleased! They were worried about how I would get on in the pool at the school here, since I couldn't swim.'

'At the school here? You're going to start school here?'

'Yes, didn't you know? We're moving here. My father has started his new job, but our house, I mean the new house we'll be living in, hasn't been done up yet. That's why we're living at the hotel in the meantime. Until our house, I mean our new house, is ready. But I don't think it'll ever be ready.'

She raised her eyes to the heavens. 'Honestly, builders,' she murmured.

'I see,' I said. 'So your father has started work in the village?'

'You're so slow, Sedd. That's what I always say.' She prodded me with her fist as usual, but I could tell that she didn't think I was particularly slow any longer. At least not today.

'Papa is the new bank manager.'

'Oh, right,' I said.

'The previous one died, you know.'

'Yes,' I said. 'He died.'

'Lobster,' said Grandfather seriously. 'It has to be lobster. Perhaps Thermidor, or perhaps à l'américaine. And a Riesling to go with it.'

'Definitely not,' said Grandmother. 'A white Burgundy. That's the thing.'

'You're right,' Grandfather agreed. 'Burgundy. The whole bloody hog. And to follow – hm. To follow, to follow ... What do you think, Sisi? Reindeer? Elk?'

'Definitely not elk! Reindeer, mm, possibly. Perhaps grouse.'

'Grouse is not a bad idea. What do you think, Jim?'

Jim, who until now had just been listening to the negotiations, nodded in agreement: 'Grouse. There's hardly anyone who can do grouse really well. But I can. I'm thinking breast. With a reduction of stock and cherries. Best with some kir in the sauce. Pommes noisettes. Or rösti. Mushrooms. Perhaps some half cherries as a garnish. That's what I think.'

Grandfather and Grandmother nodded in satisfaction.

'And then the desserts,' said Grandmother.

Grandfather and Jim looked at each other uncertainly, but said nothing. The word *Gugelhupf* hovered unspoken in the air. Jim said:

'A refreshing ice cream concoction with meringue. And after that *Sachertorte* with the coffee. Your inspired *Sachertorte*.'

Grandfather: 'Marvellous, marvellous.'

Grandmother: 'Shouldn't we serve cheeses as well?'

'I think the latest deliveries from Oluf Lorentzen have been of doubtful quality,' said Grandfather.

'That's right enough,' said Jim.

'Besides,' Grandfather added, 'that might be – what would you call it? – rather too opulent.'

'Very well,' said Grandmother. 'Let's say that. Although strictly speaking there ought to be a cheese course in a classic dinner. Especially if it's to be the best we can provide.'

'I suggest a consommé,' said Jim. 'Simple. Elegant. Classic.'

They'd been sitting there discussing the menu for over an hour. Such menu planning sessions rarely lasted longer than fifteen minutes, but this time the grown-ups had run through quite an amazing number of suggestions and ideas, with an eagerness which seemed almost over the top.

'Or perhaps *Geeiste Gurkensuppe*,' said Grandmother thoughtfully. 'That's something you don't get every day...'

'Bordeaux,' said Grandfather. 'With the grouse. Definitely a good Bordeaux. And it must be decanted. That'll be your job, Sedd.'

'Yes, Grandfather. Of course.'

'Though perhaps consommé would be better.' Grandmother looked as if she was mentally tasting both alternatives.

'Then the question is,' said Grandfather: 'which others?'

For a moment I thought he was still thinking of the wine, but then he said: 'Just the bank manager and family, or should we invite some of the others as well?'

'Good question,' said Grandmother.

'So that it becomes a sort of welcome dinner for them? So that they get to meet some – how should I put it – central figures in our district.'

'Good question, *Schatzerl*. But in that case it shouldn't be too many. It can easily come to seem opulent in a different way, if you see what I mean?'

'Of course, of course. And we need to find a day. Or rather an evening. Sedd?'

'Yes, Grandfather?'

'Has this Karoline said anything about how long her parents will be staying at the hotel?'

'And her, Grandfather.'

'Pardon?'

'And her, Grandfather. She's staying too.'

'Well yes, of course, her too, of course, but has she said anything about it? That's what I'm asking.'

'No. She hasn't.'

'Right.'

'Why don't you just ask them yourself?'

'It would be practical to know in confidence, Sedd, I'm sure you can see that. This is important, you understand.'

'Yes,' I said.

'After Bjørn's passing and all that. It is important to establish a good personal relationship with the new bank manager. If only we had known about this a bit earlier.'

'Yes,' Grandmother interposed: 'why didn't you tell us about it earlier, *Büberl*?'

'I haven't known for very long,' I said. 'Besides, I had no idea it was so important. No idea at all.'

They looked at me, scandalized.

'But you must realise, Sedd,' said Grandfather, 'how important it is. A bank manager is always important.'

'I do now,' I said.

'Anyway,' – he turned to Grandmother again – 'many or just a few? Or just them? And Bordeaux?'

'Bordeaux,' said Jim.

They didn't seem to notice when I went.

24

I went up to the attic corridor in the old wing. I don't know why I did that. It was a good while since I had been there.

I walked along the corridor until I was standing outside the door to Olympus. It looked just as shut as ever. Silent and shut. Nevertheless, just for the sake of appearances, I tried the door handle. Pushed it down, pulled it towards me.

I stood there looking at it for a while, as if that would help. Idiot door, I said to myself. Then I tried the door handle once more.

This idiot door had been standing here closed for God knows how long. Perhaps it had been closed and locked for the whole of my life. Perhaps it had been standing there brooding like that ever since I was born? Perhaps Olympus contained a kind of memorial altar to my exotic, deceased doctor father? Or perhaps the room contained my mother's diaries, her collected thoughts, thousands of pages, written down from hour to hour ever since she lost her baby teeth and until the moment when she was taken by Time? Jottings which, if I could just get this confounded door open, would tell me everything, everything I wanted to know, absolutely everything I was wondering about regarding my mother, about who she was, about why she had fallen for this Indian from Bergen, as well of course as why she had let herself be taken by Time, left us all in the lurch and wasn't here any more.

Not so much as a postcard. I had occasionally overheard Grandmother making this remark to Grandfather. In Norwegian or German. *Nicht mal eine Postkarte.* She always thought I was too far away to hear, or perhaps this was just something I imagined, that it was a kind of coded signal from her to him, a brief departure from the norm of never discussing what could anyway not be altered. Not even a postcard. Although it may be that I was just imagining things, and that this remark, which was not uttered particularly often, was just a heartfelt exclamation that some guest or other that we had made a special effort for, or a bridal couple whose youthful happiness had been polished to a shine by Grandfather and Grandmother, had not even bothered to send so much as a postcard with a picture of Ålesund to say thank you.

I gave the door a kick. Well, not really a kick, more a nudge with my trainer.

Perhaps when all was said and done there was nothing behind this door, nothing of any significance, just an old-fashioned, unused hotel room with faded flowery wallpaper, a storeroom like the other rooms up here, with dusty old ornaments which no-one had gone to the bother of throwing away, boxes of old tourist brochures and cardboard boxes full of loose-leaf files of curling yellow invoices. Perhaps someone had simply lost the key. It was possible. Lost it on the way down the stairs, on the way across the yard, on the way across the grass, across the terrace, through the rooms, in a crack in the floor, behind some moulding, under a flagstone, between two plant bulbs, down a hole. And that was all it was, and nothing odd about it.

There was a sound on the stairs. Light footsteps, in shoes without high heels, but I heard it.

'Sedd?'

I didn't answer.

'Sedd? Are you there?'

The next moment Karoline's face emerged round the corner. At the corner, in the half-light.

'So this is where you are?'

'This area,' I said, 'is closed to the public.'

'Synnøve said she'd seen you go up here.'

'Because of the fire risk. This wing is closed to guests because of the fire risk.'

She came right up to me.

'Are you crying?' She looked at me wonderingly.

'No,' I said.

I turned my face towards the door again. For a while neither of us said anything. She stood quite still beside me in the dark corridor, but she didn't pester me, thank goodness; she didn't look at me either. She looked at the door. For a moment she lifted her hand as if to take hold of the door handle, but let it fall again at once.

There we stood. Then she whispered solemnly:

'What is it about that door?'

'It's just a door,' I whispered back. 'Nothing special about it.'

'Oh. I see.'

We were quiet for a little longer, standing with our faces turned to the door. 'Shall we go swimming?' I asked, but she said:

'What's in there?'

'I don't know. A lumber room. Perhaps something is stored here.'

'Oh, right. Do you often come here?'

'No.'

'No. OK.'

We were still again. For quite a while, actually. For so long that Karoline finally whispered, still solemn:

'Are we going to stand here looking at it for a long time? Is that the usual thing?'

'Usual?'

'Yes, I mean, when you come up here?'

'Yes. I mean no. I hardly ever come up here.'

'Oh, I see.' She looked as if she was weighing up my answer. Then she asked: 'Are you sure it's locked?'

'Quite sure.'

'Well,' said Karoline, 'we won't get any further, then.' She smiled. Then she took my hand. Quickly and cautiously, but nevertheless: she took it. Then she lifted our hands up to the door handle, and together we pressed it down. For a moment I thought, now this is going to be like a film, one of Walt Disney's films perhaps, who with his immortal artistic genius created impressive film stories where absolutely anything can happen, and that the door would now move, no, would *glide* open, to the accompaniment of stardust and harpstrings. But no. Of course not. It remained just as stolidly immovable.

Karoline let go of my hand. 'Would you believe it,' she said.

So we went for a swim. She was getting better with every day that passed.

In Dr Helgesen's waiting room there was a smell of soap and a multitude of medicines, all the medicines you never get from your doctor, but which smell good. My door is always open. But it wasn't, on the contrary it was closed, because right now there was an old woman in there, just as before her there had been a different old woman in there, and before her again another one – and still there were two old women in front of me in the queue in the waiting room, and a further three who had arrived after me, so that I felt almost like the black sheep in the flock; a black pearl in a whole string of mother-of-pearl-pale, suffering women without end, and I suddenly thought that the medical profession is actually perhaps not something to aspire to, if you look at it in the round. It is important to be able to look at things in the round.

I had not made an appointment or anything like that, but taken the GP at his word, that his door was always open, and he had looked at me in surprise when he popped his head out of the door to call in one of the sufferers, nodded shortly, and so here I sat.

And suddenly I wished I hadn't come. Here I sat, not sick at all, without so much as the beginnings of an early autumn head cold, and all at once I thought I'd better invent something; I could come up with some suitably dramatic symptoms, symptoms which demanded immediate attention, and thereby a visit to the doctor's, although without indicating any acute physical illness. And I tried feverishly to think of some indeterminate signs of illness; feverishly, although I didn't have a fever, it would be easy for Dr Helgesen to establish that. I cleared my throat cautiously a few times in order to check whether there was any suggestion of a sore throat, but no. A sore throat would in any case be ruled out if the doctor so much as glanced into my mouth.

Eyes. Perhaps I could say that I could see fuzzy specks in my field of vision. Specks which came and went, as it were. But then perhaps he would prescribe glasses, glasses which I had to wear all the time, and I really didn't want to do that. Stomach pains was of course a possibility, but with stomach pains you have to know what you're doing. You have to know where the various organs are located, and so forth, so that you don't by mistake happen to explain that you feel pain in an area which means that the doctor is seriously alarmed and immediately gets you up on the operating table in order to remove your appendix, for example, or even more vital organs. So I didn't dare do that. It would be good to have a father who was a doctor, and who was also alive. Then you would have grown up with the location of all the organs and their Latin designations as an everyday topic at the breakfast table. You would have swallowed your cornflakes down your *oesophagus*, your father would have explained patiently, before he got up and went out to stretch his *femora* and *tibiae*, and you would have sat there looking after him, proud, moved, brimming over with medical knowledge, and felt your filial love coursing warmly through your *vena cava superior* and *inferior*. But that's not how things were; the door opened and Dr Helgesen looked at me with a friendly expression: 'I think you can come in now, Sedd.'

He was calling me in out of turn, even though a couple of the women who were before me did not look good at all, and straight away I felt quite ill. It could be that without being aware of it in the slightest, I was displaying symptoms which to the doctor's gimlet-sharp eyes could immediately be interpreted as elements of a serious clinical condition.

'Do sit down.'

I sat down. The doctor looked at me with tired blue eyes, but then he smiled reassuringly, and I understood that this day would not be my last.

'Well, Sedd,' he said, 'how are things?'

'Things are fine. Very good, actually.'

'Yes?'

'Great. I've never felt better.'

'That's good to hear.'

'It's been a really interesting summer. Really interesting. Grandfather and I were in Oslo when the bomb went off at the railway station.'

'Goodness!'

'It was very dramatic. But we weren't hurt. We were some distance away.'

'Well, that was a good thing. Gracious me.'

'And then we had a group of high-flying German engineers as guests, and I had to be their guide on trips into the mountains. They came for the fishing.'

'I see.'

'None of them drowned.'

'Well, that's good to hear.'

'But I've done quite a bit of swimming.'

'Splendid. Splendid.'

'And taken photos. I inherited Bjørn Berge's Leica. It has been very stimulating, learning how to take photographs.'

'Yes, it must be. A Leica, that's not bad, you know. But they're not easy. I do a bit of photography myself.'

'I was lucky to get some good tips from one of the German engineers. They're good at things like that, Germans, you know. I learnt a lot.'

'And apart from that, Sedd?'

'Apart from that, things are fine.'

'I'm glad to hear that. And all is well with your Grandmother and Grandfather?'

'Really well. They're both really well. Grandfather is as frisky as a foal, he says so himself. Running around in the mountains at all hours. The soles of Grandmother's feet hurt, but it's nothing to worry about, they've always been like that.'

'Always.'

'So everything is normal, fortunately.'

'That is fortunate. But times are tough in the hotel business, I understand.'

'Times are tough. But we'll get through.'

'Let's hope so.'

'Grandfather says that after the dark times come the lighter ones, and it's been like that for the whole of Fåvnesheim's history.'

'I'm sure that's right. And are you sleeping well at night?'

'Not too well, actually. Just recently.'

Dr Helgesen pulled over a blue pad and drew a signpost at the top of the page. Then he wrote some numbers and words in the kind of writing which only chemists can read. I suppose that is part of the duty of confidentiality.

'Why,' I asked, 'did you draw a signpost?'

'A signpost?'

'Yes, at the top of the prescription?'

'Oh, that.' He smiled. 'It's not a signpost. It's a cross.'

'Interesting.'

'That's what doctors have always done. It's a tradition.'

'Very interesting tradition.'

'It means: in God's name. And after that I write Rp., and that means *recipe*, which is where the word for prescription comes from, and that means "one takes". So that is what the patient is supposed to take. In your case Phenergan, some very, very mild pills to help you sleep. One tablet half an hour before bed.'

'That is really informative, Dr Helgesen.'

'Do you think so?'

'My father was a doctor.'

Dr Helgesen looked at me:

'Yes. He was.'

'Did you know him?'
'Yes. I knew him well.'

25

There you lie, grand hotel, almost empty, like a sleeping dragon in the autumn dusk. In our grandfather's house are many rooms, but only a few are occupied and even fewer booked. There are lights from the windows on the ground floor, the lamps in the parking area outside are lit, but otherwise, from wing to wing, in all the extensions which a century has added, practically all the windows are dark rectangles in the grey mass. In one place there is a light, and in there sits the daughter of this new bank manager; I know what she is doing. She is drawing hearts. It's a habit of hers. I've already found at least one. One afternoon, after we'd been swimming, I found it under my clothes in the changing room. But one is a professional after all, one is in the hotel business, and one displays no reaction in such circumstances. One morning when we'd been playing minigolf, she simply sat down: sat down right next to me as I stood slotting the golf clubs into the golf bag, as if she were a dog, and looked up at me. She is an incredible nuisance. Nothing is too good for our guests, as Grandfather always says, but there are limits.

Somewhere inside there, in that remarkable hotel, my grandmother is starching napkins. I know that's what she's doing. She has perfected her own technique, according to a secret Austrian formula which no doubt dates from the time of Haydn or some such thing, and she is starching the finest damask napkins; they are to stand there like shining icebergs, gleaming on the service plates as the guests take their places at table.

Grandfather is polishing shoes. He polishes and rubs and polishes again until they are so shiny that you can see your face in them. Here he uses an old Norwegian formula which probably goes back to the time of Olav Tryggvason: he spits. Everyone knows that the old saga kings were masters of spitting. So they must have had extremely shiny footwear, because when you've been standing there for an hour carefully polishing the leather – first with shoecream and then with wax – you have to spit on it and rub it in, square centimetre by square centimetre, again and again, until you finally have shoes worthy of a gentleman. So there he stands. He spits and rubs, with a patient expression, his usual one, where you can't make out whether he is thoughtful or absent-minded.

In the kitchen it is light and warm, a pan of stock is simmering, a sauteuse is bubbling. Jim is juggling dressings, potatoes, root vegetables.

There are lobsters in the aquarium again. Large, black and full of life. For the time being at least. They have taken up strategic positions on the bottom of the large tank, fourteen of them in all, even though there will only be twelve guests at dinner, but Jim has had two extra delivered, for good measure, as he says, as he always says, as he usually says. But I know why. It's because neither Jim nor I feel that Fåvnesheim is a complete culinary institution without lobsters in the aquarium. So whilst twelve of them will rise up to be clad in the cardinal's red robes of death, two of them will remain in order to keep the aquarium inhabited. It's not good to have empty tanks, empty rooms, or indeed empty anything. Stamp boxes. Tills.

This evening, whilst the beams of lights from the cars on their way up pick out the landscape along the winding road like shining parallellograms, it is as if the hotel is lying there waiting. If you listen extra hard, it's as if you can hear it breathing. If you walk from room to room, from wing to wing, you can feel its breath in the air, almost like a grey film. It rests on the portraits in the Heimdal room, it billows over the green baize of the billiard table, it creeps like a tidal surge along the many long, empty corridors.

As you walk from room to room you can hear it sighing. It seeps out of the closed-off corridor on the attic floor in the old wing, it flows down the stairs and spreads out.

On evenings like this you have to go out. You have to see the hotel from a distance, from a knoll, from the nearest hummock, as it lies there coiled around itself. Then you have to turn your back. You have to look the other way, towards the mountains, where the dusk has already turned all the autumn colours grey-blue, where the low clouds are scudding across and seem to be brushing the plateau, where there is nothing.

But then you have to turn back again. Soon the first car will drive into the entrance, soon the guests will fill the rooms with laughter and well-bred conversation, soon Grandmother will light all the candles: thin, elegant candles of the finest quality from Glasmagasinet in Oslo, and light and laughter will banish the grey mist for a brief hour. Tonight – this evening – is crucial.

I have understood that now.

It is not many paces back to the hotel, but it's strangely slow going, even if it is downhill. Suddenly I feel a sense of urgency. Suddenly I get the feeling that what is coming now, this dinner with, so to speak, the same twelve people as last time – or at least the same twelve roles, just with two of the actors exchanged for new ones – is simply a repetition. That a new rescue mission is at hand. Just a much greater one than on the last occasion. And I notice that I take several deep breaths, as if to prepare myself.

The consommé had just been served, with meatballs this time, which floated like small woolly clouds in the clear shining broth.

Well-bred conversation. The mayor and his wife. The deputy mayor. Dr Helgesen and his wife. The head of tourism and his wife. Acting local authority treasurer Herr Knudsen.

And of course the guests of honour for whom all this had been arranged, the evening's social focus: the new bank manager and his wife. Karoline had been deeply offended when she was told by her parents that she was not going to eat with the grown-ups, but brightened up when it transpired that she was going to eat with me and Jim, or Jim and me to be more correct. Now she was sitting swinging her legs on one of the kitchen benches as she watched us working with intense concentration. She was as still as a mouse while she watched. The only time she uttered a sound was when Jim dexterously fished the lobsters out of the tank and dropped them headfirst into the large pot for one minute, after which he split them in two lengthwise. That she obviously thought was disgusting, and she said so too, but Jim just laughed and told her they felt nothing, and she actually looked as if she believed him.

Grandfather gave a speech of welcome. We only picked up fragments of it, either as we were clearing away or via a few words which reached us through the serving hatch, about how pleased he and Sisi were, what an honour, how good to get to know you, and so on, and then of course the district, the district's opportunities, potential, development, and from that naturally to Fåvnesheim Hotel itself, how so many distinguished gatherings and parties had been held there over the decades; after dinner he himself would have the pleasure of explaining a little more about this history, which was so long, so rich, so exciting, because we shall assemble for drinks in the Heimdal room after the meal, but let me just sketch out a few main points in advance ... .

The speech went on, but Jim was as always a master of timing. He had in addition made sure he had some room for manoeuvre by including a little scallop dish, which could be prepared in a twinkling, between the consommé and the lobster. Salad and trimmings were already prettily and symmetrically arranged on twelve plates, and the browned almonds in butter were straining at the leash on the hotplate.

The scallops needed only a few seconds on each side in the frying pan, and everything would be ready to go.

'There's bound to be more speeches you know, Sedd, that's for sure. So we need elbow room here.'

He was right. Grandfather had now finally arrived at the present day, when Fåvnesheim stood proud as the very incarnation of a modern institution, with a swimming pool which held 170,000 litres, sauna, exercise room, billiard tables and minigolf, ready to meet the future, with open eyes, optimism and willingness to adapt, but at the same time with the rich traditions of a classical kitchen which would demonstrate its skills to the full this evening, because only the best was good enough and so on, without meaning to sound immodest, ha ha, not at all, but the kitchen and its master chef were the very heart of Fåvnesheim, if not its soul, yes indeed, and now he hoped that our newly-arrived friends would be happy here, heartily welcome once more, and take us as you find us. As we say up here.

Polite applause. The head of tourism seized the chance to speak at once.

'What did I say,' said Jim, resignedly pushing the frying pan off the hotplate, resting the small of his back against a kitchen table and crossing his arms. A new monotonous hum of speech came from within. The head of tourism just wanted to agree with what my grandfather had said, and in addition to elaborate on a couple of points. Mountain and plateau, lake and waterfall, a terrain for both summer and winter, but also for spring and autumn, in brief a terrain for all seasons, and here we had plans. Big plans. And of course it was to be hoped that the bank, here represented by the new bank manager, whom everyone wished heartily welcome with his new family, would continue his good and natural engagement in this vital work – naturally in collaboration with both the mayor and the treasurer, who are sitting there and sitting there, and of course not forgetting the political leadership, which naturally must not be forgotten either, not in the slightest, and that these vital interests had meant so much to Bjørn Berge, poor Bjørn, had been close to his heart, but then as we know his heart regrettably failed. Cough. Eh. Yes, and so on and so on and heartily welcome in our midst, and so on and so on.

'Scallops!' exclaimed Jim the moment the glasses in the room clinked. And they were already in the pan and on the point of being served when someone in there tapped on a glass again, and Jim cursed. 'Bloody fucking speechifyers! Fucking arseholes!'

Karoline giggled.

Incredibly, it was Grandfather who had tapped on his glass again. It transpired that he would just like to elaborate a little on what the head of tourism had said. It was something about the future and opportunities which he had perhaps not given adequate expression to, not fully and completely, when he wished them welcome, because naturally it was vital for the hotel as well, as the ancient and venerable institution it was in the community, indeed in the whole district, and with its venerable history, which he would have the pleasure of explaining more fully after the meal, as already mentioned, to have a good relationship with the bank, whose engagement in Fåvnesheim throughout its history had constituted a central pillar, not to say a wall of the whole enterprise, ha ha, and in which Bjørn Berge's help and continually renewed interest, and help, had been of invaluable help.

The scallops had long since gone cold, and went in the bin. With the patience of an angel, though not exactly the language of an angel, Jim prepared twelve new scallops. And when the somewhat scattered applause had died down in there, he cast a critical glance through the serving hatch.

'Psst, Sedd,' he said, half turning to me: 'D'you think there'll be any more now? Or are they done babblin'?'

'I've no idea, Jim.'

He peered out at the gathering like a sea captain, a pilot, searching for signs of reefs and shallows ahead.

'Go fetch your grandmother.'

It wasn't a question, it was an order.

I went. Whispered. I hardly had to say two words in Grandmother's ear before she stood up, excused herself and came out to the kitchen with me.

She looked completely desperate.

'Excuse me, Fru Zacchariassen,' said Jim, 'but are any more of them going to say something now, or what?'

'I don't know. I don't think so.'

'Because I've only got these twelve scallops left,' said Jim, pointing critically at the pale shellfish lying ready on a plate.

'I don't think so, Jim. I really hope not.' She had her hands clasped in front of her. Then she raised them to her face and turned to me: 'Ach, Sedd, how *could* he? It was so frightful. *Es ist alles nur so schrecklich!*'

For a moment I thought she was going to cry. But then she pulled herself together, smoothed out her face, straightened her pearl necklace and rejoined the social group.

The sound of well-bred conversation intensified in there, I went round and refilled the glasses, and when I got back, Jim looked at me decisively:

'Right, we'll go with the scallops,' he decreed.

The moment the butter had begun to settle in the pan the scallops were added. First they browned nicely on one side, then on the other, and they were ready, perfect, delectable, and just warmed through sufficiently as not to be chewy, when someone tapped on a glass in there once more.

It was the mayor. Jim's face was white. So was Karoline's, but that was mostly because she was shocked to see someone get so angry. I don't believe that anyone in the West End of Oslo gets so angry as they do in a restaurant kitchen. So in many ways this was very educational for her. Altogether, I pondered in order to avoid listening to everything Jim was now saying, Karoline had learnt a lot during her weeks up here. A great deal. To play minigolf. To fish. To swim. And to be rescued.

I interrupted the stream of colourful words and expressions which were pouring out of Jim:

'They'll have to have them cold, Jim.'

'Fucking eejits!'

Karoline giggled.

'We'll squeeze some lemon over them, Jim,' I comforted him. 'And they'll have the hot butter on them.'

'They'll be chewy,' Jim said darkly.

'I know.'

'They *shouldn't* be chewy! That's not how they should be.'

'No.'

And therefore, the mayor concluded, he too, and his wife, of course, would like to bid the new bank manager heartily welcome to the community, a community for all seasons, which had so incredibly, incredibly, incredibly much to offer, in all seasons, as they would now certainly discover, now they had arrived here, with us, amongst us, in our midst, and once again let me bid you heartily welcome amongst us, and thank you for listening.

They got the scallops chewy.

Whilst they were chewing, Jim embarked on the final stages of Lobster Thermidor.

In reality it is not a difficult dish. But it demands attention and timing. The lightly-cooked lobsters lay already split in half, spread out like butterflies, with the lobster flesh in the shells. All that remained was to pour sauce into them, scatter cheese over and cook them *au gratin* for three minutes. With his usual precision Jim poured the sauce, whilst I scattered cheese, lobster by lobster. Into the oven. Jim stood there like a concerned stoker, watching as they slowly began to bubble. Karoline started to ask about something, but Jim just hushed her, with a dark expression and without taking his eyes from the contents of the oven.

The second they were ready the tray came out quickly. Jim deftly flipped the lobsters over onto the plates, where the trimmings were already arranged, without one single split lobster falling apart; they still hung together like butterfly wings. After that: finely chopped chives, another soupçon of sauce, and then they were borne in. This time Jim insisted on serving them himself, whilst I poured the wine.

As was only proper, he served Karoline's mother first. From the other side of the table, where I was pouring wine for the mayor, I could see her looking up at Jim and shaking her head regretfully, smiling, and Jim himself made a grimace which was supposed to represent an apologetic expression; he lifted the plate of Lobster Thermidor, his masterpiece, up again from the service plate in front of her, and put it down in front of the next person instead.

The back of his neck was red as he disappeared into the kitchen to fetch some more. I followed.

As soon as I had got through the kitchen door, he snarled:

'Sedd, for Christ's sake, she doesn't eat crustaceans. They make her ill! Bloody hell! Get out there with the rest now, quick, whilst I throw together a salad with a poached egg for the lady!'

Off I went. Behind me, Jim, grim-faced: 'Damnation, damnation, damnation!'

When they'd all been served, we stood there in the kitchen looking at the lonely, uneaten lobster.

'Why didn't you say,' I asked Karoline, 'that your mother can't eat lobster? I asked you if there was anything they didn't eat?'

She looked at me unhappily:

'I didn't know. I really didn't know. We never have lobster!'

'Well, there's a reason for that, isn't there,' Jim muttered. 'Oh well. Oh well. It happens,' he said with as much self-control as he could muster. But I could see he was seething.

More speeches. More of the same. The deputy mayor this time. Jim had anticipated this, had the fillet of reindeer under control. They were already grilled and lay resting in the warming cupboard. The sauce was in a pan, fine and glossy, and had only to be combined with a little cold butter in order to be smooth and gleaming, and the cantarelles just needed a quick toss in the frying pan. The rösti potatoes were on the hotplates, everything under control.

'Now I hope you're not going to tell me your mother doesn't eat mushrooms either,' said Jim darkly to Karoline.

'She eats mushrooms,' Karoline informed him. 'Oh yes. I'm almost certain.'

The speech was nearing its close, more of the same: progress, future, growth and development.

Everyone clapped, and when the buzz of conversation out there began to rise, we set about serving.

Carefully, with a finely sharpened knife, Jim sliced the fillet, whilst I whipped butter into the hot but not boiling sauce. Then he poured a neat mirror of sauce onto six of the twelve hot plates, arranged the pieces of meat attractively on top of it, added the rösti, together with the mushrooms, which were just cooked, and finished off with fresh chervil and a perfect half-sphere of rowan jelly.

As soon as those six plates were ready, he nodded to me: 'Pour the wine. I'll finish the rest.'

When I came back after pouring the red wine, all twelve plates were ready to go, and Jim nodded, 'Service!'

I picked up two plates with either end of a cloth, lifted them up from the table, and at that moment the electricity went.

For a moment nothing happened, everything was pitch black, and then I put the plates down again with two bangs and pulled my hands away. Jim's voice in the darkness:

'Stand still, completely still. Don't move. Not so much as a millimetre! Wait here; I'll fetch a light.'

I heard him going out of the kitchen door in the direction of the stores, bumping into things and cursing under his breath. Not so much as a millimetre, he had said, otherwise I'll cut off your noses a slice at a time. At the same time I heard voices out there rising and falling in surprised tones, and then Grandmother was standing in the doorway, holding up one of the expensive candles from Glasmagasinet.

'What's happening?' she asked.

'The power went,' I said.

'Yes, thank you, Sedd, so much I had understood.'

'The food's ready,' I said, 'and Jim's fetching lights.'

In the glow of the candle I could see her putting on a brave smile: 'Well then, it'll be dinner by candlelight. I'll ask Grandfather to go to the switchboard room and see if it's the fuses.'

Then she disappeared again, taking with her the light and her smile.

It seemed even darker now. I stood completely still. Then I felt Karoline's hand clasping mine.

All she whispered was: 'Sedd.'

I didn't answer. She said no more. Just came closer, with her whole self. Breathed.

But then Jim was there with lights, and Karoline was standing where she had always stood, and Jim swore terribly, and everything was as before – apart from the lack of light, of course.

Somehow or other we managed to balance the plates, with food which was now half cold, out to the company. Grandfather had left the table, but Jim put a plate in his place anyway.

'Bloody hell,' said Jim when we'd finished serving.

'What do we do now, Jim?' I asked.

'One thing's for sure,' muttered Jim, 'if Zacchariassen doesn't find anything wrong with the fuses, but there's a problem with the cable, then the crème brulée won't be caramelised.'

'No,' I whispered. We could hear Grandfather coming back to the company.

'I must apologise,' he said, 'I really must apologise. This is most lamentable.'

The guests tried to reassure him, but he continued:

'There must be something wrong with the electricity supply. The fuses were fine. I am so sorry. Let's hope that it isn't long before the power returns, but you never know.'

The others said that it didn't matter at all, that the food and wine were excellent, and the deputy mayor made a little speech whilst they were eating about the urgency of developing the infrastructure.

The power did not return. They were served the crème brulée without a sugar crust, but with a sprinkling of grated chocolate, improvised by Jim and rechristened Crème Fåvnesheim, and it was quite a success.

But it was obvious that they couldn't have coffee, and the planned drinks in the Heimdal room with accompanying historical lecture came to nothing. Instead they were all forced to go home early. Jim conducted Karoline and her parents up to their rooms, equipped with a packet of candles, a torch and matches, whilst Grandmother, Grandfather and I escorted the guests out to their waiting cars, under a shower of excuses on my grandparents' parts. The guests protested, like good guests should, that everything was fine and such things can happen to the best of us.

I accompanied Dr Helgesen and his wife to their car.

He stood still for a moment, peering out at the road.

'Odd,' he said, 'that's very odd.'

'What is?' I said.

'There's a light,' he said, nodding slightly at the two street lights which the council had installed just here, by the turn-off to the hotel.

'Yes, it is odd,' I agreed. 'That must mean that the power failure is local.'

'Yes, it must be local,' said Dr Helgesen, got into his car and drove off.

26

It is important to act. That's actually my motto. Only if you act do you become a man of action. That's what Grandfather has always said too.

Grandfather acted. He remained sitting in the living room in our private quarters until far into the night, thinking about the situation, together with a lighted candle and a bottle of Dubonnet. Grandmother, who was distraught after all the catastrophes during the dinner, merely looked indignantly at him before she went to bed. I don't believe that she understood what I understood instinctively, which is that a man of action needs to think before he acts. And once he has thought, he can fall asleep in his chair with his mind at ease.

But as soon as dawn arrived Grandfather was on his feet; he washed and groomed himself and got dressed, as immaculately as ever. After that he got into his Vauxhall and drove down to the village. In the meantime we had a cold breakfast. Jim was crabby because he didn't get his coffee, and when I went into the dining room to see whether Karoline and her parents needed anything, they had already left the table and driven down to the village as well.

In good time before lunch Grandfather returned, smiling, and said that he had been along to complain to the electricity company. They had taken his complaint very seriously, and were going to send a fitter up immediately. He would be here at any moment.

And sure enough, in less than an hour the green van arrived, parked out on the road and out got a stout man in overalls. He strolled down to the hotel, without having the time to so much as say hello, but plodded resolutely over to the door to the switchboard room, which was at the short end of the west wing, in the cellar. He unlocked the door and let himself in, staying inside for a couple of minutes before he came out again, locked the door behind him, plodded just as resolutely back to the green van, and drove off. Then Jim got his coffee and everything was as before.

That just shows that decisive action is necessary if you want quick results.

Electricity is a very practical thing. Everyone who has had to manage without knows that. Since Edison invented electricity, the world has become a different place. But it has also become much more vulnerable. It only takes a couple of crossed wires, a short circuit, a defective fuse or a tiny failure of the switchboard, and immediately civilisation is threatened. It is a thought-provoking thought. At any time, indeed at any moment of the day, all the modern blessings we are accustomed to regarding as a matter of course can be taken from us: no coffee, no TV, no radio and no light. You can't get very far on batteries. In such a harsh climate as in Norway, where nature is particularly brutal, we are especially exposed to potential breakdowns of civilisation. Particularly when the weather is bad, of course, but in principle even on a perfectly ordinary Thursday evening in the middle of August, whilst the leading citizens of a dynamic and forward-looking community are sitting at table about to enjoy a delicious gourmet meal – suddenly the electricity goes, and they are surrounded on all sides by the elements, high up in the mountains. For the moment they are protected by the walls and the accumulated warmth, but quite soon it will be ice-cold in the rooms, and the breakdown will be a fact. From there it is a short distance to freezing to death and cannibalism. There are historical examples of this. So it's a good thing Grandfather was a man of action.

The following Monday Karoline's father was to take over his new post officially, and at the same time their house would be ready for them to move in. So on the Sunday I took

Karoline out for a farewell hike in the mountains. There was radiant sunshine and glorious autumn colours, but the hike was odd. Karoline, who normally babbled like a waterfall, or at least like a rippling stream, was almost completely silent. I had to drag words out of her. I even tried singing 'Mannen og kråka', but she just looked at me as if I was doing something abnormally stupid, so I stopped after the first verse.

I picked out a small hummock and decided to declare we were halfway. We sat down and got out our sandwiches.

Karoline chewed without saying anything. She wouldn't meet my eyes either.

'You're starting school on Wednesday,' I said experimentally. 'Are you excited?'

'No. A bit.'

'It'll be fun to make some new friends, won't it?'

'Perhaps.'

'Friends of your own age?'

She didn't answer. Just looked away.

'It's always exciting to make new friends,' I insisted. No reaction. So I didn't say anything more either. She ate her food quickly and drank up her mug of juice as if we were in a hurry. Screwed up the greaseproof paper, put it in the sandwich box, thrust the box into her rucksack and stood up.

'Come on,' she said, 'let's go home.'

Obediently I got up and followed her. She set off at a smart pace back towards Fåvnesheim.

We separated in reception. 'Thanks for coming with me, Karoline,' I said. 'Thank you,' she said without turning round, and vanished in the direction of her room.

I could hear voices from the Heimdal room. It was Grandfather and Karoline's father. They looked up as I came in, Grandfather with a strange crooked smile, whilst Karoline's father looked at me seriously, perhaps slightly irritated.

'Am I interrupting?'

'A little bit, perhaps,' said Grandfather. 'I was telling the bank manager here about the history of this place, since I had no chance to do so when it got so dark on the evening of our dinner.'

'Yes, he was,' Karoline's father agreed.

'And then I've brought him up to date, you know, the ongoing situation, and so forth.'

Karoline's father took a sip from his coffee cup.

'We have brilliant prospects coming up,' said Grandfather, 'isn't that right, Sedd?'

'Yes, Grandfather,' I said.

'Lots of autumn weddings, and the autumn holidays are looking good.'

'Oh yes,' I said. 'There will be loads to do. But I don't want to disturb you.'

'That's OK, Sedd. Quite OK. I thought you'd gone for a walk with Karoline?'

'I did, Grandfather. But we didn't go so far today.'

'I say, Sedd,' said Karoline's father, 'I'd just like to say how kind and considerate you've been with Karoline. We have really appreciated it, we'd like you to know that. Her mother and I have been so busy with our new house and everything else.'

'Oh,' I said lightly, 'don't mention it. It was a pleasure. Nothing is too much for our guests. That's our motto, you know.'

'Yes, that's our motto,' Grandfather agreed.

Karoline's father smiled suddenly.

'Well, well,' he said, 'that's excellent.'

'Shall I bring more coffee?' I asked.

'No, Sedd,' said Grandfather. 'That's not necessary. Thank you anyway.'

'You're welcome,' I said.

'Thank you, Sedd. Thanks again, son.'

In the kitchen I found Grandmother and Jim. They looked sombre.

'Has someone died, Jim?' I asked.

'Oh no,' said Jim. 'No, no. Don't worry. Everything's OK. But these are difficult times, aren't they, Fru Zacchariassen?'

'*Ach, ja*. They are. They are. We – yes, you are old enough to understand this now, Sedd – we are worried that we may have to make some cuts in the number of staff.'

'There aren't many left anyway,' I said without thinking.

'True enough, Sedd; there aren't many. So it's possible we'll have to hire fewer people when we need extra help. And we'll have to do more ourselves anyway. *Verstehst du*?'

'Yes, Grandmother, that's all right.'

'Oh, you are *ein braver Bub*. That's what I've always said.'

'There'll be quite a lot more to do, you know, Sedd,' said Jim. 'Are you up for that? We lads will have to clean the corridors as well now.'

'That's all right,' I said.

'That's just what I said, Fru Zacchariassen, a grown-up lad isn't afraid of mops and buckets.'

'That's quite all right,' I said, swallowing. 'So long as *you* don't have to leave, anyway.'

'Oh no,' said Jim, laughing, '*I'm* not leaving, you know. That's not going to happen.'

'But Synnøve will have to cut her hours a little.' Grandmother looked at Jim, worried. 'Do you think she'll agree to that, Jim? I'll have to take on a few more hours in reception myself instead.'

'I'm sure she'll understand, Fru Zacchariassen. Synnøve has been here so long.'

'That's just it,' said Grandmother.

'Needs must,' said Jim.

'Just so long as there isn't a strike at the off-licences,' Grandmother added worriedly.

'Oh no,' Jim asserted. 'There won't be. And if there is, we'll have to lay in a stock. Buy everything we need in good time. We'll manage fine.'

'Yes,' sighed Grandmother, 'I'm sure we will. I'm worrying too much.'

'Perhaps you ought to do some baking, Grandmother?' I suggested. 'That normally takes your mind off things?'

'*Ach, nein, Buberl*. I don't think I can do that. I don't think I can do that now.'

She shrugged her shoulders in resignation.

'I've got masses of flour and eggs, Fru Zacchariassen,' said Jim comfortingly. 'Masses of flour and eggs.'

'Bjørn, our dear Bjørn, God rest his soul, he would never have let this happen,' said Grandmother despondently. 'Never.'

'No, Grandmother,' I chimed in. 'He was so fond of cake. After all, it was his –'

They looked at me, horrified.

'… I mean, Bjørn Berge was a real gentleman.'

'Yes, he was,' Grandmother agreed. 'Ach, Jim, I'm afraid. I'm afraid that this new one is not a real gentleman.'

27

And suddenly they had left, Karoline and her parents, checked out, gone away, and the summer was over. She didn't even say goodbye. They were just gone, she was gone, like a tuft of cotton grass blown away to God knows where, although I knew where they were going. To the bank manager's house, the yellow house which had become a green one, and in which the kitchen and bathroom and everything else had no doubt been renovated at great expense, in order to be worthy of a new and modern bank manager.

When school began I did see her again, but she hardly said hello. Just hurried past me in one of the corridors, with new red jeans on her thin legs and a fashionable denim jacket with little patches of fur, as well as a smart new leather satchel. She was together with two other girls with the same thin legs and arms, and I said hi, in the normal way, and she said hi back, I'll give her that, but you could hardly hear it.

It didn't really matter, to be honest, now that our commercial relationship had ceased, and I was released from her pushiness every hour of the day; after all, I wasn't some kind of playschool organiser whose job it was to dream up leisure activities, so that wasn't a problem, but I do think she might have behaved a bit better, when all's said and done. But it's impossible to be friends with someone as young as that, everyone knows that. Everyone knows that youth is a resource which is wasted on the young, as Grandfather always said. Young people simply don't understand how fortunate they are, much less what is good for them.

After that the wedding season began again, and pretty quickly too, with two weddings on the last two weekends in August. And as there were fewer of us, our areas of responsibility expanded. And by responsibility I mean, of course, tasks. If one of my tasks had been to entertain Karoline as well, in the midst of all the wedding preparations, I wouldn't have had time for anything else, and certainly not for homework. Not to mention photography, which had faded into the background as Karoline's leisure activities had occupied the foreground. Besides, my extra earnings for the summer had not been adequate recompense for my efforts, not even with Karoline's contribution for all the games of golf, so my plans for a darkroom were still shrouded in darkness, so to speak.

Amongst my many new duties was to help Jim with transporting provisions. Up to now he had had the assistance of Ivar, who helped at the hotel from time to time, but now Grandfather had decided to cut Ivar. I can well understand that. Ivar was a good enough fellow, but it is absolutely unbelievable how much a labourer has to be paid nowadays for doing the simplest things with his labour. Shifting crates of bottles for example. Of course it's heavy work, it certainly is that, but there's no way it's worth such large sums as Ivar required for what is after all an extremely primitive form of work, so I think Grandfather was quite correct in his reasoning. It wasn't too difficult for me to manage well enough; I worked that out when Jim and I went down to the off-licence a few days before the first wedding to pick up the drinks that had been ordered. The boxes were already neatly stacked in the store-room, and Skarpjordet, the storekeeper, was ready with the invoice. He smiled broadly at Jim, said hello to me and goodness how I had shot up and all that, and, ha ha, that I was still too young to drink what I was carrying.

Jim was always nervous in the proximity of so many bottles, I knew that, but he concealed it well and just winked at Skarpjordet and said he would count them carefully when we got back to Fåvnesheim again, so I'd better not try it.

'Ha ha,' I said.

'By the way,' said Skarpjordet as we started moving the boxes, 'ask your grandfather, I mean Herr Zacchariassen, to think about putting in a new order straight away. I mean, if he needs any supplies, and I suppose he will, for more weddings later this autumn and all that.'

Jim, who was keen to demonstrate that he had a higher rank than me, since I was just a porter in this situation, after all, said:

'You don't think this strike will come to anything, do you, Skarpjordet?'

'God knows,' said the storekeeper. 'God knows. Things look pretty deadlocked, it said on the news this afternoon. You see,' he explained as he glanced over at me, 'I have my travel radio on in the office now and then. Not in the shop, of course.'

'Do you think it'll go on for long, then? I mean, if there is a strike?'

Jim looked at him in disbelief, but Skarpjordet just shrugged:

'Don't ask me. Don't ask me. No-one understands what they're thinking down there in Oslo.'

'You just can't do that,' said Jim, 'stopping a whole country from drinking.'

There was pent-up anger in his voice.

'You might well say that,' said Skarpjordet. 'This is bloody well worse than the Soviet Union.'

'Yep, just like the Soviet Union,' agreed Jim.

'But you're right, Jim. They can't stop a whole country getting hold of something to drink. It's nothing short of prohibition.'

'Yep, nothing short of prohibition,' said Jim gloomily.

'So if there's a strike,' said Skarpjordet, 'I can't believe that Prime Minister Willoch will put up with it. Willoch is a man of action.'

'I heard,' I began, 'that Willoch is teetotal... .'

They looked at me in horror.

'Willoch?'

'Teetotal? But he's a Conservative!'

'Well,' I began uncertainly, 'perhaps it's more that he only drinks in moderation, when I come to think about it.'

'Oh, in moderation, well, that's a different kettle of fish, son!' Skarpjordet looked relieved and added: 'It's bound to go to arbitration, that's what'll happen.'

'Yes, they'll have to do that, that's for sure,' Jim nodded.

'But just to be on the safe side,' Skarpjordet went on, 'because it might take some time. If there is any strike after all this. It can always take some time, can't it, before they agree to arbitration, so that they feel they've made their point by striking, if you like. So I think ...'

'I'll let Zacchariassen know,' said Jim decisively. 'It would be smart to be on the safe side, of course.'

'Good, good. That's right. And by the way, while you're talking to him, Jim ...' Skarpjordet shuffled his papers: 'Can you remind him about this?'

He handed Jim a piece of paper. Jim studied it and frowned.

'And this,' said Skarpjordet in a low voice. 'And this.'

Jim cleared his throat and glanced at the papers. Then he pushed them into his inside pocket.

'Of course, Skarpjordet. Of course I'll do that.'

'Good, Jim. Thanks for that. OK, boys, let's get the stuff moved!'

On the way home I asked Jim if we could stop by Titlestad's photo shop. I had a couple of rolls of film with me which needed developing, and I needed some new ones.

In Titlestad's photo shop everything was as it always was. Cameras, lenses and other equipment glinted in the glass-fronted cupboards, on the walls hung examples of representative family pictures in representative family frames, and behind the counter stood Titlestad, large and weighty, looming up in the vinegary-smelling gloom of the shop. Given that he was a man who dealt in light and dark, Titlestad had definitely chosen to imbue his shop most strongly with the latter element. Only when you wanted to look at prints did he switch on the Luxo lamp over the counter. It suddenly struck me how strange it was to find a photo shop in semi-darkness – but on the other hand: you shouldn't judge. Perhaps Titlestad had one of those rare illnesses which made him shun the light. Or perhaps he simply didn't want to be exposed. You shouldn't judge, as I said, so I started brightly: 'Good afternoon, Titlestad! Nice weather today!'

Titlestad just looked at me sourly.

'I'd like to have these two films developed,' I said, putting them on the counter. 'And then I'd like two rolls of Kodacolour 100 ASA, 24 exposures.'

Titlestad stood behind his counter, completely immovable. He made no move to pick up the films or get out any new ones. Instead he just looked even sourer, staring at me without blinking, and I thought for a moment that it really couldn't be altogether good for your health to stand here in the smell of chemicals all day. Perhaps you went kind of sour inside if you just stood like that for enough years.

I said no more, just looked enquiringly at him. He stared back, still without blinking, like the eye of a camera during a long exposure, completely motionless.

A fat, lazily-buzzing autumn fly circled one of the vitrines in vaguely elliptical orbits. Otherwise all was unmoving, as if the moment was frozen and time stood still. Titlestad stood there like some kind of monument, but with less life.

He stared. I stared.

In the end he actually did move, he placed his hands on the counter and shook his head.

'Sorry,' he said heavily. 'Sorry. Can't do.'

'Can't do?' I said. 'Is there something wrong with the developer?'

'Listen,' he said. 'I can't put any more film-developing on the slate. And I can't provide any more films on the slate either.'

'Oh,' I said, 'has the business changed its sales policy? That's not a problem. I can pay in cash.'

I pulled out my wallet and counted out an appreciable number of the ten-kroner notes Karoline had provided me with during the summer. Put them on the counter.

He took the money. 'Thank you,' he said. But he gave no sign of accepting my films or getting out any new ones.

'Yes?' I said. Glanced at the two films between us. Glanced up at him again.

'And then there's the rest.'

'The rest?'

'Yes, the rest.'

'But I've just given you three hundred and sixty kroner. That should be enough for both the developing and the films.'

'That's only a fraction of what you owe,' said Titlestad, just as sourly.

'Owe?' I exclaimed with what I would call a suitably quivering but temporarily controlled indignation. 'I don't owe anything! I get things here, I mean, I'm a customer here on my grandfather's account.'

'Yes, you say that. You say that.'

'Say that? It's actually a fact. You only need to ask Grandfather. Herr Zacchariassen the hotel manager.'

'Herr Zacchariassen, yes. Herr Zacchariassen is a difficult man to get hold of. So you'll have to find a different photographer's for your purchases. I'm not going to be a part of this any longer, at least not until you've told your grandfather that you get things here on credit and persuade him to settle up. Understood?'

'Understood? But this must be a misunderstanding. My grandfather has an account here.'

'Not any more.'

'In that case I'd like my money back,' I said. 'Then I can go to a different photo shop with them. When I make a trip to Oslo, for example.'

'Your money? I rather think it's my money.'

I stood there looking at him. At times it happens that words fail even the most accomplished speaker, even if the person in question got a distinction in spoken Norwegian.

I simply didn't know what to say. I felt that at this juncture I ought to say something incisive, something crushing, but instead I could only manage a pitiful: 'But I need that money.'

'So do I,' said Titlestad, turning his back. The audience was clearly over. For a few moments longer I remained standing there, fumbling inside myself for something to say, but the photographer's broad back did not invite any further exchange of views.

So I went. I scooped up the films on the counter and went. Outside the autumn light was sharp. Jim was standing by the van, smoking.

'That took long enough,' he said, dropping his fag-end.

'Yes,' I said.

'Anything wrong?' said Jim.

'No,' I said.

'Did you get what you wanted?'

'No,' I said. 'He wouldn't give me the films. Even though I paid for them out of my own pocket. Three hundred and sixty kroner.' Jim looked at me thoughtfully.

'Three hundred and sixty kroner,' he said. 'You gave him three hundred and sixty kroner? And he wouldn't give you any films?'

I shook my head. Jim scratched his ear, mulling it over. 'Hm,' he said. 'That won't do.'

There was a dangerous gleam in his eye as he looked over at the door to the shop.

'Come on, Jim,' I said. 'Let's go.'

'Hm,' said Jim, looking over at the shop once more.

'It was just a misunderstanding, Jim,' I said. 'I don't think he believed that Grandfather had given me permission to –'

'Get in the van and wait, Sedd.'

I got in the van whilst Jim went into the shop with resolute tread. Even through the car window I could hear him slamming the door.

Then nothing happened for a long time. Until the door crashed open again and Jim reappeared, red-faced and with his hair standing on end, as he marched equally resolutely back to the van. He got in and shut the door hard.

'Here,' he said, passing me a paper bag. 'Here are your films.'

He turned the key in the ignition, and we drove off. In the bag were six rolls of Kodacolour 100 ASA, ready for use.

28

According to Grandfather, strikes at the off-licences were something the riff-raff in the country dreamt up in order to ruin us honest business people in particular, and otherwise to torment the population in general. We had enough drinks for the first wedding of the season, thank goodness, so things weren't desperate yet. 'But it's too bad,' said Grandfather, as he and Grandmother sat in their private living room discussing the coming weekend's wedding, 'that a small band of rabble-rousers who've all got secure jobs are able to hold a gun to the heads of all those who are really trying to create something in this country.'

Grandmother nodded.

'Those of us who create employment,' said Grandfather. 'Someone has to create it. It doesn't create itself. Just the opposite. But there's no-one who thinks about that. Someone has to create employment and opportunities, growth and future prospects, yes. But there's no-one who thinks about those of us who are creating future prospects, least of all those who have secure government jobs to go to down there in Hasle.'

'*Nein, Schatz.*'

'Besides, it's utter nonsense having state-owned off-licences. What's the point of that? I mean, what are we doing with such a hopeless arrangement? It's only because we've copied the Swedes, which is just typical – and no doubt the Swedes got the idea from the Soviet Union.'

'I don't think they have state-owned stores in –'

'Well, from some other Communist dictatorship, then! In a free land a free man can buy free whisky over a free counter, when he wants and where he wants, without it being anyone else's business!'

'*Ja, Schatz.*'

'Fortunately we've finally got a decent government. So it won't take long for them to put the riff-raff in place.'

'But, *Liebling*, perhaps just to make sure we ought to –'

'They'll get a week at the most, I'll lay odds on that, and then Willoch will sort them out.'

'Yes, but in any case, you never know, don't you think?'

'In China! They have state-owned off-licences there. In China a free man can't just walk into a shop and buy rice wine, can he, because there are no free men in China! That's how these chickens want things to be, just like in China.'

'*Ja, Schatzerl*, I'm sure that's true, but can't you, since you're a free man, just ring Skarpjordet and order some alcohol so that we have enough for the next two wedding weekends as well?'

'It won't be necessary, Sisi. I guarantee it. Just wait and see what happens when Willoch gets his trousers on.'

'It's possible that he will want to press them first, *Liebling.*'

'Press them? Of course he'll press them! Crush them, that's what he'll do! Riff-raff strikers like that deserve no better!'

'It was the trousers I was thinking of, dear.'

'Trousers? What trousers?'

'Willoch's trousers. He's always so nicely dressed.'

'What on earth have the Prime Minister's trousers got to do with this?' Grandfather looked at her in astonishment.

'I just mean, *Schatzerl,* that it is possible, because you never know, you really never know, that it will take a little longer for Willoch to sort them out than you, a free man, might believe, so in that case, *bitte, sei nun mal endlich vernünftig* and order drinks from Skarpjordet for the next two wedding weekends before his stock runs out! *Bitte!*'

Grandfather looked at her, crestfallen.

I said: 'Our teacher Herr Dahl said that the state alcohol system is a relic from the time of prohibition, which we shared with the USA.'

'It's good that you learn about such things,' said Grandfather. 'All right. I'll do that, Sisi, of course.'

'Good. Because you don't want to risk us running out of drinks later in the autumn?'

'No,' admitted Grandfather, 'but just you wait. Mark my words. As soon as Willoch …'

'Besides,' Grandmother interrupted, 'we can get them on sale or return. We ought to buy enough for three months.'

'But there'll be so much to carry,' Grandfather began.

'*Quatsch*! Sedd and Jim can make several trips. The most important thing is that we have enough to get by.'

'Yes,' said Grandfather, 'you're right of course, Sisi. I'll sort it out tomorrow.'

'Why not today? It's only just after three.'

'It's Wednesday, and on Wednesdays Skarpjordet leaves the office early. But I'll ring him tomorrow morning, as soon as it's open, that miserable prohibition store.'

The next day was Thursday, reasonably enough, since the day before had been a Wednesday, when Skarpjordet, the storekeeper, normally went home early. Unfortunately, Grandfather informed us when Grandmother enquired, Skarpjordet was not at work that day either, but had left for a meeting in Oslo which would update storekeepers on the progress of the strike negotiations.

'Well, just leave an order with the staff,' said Grandmother, 'that's no problem, surely.'

'Oh, but it is,' said Grandfather, 'they're useless. They just mess things up. Hopeless. Government employees, you know. Can't you remember that time we got Dubonnet instead of Cinzano? Or when we suddenly found ourselves with two boxes of white burgundy instead of one white and one red? Oh no, as manager of the hotel I prefer to conduct business directly with Skarpjordet himself.'

'Yes, but, *ausnahmsweise*, because the situation is extraordinary. They said on the news at 12 today that the shelves of the alcohol stores in the larger towns are already being –'

'Skarpjordet will be back at nine o'clock in the morning, Sisi, we have plenty of time. I'm quite certain.'

The next day was Friday, of course, since the day before had been a Thursday, something which had been determined by it following on from a Wednesday, and Grandmother was insistent, but now it had suddenly become urgent to get things ready for the wedding, the filter in the swimming pool needed changing, and Grandfather just replied irritatedly to Grandmother that he really didn't have time right now. There was a great deal to do to get the premises in tip-top condition for the autumn, and suddenly, and obviously enough, since that day had been a Friday, it was Saturday. As is known, alcohol stores do open on Saturdays, at least for a few minutes, but to start with their managers are not present on Saturdays, as Grandfather explained, and secondly the hotel was already in the process of filling up with festive wedding guests, from near and far, expectant, hungry and thirsty. They ate and drank all weekend, at length and with a good appetite, early and late. And then it was Monday.

29

The day the first fog of autumn arrived I was going to go home with Hans. Not for anything special, we were just going to do what we always did, look at stamps and that kind of thing. But as we arrived at their house, his father popped up from the foggy shroud, like a troll-in-the-box, large and built like a quarryman. I had always thought that Hans's father was a bit scary, so I jumped. Hans jumped too, although he ought to be used to him, after all. The thing was that Hans couldn't invite anyone home that day, and what was he thinking of? Did he never stop to think what he was doing? Could he never remember anything? Hans looked guiltily at the troll, but still didn't look as if he remembered anything at all; then I could see a light go on in his head as he was reminded in no uncertain terms that today was the day they were going to visit Aunt Ninne, and he had known that for several weeks; they had reminded him about it yesterday and the day before and the day before that again, and most recently they had reminded him today at the breakfast table: Hans, they had said, you mustn't forget that we're going to see Aunt Ninne, they had said, straight after school, just remember that, son, and don't forget, but what did Hans do? 'I'm sorry about this, Sedd, it's very unfortunate, but Hans can't have a friend round after school today, you see, because Hans is coming with us to visit Aunt Ninne, you understand, and he's known about it for a long time, and perhaps you'd like to come into the house and ring up Fåvnesheim, so they can come down and pick you up; I haven't the time to drive you all the way up there before we go to Aunt Ninne's because we have to go right now. But you can wait in here until you're picked up, that's the least we can do, since Hans remembers nothing and when are you going to learn, Hans?'

I went in to make the call, while Hans remained outside to receive further admonitions about his dreadful memory. Inside, Hans's mother and sister were ready to leave, off to see Aunt Ninne, and I explained the situation. 'That Hans, I don't know, he never remembers anything,' that Hans's mother sighed, and she got out a bottle of pop and a bag of crisps, so that I would have something to keep me going whilst I waited for my lift. 'Hans is completely hopeless,' his big sister groaned.

'The telephone's over there, you can watch TV if you like, just remember to make sure the door's properly shut when you leave, and we're really sorry about this, Sedd,' said his mother in a cloud of sudden concern, patted me on the cheek and vanished out into the pea-souper, where her husband was still reading the riot act about chronic memory loss.

Straight after that I heard them driving off. I went over to the phone and dialled the number home. It rang once, then you could just hear the three pips which meant there was a fault on the line. I got the dialling tone again and tried the telephone number for reception. Same result. I tried both numbers twice more, then I gave up. The line was down or something. Norway is a proud but weather-beaten land, that much is sure. The agreement was that Jim was going to pick me up in three hours, at six o'clock, so I had plenty of time to kill.

I sat down in front of the television with my pop and crisps, in the large leather armchair where Hans's father normally sat. On TV they were just showing the end of an afternoon programme about Swiss clock-makers, which must have been quite interesting, but then it was over and they went back to the test card.

I switched off and tried to ring home again. Same result. The miracles of telecommunication were clearly not entirely on my side today, with a fault on the phone and the test card on TV.

I drank the rest of my pop, then set about exploring. Very carefully, of course, so that no-one could see that I'd been prying. Not that I found anything very interesting. In Hans's sister's room there were only horsey things, and in his parents' bedroom everything was so painfully neat that I daren't even go in. In a cupboard in the corridor on the first floor there were boxes of bottles, wine and brandy, liqueurs and port, so that for a moment I began to be worried that Hans's parents were secret drinkers, but then I realised that they had taken precautions and stashed bottles away before the strike. Grandfather hadn't stashed, and now the shelves of the off-licence were sparsely stocked, but he had managed to scrape together enough drinks for one more wedding, and anyway the strike would be over any day. In a little metal cabinet in the hall there were masses of keys hanging on hooks. There were cellar keys, attic keys, shed keys, garage keys and bicycle keys, all neatly labelled with green key tabs, and in addition two sets of keys for the quarry, even though I had imagined that most of the activity there happened out in the open, but here there were keys to the gate, the office, the dynamite store, the warming shed, the cloakroom, and still more. There were also two extra sets of house keys for the house I was in. I picked up one of them, and one of the sets of keys for the quarry, without really thinking about it, as well as the shed key, and went out to see if there was anything exciting in it, but there wasn't. So I went in again and up to Hans's room, to see whether he had any secrets. Hans had no secrets, just stamps and model aeroplanes.

I went down again and rang home. Same signal. And all at once, as I sat there in the hall with the stone floor, it was as if this house, so tidy and boring, with the test card on the TV, started to get on my nerves. It was even more boring here than normal.

I decided to go for a walk. Jim wouldn't be coming to pick me up until 6 o'clock in any case. So I put my coat on, and shoved the house key into my pocket just in case I needed to go back in to get warm again or go to the toilet before Jim came.

Then I set off down the hill.

There was no-one to be seen as I walked down the road, and not a single car came along. Thick greyish-white fog lay over everything, and seemed to blur all the lights. The pine trees stretched long fingers into the patches of light. For a moment I thought, as I can think occasionally when I'm alone on a walk, that I was the only one alive and the world was empty. I knew that it wasn't like that, but I thought it anyway, and that thought had actually never frightened me, just perhaps made me melancholy for a moment. What was it Dr Helgesen had said?

I knew him well. A brilliant doctor. From India, but trained in Manchester. A proper original, that's what he was. After working as a doctor in a little town in North England for 25 years, without taking any holiday, because Indians never take any holiday, at least that's what he told me, he took a holiday anyway. He got on the ferry in Newcastle and crossed the North Sea to Norway. He was only going to stay for a week. But when he'd seen his first fjord and his third waterfall, he was hooked. 'You know what, Dr Helgesen,' he said to me, laughing, 'I thought I had arrived in Paradise.' He'd never seen anything so spectacular. So he hurried back to England, sold his house, packed all his possessions, sorted out a residence permit, gathered up his wife and two children and moved to Norway. Learnt Norwegian pretty well. But as he said, 'Dr Helgesen, everyone here is so friendly and many people speak English, and they're all so hospitable. The most important thing is that I know the names of the illnesses and the organs. Not even Norwegians know the names of all their organs.'

And then? Well, after a while he passed all the extra exams he needed in Bergen and got a job in Valdres, and everything went pretty well there until the first snowfall. That is to say, Dr Kumar, Vikram, loved the snow. He slipped and he fell and enjoyed it every time. His wife however did not share his enthusiasm. But he told me that she bore it bravely as long as she could, and no doubt a bit longer than that, but when the second winter came she took the children with her and returned to England. 'Can you understand it, Dr Helgesen,' he said, 'that anyone would want to exchange clean, white, ice-cold Norwegian snow for rainstorms, umbrellas and Wellingtons?' But he didn't hold it against her, because he was the one who wanted to stay. After that he moved here, and in the short time I knew him he was an excellent and well-liked district locum, even if he was a good way into his fifties. Or perhaps precisely because of that. So many young doctors come out to the country, stay for a while and disappear again as soon as the towns call them. People don't like that. People like doctors who are older than them, or at least properly grown up and able to convey experience and authority. I'm sure it helps to have grey hair. Or at least to be beginning to show streaks of grey. It's probable that doctors whose hair is beginning to turn grey have a higher success rate. Your father, Vikram, had plenty of white hairs amongst all the black ones. He was patient, smiling and attentive, and almost always made the correct diagnosis. And if anything went wrong, he kept checking up on the patient until he was sure that everything was on the right track again.

Were people sceptical because he was Indian? Of course they were. Some of the elderly ladies were worried that he was going to breathe garlic on them. But Dr Kumar, who believed that he really ought to have been reincarnated as a Norwegian, had practically shifted to a completely Norwegian diet. It tastes of nothing, he said, nothing at all, but it feels right. And since he was so charming and there was no whiff of spice about him, he was a hit, even with the elderly ladies, but not just with them.

No. Not just with them at all. Not at all. Several times a year he drove over the mountains to take the boat to England and visit his wife, or ex-wife, I'm not quite sure what they were, what she was, because he talked about her sometimes as the one and sometimes as the other, and of course to visit his children. 'And you can be sure, Dr Helgesen, that I get told off then! Oh, I get told off so much! It's really terrible, but I suppose I've deserved it. I accept it as my punishment, you understand, Dr Helgesen. That's why I go. So I'll escape being punished later.'

So that's why he drove over the mountain, on the way to his punishment, but it sometimes happened that he stopped for a night at Fåvnesheim to fortify himself a little in advance. Jim was already there then, and in addition the standard was, to be perfectly honest, somewhat higher than it is today, so he wanted to treat himself to an outstanding meal, and besides –

Besides. Besides, the manager and his wife had a daughter. Well, you can probably hardly remember her, but she was extremely charming, your mother, even though she was …

… young. Yes. She was very young. So young, I believe, that your grandparents, and now I'm talking to you as an adult, had no idea of what was developing each time the charming, exotic district doctor came visiting. After a while he began to come even when he wasn't on the way to be punished in Lincolnshire. She was seventeen, he was fifty-six. These things happen.

What happened? It happened. Suddenly one evening, or rather in the middle of the night, around three o'clock, I was summoned to the hotel in an emergency. Your grandmother, white as a sheet, met me without a word, and without a word she showed me up to Dr Kumar's room, where your grandfather was trying to comfort your mother, who was having an attack of hysterics on the edge of the bed and would not let go the hand of Dr Kumar, who was lying dead in the bed. There was no doubt. He was dead. No doubt of what had happened.

Then it happened. Yes, then it happened. Nine months later, exactly on the due date. To the day. Or rather the night. You came into the world at three o'clock in the morning.

'At three in the morning. I see. That must be why I sleep so badly.'

'I don't think so. And are you sure your grandparents have never told you anything about all of this?'

'It's a very interesting story, actually. Very unusual.'

'And they haven't told you a word about it?'

'Not that I can remember.'

The fog lay in long streaks along the road through the prosperous residential district. I wandered aimlessly, without purpose, just let myself glide along in the greyness, as if in a sticky liquid, which obscured everything and made it almost unrecognisable. I walked. And suddenly I discovered that I was now, entirely by chance, I'm sure of that, standing outside the bank manager's house, Bjørn and Yvonne Berge's old house, which was where Karoline and her parents now lived and which had been yellow and was now green, but in the fog all bank managers' houses are grey.

For a while I stood there looking over the fence; there was a warm yellow glow from some of the windows on the ground floor. I could see Karoline's mother in the kitchen window; she was no doubt busy preparing dinner, like mothers do, I suppose. In the living room, no doubt in a Stressless, the twin of the armchair belonging to Hans's father, there sat no doubt Karoline's father, stressing less, whilst reading the evening paper like fathers do. Some fathers are so considerate as to refrain from dying at the moment of conception. I have actually had sufficient information about this, not just in general studies at school but also in the smutty books *A Child is Born* and *Show Me!* so that I can imagine exactly how this happened. My exotic father, Vikram, in his enthusiasm for Norway, is labouring away on top of a far-too-young girl, experiences the ultimate union with his new native land, so to speak, and as he shouts Ah and she shouts Oh and he empties himself into her, dispatches an eager and vigorous delegation of sperms, pollinates her or dumps his load in her, as Jim would say, gives her a bun in the oven, after that he has nothing further to do – his life's work is done, his activity ceased, he is in the past, going as he comes, departed, deceased, vanished into Time, or out of it, at the same time as he slides out of little Frøken Norway, disappeared, kaput, in a word dead, and has no more to say, except perhaps a little squeak. He is a dead father. He is completely stressless and will never sit there with the evening paper. And the girl lying there no doubt has what you could call an emotional reaction, because that's what it's called. Whether she cries or screams is all one, doesn't matter, means nothing, is immaterial, irrelevant, has no bearing on the facts, not worth thinking about, not in the slightest. Just as it is completely immaterial in the chain of events whether she ended up, a few years later, in Amsterdam or Copenhagen, in Morocco or Tunis, in Nepal or Bhutan, or whether she actually achieved her goal of joining an ashram in India or the international company of witches. It doesn't matter, alive or dead, for she was taken by Time, left Fåvnesheim and the rest like a foxy-red sheen in the air, striding quickly through the rooms; I can remember that there was a lot of shouting and screaming that day, and Grandmother was crying. I was crying too, standing in my cot, arms outstretched, my own crying like a sound outside myself in the air. Then she was there for a brief moment, said something, kissed me on top of the head, and then she was gone. More crying in the air, and after that I remember no more.

Perhaps, I thought, there are some children somewhere in Lincolnshire who have also cried for a father who never came home again.

Up the road came Karoline, clearly on the way home from school, or perhaps from a friend's, wearing her satchel. She caught sight of me, and it looked as if she lit up in the fog, at any rate she walked faster.

'Hi Sedd, hi,' she said when she was no closer than ten steps away.

'Hi!'

'How strange to see you here. Are you coming to our house?'

'I'm just out for a walk,' I replied. 'I was supposed to go home with someone, but it didn't work out. So I'm going for a walk instead. It's good to go for a walk.'

'Who was it?'

'What do you mean?'

She looked at me with a kind of suspicious gleam in her eye:

'Who were you going home with?'

'No-one special.'

'Oh.'

'Someone from my class.'

'Oh. I see. D'you want some gum?'

'No thanks.'

'I'll have one then. It's good for stress.'

From a pocket in her corduroy jacket she pulled a long packet of Hubba Bubba, pink flavour. She manoeuvred a fat cushion-shaped piece into her mouth and began to hub and bub.

'You know, Sedd,' she said as her jaws worked, 'it's strange that I should meet you just now.'

'Is it?'

She looked down at the asphalt. With her right foot she drew a kind of invisible half-circle in front of where she was standing.

'On Saturday,' she chewed, 'it's my birthday.'

'Happy birthday,' I said. 'Happy birthday in advance.'

'Yes. And I was just thinking ... I mean.'

She drew several more invisible half-circles with her foot, feverishly, whilst she chewed to reduce stress.

'What were you thinking?'

'I was thinking I wouldn't have a party. I don't really know anybody here.'

'That's a shame.'

'Apart from you, of course,' she added quickly. 'Apart from you, Sedd. You were so cool this summer and that, you know.

So I was wondering – and anyway, I think I'm too old for those kids' parties, I'll be twelve after all. So you see?'

I thought hard. 'Not really,' I said.

'Oh, don't be so slow, Sedd. Sometimes you're just so slow.'

'Yes.'

'I was wondering if you'd perhaps come round and have dinner with me and my parents, and then after that you and I could go to the cinema or something.'

I thought about it. 'OK,' I said, 'that would be nice. What shall we see?'

'I thought we should see *Arthur*. It's on now. I've heard it's really super.'

'I've heard that too.'

'I talked to Mama and Papa about it anyway, and they're fine with it. They think it's a nice idea. Besides, I can do what I like.'

'OK,' I said. 'But are you sure you don't want a party?'

She pulled a face:

'Parties like that are stupid. Even more stupid than you. But I've got to go now. I'm late for dinner.'

'OK,' I said. 'See you on Saturday then.' She was already on her way in through the gate and didn't turn round, but I could hear her blowing a large bubble which burst. Out of the bubble came the words: 'Come at six, then.'

'Right you are, six it is,' I said. 'Bye for now.'

But she had already disappeared up the driveway on her long thin legs, and was gone.

I walked around the district some more. The fog wandered about too. It was only when it was getting near six that I walked up to Hans's house again. I didn't open the door, just stood waiting for Jim, who turned up at five past six to collect me.

'Did you have a good time with Hans?' he asked.

'Yes, great,' I said.

As we climbed up higher we left the fog behind us. Then we were home.

314

30

These things happen: suddenly my uniform, the stylish red one, was too small. That happens, as I said, and there's nothing that can be done about it; for the last wedding before the summer holidays it had still been big enough, but for the first autumn wedding it had become so small, or perhaps I had become so large, that it was creaking at the joints, or rather bursting at the seams. You're growing so fast you'll soon be too big for your boots, said the grown-ups and so on, but no-one made any move to order a new uniform, and in any case it didn't really matter. To be quite honest, it was no longer necessary. Because after the last autumn wedding, when I had worn the outfit Grandfather and I had acquired at Ferner Jacobsen's, there were no more weddings. In direct contravention of the prognoses of all clever and perspicacious men, Prime Minister Willoch did not recognise the needs of the travel business and the restaurant business, but allowed the wretches at Hasle in Oslo to carry on striking, week in and week out, whilst the country's hotel guests, not least the wedding guests, were on the point of expiring of thirst. At least, that is, at the hotels and other premises where they had not had foresight enough to lay in a stock. Cancellations arrived like pearls on a string; or rather they did after we had our phone and telex connections restored, a stubborn fault which cut Fåvnesheim off from the rest of the world for several days, or the rest of the world from Fåvnesheim, depending on how you look at it, until finally Grandfather drove down to the village to sort it out. Then the connection was restored instantly, and with it came the cancellations.

'Drive over to Sweden,' said Grandmother crossly, 'why don't you drive over to Sweden?'

'It's a long way to Sweden,' said Grandfather, looking at her with a pained expression.

'*Quatsch*,' Grandmother declared. 'We can't allow one wedding after the other to go elsewhere, simply because our guests decide to move their celebrations to places where there is something to drink. If the mountain won't come to Mohammed, then Zacchariassen the hotel owner will have to go to a Swedish store.'

'The wine you get in Sweden isn't of the same quality,' Grandfather suggested tentatively.

'*Quatsch!* Quality? As if Norwegians have ever worried about the quality of their drink? The only thing that counts *hier im Lande* is that there is *enough*. *Das weisst du doch, Schatz!*'

Grandfather made no answer. Just looked at her for a long time with the same pained expression. He glanced briefly in my direction, and then back at Grandmother in the way he always did when he wanted to telegraph that this was not for my ears. But Grandmother just looked at him challengingly:

'Well?' she demanded. 'What's it to be?'

Then Grandfather lost his temper. He lost it visibly, just like when you see someone lose their grip on a boat railing and fall backwards and under the water:

'*I can't drive to Sweden to buy stuff!* Just get it into your head, *Mensch!* It's not going to happen! Just try to understand, for fuck's sake.'

He turned on his heel and simply left Grandmother behind, without so much as a glance in my direction, his face dark red. 'Fuck' was actually a really strong expression coming from him, so strong that for a moment it seemed that the whole atmosphere had become electric, as if there were sparks coming from him, and for the first time I understood how swearing could make the air turn blue.

Grandmother just stood there, startled, for once in her life silenced, and stared after him. She didn't follow him. Instead she, too, turned on her heel and marched off in the opposite direction, whilst starting to mutter something about going home to Vienna, where there was no alcohol strike.

The lobby was completely empty. No guests, no casual visitors. Jim was out hiking, Synnøve was not at work. None of the other staff were there either. Without guests you don't need staff, neither do you need a piccolo uniform with a piccolo in it. You just need someone to register how empty everything is. Neither the telex nor the telephone made any noise, despite the fact that they were now working again.

I went out to the kitchen. Where I always used to go when I was little and the grown-ups were at war. Slips, slapped, have slopped. In the warmth from the ovens where Jim was I could be sure of finding a safe place, surrounded by smells and tastes. But now all the bench surfaces were empty and scoured with steel powder, there was no pot of stock bubbling away, and not so much as a tray of bread rolls baking in the oven and spreading their aroma. The neon light on the ceiling was cold and bluish-white, humming gently; the dynamo for the freezer was rumbling. Everything was missing, not just Jim. A kitchen with no food and no cook is not very comforting. You don't even feel hungry, just sad.

It suddenly occurred to me that they might not remember that someone had to drive me down to my appointment with Karoline. I returned to reception to see if I could find any of them, but it was empty as before. It was empty in the lounges and the dining room, empty in the bar and the billiard room, empty in the swimming hall, empty in the private quarters. I went from room to room.

I looked at the clock; perhaps they had gone for a walk, I thought, both of them, or perhaps Grandmother had got in the car and driven off, possibly on her way to Vienna as usual. I looked out at the parking place, but the cars were still there. So I looked at the clock again and this time I registered what it said. I still had good time. Despite everything, I thought,

Grandfather was a man of his word, no reason to believe anything else, and he had promised to drive me down.

So I went up to my room, got out my outfit from Ferner Jacobsen, brushed it, checked that my shirt was clean and freshly ironed. Then I cleaned my shoes. Combed my hair. Got changed. No-one would be able to complain that I was not smartly dressed for poor Karoline's birthday. Everything for the customer. Nothing is too good for our guests.

When I was fully attired, I surveyed the effect in the mirror. I must admit that the result was creditable; I could have featured directly in an advert for advanced tailoring.

Then I went down to reception. It was as empty as ever, and I sat down to wait.

And sure enough. At the exact moment he had promised, Grandfather suddenly appeared before me, wearing his anorak and boots. He must have been for a walk. 'You look very elegant,' he said. He jingled his car keys in his left hand.

'Shall we go?' he said.

The cool blue darkness outside the cinema, the moment we came outside, was as always completely different from the darkness inside the auditorium. So there we stood, Karoline putting on her coat and scarf whilst I shivered a little in my stylish blazer.

'That was lots of fun,' Karoline enthused as we started walking. 'I think it's the funniest film I've ever seen. Oh yes, it must be. Mm.'

All I had to do now was see her home.

'Don't you think it was great fun, Sedd?'

'Oh yes. Great fun.'

'Sometimes you're so slow.'

'Superfunny, actually.'

'I didn't notice you laughing much.'

'I was laughing inside. That's what a lot of people do. It's quite a convenient way of laughing. You don't disturb other people.'

'Oh.'

I could see that she wanted to take my arm, but I pretended not to notice and held my left arm tightly against my side.

'You don't laugh like Arthur does, that's for sure. When he was drunk, I mean. Oh yes, how funny was that!'

'I think perhaps Dudley Moore is the world's funniest actor,' I said.

'Is that what he's called? But she was good as well, that actress. Very funny.'

'Liza Minnelli,' I said.

'But not as funny as he was. Duddey or whatever he's called. Arthur. He must be the funniest actor in the world.'

'Yes.'

She walked along beside me for a while, quite close, without saying anything. Then she simply pushed her hand resolutely inside my arm. I let her do it. The darkness from the auditorium seemed to be following us still, warm and brown.

And it was this hand which had been wandering in the darkness of the cinema, in the midst of an outburst of laughter, suddenly flickering, fluttering, eager and aimless, but nevertheless with a goal in mind, until in the end I had to seize it in the air and let it finish up in mine, almost like when you put a baby bird back in the nest. And there it had stayed, more or less, through more outbursts of laughter, whilst Arthur lost his friend the butler and was slowly getting closer to losing his inheritance, against the background of yet more laughter; just a couple of excursions, otherwise it rested there quietly whilst the rest of us laughed.

But now her arm was much more determined; it pulled me from lamp to lamp beneath the lamp-posts, on the way to what I hoped would be the end of a long evening.

On the way? The bank manager's villa, which had been yellow but was now green, was not in the direction we were going.

'Just think of having so much money,' said Karoline dreamily. 'So much money that you can do what you want, use as much as you want, buy the most expensive things every day and drive a racing car without ever being worried that it might get used up.'

'That must be nice,' I agreed. 'And very practical.'

'Mm. Be able to travel where you want. To the South.'

'The infernal South,' I said.

'What? The inferwhat?'

'It's just what we in the hotel business call it.'

'Oh? Why? I would really like to go to the South. … One of those places with warm blue evenings. And then –'

'Norwegians aren't interested in having a holiday in their own country any more. That's why we have the slogan "Norway – discover your own country". They ought to.'

'Ought to what?'

'Travel around Norway more and stay in hotels here, and less in the South.'

She said nothing. Just pulled me along by the arm, further and further away from the bank manager's house and rescue in the form of a waiting grandfather with the car. I guessed that he was probably there already, it had to be after 11 o'clock, but I couldn't see my watch, which was on the wrist which belonged to the arm which Karoline had kidnapped.

A burnt pepper steak, tough as old boots, pepper sauce, baked-to-death tomato and a baked potato the size of a child's head, together with two smiling but slightly ill-at-ease bank manager parents, over the red-checked tablecloths at Antonio's, formerly the village café, now taken over by a Turk called Ufuk, but you couldn't call a restaurant that, regardless of how good or bad the owner was at preparing food. So there we sat, with an endless steak and a bottomless potato, and conversed awkwardly, and they asked me polite questions and listened attentively to what interests I had (photography), what sport I liked (skiing), what I did in my spare time (fishing, Red Cross Training Corps) and so on and so forth, and how were things at home? – whilst Karoline intermittently blushed at the whole set-up, at seeing me sitting there at table together with her parents, or was obviously embarrassed by the questions, which she made very clear she thought were hopelessly childish, in a way which made her seem pretty childish.

How were things at home? Oh, you know … Those devils over at Hasle would never stop striking, so it's obvious that we're losing quite a lot of guests. But that must be true across the whole business.

And Karoline's father had looked at me with a friendly expression and nodded seriously and said he could understand it, because the situation was extraordinary for everyone, that was true enough, and Karoline's mother asked me hastily at the same time whether I would like another coke.

We walked. It was pretty chilly and there weren't so many people about, and the darkness between the street lamps swallowed us up and then released us again.

'That's where Papa works,' said Karoline, stopping. We were standing outside the bank. A white box, with lots of tall windows, and three large ones in front of the counters. It was completely dark inside.

'That's where the money sleeps, in there,' she said in a low voice. She uttered a strange little laugh.

'Then we'd better hope the money isn't afraid of the dark,' I said, and she laughed the same little laugh again. Held on tighter to my arm.

'Sometimes,' she whispered, 'sometimes I've stolen Papa's keys to the bank.'

'Have you?'

'Yes,' she whispered again, 'and then I've come down here after dark, without them knowing. And let myself in.'

The last sentence was almost inaudible, like a breath.

'But …' I began. 'Isn't there an alarm? And why do you – '

'There's lots of money,' she whispered just as quietly. Then she laughed again, but this time shakily, making a noise that was almost scary. 'Besides,' she went on, 'there's just a button in a box inside the door, and the key to that box is on the bunch of keys as well. So that takes care of that.'

She pressed her face against my shoulder.

'But Karoline,' I said. 'do you go into the bank to – I mean, don't you get pocket money?'

'Oh yes,' came the muffled reply from my armpit.

'So why …'

'You're so slow,' she mumbled from down there.

Then she said no more for a while, just stayed where she was. I didn't know what to do, just stood stock still.

Suddenly she looked up.

'I thought perhaps,' she said with the same slight shakiness in her voice, 'we could go into the bank now. Kind of take a look round.'

She let go of my arm as she said that, and I hastily manoeuvred my wrist up to eye level.

'Erm … I don't know.'

'Come on,' she said with a little more assurance. 'It's really fun, you know. In amongst the money. It's fast asleep. Completely quiet. Money doesn't snore.'

'Well,' I said, 'I'd like to …' She got hold of my hand and pressed it against the breast pocket of her coat. 'I've got them in here,' she said. 'The keys.'

'Yes, right,' I said, 'but perhaps another time. I think Grandfather must be waiting for me by now. And I'm sure your parents are too. They'll be beginning to wonder what we're up to.'

I decided to try a bit of psychology, and winked at her. It worked.

'I get it,' she said. 'I get it.'

She looked at me conspiratorially, then she shut her eyes. Stood quite still.

I twisted my hand out of her grip, then took hold of her hand and pulled her along, away from the scene of her crimes.

'Come on,' I said cheerfully, 'Grandfather gets cross if he has to wait. And I do mean cross.'

'You and that grandfather of yours,' said Karoline, a bit peeved, but she didn't pull her hand away.

When we'd gone a bit further she said: 'Anyway, Papa says your grandfather is insolvent.'

'Insolvent? What does that mean?'

'Ugh, you're so slow. Insolvent is when you don't have the money to pay for your minigolf lessons. Insolvent means you can't keep your head above water. That's what your grandfather is.'

I said nothing.

'Just like Arthur, if he hadn't rescued everything at the last minute, he would have been taken by insolvency.'

'He would never have survived that,' I said.

At Karoline's house the grown-ups were sitting waiting for us. They were waiting in the living room. Grandfather was holding a glass with a watery brown liquid in, and had a satisfied air. Karoline's mother had put out some cakes.

All three wanted to know if it had been a good film, and Karoline and I could agree wholeheartedly on that. They also wanted to know if it was as funny as they had heard, and we could agree on that too. Finally they wanted to know, as they looked a bit speculatively at Karoline and me, whether we had had a good time. We had. So there was nothing left other than to say goodnight; Grandfather thanked them profusely for the drink, which had been just the right strength for him still to be perfectly able to drive, and for the coffee and cakes, not forgetting the pleasant chat, which had been extremely pleasant, indeed, both pleasant and productive. 'Yes, you understand, Herr Ekenes.'

Karoline and I said goodbye briefly. She looked at me sideways and said see you. Karoline's parents thanked me for coming along to help celebrate Karoline's birthday, and I remembered to thank them for the delicious steak at Antonio's.

After lots of thanks in all directions we got into the Vauxhall and drove up the hill. Grandfather was in unusually high spirits.

'Nice girl, that Karoline,' he chuckled, winking at me.

'Come off it, Grandfather.'

'I think she fancies you, my lad. Yes indeedy.'

'Come off it, Grandfather. She's just a kid.'

'Perhaps that's the future mistress of Fåvnesheim you have there, Sedd. Who knows?'

'Don't say that, Grandfather. I only went along to be nice. And because they've been such good guests.'

'Is that so. OK, Sedd, that's fine. That's fine. No doubt very clever of you.'

We drove for a while in silence whilst the road twisted upwards. When we were driving into the mountains, Grandfather said: 'He's actually quite a friendly fellow, you know.'

'Who is?'

'The bank manager. The new one. Karoline's father.'

'Oh yes, he's friendly. A decent sort of chap.'

'I thought he was much more difficult than Bjørn Berge. To tell you the truth, I've been worried for a while. I really have. But you'll see, he'll learn to fit in. Yes. Fit in to the place and the circumstances. Just like following the golden rules of mountaineering.'

'Humans are adaptable animals,' I said.

'You'll see, it'll all fall into place in the end,' said Grandfather, almost dreamily. 'He understands everything now. The alcohol strike and everything.'

'Well, that's good.'

'Good? It's more than good. It's our salvation, don't you see, Sedd? Now we have some breathing space. So now it's all hands on deck.'

'Yes.'

'We have to turn the ship around.'

'Yes.'

'Hoist all the sails.'

'All the sails, Grandfather.'

'I know you understand, Sedd, that times are hard. With the infernal South and all that. And that scum down in Hasle.

And this so-called Conservative government which is letting the country go thirsty. Die of thirst. That's how things stand.'

'Things are pretty bad, Grandfather.'

'And all the taxes on top of that. And VAT. And employers' contributions. It's not exactly got any easier, I can tell you. But now – let's hope things will change.'

'I'm sure they will, Grandfather. Fåvnesheim's history shows very clearly that things always work out.'

Once we were home, Grandfather installed himself in his comfortable armchair with a glass of something distinctly less watery, reading a book on the history of war. It occurred to me that it was a long time since I had seen him sitting like that, reading happily, smiling to himself, with a snifter in his glass just for the pleasure of it.

Grandmother and I went to bed quite early, but I think Grandfather sat there for quite a while, relaxing.

Relaxing is something you can do when you've properly deserved it, and this time I thought Grandfather really had.

31

But the next day the bailiff was standing in the front drive. He had with him a couple of people I didn't recognise; a serious-looking pale woman in a grey skirt and dark jacket, together with a man in a boiler suit with a toolbox. The black and white bailiff's car was standing in the empty guests' car park, beside a red van.

I was alone in reception and was the first to see them. Perhaps, I thought, they're searching for a dangerous criminal who's escaped. The woman in the grey skirt looked just as if she could be a plain-clothes investigator from Special Branch in Oslo. I didn't know exactly what plain-clothes female investigators would normally look like, but if I were to imagine a female plain-clothes investigator, I would have imagined her precisely like that. What the man in the boiler suit was doing with them was a bit more difficult to work out, but it was possible that he was a police technician. He could well have both fingerprinting equipment and plaster of Paris to make impressions of tyre tracks and footprints in his toolbox. It must be said it had never happened before, at least as far as I knew, that there had been a dangerous convict at large in our district; if there had, the person concerned had only been passing through. But there's a first time for everything, and forewarned is forearmed when you're fighting serious crime. Lawlessness is increasing at all levels of society, everywhere, and you really don't know what to expect any more. One day some youths explode a gigantic charge of dynamite in a quarry in Oslo, probably because they've been sniffing Lynol, and the next a madman explodes a bomb at Oslo station in order to extort money from the authorities. Perhaps he'd been sniffing Lynol as well, it's not easy to say. And before that again there was that man who wanted to blow up the bridge at Alta up in Finnmark, but he was certainly not under the influence of Lynol. He was blinded by civil unrest, is how Grandfather explained it. So things are falling apart on all sides, and it is vital to assist the police as much as possible in their important work, and with this uppermost in my mind I went out to see the bailiff and enquire in what way we could best offer this assistance.

Normally the bailiff was friendly and relaxed, at least on the occasions when I had met him, but then I'm not a criminal. But today he was strangely serious and formal.

'Hi Sedd,' he said, not smiling.

'Good morning, how can I help you?'

He looked down. Then he looked up again and said, still seriously:

'We need to talk to your grandfather, Sedd. Is he at home?'

'He's sleeping in today. Just this once. I think he needed a bit of a rest.'

The bailiff and the plain-clothes woman looked at their watches simultaneously.

'It's five to ten,' said the woman to the bailiff.

'So it is,' agreed the bailiff. 'Sedd,' he said, 'would you mind going in and waking your grandfather at once and asking him to be quick. We need to talk to him.'

He looked at his watch again.

'OK,' I said, 'of course, but perhaps you'd like to come in and have a cup of coffee whilst you're waiting? It's pretty chilly today.'

The man I assumed was a police technician brightened up at this suggestion, and looked as if he would be very happy to have a cup of coffee. Police technicians have to be outside in all weathers, and no doubt they're often freezing. They must see a lot of nasty things as well. But the bailiff said:

'No thank you, Sedd. That won't be necessary.'

'Is there anything else I can help you with while you're waiting, then?' I asked.

'No thank you. Just be quick. Go and fetch your grandfather.'

I went. They stayed where they were, in front of the hotel, without moving, with their faces turned towards the main entrance.

Inside reception I met Grandmother, who seemed agitated. Presumably she had caught sight of the investigators from a window.

'*Was ist los?*' she asked.

'I don't quite know, Grandmother, but I think perhaps the bailiff and the two investigators are searching for someone. I think so. But they won't tell me anything. Anyway, they want to talk to Grandfather.'

She looked appraisingly at the three figures standing formally outside the entrance.

'Go and wake him up, Sedd. Right now. *Sofort!* I'll go out and talk to them.'

'All right, Grandmother.'

'And fetch Jim as well if you see him.'

'Will do, Grandmother.'

Grandfather was deeply asleep, as if he hadn't slept properly for a long time and had decided on precisely this morning to make up for lost time. In addition he smelt quite strongly of the well-deserved snifters he had imbibed just for the pleasure of it the evening before. So it took a while to rouse him, but as soon as he understood that none other than the bailiff was waiting outside, together with two investigators, he was on his feet at once, like the law-abiding citizen he was, ready to provide assistance to the police. He hurried out to the bathroom to get ready in a jiffy.

In the meantime I went out to the staff wing and knocked on Jim's door. Jim was up, but he wasn't dressed either. When I explained that the police had arrived, he too wasn't slow to get his togs on. He pulled on his trousers, thrust his arms into his cook's jacket, shoved his feet into his clogs and set off at a run.

When I got back to reception, I could see Grandmother and Jim standing talking to the three visitors, and I could see that it was quite a loud conversation. Grandmother was holding her head and wagging her right index finger threateningly. Jim was gesticulating with both hands whilst he walked to and fro along the row of police officers.

A little later Grandfather came down, just as well-groomed as always.

As soon as he went outside things seemed to calm down a little, at least to start with. The woman in the grey skirt took some papers out of her briefcase and showed them to Grandfather and Grandmother.

Grandmother held her head, but didn't wag her finger. Grandfather took one of the papers and waved his hand, courteous and smiling, and clearly had a great deal to say.

I thought: I ought to go out to them.

I thought: I won't go out to them. I'll stay in here and soon the police will leave and afterwards everything will be as before.

The man in the boiler suit began to rummage in his toolbox. He got out a screwdriver and a hand drill. He walked across to the main door, then stopped and considered the lock.

Jim followed. He tugged the door open, and I heard him say: 'Look here, just a minute. Just wait a fucking minute.'

Grandfather gave the paper back to the woman, then he beckoned the bailiff into reception with him, right across to the counter where I was standing.

'Sedd,' he said grimly, 'could you please go somewhere else. Up to your room or something.'

'But Grandfather –'

'Do as I say. The bailiff and I need to make a call. On our own. It's important.'

329

The bailiff: 'With all due respect, Zacchariassen – none of this should be news to you. You've had every chance to make that phone call long since.'

Grandfather: 'I apologise, as I said, but I can only repeat –'

Bailiff: 'You were fully informed of the date and time long ago. There's no doubt about it. But by all means make that call to the bank.'

'Sedd,' said Grandfather, 'off you go!'

I went. But not up to my room. Instead I went up to the corridor in the west wing and stood by the window on the second floor looking down at the area in front of the entrance. The grey woman was standing motionless in the same place as before, Grandmother was walking aimlessly up and down whilst obviously speaking German to her, and Jim had obviously parked the man with the toolbox at a safe distance from the house, and was standing on guard between him and the entrance.

I don't know how long I stood there. Perhaps ten, perhaps twenty minutes. It was suddenly difficult to breathe. You can manage with very little oxygen for a long time, actually. Then suddenly Grandfather and the bailiff came out again; they shook hands, Grandfather smiled courteously, and the delegation got back into their cars and drove off.

Grandfather and Jim came in. Jim had put his arm around Grandfather's shoulders.

Grandmother carried on walking up and down on her own for a while, still talking. Now she was wagging her finger as well.

32

What counts is not to talk about it. I understand that now. What counts is not to talk about it, because then it doesn't count. What doesn't count doesn't matter. So long as you don't talk about the accounts, they don't count, not even if the bailiff arrives at the front entrance for the third time to hold you to account; it still doesn't count – at least not so long as he has to leave for the third time, just as he did the second time, just as he did the first time, with empty hands. Or unfinished business, which I understand is what you call what doesn't count. A very unequal business, if you ask me. If it had counted, it would have consisted in one side taking everything whilst the other side got nothing, rather like when you throw snow into the air from a child's spade: I started off with so much – I gave away so much – I was left with so much. But there is never anything left, everyone knows that; the snowflakes are whirled away in the air and fall down on more snow, there's snow everywhere, but your spade is empty. Apart perhaps from a few flakes.

So what counts is not to talk about it. What counts is not to lift up the spade and say the magic words, 'I started off with so much,' because then it is possible, I gave away so much, that you will see where things are headed, that someone departs in all seriousness for Vienna, that rooms must be emptied, staff dismissed, that four generations of valiant heroes are tipped out into the snow, become snow, and that the fifth generation is left staring into thin air: I was left with so much. Counts, accounted, has discounted.

The snow came early that autumn. It lay like a heavy white sleep over Fåvnesheim, it snowed and snowed, everything was covered in snow, and much good it did us now that those miserable devils down at Hasle finally called off the strike. The time for weddings was past, and our only hope now was the Christmas dinners.

I wish I had taken a photo of Grandfather during this time, when things were so strange. His gaze was blank. His eyes simply wandered. The hotel was empty, with the exception of Jim, Grandmother and me, but despite that he was in his place behind the counter in reception every day, impeccably dressed, managing. Synnøve was on temporary leave, as he expressed it. If you went over to reception, he suddenly found something to do elsewhere. There was so much to keep in order in a large hotel, and he was busy. Grandmother was busy as well. There was so much to get ready for the winter season. An endless number of rooms in an endless number of wings.

The lights went out again, and came back on again. According to Grandfather there were maintenance issues with the cables. On the front page of *Aftenposten* the adverts for trips to the infernal South just got larger and larger. In the end they took over the front page completely. In the final days before *Aftenposten* stopped coming the newspaper consisted entirely of adverts full of parasols and boring beaches, so that the news about the really important things in the world was squeezed into two narrow columns to the left of the death notices. The deceased requested no flowers. Negotiations about a nuclear weapons treaty. A loving heart is stilled. Come to beautiful Benidorm.

'It must be possible, *Schatz*,' said Grandmother one day at the kitchen table, whilst we were eating a late breakfast and it was snowing and snowing outside, 'to get this new bank manager to agree to some arrangement?'

Grandfather looked up from his slice of bread with herring salad, since he no longer had any *Aftenposten* to look up from, inclined his head in my direction and looked warningly at her. Then he looked down at the herring salad again and studied it closely. He said nothing. I made haste to follow his example and attempted to read the cumin cheese.

'Really, my dear,' said Grandmother. Then she did something I hardly ever saw her do; she laid her hand over Grandfather's wrist across the table. Grandfather still made no answer, but he stopped chewing and sat staring down at his food.

'I've had enough to eat,' I said enthusiastically. 'That was very nice, thank you. May I be excused?'

'That's fine,' said Grandmother. 'Off you go then, *Buberl*.'

I got up and left. The two of them were sitting quite still in the same positions, like two wax figures, motionless, as I pushed my chair back under the table, but not as far as it would go, because that doesn't look good. There always has to be a certain space between the back of the chair and the table. Actually not everyone knows that.

They were sitting there as I closed the door behind me. Just the same. And I think they remained sitting like that during the couple of minutes' silence which followed, because from where I was standing against the wall of the corridor outside the kitchen, quite still, breathing gently through my open mouth, I couldn't hear so much as the sound of a breadcrumb falling from in there. But in the end Grandmother said, unusually softly and gently for her: '*Er ist doch kein Unmensch*, this new one.'

'No,' said Grandfather, 'but he is new.'

'But if you –'

'He doesn't understand what Fåvnesheim means to the community.'

'No, but –'

'What it means, and what it has meant. He says there are new demands these days. The bank is part of a group now.'

'Yes, but *das wusstest du doch*. It's been like that for quite a while?'

'Yes it has, Sisi. I know that. But Bjørn Berge, good old Bjørn, would never have thought of applying it retrospectively. Bjørn Berge had read the Constitution, after all.'

'I don't think there's anything about that in –'

'What did you say?'

'Oh, nothing. Nothing.'

'Right.'

'But it must be possible to reason with him, nevertheless?'

'Sisi, you mustn't bother your head about this.'

'*Aber wirklich. Es ist doch mein Kopf.*'

'Besides, I'm sure I've done that already. He understood that this alcohol strike was an extraordinary circumstance. But now – it's snowing.'

'*Ja, und?* So much the better. We'll start offering Christmas dinners early. We need to sell lots of expensive Christmas dinners. It'll all work out, you'll see.'

...

'Lots of Christmas dinners. Do you hear? But my dear ...'

...

'Come now! We'll work it out, you'll see. Perhaps we can even manage a winter wedding or two.'

...

'Then he'll just have to give you an extension. Perhaps even increase your credit a bit. Until we get the ship on an even keel. Don't you think that'll be possible? It has to be possible.'

...

'Well, I'll go and talk to him. Besides, Karoline and Sedd are such good friends.'

'But you must understand, Sisi, I have tried that. With precisely that argument about the ship.'

'*Ja?*'

'He understood what I was saying, I think. But it was as if it made no difference. There are certain demands, he said. Certain demands.'

'*Quatsch,*' said Grandmother. '*I'll* go and talk to him. Then you'll see he'll be more accommodating.'

'I don't think this is anything you should bother –'

'*Schluss jetzt!* It's my head, as I said. Thanks for the meal. As you Norwegians say.'

'Thanks for the meal.'

That afternoon, when I went out to the toolshed to find some ski wax, I looked for Grandfather's box at the same time. It wasn't there.

When I got home from my ski trip, I noticed that there was a light in the office behind reception. I peeped in through the window. Grandmother was bent over the writing table with Grandfather's box in front of her. On the table lay a large white covering of papers and envelopes.

I left my skis outside the main entrance and went in through the half-dark reception. In there, in the lobby between the postcard racks and the brown leather armchairs, I found Grandfather. He was pacing to and fro, from one side to the other of the large space. We pretended not to see each other, and I went up to the private apartments.

The next day, Sunday, Grandmother got into the car and drove down to the village, even though she didn't like driving when the roads weren't cleared of snow. She took me with her, so as to have someone to clear the snow away, she said. But it was me that had to remind her that in that case we ought to take a spade with us.

We got through somehow or other, and I didn't need to shovel snow. Down at the bank manager's, in the house that had been yellow, the family was at home. There was light coming from the kitchen and living room windows. The drive was newly cleared and the gate was open, but we parked down on the road.

At a fast and resolute pace, Grandmother approached the front door with me in tow. When I say in tow, that's because to be honest I was slightly sceptical about the whole thing. Grandmother had not said much in the car, apart from the fact that it was a good thing I was with her to clear snow, and that it was a good thing I was with her since Karoline had become so attached to me. It was this last statement I didn't like. It was as if it didn't occur to Grandmother to ask whether I had become attached to Karoline. It was entirely possible that I hadn't, after all. I think everyone ought to be able to decide for themselves who they get attached to. Attachments must be a personal matter. So I had a feeling that I had come along, in tow, as a kind of pawn, or a go-between, and that made me sceptical. I think everyone ought to be able to decide for themselves whether they want to be a go-between. But I didn't protest, because it wouldn't have made any difference. Not with Grandmother, who was now ringing the front doorbell with a long, trembling, Austrian index finger.

It was Karoline's mother who opened the door. She looked surprised, and that was not so strange, because we hadn't said we were coming. But when Grandmother in her most charming way apologized for the intrusion and asked if she could speak to the bank manager on an urgent matter, she let us in. Karoline's father came out into the hall at the same moment; he and his wife exchanged wondering glances, whilst Grandmother repeated her apologies for disturbing them on a Sunday and asked if she could please have a word with him.

Karoline was standing at the top of the stairs, watching. It was a little while before I noticed her. She was standing observing the whole scene with large, grey, serious eyes.

'... yes, and I brought Sedd with me too,' said Grandmother brightly; 'he was so keen to come along and say hello to Karoline.'

'And to clear snow, Grandmother,' I said in a low voice. 'Mainly to clear snow.'

'Ha ha, *ja, selbstverständlich,* that too. *Natürlich.* We really have had a lot of snow up in the mountains now; never seen anything like it.'

'It's easy to get stuck, then,' said Karoline's father.

'Very easy,' I said.

'Yes,' said Grandmother. 'Very easy.'

'Well then, perhaps you and I should go into the living room, Fru Zacchariassen, and Sedd and Karoline can keep each other company while we talk. Perhaps there might be a drop of coffee going?' He looked at his wife.

'I was just going to make some more, do go in.'

'Thank you,' said Grandmother. She disappeared into the living room with the bank manager, and Karoline's mother went out to the kitchen.

I looked up the stairs. Karoline and her large grey eyes were still there.

'You're so slow,' she said.

'Do you think so,' I said. I started to walk up the stairs. I didn't like the fact that she was on a higher level. She could easily get the idea that I was a sort of pawn, or a go-between. Or a trophy.

'Clearing snow, eh?' she said when I was halfway up. But when I'd reached the same height as her she said no more, just led the way to her room.

Her room was childish and girly, just as I expected. Actually it was a little bit like my own room, which was really my mother's room. And she was a girl, of course.

Karoline sat down on the bed. I sat on the chair. It suddenly occurred to me that I couldn't remember having been alone in a girl's room before. What was it correct to talk about in such a situation?

'Nice room,' I said.

'Thanks.'

'Very nice.'

'It's just been redecorated,' Karoline declared.

'Has it? I mean, of course, I know that.'

'You're so slow.'

After that we said no more for quite a while. The greyish-white light reflecting off the snow outside made everything look veiled; it was as if the room lost its depth and it was difficult to judge distances, such as the distance from me to where she was sitting on the bed. Then I found it difficult to see her. She swam away in the light.

'But Sedd...'

I looked down at my boots, which I had completely forgotten to take off in the hall. That was not good. Now they were dripping. There were already two little pools in front of the toes.

'But Sedd ... are you crying?'

'No,' I said. 'I don't think so.'

She was standing beside me. Quite still, for a long time. Now there were pools by the heels of my boots as well. Then she carefully placed her hands around my head.

She said my name. My whole name. She didn't pronounce it properly, but that was only to be expected. Not everyone is used to foreign-sounding names.

It was quiet for a while. Then she said: 'I'm sure there'll be a way out.'

'Do you think so?' I said. I didn't look up. But she raised my face up so I had to look at her. Again she was on a higher level, but she didn't make use of that, she just said: 'We'll sort this out. You and I. I promise.'

'Do you think so?'

'Of course. Definitely. You're so slow.'

'Yes.'

There was a knock on the door. The next moment I was standing by the window looking out at all the whiteness, while Karoline in one bound was across the room to open the door.

It was her mother. 'I think Sedd and his grandmother are going home now,' she said.

'Oh,' said Karoline.

'Yes. It's a long way back up there, you know, darling. And it doesn't look as if the snow's going to stop. They can't stay the night, after all,' she said, making a joke of it.

'No,' said Karoline thoughtfully. 'Have they finished talking then?'

'Yes. They have. Sedd. Sedd?'

I turned round.

'I think they've reached an agreement, Sedd,' said Karoline's mother.

'Right,' I said.

'We're coming straight down,' said Karoline. 'I just have to say something to Sedd first.'

When we were alone again, she said it. And then she asked me about something secret.

'Yes,' I said. 'OK.'

'Then it's a deal,' said Karoline.

In the car on the way home Grandmother was in high spirits. She was humming selected Austrian hits, and it was obvious that she was pleased with her efforts and the result.

'You'll see, Sedd,' she said, 'it'll all be sorted out.'

'Yes, Grandmother,' I said. But I was wondering at how easy it seemed to be for people to say that everything would be sorted. After all, it was the second time in less than an hour that someone had said just that.

'Now, Sedd, *Buberl,* we've got a reprieve. We've bought some time.'

'Right, Grandmother.'

'Now we've just got to do what's necessary. What we have to do. Then hopefully it will all be sorted.'

It wasn't necessary to shovel any snow on the way back either.

33

'No way,' said Grandfather, turning pale, 'no way. Never again.'

Grandmother looked steadily at him.

'We have to, *Schatz*,' she said heavily.

'Rubbish,' said Grandfather, 'we don't have to do anything, not at all.'

'It's a very lucrative affair,' said Grandmother. 'They'll pay triple prices. In fact I think they're prepared to go even higher. It's difficult to refuse such an opportunity. Besides, there are no other hotels in the whole of southern Norway which will take them.'

'That doesn't surprise me,' said Grandfather.

'Well?'

'It's out of the question,' said Grandfather. 'Completely out of the question. After last time –'

'I've looked into it,' said Grandmother. 'They've tried everywhere else and been refused.'

'And they should be refused here too,' said Grandfather. 'I don't want them here again.'

'*Liebling*,' said Grandmother, 'I don't think we have any choice. They've aleady written to the hotel three times to ask.'

'Have they?'

'They have, yes. But you wouldn't know that. The letters were buried in your secret treasure box.'

Grandfather did not answer.

'Would it help if we included a clause that they would be financially liable for any potential damage or extra expense?' Grandmother stared directly at him like an Austrian eagle.

Grandfather knew all too well that she was not to be trifled with when she was in an imperial mood.

'If we can earn as much as that,' she said emphatically, 'we might be able to get over the hump. The bank is willing to allow us a little more credit one last time, so that we can pay tax and employer's contributions.'

'And VAT.'

'VAT, yes. I'd quite forgotten that. That was also buried, together with –'

'Sisi …'

' – together with all the other horrors, and really, what sort of a man are you? I've been wondering about that ever since I came to this dreadful country.'

'Sisi … Well,' said Grandfather. 'I seem to remember that Jim threatened to resign last time they were here.'

'I'd quite forgotten that,' said Grandmother, worried.

'Well,' said Grandfather. 'If Jim can be persuaded, which I very much doubt, then in God's name we'll do it. But Jim must go along with it. We can't cope without Jim.'

'No,' said Grandmother. 'We can't cope without Jim.'

'Bloody hell, are you mad?' Jim looked at Grandfather in dismay. 'No, Zacchariassen,' he said, 'that's not going to happen. No way. Never. Never again. Over my dead body.'

'But Jim,' Grandfather begged him, 'this is an extremely lucrative affair. They'll pay –'

'Zacchariassen,' said Jim sharply. 'I said it last time they'd been here, and I'll say it again: in that case I'll resign. On the spot.'

'But Jim, dear –' Grandmother began.

'I don't care if they pay a million! It'll be the death of me. And it won't make any difference if these people promise to arrange a state funeral in Nidaros Cathedral – I won't do it. No way. Completely out of the question.'

'But Jim –'

'Don't Jim me.'

Grandmother looked at him, affronted, whilst Grandfather held out his hands in resignation and sighed.

'Oh well,' he said, 'I can't say that I don't understand you, Jim. Believe me. I do understand. Hand on heart, I can't say anything else.'

'Good,' muttered Jim.

'And I respect you and your decision,' said Grandfather mildly. 'I understand and respect you absolutely. You know that, Jim.'

'Yes,' said Jim. 'I know that.'

'I hope you've never doubted it,' said Grandfather.

'No,' said Jim, who thought he'd won the day, 'I've never doubted that.'

'You know that for Sisi and me you're almost like a son, Jim.'

Jim swallowed.

'And for Sedd here –' Grandfather waved a hand in my direction ' – for Sedd you're like an older brother, almost a father substitute, because I'm too old for that, after all.'

Jim swallowed again and looked down at the kitchen counter.

'Isn't it nearly sixteen years you've been here?' asked Grandfather.

'Seventeen.'

'Seventeen, is it.' Grandfather sighed. 'Goodness, how time passes. Seventeen, yes. Back then Elisabeth was still – my goodness me. You know, Jim, it must be said that you're a pillar of our existence for Sisi and me. Sedd is still young –' once again he waved his arm in my direction '– and Fåvnesheim needs you, Jim. That's for sure. We need you. And now we need this Christmas party. We really do.'

Jim looked at Grandmother. Then he looked at me.

I nodded.

'All right,' said Jim, 'we'll do it. They can come. On one condition.'

Grandfather cheered up: 'Yes?'

'This must be absolutely the last time,' said Jim. 'Next year and every year after that those bloody Frankensteins will have to find a different place for their pagan rites. Even if they have to travel to the Faroe Islands. The other condition is – '

'You said one condition, Jim. One.'

'Well, all right, two then,' said Jim, irritated. 'I want a double Christmas bonus and an extra week's holiday. No, just a moment, a treble bonus.'

'Now, now,' said Grandfather.

'All right, double will do, then,' said Jim. 'But it's not to go on my wages slip.'

'All right, that's agreed, Jim,' said Grandfather, relieved. He left the kitchen hurriedly, and I could see that he was already working out how much Jim's demands would swallow up of the income; but his tread was so light that I understood that this must be in all ways a lucrative affair.

'God have mercy on us all,' said Jim heavily. 'Yes,' he added, 'you're too young to be able to remember last time they were here – you were asleep in bed. The only one who did sleep, I think.'

'But Jim,' I asked, 'who *are* these people?'

'You'll find that out soon enough, lad,' said Jim gloomily. 'They'll be the death of us. You mark my words.'

In the days before the approaching Christmas party Grand-mother instituted various precautions. I'm not quite sure why you call them pre-cautions; we were hardly being cautious about it. But then you can't institute them afterwards either, no-one ever talks of post-cautions. Whatever you decide to call them, there's one thing which is sure, namely that you can never be sure in advance exactly what kind of misfortunes will occur.

There were many things which had to be done. We would have a hotel full, and had to try to reengage the staff we'd had to let go earlier. Synnøve came to the rescue, of course. But many of the rest had found other things to do, and it was quite clear that there were too few of us. Besides,

Grandmother and Grandfather were preoccupied with the calculations – for every helping hand we had to pay for there would be less money left to pay tax, employer's contributions, not forgetting VAT, let us not forget that, and above all: to pay the first large instalment of the bank's extended loan, which from now on had to be paid punctually on the 20th of each month, if we were to avoid further visits to our front door by the representatives of law and order.

Because of this, Grandfather and Grandmother were opposed to hiring a larger staff than was absolutely necessary, and Jim agreed (as so often before) to assume another role, and the silk waistcoat which went with it, and become a bartender after the meal. It's true that he thought that drinks with slices of orange and lurid colours were a load of muck; anything beyond gin and tonic seemed pointless to him. On the other hand he was good at selling drinks to the guests, and the main thing here was to sell, with as much profit as possible. But, Jim said, if he was to take care of the bar, we would need a couple of extra hands for the washing up and clearing up in the kitchen. You couldn't expect me, Sedd, to do all that on my own.

Grandfather thought that I could manage that on my own, and I thought so too, but Grandmother had assumed the mantle of leadership completely and had a new and, she maintained, good idea. She just wouldn't tell us what it involved. She restricted herself to looking inspired and telling Jim I'll sort this out, don't worry.

After that she returned to her own preparations, which mainly involved clearing away art and old photographs, vases and ornaments, precious agricultural antiques, and not least rolling up and tying ropes around several carpets in the lounges. Jim and I had to carry everything out to be stored in the shed beside the ski store. The Thaulow and Wentzel pictures went the same way, securely padded and wrapped. I found it difficult to comprehend why it was necessary to institute all these precautions in advance, but Jim made no objections.

The Christmas party was to take place on a Saturday, and from the Tuesday onwards Jim was busy prepping in the kitchen. Although we otherwise normally served steak on such occasions, for Christmas as well, it had been decided that this time we were going to serve spare ribs, which are the cheapest to buy. And Jim had scoured the country for the cheapest of all. 'They'll just have to put up with it,' he said; 'no-one else will entertain them. Besides, it's not the food they come for.'

I chopped up two dozen cabbages, second-rate goods, for sauerkraut, and Jim made pork meatballs with a high percentage of flour.

Then Saturday arrived and with it Karoline arrived too. Of course. The rest of the staff were already in place and getting on with things, me too, when Grandmother came into the kitchen, beaming, with Karoline in tow.

'Here is your kitchen assistant, Jim,' she announced, winking at me. Karoline looked embarrassed, and Jim stared at Grandmother, thunderstruck. But he said nothing.

'I mean, since she was such a good help last time,' began Grandmother, and Jim said: 'That's quite all right, Fru Zacchariassen.'

'I've arranged with her parents,' said Grandmother, 'that they'll come to collect her tomorrow morning. Sedd, could you please show her up to her room; she's staying in 321, the little room. And then bring her down here again and put her to work.'

Karoline and I looked at each other.

'OK, Grandmother,' I said.

As I carried her small case and walked up the stairs in front of her, I was thinking strong and disciplined thoughts. Nothing is too good for our guests. Or rather: nothing is too good for our bank.

I put her case down inside the door with a little bang.

'There you are,' I said. 'Welcome. This is where you're staying.'

'Thank you.'

'Are you going to wear a blouse and skirt while you're working in the kitchen?'

'Yes,' she said. 'I'll be fine like that.'

'As you like.'

On the way downstairs again, she said:

'I thought perhaps you'd come for a swim afterwards?'

'No.'

'Or perhaps you could teach me to play billiards.'

'No. We don't have time.'

'Oh, right.'

'There's masses to do. There'll be over a hundred guests.'

'Right. Later then, perhaps?'

'We'll see.'

Down in the kitchen I put on a white jacket and apron, and Karoline was given an apron which had to be tied round her three times so that she didn't drown in it.

Then the Christmas party could begin. The first bus-full of guests arrived around four o'clock, just as it was beginning to get properly dark.

Three buses arrived in all, from west and east, south and north, and it was a remarkably quiet and correct gathering. In fact, I would almost call it a sombre gathering.

All the gentlemen looked exactly the same. You couldn't say they looked the same the way that all gentlemen in dark suits do. They weren't just wearing dark suits, they were wearing extremely dark suits. I'm sure that any impartial witness describing these gentlemen's suits would say that they were abnormally dark. They were as black as coal. The same was true of the gentlemen's ties, which were also extremely dark. Furthermore, the ties were impeccably tied with double Windsor knots, one of the more advanced knots Grandfather had taught me, and which it is important for people in representative positions to master. So it was easy to see that the gentlemen in suits and ties who streamed out of the buses and into the hotel one after the other had some kind of representative function. The number of ladies I would estimate at about a quarter, and most of them were also suitably respectably dressed, in dark, straight, knee-length skirts with matching white blouses and dark jackets.

Jim and I carried cases. Karoline helped with a few of the lighter pieces of luggage. It was as if the hotel had been filled by a group of preachers, and a cloud of seriousness and respectability hovered over them as we showed them to their rooms. No loud laughter, hardly a smile. I suggested to Jim that they seemed like very easy guests, but Jim merely whispered through clenched teeth that it had been like that last time as well, and just you wait.

It was a while until dinner, and when we'd finished carrying cases, Karoline suddenly set off, pulling me by the arm.

'I want you to show me your room,' she said, but she was the one who went first into the private apartments, and I followed her up the stairs, as if she already knew where it was.

I wanted to put the light on, but she stopped me. For quite a while she just stood close to me in the darkness, with her arms around my neck, breathing.

I stood quite still. Didn't move a muscle. But when she pulled my head down towards her face, I pulled away and switched on the light.

'We haven't time for this,' I declared soberly. 'We have a hotel full of guests.'

'You're so slow,' she said, pouting. 'Look here!'

She went over to my desk. Then she began to pull money out of her pockets. There were blue notes and green notes, and a whole bundle of red notes, and in between there were some rust-coloured ones as well. She just went on and on dropping notes on the desk.

'There!' she said. 'It's yours!'

I stood there staring at all the capital.

'But Karoline,' I said, 'where does all this money come from? What is it you're up to?'

Again she was suddenly right next to me: 'They'll never guess it's me,' she said in a low voice. 'It's just a matter of taking a bit here and a bit there.'

She said no more. Just leaned against me with her eyes closed.

'But Karoline,' I said after a while, 'what am I to do with all this money?'

She shrugged.

'Take it, of course,' she said. 'Perhaps it'll help. There's more where that came from.'

I sat down on the bed. Shook my head. 'I can't do that,' I said. 'You must understand that.'

She sat down beside me.

'If we had some dynamite,' she giggled, 'we could blow up the vault. We could just go in and do it.'

'Become bank robbers, you mean?'

'Oh, yes.' She bit her bottom lip at the thought.

I got up, went over to the desk and opened the top drawer.

'Here,' I said as I sat down beside her again: 'Here's some dynamite.' I showed her the bunch of keys.

'Dynamite?'

'Yes,' I said, 'one of these keys opens the gate to the quarry. They belong to Hans's father. He's the manager.'

'Did you steal them?' The question came with a strange, hectic breathiness.

'Yes,' I said, 'I mean no.'

'Cool.'

'I just forgot to give them back.'

'Right.'

'I thought perhaps there wasn't any rush.'

'I see.'

Without more ado she took the bunch of keys and put it in her pocket.

'Now we can blow up the bank,' she giggled. 'Properly. We can do a real job.'

'No, we can't,' I said emphatically, but she just went on:

'You know that lot there' – she nodded at the heap of notes on the desk – 'that won't go far. Not compared to what your grandfather owes.'

'I don't know anything about that,' I said.

'He owes loads,' said Karoline. 'The hotel has masses of overdue bills. Old debts. Creditors who've never been paid. I've heard Papa and Mama talking about it.'

'Really,' I said. 'Well, that's interesting. But I can't leave all this money lying about here.'

'Well, put it somewhere else, then. You're so slow sometimes.'

I got up, gathered the notes together and swept them down into the drawer.

She was standing right next to me again. 'So now we're going to be bank robbers,' she said. 'Safe crackers.'

'Now we're going downstairs to do some work,' I said, helplessly.

'And tomorrow morning,' she said, 'I want to go swimming with you. I've got really good.'

'The guests are waiting,' I said, desperately.

She looked at me with a glance that was both serious and mocking:

'I suppose they are.'

The guests appeared transformed. There is no better word for it. They had gathered in the lounge for a little refreshment before the meal, and Grandmother had made a special point of setting out the smallest flutes. It is true that the gentlemen still looked as if they had a layer of representativeness smeared over their faces like vaseline, but on several of them the layer was in the process of disintegrating. They had had time to change into Hawaiian shirts or other forms of colourful clothing, and a few of them had refreshed themselves sufficiently in their rooms even before this first refreshment for them already to be unsteady on their feet. They compensated for this by singing a song. We would have the opportunity to hear this song several times during the course of the evening:

We have an ancient burial ground where graves are
squashed up tight
But still there's room for many many more.
We keep an eye on people who look pale and none too
bright
To gather all the souls we can to bury more and more.

This was just the first verse. There were many verses. The
second verse, for example, went as follows:

We have an ancient Daimler-Benz all lined in solemn black
To whisk you to the crematorium door
We drive at quite a dash to the cemetery and back
We gather all the souls we can to bury more and more.

Karoline clearly thought that this grotesque song was quite
fun, but I could see as we went round with trays of glasses
that Grandmother was deeply shocked. The most refreshed
had not managed to snuffle their way to the third verse before
the company sat down to dinner; so instead it was sung there
as a rousing chorus. However, the evening began with the
president of the Association of Norwegian Funeral Directors
welcoming his members to this year's traditional Christmas
party, a much-loved ritual, held this year for the second time
at Fåvnesheim, a place he reckoned at least a few of those
present might remember vaguely. 'We will now be served
gravlax,' the president added. 'And that will be followed by
Christmas dinner, with ice cream flambé for dessert. It is not
so easy,' he went on, 'especially in small communities, as you
know, to carry out the tasks and assume the heavy duties we
all have. Many people don't understand our profession, they
fear it, and at the same time we are indispensable. People die'
(here the company nodded solemnly) 'and we stand ready
to receive them. We receive them with solicitous hands and
prepare them respectfully for the last journey, which now
awaits them, as the poet Wergeland says. In the midst of life
we are in death – but we, my friends, we know better than

anyone else that in the midst of death we are also in the midst of life' (the company uttered small cries of agreement: 'the midst of life!'); 'we are people too, behind our sympathy, our considerate hands, our professional demeanour. We too stand in the midst of life, even in the darkest hour for the family of the deceased. We see terrible things, we see the grief of our fellow humans, but as the poet Kingo says: Sorrow and joy, they walk together.' (Company: 'Joy!') 'So it will do us good, we who are constrained by the shared secrets of our profession, indeed, constrained in so many ways, once again to join together with – erm – like-minded colleagues for a brief interval. A hearty welcome to our Christmas party, and skål!' (Company: 'Skål!')

As we stood there in the service area, listening, Jim whispered grimly to Karoline and me: 'You see, these are people who can never let their hair down where they work, so now they're going to let their hair down. That's what he's trying to say.'

The gravlax was served, with a tiny glass of sherry for each person. It was hardly larger than a thimble. However, there were several people who preferred to partake of their own supplies from shiny silver hip flasks, whilst the association's general secretary made a short speech over the gravlax, appropriately enough, in which he remembered those of the association's members who in the course of the past year had shifted roles to become customers, and followed by distributing the association's annual awards. For example, Brynhildsen's firm in Volda had distinguished itself after the tragic avalanche; that was certainly not an easy situation to handle, indeed it was not. Hellberg's firm in Trondheim was celebrating its jubilee, and we are so fortunate as to have with us this evening the fourth generation Hellberg and his wife, who is also active in the firm; they will in addition be celebrating their silver wedding during the coming year, so let us wish them well and drink to them – but I think we need a small refill …?

Jim threw a questioning glance from the service area across the room to Grandfather, who was standing by the entrance. Grandfather nodded resignedly that we could pour a further few millimetres of Dry Sack.

Our actions reminded me of that film about heavy water. One of Grandfather's favourite films. In that film the heroes from Telemark, who all play themselves, apart from Henki Kolstad who simply is himself, walk and walk through the snowstorms and over wide white plains. They walk and walk in order to reach Norsk Hydro's factory at Rjukan, and it's a long way. They walk and they walk. And in between the walking and the sound of their skis we watch a drop falling from a spout. Slowly. A tiny precious drop of heavy water. Then another. And then we see the heroes of Telemark walking onwards. The hotel's alcohol policy this evening adhered to the heavy water principle. But it didn't make much difference. Either because the shiny silver hip flasks were so numerous, or because these people otherwise never drank.

As early as the first serving of spare ribs the hats and masks began to appear. We were particularly impressed by two people who ran around on all fours between the tables wearing pig masks.

Karoline, Jim and I watched the company from the service area.

'Death will never be the same again,' was Jim's comment.

'No,' I said, swallowing. I couldn't think of anything else to say.

But Karoline was staring fascinated at this unfolding of life in the midst of death. Out on the floor in the dining room two of the lady funeral directors had undertaken to herd the two four-legged creatures back to their places.

'Something you should notice,' said Jim: 'Do you see anyone who's missing?'

I didn't understand what he meant.

'Do you realise we can't see Gottlob Uttorpet or any of his staff here this evening?'

Jim was right. The pale, quiet, always solemn Uttorpet, our local funeral director, with hair as thin and yellow as a fluffy chick, was absent. Neither was the always friendly but silent Fru Uttorpet present.

'You see,' said Jim, 'the local members don't come to the party. They're not allowed. They might frighten the staff and waiters so that they put them off dying.'

'But it can't be easy,' said Karoline. I could see that she was shuddering, but fascinated at the same time. 'They must see lots of horrible things?'

'Sure,' said Jim. 'Sure they must. Come on, time for second helpings of main course.'

When we'd finished taking the dishes round again, Karoline insisted on dragging me off to the refrigerated room to get a bottle of Solo.

'You can get it yourself,' I said. 'You know where it is.'

'I know, but it's a bit creepy there,' she declared.

'There's nothing creepy about vegetables,' I said.

But I went along anyway. Inside the refrigerated room she pulled me close to her again, and looked up at me expectantly. But I didn't want to.

'Didn't you want a Solo,' I said. She was just a little kid, after all.

She pushed me away. 'You're so slow.' She got her Solo and we went out again to Jim, who was standing watching the party with interest through the serving hatch.

'Time to clear,' he said. 'After that we must get the ice cream flambé ready. Last time they had ris à l'amande with red sauce and almonds. That didn't go too well. No-one found the almond. But they were desperate to find it anyway. It took us a whole day to clean up the rice. Let's hope there's less mess with Omelette à la norvégienne.'

It is actually possible to flambé ice cream. You just have to get it served quickly. The idea was that everyone would get a little ice bombe with a meringue topping in an individual bowl with a blue flame on top. As we were putting the bowls out on large serving trays, we could hear the company joining in with another verse of their song:

A number of our clients are too fond of food and drink
And nothing gives us greater joy to see.
In a pink and silver coffin we'll escort you to the brink
And lower you into your grave with glee.

At a sign from Jim, Karoline and I and the two hired waiters began to set fire to the brandy on the finished desserts; it looked really festive. Karoline stared at the flames with wide eyes, but only for a few seconds, because the trays were whisked off straight away to the dining room, where the dessert was met with ovations; a few people even raised their paper hats devoutly. So it is no exaggeration to say that the dessert was a success.

Unfortunately it is the case with dishes like these which need to be served flaming that the last ones to be served – regardless of how quick the servers are on their feet – arrive at the table with dying flames, or with no flame at all. This is unavoidable. Normally this elicits an expression of assumed but polite disappointment from the unlucky ones, but that's just the way it is, and they eat it without any fuss.

Not this time. This time the disappointment was real. And great. And the desire to remedy it was equally great. The hip flasks came out.

It is quite amazing how many kinds of spirit you can use to flambé. That was something I learnt that evening. Akvavit, cognac, whisky, vodka, gin, moonshine, methylated spirits – everything works, so long as you pour enough on, and everything gives off its own characteristic aroma as it burns. Furthermore, it becomes evident that both Christmas cakes and the chocolate served with the coffee can be ignited, when the ice cream bombes have been eaten. Unfortunately Jim had not reckoned with the fact that these were people who had quite advanced knowledge of the processes of combustion, at times of quite large quantities, and therefore were not nervous about playing with fire. It soon emerged that floral decorations, serviettes, serviette rings of yellow birchwood and crocheted table mats can be flambéed with varying degrees of success, although it is possible that some of the inicipient fires were caused by accident.

Finally we managed to remove the gang to the adjoining rooms, where there was to be dancing and a drinks bar, whilst we surveyed the damage. Grandfather's expression was dark, Grandmother was crying. But Karoline stared at the ruins, fascinated.

Inside the dance hall stood Johnny West's Limelight Band, ready to meet the advancing hordes.

And here it must be stated at once that Johnny and his men were as solid as besequinned pillars that evening. In addition to his real, true life as a performer, Johnny West led a shadowy existence as a science teacher in secondary school, so he had quite a wide range of experience. Many people believe that chemistry is an easy subject. But Vestby the science teacher knew that it's not enough to make things explode or burst into flames. That can be done in no time. Chemistry is about making things explode, or burst into flames, in slow and long-drawn-out ways. Here a good teacher can learn a great deal from a good performer. It's a matter of letting the tension build slowly. That's how it is with chemistry, and that's how it is with performing. When Vestby the teacher went into a telephone kiosk in the early evening and Johnny West emerged from it a few seconds later with sequins and everything, he was invulnerable. No naked dancing on the dance floor, no beer glasses or half-eaten hot dogs flying through the air could make him and his men wobble behind their amplifiers, their drum set and their Hammond organ. Clad in hard-wearing made-to-measure suits, with blue waistcoats, sumptuous shirt fronts and jackets with sequinned stripes, they were as steady as mountains. Johnny West was the front man, steadfast, just like the greatest science teacher of them all, Galileo Galilei, before

355

the court of the holy inquisition in the midst of the paradigm shift.

Although they were put under severe strain that evening. From early on it became clear that the partygoers' expectations with regard to ecstasy and climax did not entirely follow the same progression as Johnny West had planned. Already by halfway through the romantic Swedish ballad 'Ten Thousand Red Roses', the funeral directors' attention began to wander, and they launched into yet another verse of their dreadful song, which in a strange way could be sung in canon with the more high-flown music; this is what is called counterpoint.

A timer on a bomb ticked home, a plane fell from the sky
Our Daimler plucked up bodies by the score.
Titanic was a great success, our boat was just nearby
We dived and pulled them out again to bury them once more.

So the band shifted to cruder music, like 'Skateboard' and 'Waterloo', and had to leapfrog over the songs Grandmother had insisted on including, such as Tom Jones' 'Delilah' and Wenche Myhre's 'I'll be Marching at your Side, Soldier Boy'. At the same time they couldn't progress so rapidly that they reached deathless hits like 'Dancing Queen' and 'By the Rivers of Babylon' so early in the evening. The result was that Johnny West and his heroic crew had to keep the tempo going the whole time with a string of energetic numbers which completely wore them out, with 'Blue Suede Shoes', 'Twist and Shout', 'These Boots are Made for Walking' and suchlike heavy beats without a break, although I think they could just as well have played 'Dancing Queen' all evening. It was the only number which seemed to satisfy the company one hundred per cent. That, and perhaps 'In the Ghetto'. But as soon as Johnny attempted a more artistic and sensitive song, such as 'Happy Street', interest waned. Large dark stains had spread from the armpits of their suits, the saxophonist had gone pink in the face and Johnny West was leaning heavily on the microphone stand as he for the third time launched into 'See that girl, watch that scene, diggin' the Dancing Queen'.

As if at a sudden signal, the dance floor was completely filled. It was fascinating to see how this one song, of Swedish origin, could instantaneously gather together a crowd which by this time had begun to be extremely unstructured and inattentive.

Karoline took hold of my hand. Pulled at it. 'Come on,' she said. At least that's what I thought she said from reading her lips. She wanted to dance.

Without thinking any more about it I let myself be pulled out onto the dance floor, which was already rather overcrowded. We were whirled into a throng of Hawaiian shirts and waving arms, so we had to dance close. Very close. Karoline practically hung around my neck. Every time I tried to pull back a little, she came with me, like a millstone. I am not a good dancer. The staff and hotel representatives are not allowed to dance with the guests, you see. It's called mingling, and it's strictly forbidden. I was reminded of this when there was suddenly an opening in the crowd of dancers, and Grandfather, who was overseeing the room, caught sight of me. He looked at me severely.

But then we were sucked back into the whirlpool of the night's dancing queens, kings and other aristocrats of varying importance; Karoline pulled my head down to hers, or perhaps she was standing on tiptoe, and put her mouth on mine.

It tasted quite nice, much better than when I had saved her up at Blåvann, warm and cold at the same time like flambéed ice cream, and I stood quite still. It was as if I could feel the whole of her through my mouth, from the crown of her head to the tips of her toes, but then I caught a new glimpse of Grandfather from the corner of my eye, shaking his head and signalling that I should leave the dance floor immediately.

Just another second, and I pushed her away, as gently as I could, gently, I did try to be gentle, but I had to tear myself away. She looked at me angrily. Since then I have wondered many times what would have happened if I had allowed two seconds to elapse, or maybe three.

She looked at me with glittering eyes. She said something, but this time I couldn't read her lips. I only saw them. Her lips. They just moved. And I'm certain, absolutely certain, or at least almost, that she didn't manage to read from my lips what I was saying to her, which is that I was not allowed to dance with guests, it is forbidden. I am convinced that she didn't understand it, because she had turned her back on me before I had even finished saying it, and disappeared into the tumult of dancing bodies.

In the pause I couldn't find her. It was also in the pause that things began to go badly wrong. When Johnny West was no longer there like Espen Askeladd with his pipe, the king's hares were scattered to the winds, and all the hares had something in their glasses. Suddenly they had occupied the whole hotel, all the lounges and rooms, with their glasses and bottles and hip flasks, and there wasn't a great deal we could do. Every now and then they returned to the bar to collect supplies and take another turn on the dance floor if the band was playing 'Dancing Queen' again, before they once more disappeared beyond the official party area.

I cleared away. We cleared away. We carried bottles, glasses and plates. Ashtrays. More glasses. As I was carrying a heavy tray of glasses through one of the rooms, I caught sight of Karoline. A little behind some of the partygoers, just a passing glimpse. She was sitting on the arm of a sofa, talking to one of the younger men, a pale red-haired guy. She had a glass in her hand.

I could not put down the tray. When I had carried it out to the kitchen and emptied and filled a machine, I hurried out again. But the sofa was empty. For a while I wandered about from room to room looking for her in the crowd of noisy and drunken guests, but I couldn't see her anywhere. And after that I had to clear away some more. Around midnight many of the guests got carried away in spontaneous fun and games in the snow outside. That soon developed into a fairly violent snowball war. Two firms from the Møre district, who were clearly in competition with each other for the same group of customers in their daily work, were battling each other with treacherous projectiles in which lumps of ice were concealed in the snowballs. The funeral procession consultants in a firm from Sarpsborg were obviously not on good terms with the chauffeurs in the same firm. The first nose began to spurt blood; a great hulk from Sarpsborg had got one of the ice clumps from the Møre district full in the face. He dried his nose on his sleeve and squinted threateningly at the civil war combattants from Møre, upon which the whole of Sarpsborg gathered around the injured man and pitched into battle against the Mørings, who also closed ranks.

Jim, Grandfather, a couple of the waiters and I stood powerless in the doorway, watching. We had extremely limited powers of sanction if we did not ourselves want to become a part of the inferno of white which was now unfolding in front of the hotel.

'Oh well,' sighed Grandfather, 'better let them fight it out. Out here they're only damaging each other, at least.'

He turned his back on the mortal enemies and strode resolutely back into the hotel in order to keep the ship on a relatively even keel. We followed him, somewhat doubtfully, as we glanced back for the final time at the winter war, which had now decisively entered a more brutal phase. Then I saw Karoline. She had her coat on and was lying on her back in the snow, making snow angels.

I wanted to go and fetch her, but Grandfather pulled me along. There was something which needed to be done; I don't remember what any more. But I registered that the guy with red hair was helping her up.

Later I caught another glimpse of her, alone, on her way up the stairs to the rooms. I was standing in reception, behind the counter, helping with something; I don't remember what any more. I could see her back, which looked slightly forlorn, but she was walking steadily enough. Just then I hadn't the time to follow her. It was a matter of crisis management now. At one moment we had to separate two gentlemen in the throes of mutual recriminations, at another the potted plants in the Heimdal room needed rescuing, and then we had to prevent three merry men taking down the elk head from the wall. My great-grandfather's collection of prizes from the National Riflemen's Games, his silver cups, had been used as drinking vessels before we could intervene. On the billiard table a lady was in the process of performing a striptease for a man who was not her husband; the husband, however, arrived promptly and carried off the man his wife was not married to. Later we found the latter imprisoned in a cubicle in the men's toilet in the cellar, where he was making dreadful noises. We decided to leave the tie which fastened the doorhandle to the water pipe in place, so that he couldn't get out. That seemed the safest thing to do.

All these incidents were, taken singly, things we in the profession have seen before. What was different this night was that we saw all the phenomena at the same time. Grandmother had gone to bed, pale with fear. Outside the hotel, in the dance hall, in all the lounges and dining rooms, as well as in many of the bedrooms, the Christmas party raged on, and Grandfather did not dare close the bar for fear that it would be reopened. The only thing we were reasonably sure about was that the swimming pool was literally under lock and key: in addition to the normal locks, Jim and Grandfather had threaded a thick chain through the door handles and secured it with a substantial padlock.

Around one o'clock I finally had time, a few minutes, a few spare moments, a few seconds' grace, to run up and knock on the door of Karoline's room. But she didn't open. I stood outside for a while, knocking several times and calling her name. But she was asleep.

Around half-past one, when I was standing in reception again, a breathless Jim came running up from the cellar to announce that there was a flood. After having slept for a while in his cubicle, the imprisoned Don Juan had attacked the door again with renewed strength and managed to get it open. However, polyester is a strong modern material, and the tie had not given way during the prison breakout; the door was also still in one piece, but something had to give, and it was the water pipe, which had broken away at the joint. Cold water was now spurting up from it against the wall; the floor of the toilets was already swimming in water, and it was beginning to seep out over the carpet in the corridor outside.

'Should we ring the sheriff?' asked Jim.

'The sheriff,' said Grandfather, 'have you gone mad, Jim? The important thing is to switch off the stopcock.'

Jim ran off to switch off the stopcock.

'The sheriff,' muttered Grandfather indignantly; 'I think he's lost his wits. If the sheriff comes now, we'll lose our licence from here to the second coming. No, we have to cope with this ourselves, Sedd. That's how things are.'

'That's how things are,' I nodded.

Since the water supply was now cut off, the next day's breakfast was now under threat, not to speak of the urgent need for the hotel not to see all its bathrooms transformed into bomb sites, so immediate action was required. The water pipe had to be repaired at all costs. 'Otherwise,' said Grandfather, 'we'll have to clean up vomit and disinfect bathrooms for the next three weeks, so get to it, lads!'

We got to it. Equipped with water pump pliers, hacksaw, monkey wrench, packing, thread seal tape and anything else we could find in the toolshed, we knelt in the wet toilet room and tried to bend the broken pipe back into place. From somewhere on the floor above we could hear a faint bellowing. It might have been the newly-released lover, it might have been something else entirely. It was impossible to say.

'Fucking hell,' said Jim. 'D'you see now why I said no, Sedd? Never again, I said. Never again. No Christmas bonus or extra holiday is worth this. Nothing! D'you hear, Sedd?'

'But it's a lucrative affair, Jim,' I said.

Jim paused for a moment in bending the pipe and stared at me with bloodshot eyes: 'If you say that once more, Sedd, I'll clout you with this wrench. Just so's you know.'

After some time we managed to wrestle the two ends of the pipe back into position. And after a further struggle we got a sleeve screwed over it and secured some packing round it.

'There,' said Jim. 'That should do it.' He got up. We stumbled back up to reception, wet to the skin.

'You do know,' said Jim, 'that I would never think of clouting you with the wrench.'

'I know,' I said.

'It's your grandfather I feel like clouting,' said Jim.

'I know.'

On the ground floor things had begun to calm down. The dance hall was empty, apart from a group in the corner, a couple of sleeping ladies and Grandfather, who was bravely guarding the precious and dangerous bottles behind the counter. It was getting on for half-past two, and it looked as if Attila's hordes had called it a night. The odd partygoer was still teetering around through the rooms, incapable of finding rest or himself. Out in the yard the battle had long since died down and only a few brown bloodstains in the snow bore witness to the showdown between Østfold and Møre. It was only in a couple of rooms at the end of the new wing that there was still life. Singing, shouting and the peculiar shrieks like car alarms emitted by drunken women over forty, could still be heard from up there. Grandfather assessed the situation like an experienced firefighter: from the sound of the epilogue he judged that the fire was dying down, that the combustible material would soon run out, and that the whole thing would shortly be extinguished of its own accord. So he concluded that the few who were still conscious could carry on without any risk until they fell asleep. He discharged most of the extra staff, stationed a night porter in reception and said goodnight. Exhausted, we went to bed. Actually Jim had an agreement with Johnny West and his brave boys to share a beer after the performance, but the leak had taken some time to repair, so The Limelight Band had driven back to town.

At five o'clock I was woken by someone running up the stairs and beginning to bang loudly on Grandfather's door. He must have been sleeping deeply after the strains of the evening and night, because it was a while before he answered. I could hear an excited voice which I thought belonged to the night porter, then an exclamation from Grandfather, but I couldn't make out what was being said. But I could hear that Grandfather was out of bed in a flash. Straight after I could hear Grandmother's voice in the corridor, high-pitched and piercing, and immediately after that hurried footsteps on the stairs.

I sat up in bed. It's a funny thing: it's as if you know somehow when something serious has happened. There's never any doubt about it. Tired as I was, I debated for a moment whether I should carry on sleeping, but then I pulled myself together. There are far too many young people these days who have no sense of responsibility. That's their problem. Perhaps they don't understand what the word responsibility means. But if you've been born and bred so to speak with the prospect of inheriting a hotel, then you understand what responsibility is. Then you can't just stay in bed. Regardless of how young or tired you are.

So I got my clothes on and ran down the stairs and out into reception.

There I found a state of emergency. Two crying women, both of them still wearing their party dresses, were standing in a corner, sobbing. The night porter was trying to comfort them.

Neither my grandparents nor Jim were to be seen. But in another corner, also crying, I caught sight of another of the female guests, and then I understood, understood instinctively what had happened, because she was not only deathly pale and in shock, she was wearing nothing but a swimming costume and swimming hat, if you don't count the pale blue towel she had round her shoulders.

Without stopping, I left reception and ran down to the swimming area; the wide, shallow slate steps which Grandfather was so proud of. Sure enough. The two large barred glass doors stood wide open. From one of the square black handles hung the chain, dangling, with the padlock intact. On the floor, by the door, lay the hotel's long bolt cutter.

And I knew. Knew without even needing to think about it what had happened. Of course I knew. Someone, that is to say Jim and I, or rather: Jim or I, or I or Jim – someone, that is we, or one of us, had forgotten to lock the toolshed after we had rescued the hotel's water supply. That was what had happened. Suddenly I could feel my heart hammering. I could feel it at the top of my breast and in my neck, and right out in my fingers and toes. This heart. The picture on my retina seemed to waver in time to my heartbeats. But there weren't many steps out into the swimming hall, and I had to take them, and I took them quickly, in time to my heartbeats, and felt my knees growing cold with each step.

In the swimming hall I saw exactly what I had already realised I would see. It was as if I took it all in at once. Every single detail. The lighted night lamps. The blinds half pulled down in the panorama windows. An overturned recliner. The rubber balls and swimming rings in the bin by the end of the pool. Grandfather and Grandmother at the other end, right on the edge of the pool. Grandmother's head on Grandfather's shoulder. The smell of chlorine. The gurgling noise from the water intake. And out in the pool, like a butterfly in a display case, motionless and with its wings outstretched, a small figure in a short dress. The dress was perfectly spread out, as was the long hair, the arms outstretched. Only the fact that one shoe was missing disturbed the symmetry.

Fully dressed and in water up to his shoulders, Jim was already on his way out to her. For a few more seconds she lay there untouched, like an impression, suspended in rocking timelessness, and then Jim reached her.

I stood there watching it all. Watching, and understanding, I didn't need to think. It was not necessary to think in order to understand what I was watching. What Jim was now carrying back to the edge of the pool with long, unsteady underwater strides, that dishevelled, wet, drowned figure, from which hair, dress, arms and legs hung down with sudden weight – that had been Karoline, the peace angel of the snowball war, who had lain there looking up into all the blackness from all the whiteness, whilst snowballs whistled past her and with her arms and legs she slowly made her last impression on the world.

On one of the recliners by the pool lay her swimsuit. And a towel.

As yet I was invisible. As yet no-one had noticed that I was standing on the pool tiles, in my outdoor shoes as well. Again I felt a sense of responsibility surging through me; at least, I assumed that was what I felt, and I thought my first thought. I thought that it was enough for those who were here already, without having to start taking care of me. I can't rule out the possibility that I was also thinking of the unlocked toolshed. But I don't believe I was thinking of that. I might of course have been thinking of other things, perhaps that Karoline must have known that the large bolt cutter was in that shed, I don't know. I turned my back on what I had seen and walked, still invisible, back the way I had just come, through the opened doors. Walked up the shallow slate steps, up from the warmth and the smell of chlorine and into reception.

There everything was still as it had been. The ladies were standing there crying. And I sat down in one of the armchairs, and I'm certain that I seemed exactly as I had before.

34

Tap, tap.

...

Tap, tap.

...

Tap, tap, tap.

(Someone's tapping.)

Tap, tap, tap. 'Sedd, dear.'

(Who's that knocking on my door?)

Tap, tap. 'Sedd, *Liebling*; it's Grandmother.'

(It's Grandmother knocking on my door.)

Tap, tap.

(Yes, right. Tap, tap. I have heard it now.)

'Won't you open the door, dear?' Tap, tap.

(And so faintly you came tapping, tapping at my chamber door. Tap, tap.)

'The doctor's here, Sedd. He'd like to talk to you.' Tap, tap. Tap tap tapping.

(Would he, right. Just so. I thought he was normally in the South at times like this. Together with all the other sunburnt bank customers.)

...

(There. I think they've given up now. Lovely to have some peace. *Über allen Gipfeln ist Ruh*.)

Tap, tap, tap.

...

(Shouldn't jump to conclusions like that.)

'Sedd, my lad. It's Grandfather.'

'And Dr Helgesen.'

And Dr Helgesen, yes.

...

'Dr Helgesen would like to talk to you, Sedd.'
'I think you need someone to talk to right now, Sedd.'
(Is that what you think, doctor. Just so.)
Tap, tap.
But I don't want to talk to him. (I don't want to talk to him.)

...

(As if I haven't talked enough. Soon this tapping and this talking will have to stop. There are limits to how much tapping a man can take, and how much talking. After all, when it comes down to it they are just sounds without meaning; sounds which want nothing, mean nothing, are nothing. Myself, I can only utter one word, a word with four syllables, and that is a word I don't want to say; I can't bear it. I'd rather take a pill. A doctor pill.

Outside I can see the reflected lights of the cars coming and going.)

Tap, tap.

(How many days have passed? I don't know. Three perhaps, but these December days are so short it's hardly worth counting them.)

Tap, tap.

(Jim was here with sandwiches. He keeps coming with sandwiches. But he doesn't knock. He just puts them down outside the door, and that's good, and then he says: 'It's Jim here. I've brought some sandwiches. I'll put them down outside the door.'

That's good. Jim's sandwiches are good. But recently, the last few days, or maybe it's the last week, it's not easy to say, I've had the feeling that Grandfather and Grandmother and Dr Helgesen are trying to starve me out. Mean as they are. Knock me out and starve me out. Together with the sheriff, although I've already talked to him. But I think they want me to talk to him again. Much good that's going to do. I've already said what I have to say, and it doesn't change anything anyway. Four syllables. One word. It's like 'Twenty Questions' with Rolf Kirkvaag. Animal. Animals are human. Were human. Vegetable. Mineral.

Or perhaps, it occurred to me, they want me to talk to the sheriff so that the hotel is not taken over by the state. It would be an extremely impractical situation if it were, that's true. We can all agree on that. But I really think I've done enough in that direction. Even though I can't say that I've been particularly successful. I didn't manage to save Bjørn Berge when he slumped down after having eaten too much of Grandmother's poisonous *Gugelhupf*. And the later rescue mission, the one in the boat, the one from the boat, the one in the cold dark water, that was merely a postponement. It was no good teaching her to swim either. Four syllables. Because she just forgot it again when it came to it. At the crucial moment. Besides, she stole. She stole from her parents, and she stole something from me. Fumbled greedily for something, though I didn't think she knew what it was. She was a thief, and now she's dead and lying in her coffin, presumably in a chapel in Oslo, waiting. Because she's not going to be buried here, so much I have gathered. She's going home to where she came from. And as I understand it, her parents are going too. So I suppose eventually we'll get a new bank manager, tap tap, who can come tapping at our chamber door.

Perhaps it's just as well.

At night when I'm sleeping, I don't sleep. Even though I've tried taking masses of Phenergan. Masses. But they're too weak, I don't believe they are real sleeping pills. Instead I'm floating around in the warm water of the pool. It's quite still, apart from the gurgling noise of the pump. Somewhere out there in the water I can see her hair, as I did once before; I try to get hold of it, as I did once before, but I can't reach it. That's how the nights pass, or is it the days? As I said, it's actually difficult to count.)

Tap, tap.

...

(But they were professionals. I have to say that. Of course it's the least you'd expect. Even before the ambulance arrived, and the sheriff arrived, and that took some time, the most sober of the funeral managers had laid her out and combed her hair and swathed her most skilfully in two of the hotel's sheets which we never saw again. We didn't see anything of the final payment for the Christmas party either, after what had happened. The whole thing had been unacceptable, we were told, what with a fatal accident and everything else. Blue lights in the yard. Police interrogation. Who had been where, and when? Difficult enough to work out as it was, but with the state most people had been in, so late at night, it was a chain of events that not even Derrick would have been able to figure out. Blue lights in the yard, as I said. Grief-stricken parents.)

'You were supposed to keep an eye on her.'
Yes.
'But you were supposed to keep an eye on her.'
I thought –
'Yes, but you were supposed to keep an eye on her.'
...
'She couldn't swim!'
...

('Take a picture of me, Sedd.'
'No.'
'Take a picture of me. Just one. Please.'
'It costs a lot of money to take pictures.'
'Just one? So that you've got one of me?'
'No. I've got more important subjects.'
'You're so slow.')

35

Time is a strange thing. Though thing is perhaps not the right word. In a way, Grandfather used to say, time is something which is coming. But it's also something which is passing, Grandmother used to add. There you have the difference between us two, Grandfather would reply to that. Someone who thinks time is coming is looking forwards, optimistically expecting the future, whilst someone who thinks that time is passing is looking backwards, longing for what has been. Like Austria, for example. Whilst Grandfather always thought of the coming opportunities, of the development of the village and the district and so on.

But I really don't know. Perhaps time is something which neither comes nor passes, but a kind of knife-blade shearing through the universe, mercilessly, steadily, like when you trim skin and sinews from a fine piece of meat – and right on the edge of this knife-blade is where we are, living our short lives, with shreds of meat and fibre whistling around our ears. At least, I often think it's like that. We're the ones who are moving, and we can't jump either forwards or backwards, but just have to hang on as best we can.

That's how it came about that it had suddenly become a new year, almost without me having noticed Christmas and New Year's Eve, other than as faint flashes of forced celebration and obligatory attempts at enjoyment. I can just about remember the roast venison Jim served up on Christmas Eve, rescued from the deepest recesses of the freezer room, and I remember Grandmother's Christmas cakes, perfect as always. *Vanillekipferl. Linzer Augen.* The only thing she didn't bake this year was the Norwegian poor man's cake.

Synnøve was gone, the staff were gone, and I had gathered that the hotel was, to all intents and purposes, closed, although no-one said as much.

But Jim stayed. Of course he did. No-one thought there was anything strange about that. Anyway, where would he go? Fåvnesheim was his home. On New Year's Eve he pulled out four deep-frozen lobsters from even deeper recesses of the freezer room; a reminder of better times. They were served à l'américaine. That too I remember as a flash. And I remember that Grandfather, as if nothing at all had happened, was standing every day behind the counter in reception, where all was completely quiet, like the captain on the bridge of a ship which has run aground, whilst Grandmother kept herself busy in some other way.

She was packing. She had begun packing a little bit, she said, but she was packing quite a lot. Jim helped her. Packed away even more pictures and antiques than those which had been salvaged before the Christmas party, and wheeled them out to the storage shed on the luggage trolley. Some from the lounges and living rooms, some from the private apartments. Grandfather didn't even glance up as they trundled past with new packages. As for me, I think I kept out of it as much as possible, and let time pass, or come, it was all one, and I just hung on. Mostly it was dark, but it was of course winter.

Until that night.

I woke up. To start with I didn't know what it was. But I woke up. Woke without knowing why, though I knew, as clearly as pitch-black ink, that there was a why, there was a reason.

I was wide awake. Was it the strange pulsating ringing which had woken me? Or was it the red glow I could make out through the crack above the blind? For a moment I lay quite still under the duvet, registering that something was wrong. I just didn't understand what it was.

Then someone began hammering at the door. The door handle was jiggled repeatedly, and I could hear the voices of all three outside: Grandfather, Grandmother and Jim. They called my name again and again.

At the same moment I realised that it was the alarm bells which were ringing. Now I could also make out what the voices were saying; they were saying that there was a fire, there's a fire, Sedd, there's a fire!

I jumped out of bed. Outside were my grandparents and Jim, all wearing outdoor clothes, looking at me seriously.

'We have to evacuate,' said Jim. 'There's a fire.'

Grandfather: 'Get your clothes on, lad.'

Grandmother: 'It's in the new wing, so you've got a bit of time. If we start now, I'm sure you'll be able to save quite a lot.'

Without waiting, Jim barged into the room with some large cardboard boxes. He began at once to sweep everything I owned down into them from shelves and drawers.

'Schoolbooks,' Grandmother said, 'don't forget the schoolbooks, Jim.'

'The camera,' I said as I pulled a jumper over my head. 'Be careful with the camera.'

Jim was careful with the camera. But the rest happened at breakneck speed. Before I'd got my shoelaces done up Jim had pulled out every single drawer and unsentimentally emptied the contents into the boxes. 'After this you can finally get round to sorting your things out a bit,' he remarked, and attacked the wardrobe. 'Right,' he said, 'get started carrying it out.'

I carried. Down the stairs and through the private apartments, which were already strangely denuded of most private things, and out into the yard where I heaved the box on top of some other cardboard boxes which were already piled up there. I didn't think, just acted. As I turned round again to go in and get the next box, I could see how the flames were leaping out under the eaves in the new wing. In just a few minutes it would all be engulfed. Then the west wing and the reception wing would follow, the private quarters and staff quarters, the old wing with the kitchen, and finally the swimming area and the east wing with the dining room and all the lounges.

If the fire reached as far as that before the fire engine arrived from the village.

I met Jim in the doorway, on his way out with another box.

'How long will it take the fire service to get up here, do you think?' I asked.

'Oh,' said Jim. 'It'll take them a while.'

I ran up to my room to collect more. In an amazingly short time the room was just about empty. I hadn't realised that it could take such a short time to leave home. When you hear about young people leaving home, it's usually a long-drawn-out business, with teenage rebellion and temperamental outbursts, but I managed it in seventeen minutes. Actually even faster than my mother had.

After that we went through more rooms. The lights were still working in this part of the house. From reception Jim and I dragged out the large old rose-painted chests, the shelf units, wooden casks and all the copper pots which were such a nightmare to polish.

'Do we have to rescue these?' I asked in mock seriousness.

Jim allowed himself a smile, but didn't answer. Just carried on. We heaved it all out into the yard.

In reception the red light on the fire alarm was flashing, and from inside the building you could hear the fire bells ringing. On and on, with short breaks, like a monotonous two-part song.

Grandfather would have liked to save the large dresser from reception, but it had taken four strong men to heave it into place, so we couldn't even think about it. On the other hand I wondered whether we shouldn't try to save the ring-binders and papers from the office, but Grandfather said it wasn't necessary. He'd already taken out the historical visitors' books and the insurance policy, he explained, and that was the most important thing.

We stood there, all four of us, some way out in the yard, watching Fåvnesheim. In the new wing the flames were licking out from several windows, and at regular intervals the glass panes shattered with muffled bangs.

Still we couldn't see or hear any fire engine.

Jim sprinted round the hotel to get to the kitchen in the old wing; there were some knives he wanted to save. Grandfather and Grandmother were standing close together. Their faces seemed to gleam in the reflected light of the flames. Grandmother had leant her head on Grandfather's shoulder.

Grandfather was looking down the whole time. Then they began to walk slowly away from Fåvnesheim, with Grandmother supporting him.

I was left alone. Watching. If the fire carried on spreading at such a speed, there wouldn't be much left to inherit.

I wasn't frightened. I don't believe I was angry either, but I was gripped by something which felt a bit like anger. Just like when I rescued Karoline in Blåvann. If you have to, you have to. I suppose that's what's called resolution.

So I straightened up, stamped my foot in the snow, once, and then I strode over to the toolshed, went in, crossed to the shelves where all the tools were kept, and picked up a crowbar.

After that I walked without looking left or right into reception and further on into the burning hotel.

There was already a strong smell of burning, but for the time being there wasn't much smoke. At least, not in reception and the neighbouring rooms. Although as I moved further into the building and came to the corridor leading to the old wing, I could see smoke seeping in under the panelled ceiling. For a moment I thought about turning round, but again I was gripped by resolution, and I carried on doggedly until I reached the stairs. Here the smoke was a little thicker, but no worse, I estimated, than that it was perfectly possible to keep going for the time being. I ran quickly up the stairs to the attic floor, switched on the light in the corridor up there and rounded the corner. The long corridor with the old rooms lay in front of me. And suddenly I was afraid. Or perhaps afraid is not the right word. I don't know. But my hands felt numb as I moved towards the locked door to Olympus. Perhaps because there was a fire, perhaps because I knew that I didn't have much time, but quite definitely because I knew that now, now or never, that door had to be opened, before it was irrevocably too late.

It was not easy. Even though I had a crowbar. Because the closed door was lined up absolutely perfectly with the frame, and I couldn't get a purchase on the smallest crack with either end of the crowbar. I tried and tried, but the wood was as hard as stone and as smooth as glass, and I managed to do no more than make thin dark scratches on the varnish. I realised that I should have brought another tool with me to make a crack between the door and the doorframe; a chisel or a knife. But I didn't have one, and there wasn't time to go and fetch such a tool either, and soon it would be too late, in vain, all over. If I went out again I wouldn't get back, I could see that. So I stood there for a while, struggling with the crowbar and that cursed door, which would never open, which was fixed solid.

When I'd been working at this for a few minutes, I'm not sure how many, I realised I would have to try a different tack. Instead of carrying on hacking away uselessly at the doorcrack, I attacked the frame itself. That was surprisingly easy. I began with the batten against the wall, which was easy to remove with three or four hefty tugs on the crowbar. The timbers in the doorframe itself offered more resistance, because they were thick and heavy and fastened with large numbers of three-inch nails, solid workmanship of the kind we don't see any more these days, but finally the outermost timber gave way, at least enough for me to be able to wedge the end of the crowbar underneath the inner one – and then I managed to prise that away, with shrill creaking sounds from the long nails, far enough to make a thin crack between the timber and the moulding. Once that crack had appeared, it was a relatively easy task to remove the moulding. And now I had created a small space between the door and the frame, down near the handle and the lock, just wide enough to be able to coax in the narrow end of the crowbar.

I got a purchase on it at once. I leaned on the crowbar with my full weight and hoped that something would give. To start with nothing happened; it was like trying to bend steel. But I got angry, started to feel desperate, and shoved even harder. I shoved. Sweat poured off me. It was starting to get quite hot. And suddenly, just as I was about to give up, about to decide I hadn't the strength, something gave way inside the door lock, audibly, with a small click, and I began to work the crowbar to and fro. The door moved slightly. I shoved. I pulled. I rocked. The door moved slightly more. It creaked. It cracked. Smoke was seeping along the ceiling. I changed my grip, rocked a bit more, then turned the crowbar round and leant on it again.

And then, all at once, the whole thing gave way; the lock sprang open with a short grating sound, and the door to Olympus was open.

I shoved it open with a kick, threw down the crowbar and put my foot on the threshold.

At that moment the light went. The corridor was as black as the inside of a sack. In front of me I could just about make out the room, with faint glowing contours created by the light of the flames, which percolated in around the edges of the drawn curtains. But I couldn't see anything.

Now that it had gone dark, I noticed more clearly what a strong smell of fire there was, or rather of smoke. And I was frightened, properly frightened, frightened to death. Sedd the Unready. I crouched down and felt behind me, on the other side of the threshold, on the floor of the corridor, for the crowbar, but I couldn't find it. So I stood up again, bending over, and moved forwards into the room. Towards the window. But I didn't get far, I stumbled over something,

something low down, a pouffe, a footstool, I don't know what, but it was hard. I fell full length on the floor and felt that I had hit myself hard on something. I could feel something warm on my upper lip, and realised that my nose was bleeding. I raised myself onto all fours and crawled further towards the window. I got hold of the radiator with my right hand, pulled myself up onto my knees and grabbed the curtains with both hands, pulling as hard as I could. Something gave way at once at the top, as though these curtains were only hanging there out of habit, and the whole lot came crashing down immediately, curtain rail, pelmet and all, and hit me on the head with a bang and buried me in a sea of rotting, dusty curtain material.

I fought to get free of the material, banged my forehead quite hard on the sharp columns of the radiator as I bent forward to get my head out of the curtains, but then, finally, I was free.

I stood up. Looked out of the window. The red flickering light from the flames was surprisingly bright, and I realised the fire must have come much closer. When I looked to the left I could see that the roof of the private apartments, only a few metres away, was on fire. I tried to open the window, but it wouldn't move. The catches were stuck. They'd been painted over several times.

Then I turned round. Now I could see the whole room and everything in it in the glowing light of the flames. It was like a darkroom illuminated by a single red bulb.

On the walls were some posters. Donovan again. Janis Joplin. The Beatles. On a chest of drawers stood a record player and a rack of records. On a shelf I could make out some paperbacks. Olympus. Just how a teenage girl would furnish her sanctuary; nothing unexpected there really. Except for one thing.

She was sitting there herself. In a wicker chair in the middle of the room, by a small round glass table, there she was. On the glass table was a teapot, a bowl of sugar and three cups. Beside them a cakestand filled with

Grandmother's unmistakable Christmas cakes. And I let out a scream. Screamed aloud in terror. Because it was her. In the armchair, motionless, with her long fox-red hair. My mother. Quite motionless, stiff, dead.

Grandfather must have stuffed her, like he did with all animals, large and small.

On the other wall I saw all the photos. And I screamed again. Because here they were; photos of my mother in all situations and at all ages. Large and small. Coloured and black and white. In her cradle, in the sandpit, on a tricycle and on the way to her first day at school. In her confirmation dress and in a trouser suit. In a leather jacket and in a skirt. With her hair fastened up and her hair down and wearing her student cap. And suddenly I remembered everything. Remembered her. Remembered exactly what she looked like, exactly what she sounded like, her voice, her laughter, her eyes, her smile: her face. And then I understood that it was not my mother sitting in that wicker chair, it wasn't her at all. When I looked again, I could see that it was a doll.

That was spooky enough. A shop-window mannequin. But its hair was like my mother's, and it was dressed like my mother in one of the photos, in the same trouser suit.

I moved a couple of steps closer. The doll sat there, stiff and artificial, and didn't look like my mother at all, it sat there drinking tea with nobody and eating cake with nobody as it stared out at nothing.

Around its neck it had a pearl necklace. Around its right wrist it had several beautiful bracelets, and on its left wrist a splendid diamond watch. On each finger there was a ring; a couple of them were a little loose and fastened with tape. And in the middle of its breast twinkled Fru Carstensen's diamond brooch, unmistakable, just as Fru Carstensen had drawn it in the sketch. Together with a piece of jewellery I assumed must be Aunt Gunvor's antique diamond pendant from St. Petersburg.

I stood there in the gloom looking at this strange frozen tableau, without understanding what I was seeing. I could not take it in. The doll's blue eyes looked straight past me, through me, through the smoke, towards the window. The stolen golden finery was glinting. I began to feel nauseous, faint, my head swam. Then things went black before my eyes, and the next moment I was on all fours, vomiting. When I opened my eyes again I could see that the corridor was on fire. Or what I could see of it through the clouds of smoke. The light wasn't red any more, it was a fierce, intense yellow colour, almost white.

It was hot. Soon everything would be gone. Soon the doll would melt, the gold would melt, the diamonds would burn up. Not everyone knows that, actually, that diamonds burn up. Like coal. That's because they *are* coal, just greatly compressed. But coal all the same. They burn up and turn to ash, even though they are the hardest material you can find. Even harder than teeth, which remain after the cremation is over. Even little girl's teeth, even little boy's teeth.

I tried to drag myself to my feet, but I couldn't manage it. Then I sank backwards, and would have sunk even further backwards, down into the dark, down into nothing, but Jim appeared in the doorway.

His face was all sooty and his eyebrows and hair were singed, and there was a long burnt rip in his jacket, but there he was. He was holding a cushion over his nose and mouth.

He gasped something. I couldn't hear what he was trying to say, but I gathered it was my name. He swayed, looked around. He caught sight of the crowbar on the floor of the corridor and picked it up. The second it was in his hand there was a hissing noise and he dropped it again with a half-stifled shout; it was red-hot. Not even a cook's fingers can pick up a red-hot crowbar without getting burnt. But then he put the cushion over his hand and picked it up again; in two strides he was across the room past me, and there was a splintering of glass. First one loud bang, followed by crunching noises as he cleared the window opening of shards. After that he knocked out the mullions.

Then he was back at my side. He still said nothing, just picked me up. With a fireman's lift he had me hanging over his shoulder, and I could feel his knees shaking, but he moved slowly but surely towards the window, put one foot on the radiator, grasped the window frame with his left hand and hauled us up onto the sill.

Then he said in a rasping voice: 'Are you ready, Sedd?'

'No,' I said behind his back. 'Did you see it? Did you see...'

'Yes,' he said. 'I know. Don't think about it.'

'But Jim,' I said.

'We've got to get out,' said Jim.

'All those pictures,' I said.

'They're just pictures.'

'But Jim.'

'You know,' said Jim, 'I promised your mother I'd look after you while she was away. Now we've got to jump, OK? Hold tight.'

Then we were in the air. It felt as if we were hanging in nothing, my stomach turned over, the cold air stung my face; then we landed with a muffled thump, much harder than I would have thought possible.

We lay in the snow, panting. I didn't lose consciousness, but I think Jim passed out for a few seconds. Then he began to move, groaning, and I managed to roll over onto my side.

'Fuck,' he said. 'I think I broke my ankle. Ow.'

'Ow,' I said in solidarity. Then I had a fit of coughing.

'Are you OK?' said Jim, then he began to cough too.

For a while we lay there, coughing. Then we managed to get up.

I had to support him on the last stretch back to the yard. In the distance, still behind several mountain ridges, I could hear the sirens. Grandmother and Grandfather were standing in the yard, Grandmother sobbing on Grandfather's shoulder. Grandfather was looking up, squinting into the light from the flames. He looked completely desperate. Then I could hear him shouting 'Sisi, here they come, look, here they come,' and she turned her face towards us; 'Thank God,' she cried, '*Gott sei Dank!*'

They began to come towards us in order to help us down the little slope to the yard. They waded through the snow, they waved, they beckoned, whilst Jim and I supported each other, step by step.

They were still a long way off, it would still take some time before we reached one another.

But they were getting closer the whole time.

Afterword

Time is central to *Lobster Life*. The narrator, Sedd, is acutely aware of the passing of time at Fåvnesheim, the Norwegian mountain hotel where he lives together with his grandparents, who run the hotel. As the seasons change, so do the guests, from summer hikers and fishers to winter skiers and partygoers, and so does the yearly rhythm of cleaning and refurbishing. The hotel has a long and proud history, which Sedd's grandfather loses no opportunity to recount at length; the Heimdal room in the hotel is given over to pictures and relics from the early days, like his father's Dunhill pipe and walking pole. From Sedd's great-great-great-grandfather, who built the original tourist cabin, onwards, the hotel has been passed down through the generations, growing in size and splendour. One day the exotically-named Sedgewick Kumar Zacchariassen will inherit all this, and he already feels the weight of history on his young shoulders.

It is not only Grandfather who is preoccupied with history and tradition; Grandmother too looks back with nostalgia to her youth in Vienna, where she trained as a hotelier and perfected the art of baking beautiful Viennese cakes, and even further back to the glorious dynasties of the Austro-Hungarian Empire. She can never quite understand how she has finished up here, in the midst of 'die grausamen Berge' – the dreadful mountains – so far from civilisation and elegant manners. And then there is Sedd's absent mother, about whom all he is told is that she was 'taken by Time'; he has no idea what that means, and has only a vague memory of her as 'a foxy-red sheen in the air' before she disappeared when he was a toddler, never to return.

The novel is set in a specific historical era, the early 1980s, and there are many incidental references to popular culture, to politics and social developments, which provide an authentic background to the story. Dramatic events which dominated the national news at that time have repercussions which reverberate as far as the isolated rural area where the hotel is situated. The bomb explosion at Oslo central station on 2nd July 1982 happens just before Sedd and his grandfather make a trip to Oslo, and Sedd is drawn to the scene of the explosion out of a curiosity which threatens to get him into serious trouble. The fifteen-week alcohol store strike in 1982 has a direct effect on Fåvnesheim, as Grandfather's faith that Prime Minister Willoch will solve matters in a few days turns out to be misplaced, and the hotel runs out of drink for its wedding parties.

The 1980s is also a time of cultural change which has a less immediate but – in the long run – more devastating effect on life in a mountain hotel. Norwegians' habits are changing, and instead of spending their holidays exploring their own spectacular countryside, they are increasingly drawn to what Grandfather often refers to as 'the infernal South'. Adverts in the daily newspaper for package holidays in Benidorm become larger and more enticing, and the postwar boom in holidays near home ebbs away. The access roads up to the mountains have improved – but that just means that people speed past when before they would have stayed. The hotel, which has had several new wings built on over the years to accommodate the growth of visitor numbers, is becoming a drain on resources rather than a source of income. Grandfather's worries about making ends meet are apparent from the first chapter, as the sudden death of the bank manager, on whom they have depended for extended credit, sets off an accelerating chain of events leading to the ultimate catastrophe.

All this is relayed to us by the adolescent Sedd, who observes and comments on what is happening. He spends much of his time with adults, either his grandparents or the hotel chef and jack-of-all-trades, Jim, who is a kind of substitute father. Sedd knows nothing about his biological father except that he is not there; his secretive grandparents have told him nothing, and he realises instinctively that for some reason he is not allowed to ask. Much of his emotional energy throughout the novel is devoted to his efforts to unravel the mystery of his origins and his mother's disappearance. To all intents and purposes he is an orphan, and his fantasies occasionally run wild. From an early age he has also been involved in various duties to do with the running of the hotel. All this has turned him into a precocious child, with knowledge and vocabulary beyond his years; he perplexes his schoolteacher with difficult questions, and loves unusual words like mnemotechnic and paradigm shift. And yet in many ways he is still emotionally immature.

Sedd approaches the mysteries of his existence like a detective, trying to piece together clues. Why is he more dark-skinned than the blond Norwegians around him, why does guests' jewellery keep disappearing, what is in the room with the locked door to which he can never find the key? He tries to discover information without revealing his motives, a procedure which leads him into several absurd situations. At the same time, he fails to grasp that adults too have hidden motives, and to understand the extent of his grandfather's self-deception. There are many clues from early on in the novel that the hotel is on the brink of ruin, and the reader can see the way things are going long before the narrator does. Sedd's supply of used stamps for his collection runs out because his grandfather has stopped opening all official letters which arrive at Fåvnesheim, the hotel in Oslo where they normally stay suddenly doesn't have a room for them, the outfitters where they buy clothes refuses their usual credit, the electricity is dramatically cut off – but it is not until Grandmother points out to him that they have almost no guests that he begins to understand there is cause for concern.

The full significance of events does not dawn on Sedd until too late. The same is true of his meeting with Karoline, the new bank manager's daughter. She is younger than he is, and he dismisses the growing signs of her devotion to him as just the antics of a child. Again, it is only with hindsight that he can acknowledge what was happening and understand his own role in the drama.

A sense of impending doom grows stronger as the story unfolds. Yet at the same time this is in many ways also a comic novel. Sedd has a keen sense of the absurd, and many of the characters he meets amuse him with their foibles: the group of German fishermen who are so weighted down with hooks and lures and spools that they would immediately sink to the bottom of Blåvann if they fell out of the boat, the Russian guest at a reception who is so enthusiastic about Johan Borgen's novel *Little Lord* that she has learnt Norwegian as a result, the shop assistant whose desire to be hyper-correct makes her mispronounce words, the photographer who spends his time in semi-darkness so as not to be over-exposed. Even individuals who appear briefly are characterized by a humorous detail which makes them stick in the mind. A bride in frothy white dress advances through the rooms of the hotel like a horizontal waterfall. American tourists in Oslo can't understand why they can't visit The Fjords in one day. A schoolteacher from Oslo accuses Grandfather of cruelty to animals for keeping a lobster with one claw, comparing it with hunting seals in the Arctic and elephants in Africa. A librarian, presumably noticing Sedd's dark skin, insists on trying to lend him a book about immigrants when what he wants is *Little Lord Fauntleroy*. And Sedd's – and the author's – delight in facts leads to several joyous digressions about such things as the history of philately and the postal service, the British and Austrian royal families, the scariness of Munch's vampires, the living arrangements on the Kon-Tiki expedition, or the competitiveness of lobsters.

It is not a coincidence that two of the intertextual references in this novel are to Johan Borgen's *Little Lord* and Frances Hodgson Burnett's *Little Lord Fauntleroy*. In all three novels the central character is a precocious and fatherless boy who has to devise strategies to cope with a puzzling adult world and an obscurely threatening inheritance. The outcomes, however, are very different. Cedric in *Little Lord Fauntleroy* is entirely a force for good, charming his embittered grandfather and securing a happy future for himself and his mother. Borgen's Wilfred Sagen is a damaged child, charismatic but deceitful, who grows up to gamble with his own life and those of others. The character of Sedd lies between these two extremes; he does his best to live up to expectations, but is hampered by a family trauma and his own limitations.

Translating this novel has been an enjoyable exercise. Most important was finding the right voice for a thirteen-year-old boy in the 1980s. Sedd's fascination with words caused a few problems; when he points out that the Norwegian word 'bonitet' comes from the French 'bonité', I had to find an alternative (pre-eminence, from the Latin eminere), or that Grandmother every now and then has a 'raptus', of which the interesting plural is 'rapti' (that has become paroxysms, another unusual word Sedd would have savoured). English does not have the polite form of address, 'De', with which the librarian addresses Sedd in Chapter 11, and neither do we distinguish between two different kinds of grandson ('sønnesønn' and 'dattersønn' for son's son and daughter's son respectively). People cannot be addressed as Bank Manager Berge or Hotel Owner Zacchariassen; but ways around this can always be found. Cultural and geographical references are much easier to locate in these days of internet searches, so there is no need to explain folk songs like 'Mannen og kråka' or street names like Karl Johans gate. I have occasionally added a word or two of explanation, such as that Annen Etage in The Hotel Continental is a restaurant or that 'All power shall reside in this chamber' is the motto of the Norwegian parliament. Translating the rollicking dirge of the funeral directors in Chapter 33 was great fun.

I am grateful to the author for answering my queries about his novel, and to my editors, John Death, Elettra Carbone and Kristin Lorentsen, for their careful reading of my translation and for the many helpful comments which have greatly improved its accuracy and consistency. Any remaining infelicities are, of course, my responsibility.

Janet Garton
Norwich, July 2019

JOHAN BORGEN

Little Lord

(translated by Janet Garton)

Wilfred - alias Little Lord - is a privileged young man growing up in upper-class society in Kristiania (Oslo) during the halcyon days before the First World War. Beneath the strikingly well-adjusted surface, however, runs a darker current; he is haunted by the sudden death of his father and driven to escape the stifling care of his mother for risky adventures in Kristiania's criminal underworld. The two sides of his personality must be kept separate, but the strain of living a double life threatens breakdown and catastrophe. This best-selling novel by one of Norway's most talented twentieth-century writers is also an evocative study of a vanished age of biplanes, variety shows, and Viennese psychiatry.

ISBN 9781909408173
UK £12.95
(Paperback, 348 pages)

VIGDIS HJORTH

A House in Norway

(translated by Charlotte Barslund)

A House in Norway tells the story of Alma, a divorced textile artist who
makes a living from weaving standards for trade unions and marching
bands. She lives alone in an old villa, and rents out an apartment in
her house to supplement her income. She is overjoyed to be given
a more creative assignment, to design a tapestry for an exhibition
to celebrate the centenary of women's suffrage in Norway, but soon
finds that it is a much more daunting task than she had anticipated.
Meanwhile, a Polish family moves into her apartment, and their
activities become a challenge to her unconscious assumptions and
her self-image as a good feminist and an open-minded liberal. Is it
possible to reconcile the desire to be tolerant and altruistic with the
imperative need for creative and personal space?

ISBN 9781909408319
UK £11.95
(Paperback, 175 pages)

AMALIE SKRAM

Betrayed

(translated by Katherine Hanson and Judith Messick)

With high hopes, Captain Riber embarks with his young bride Aurora on a voyage to exotic destinations. But they are an ill-matched pair; her naive illusions are shattered by the realities of married life and the seediness of society in foreign ports, whilst his hopes of domestic bliss are frustrated by his wife's unhappiness. Life on board ship becomes a private hell, as Aurora's obsession with Riber's adventures as a carefree bachelor begins to undermine his sanity. Ultimately both are betrayed by a hypocritical society which imposes a warped view of sexuality on its most vulnerable members.

Amalie Skram was a contemporary of Henrik Ibsen, and like him a fierce critic of repressive social mores and hypocrisy. Many of her works make an impassioned statement on the way women of all classes are imprisoned in their social roles, contributing to the great debate about sexual morality which engaged so many Nordic writers in the late nineteenth century. Her female characters are independent, rebellious, even reckless; but their upbringing and their circumstances combine to deny them the fulfilment their creator so painfully won for herself.

ISBN 9781909408494
UK £11.95
(Paperback, 136 pages)

Lightning Source UK Ltd.
Milton Keynes UK
UKHW020839191019
351913UK00009B/154/P

9 781909 408524